PHILISTINE

A TALE OF GOLIATH

OTHER BOOKS BY STEVEN L. SHREWSBURY

Hell Billy
Overkill
Thrall
Stronger Than Death
Tormentor
Hawg
Godforsaken
Bad Magick
(with Nate Southard)

Bedlam Unleashed
(with Peter Welmerink)

Black Son Rising
(with Maurice Broaddus)
(forthcoming)

COLLECTIONS

Thoroughbred
Bulletproof Soul
Depths of Savagery
Nocturnal Vacations
Blood and Steel: Legends of La Gaul Vol. 1

PHILISTINE
A TALE OF GOLIATH

STEVEN SHREWSBURY

Cover art: Matthew Perry
Cover art in this book copyright © 2013 Matthew Perry & Seventh Star
Press, LLC.

Edited by: Joshua H. Leet

Published by Seventh Star Press, LLC.

ISBN Number: 978-1-937929-45-9

Seventh Star Press
www.seventhstarpress.com
info@seventhstarpress.com

Publisher's Note:
Philistine is a work of fiction. All names, characters, and places are the
product of the author's imagination, used in fictitious manner. Any
resemblances to actual persons, places, locales, events, etc. are purely
coincidental.

Printed in the United States of America

First Edition

ACKNOWLEDGEMENTS

Thanks always to Mark Boatman, Stephen Zimmer, Angie & Chris Fulbright, B.J. "Bucky" McPherson, Peter Welmerink, Sharon Moore White, Ron Kelly, Norm Partridge, Jessica Lay, Brady Allen, Bob Freeman, Louise Bohmer, Cody Goodfellow, Tod Clark, Jim McCleod, Cheryl Lynne Staley, Gina Ranalli, Evyl Ed, Donnise, David Wilbanks,, P.S. Gifford, Martel Sardina, Lisa Mannetti, Eric S. Brown, Elizabeth Donald, Ty Schwamburger, Rhonda Wilson, Angel Lesa, R.Thomas Riley, Fred Grimm, Kriss Morton, DezM, Val, Noigeoverlord (Paul), Ali Justice, Andrew Leonard, Rita Scarlet, Jon F. Merz, Cherry Wanders (Nikki), Minh, Sharon Durham, Dean Harrison, Keevah, Jeremiah Negray, Kelli Miller, Ginger May, and Don Leonard.

Lastly, but most of all, thank you to my family, Stacey, John and Aaron.

Shrews
Rural Central Illinois

For my sons

John and Aaron
Who are already giants in my eyes

And for my Godson

Mark K. Shrewsbury Jr.

Who even I look up to
Literally

CONTENTS

"Those who have done good will enter eternal life.
Those who have done evil will enter eternal fire."

Athanasian Creed

"If I whet my glittering sword, and mine hand
take hold on judgment;I will render vengeance to mine
enemies, and will reward them that hate me."

DEUTERONOMY 32:41

Philistine

CHAPTER ONE
BEYOND NIGHT

"Come closer, you little pricks and I'll show you what God looks like."

The boast didn't bring the charging war chariot to an abrupt stop, but the javelin stabbing through its right wheel did. Spokes splintered as the heavy spearhead embedded in the ground, but the javelin's beam didn't waver as the chariot whipped about, sending the driver and his onboard supplier of lances airborne. The spear then tore up from the ground and a battle cry tinged with laughter echoed across the plain. A looming figure in front of the Philistine forces turned to the driver of the chariot, who lay prone at his feet. The Philistine drove his javelin into the driver's spine. Though the driver contorted in death, no sound came from his open mouth. After taking the life of this attacker, the warrior looked away at more chariots charging up toward their position from hidden caves beneath Mount Nebo's base. Not bothering to slay the fleeing lance supplier, the huge man set his feet, unflinching at the new challenge. Dark hair spilled from under his bronze helm, settling over expansive shoulders. Twelve fingers on his hands gripped the shaft of the javelin anew.

"So seldom do they take the easy path offered,"

the deep voice intoned as Philistine soldiers moved up behind him, the rising sun at their backs. He motioned with his chin for his shield bearer to shift to the left as the opposition came forward. At this action, the two fresh chariots adjusted their paths, ensuring them a near clash as they approached the man holding the spear. This giant's left hand spun the javelin like a wheel as he reached back to draw a sword from his back holster.

He shouted, "You need not all have to die." His voice echoed down into the caverns under the foundation of the mountain. "Give me the strongest man, your champion. I'll kill him instead of all of you *and* those two mean bitches you serve."

Those charging never heeded his words, either their minds so blinded to fate or their courage screwed in tight. Both chariots slung spears, each launched in quick succession with the second figure in the chariots feeding the drivers from woven quivers. Most men would've been impressed by the act of fearless bravado.

The champion of the Philistines wasn't most men, though.

With an action swift for a being his size, the giant ran forward. The incoming lances impacted on his plated armor and then glanced off as he reached his goal. He ducked low, took a knee, placed each weapon on either side of himself and swiped, striking each horse in the neck as they thundered near. These animals, maimed, bellowed as they pulled up as if hitting a wall. However, the carts continued forward, into the embrace of the fighter. The faces of the drivers couldn't hide their fright as their screams named their slayer.

"Goliath!"

Arms extended still, Goliath's hands chopped down, smashing into each driver's breastplate. The wicked strikes cracked their sternums, but Goliath took little time to dwell on them or their terror-stricken faces, for their momentum carried them on past. His hands grabbed their weapon suppliers by the hair. Goliath turned and held up the two screaming men from the rear of the chariots. Each figure dangled from his grip, kicking at him. The contingent of Philistines rippled with laughter as Goliath eyed each of the suppliers. One sported a deformed nose, placed higher between his eyes than normal and the other sported a head malformed from birth, explaining to Goliath why they served in such a capacity.

"You have balls, I grant you that," Goliath said to the two with a bored voice, then dashed their heads together. In but a moment, the two skulls became one mass of brain and slime, splashing on the ground before Mount Nebo. The move made even those experienced Philistine soldiers in the front ranks jump.

The bodies dropped and Goliath shook off his hands. He motioned to his shield bearer to step closer and guard his flank as more men poured out of the lower keep of Nebo. The man sporting Goliath's shield stood a head taller than the other Philistines, but still reached nowhere near the height of his master. All of the Philistine troopers stood as big men, sporting greasy locks of black hair and full beards. Every soldier, clad in short kilts, chain-mail shirts, bronze helmets, and metal leggings, gripped the pommels of swords slung at their belts.

"Come along now," Goliath shouted toward the tunnel mouth where people started to amass. Hands curled to fists, poised on his hips, he added, "Let me pass. This is all unnecessary."

Hundreds of more men and women streamed out of the long cave opening, jogging to Goliath's left or right. They fanned out in an attempt to surround the Philistine force in a pincers movement.

Disgusted, Goliath picked up his weapons and

quipped, "My cousin Neurath is getting lazy or he'd have taken these pukes into his cult on the other side of Nebo. That would've saved us this trouble." As mirth returned to the troops, Goliath spoke to his shield bearer in a softer voice, saying, "Look at them, Abimelech, they all wear false wings. Did we interrupt a children's game or a pathetic rite these religious idiots engage in?"

The thickset man supporting the shield let his eyes follow Goliath's gesture, seeing the strange clothes and feathered appendages drooping from those streaming out against them. "I cannot tell, sire. Why wear such juvenile things into battle? Why not suitable armor against us?"

Goliath gave a shrug and took up his shield. Though Abimelech used both arms to sustain the safeguard, Goliath easily handled it with one hand. He held it like a child upending a dinner plate, bouncing the edge on his waist belt while facing the belly of the mountain. "They're mongrels, Abi. See their weapons?"

"They aren't forged like our folk and they haven't our craft at smithing behind them. Their weapons are all they could steal or find."

"Such are the ways of cults that follow after gods or goddesses made of flesh."

The Philistines took up a defensive posture and a few officers rode closer to join them. Abimelech spoke up to say, "They seem willing to die to defend their goddesses, the twin ladies of Sanrevelle, and guard secrets of any rebellion those two foster amongst our ranks."

"Bah, my balls are twins and I never make a case for it." Goliath still showed no concern as the cultists kept flooding out, surrounding the Philistine force with superior numbers. "If they hadn't had the daughter of the high priest of Dagon join their cult and pray to those sister-things under the mountain, we'd not be here."

Philistine

Abimelech imparted a thoughtful nod, but his gaze wandered to the officers for a moment. He saluted the short-haired, clean-shaven man on the lead horse, saying, "General Samien." His face turned from the man riding close to Samien, the General's badger-faced adjutant and then spoke to Goliath again. "But you have always wanted to return here, sire."

Goliath's smoldering eyes focused on Abimelech. "You've known me since my birth, Abi. I have no secrets from you."

Abimelech stepped back as two more chariots charged out towards them. The Philistine formations spread out and the officers drew their swords. However, Goliath remained still. He took his shield and brained the new attackers in a slashing, side-to-side move. A smile spread on his face as Goliath gripped the handgrips tight and the shield became a bludgeon, crushing arms and spears as men flew off their chariots. The horses kept running.

Samien tightened his helmet strap, and then soothed brown hair behind his ears before nodding to his adjutant. "Proceed, Colonel Baldassare."

Orders barked from Baldassare, and the Philistine archers took a knee. Arrows notched, they leveled their bows at the encroaching cultists and fired. While this move sent many foes scurrying back to their ragged lines, a few of those from the mountain met death, staring down at the shafts in their chests with quizzical expressions. They fell to the ground, the looks in their eyes unchanged.

Goliath regarded General Samien only in passing, saying, "How's that for courage? Dumbass courage, but courage all the same."

Samien replied, "We are here for the high priest's daughter, that rare flower of short-haired beauty with violet eyes, remember?"

"Yes, General," Goliath grunted in a low voice, a tinge of comedy in his tone. "Religion first, always, even if that religion must get men killed to favor a cock teaser with hair like a boy."

General Samien's sullen eyes held no contempt for their champion, but easily read his mocking tone. "If not for the gods, you wouldn't be here." He moved his mount about and took care not to stomp on the feet of the slender teamster who stumbled near the animal. "Have a care, Yaggah," Samien admonished the wiry teamster. Since the flood of cultists cut off the Philistine rear guard, many of their teamsters became trapped in the loop and they ran between the warriors. They sought cover, as they wore no mail armor or helmets.

Whereas the champion paid the General's words little mind, Abimelech watched the carnage wrought by the archers. Several volleys from the bowmen and the twitching bodies of the felled men subdued the initial nerve of the cultists. Goliath stood by Abimelech as they watched the surrounding cultists taking up positions against the Philistine forces.

Abimelech moved in closer to his master. "Sire, whether or not the Sanrevelle sisters can indeed handle your manhood is no reason to seek them out, but I have no doubt of other motivations."

Thumbs tapping the top of his shield, Goliath's sardonic grin turned to a snarl. "For revenge, for my friend who fell at the twins' embrace long ago, and for blood." His voice rose so the army and the cultists could hear him. "That's what it's all about, right? That's what these cults desire from their breeder whores and what the priests of Baal, Dagon, and Moloch yank at their pricks over. Blood, blood, blood." His face turned grimmer and his eyes leered into the underground path. "They gotta die."

Samien tore his gaze from the champion and reined

his mount around to give orders to others in the cavalry.

From out of the cave strutted two smaller figures. "Are these the sisters come into the light of day?" one of the Philistine infantrymen asked a fellow soldier. They presently saw that though the forms out of the mountain that scurried behind these two appeared first like a horde of rats, they soon took on humanoid shapes. Goliath raised an eyebrow as the two leading figures stood on outcroppings of stone and raised their arms. Clad in baggy caftans, these two tiny men made many Philistines laugh.

One of the Philistine infantry Captains said to the soldier that spoke, "Those cannot be the sisters, Cairn. Keep your blade at the ready." When another young soldier moved up by Cairn, the Captain said, "Keep prepared, Sadik."

The youth, different only from his brethren in that he was beardless, nodded, but remained focused on the little ones.

The Captain wondered, "They send out their children to fight our champion?"

Goliath scoffed, "They aren't children, or dwarves, Captain Balzer, but small folk. They aren't from around here, see by their dusky skin?" His voice trailed off as he saw dozens of them behind the two who stood on the rocks. These swarmed around the two, who chanted and wiggled their fingers in the air.

Like a swarm of ants, they flowed forward, causing the Philistines to draw back. In another moment, these forms covered a hundred yards, speeding to Goliath's greaves before he could move. They struck him with small daggers and climbed his legs like a horde of insects.

Abimelech moved back, but drew his two short swords and sliced through a few of the tiny folk as they attacked his master. Their numbers ran so thick all

Abimelech had to do was swing and bodies rent apart. The crush of them proved so many Abimelech backed away from the champion and stumbled to his knees. One of the little ones launched himself from a heap of dying bodies, striking Abimelech in his nose with a cocked elbow.

Two on each limb, and several on his back, Goliath went to the dirt. He tried to rise up, failed, but threw off a few bodies, cursing. "Get the hell off me, you little bastards!" Repeatedly, they stabbed at him with their blades, but they broke these points and many teeth against bronze armor.

Throwing off a body every time he punched at the air, Goliath felt more of the minuscule men leap on him or tiny feet tread over his body. Some concern seized him, knowing that soon they would find a vital spot in the links or get lucky to gouge out an eye. He seized one by the ankles and swung the pygmy hard, impacting on soft flesh of others. Goliath smelt blood, rolled over, and swam in the crushed bodies before climbing back to his feet. He kicked his right leg and one of the attackers flew. Goliath aimed this projectile at the chanting man in the caftan on the right. The tiny pygmy knocked the wizard from his perch.

Watching the cultists arise to renew their own attack again, Abimelech fought off those that oppressed him, blood flying from his nose. Captain Balzer skewered bodies from Abimelech's back with a lance like he plucked fish from a river.

"Many thanks, Balzer," Abimelech spat, swinging fast and chopping more of the tiny fighters in half.

Balzer then aimed the bloody point of his spear at the cultists surrounding them. "Why don't the rest of them attack? A few did at first but fell back fast after these little ones came forth."

Goliath focused on the last tiny spellcaster, who

never stopped his incantation as his fellow wizard got bowled over. "They're waiting." Goliath glared at Abimelech and asked, "What do you see?"

Abimelech took a few breaths, wiped blood from his nose and confessed, "The day is all wrong. Though clear a moment ago, the clouds now boil overhead."

Balzer rubbed his eyes. "The sky looks like intestines, all ropey and rotten."

After a few vigorous nods, Abimelech added, "The world isn't right, but I feel the beat of a hundred hearts like a heavy footfall or the thrum of a heavy bowstring."

"Wizards, damn them," Goliath growled, eyes not blinking.

Balzer staggered. "Don't you see it? The grass is now turning black and shadows are everywhere. Can't you hear the shrill cries of strange beasts and the ground breathe?"

Hands to his sides, Goliath confessed, "No, I don't. This what you see is a spell for you all.." He then held up his shield and took a step toward the tiny wizard.

The wizard smiled with a mouth full of blackened teeth as he left his perch to stand on the ground. "You cannot see the world vacillate, great Nephlionic champion of the Sea Peoples?"

What Goliath could feel was pressure on his chest, the magick of the mage pressing against his being as he advanced. Like invisible hands wearing gauntlets made of writhing bees, the magick touched him. Goliath screwed up his will to fight off the sensation freezing the Philistines, but his vision started to blur. He stopped in his movements, but wasn't held back by the force of the magick. Goliath's rigid countenance set on the wizard as Abimelech babbled about dark canyons encroaching and the infuriated heavens.

"Keep your guts tight, Abi," Goliath ordered, but for a moment, he caught a glimpse of what approached the

Philistine army, what the wizard made them see...

The cult members out around the ridge transformed into black figures and surged headlong at the Philistines. Twisted crooks of horned demons and six-winged fallen angels, the devourers of dreams, the scavengers of blackest night. Certainly not mortal men at all, Goliath longed to spit at them. Their tortured visages glowed with yellow, catty eyes. Twisted maws emitted burning drool as dripping fangs snapped and churned. Bodies that bristled and popped with gore-oozing pustules slithered or shambled forward toward the fighting force.

An inhuman roar escaped from Goliath and he held his shield across his chest. "Bewitch us no longer, you little sonofabitch! You send death to them, all that's evil and unclean? You don't know what evil is yet." The warrior raised his shield up high over the wizard. With no more words or yells, Goliath brought the shield down, flat, crushing the tiny spellcaster under the shield. Once the shield rested near to flat on the ground, Goliath stepped on it and faced the Philistines. The army, now clear of the enchantment, saw their foes not as gibbering horrors of the ether realm but as a pathetic fighting force no match for them.

Balzer shouted, "Kill them all! Spare no man or woman, save for the high priest's daughter! Remember, she's the short-haired one!"

Goliath looked into the cave opening and stepped off his shield.

Abimelech stared at the shield and waited, but it never moved. The giant reached into a pocket on his belt and took out tiny metal rods.

"Abi?"

"Yes, sire?"

"Clean my shield, won't you?"

Abimelech sent the shield a doubtful look. "Yes, sire."

Philistine

Goliath shed his helmet and his upper body armor. "It's time I was done with this task."

Abimelech squatted by the shield as he watched the slaughter of the cultists. As the cries of death and dismemberment grew louder, he said, "Sire, is the priest's daughter within Nebo itself?"

With a shrug, Goliath turned away. "For all I know she's dead in the attack out there. What's one more life to a priest of our gods? If Samien wants her alive then let him go fetch her in the din. I go to right a wrong in life and will confront the twins. My ass grows weary of kings, priests, gods, and their desires." Goliath then reached over, grabbed Abimelech's nose and twisted it back into place.

More blood spurted from his nose, but Abimelech took a liquidy breath. "Thanks, sire."

Abimelech watched the champion of the Philistines disappear in the darkness, following his own yearning and searching for destiny.

*****

"Come along now, warrior from the Philistine realm," a sultry voice purred from all angles in the underground chamber. "Drawn nigh unto me fast. Find me amongst these cyclopean tombs of the sons of God and lay claim to that gift so many have sought after."

His mane of hair back against a rounded pillar, Goliath held his breath and tried to place the rapid footfalls. The padding of bare feet, as brisk as that of a galloping deer, traveled across his range of hearing, coming from all directions in the vast abode, much like her oppressive voice. The echoes in the stone cavity played havoc with his senses, but Goliath's resolve held. The countless candles didn't dance, their flames remaining erect as if no air moved in the enormous area. Since dozens of the thick pillars rowed themselves up in the tombs, Goliath didn't lack for a hiding place. His greatest trouble was to not pass water at the teetering voice that mocked him.

"Oh, come to me, strong man," a second female voice cooed, the accent very similar to the first, yet somewhat higher in pitch. "You know yours can be the one to take our eldritch power, such a man of primal breeding. That must've been a long journey here to the belly of Nebo, coming from a seafaring folk." The voice sliced through the air like thin branches in a windstorm. "Lay down with me and rest, great one, forever."

He found this place with ease, as the cultists and their mounts came from a cavern further across the way in the hidden sector by Nebo. However, this long ramp, strewn with cobwebs and emitting soft lights, easily called to Goliath from dim memories of his youth. Though led by his own reasons, Goliath frowned at the idea of doing Samien's work. Aside from retrieving the priest's daughter, the General wanted to find and destroy the focus of a rumored rebellion, who gave it guts and faith. Word came from the priests that the twins were guilty.

Ears and eyes failing him in this hunt amongst dozens of pillars, Goliath relied on other wits. Nostrils flaring, true to his primeval instincts, Goliath could smell his quarry and place their location as they moved nearby. With a single stride, the sinewy Philistine slid across to the next pillar, leather boots making nary a sound as he went.

A form moved swift, spinning near him. His clenched fist opened out of surprise. The attack never came, but what he held in his grip plunged to the stone floor. The metallic tinkle sounded louder than a bear's call, echoing in the stone hall. He held back a curse of Ba'al Zebul, knelt and searched with desperation for what he lost.

"You play games with us," said the voices in unison, making sweat roll from his nose in the cool extent. "Bringing toys for us to play with? There is more here than could be dreamed of, even if you could read from the Pnakotic, Pnom, or Ponape scripts. No need to translate, dear man, for the instrument of your enlightenment swings between your legs. You can embody all the power of the ages, brawny man, just take it from between our thighs and be done, forever."

Goliath's fingers felt on the floor, illuminated by erratic surges of light from beyond the pillars. He soon found that the objects he dropped lodged between the seams of the granite blocks making up the flooring. Eyes leering at the farrier rasp used for tending horseshoes, his heart sank when it proved evident that he couldn't retrieve the specially crafted tool.

The sexy voice went on to say, "Our father, Nyarlathotep, blessed us with these breathtaking abilities, for he came from outside the shifting sky." Greater peril lurked in her attitude as she invited him, saying, "Come lay with us and see what lies beyond night itself."

Against the column again, he damned himself for losing the metal shanks. Mind racing to find a replacement, he breathed deep. Right hand gripping the pommel of his broadsword tight, Goliath allowed the weight of the weapon to rest across his hairy chest and against his thick beard. As he tried to move in quietness, his boot turned over debris on the floor. Licking across his mustache, Goliath took a cautious breath and peered down at what he trod.

"He smells familiar, sister, like old wily Neurath the man-god, but different," the torrid voice declared, losing a bit of its sexual menace. The footfalls stopped for a moment. "I never forget a man, or one who fashions himself man *enough,* no?"

The lofty voice replied, "You're so adroit with anomalous scents, sister. How could he have come unto us and somehow escaped?" Every so often, as the voices echoed, a yellow glow on the walls throbbed. "No one ever has, no?" Her sardonic laughter came at him from all over, like a swarm of mosquitoes.

Goliath's boot stepped on ancient proof of this statement. Aside from the ruined skull, which lay shattered like a crystal ball, a few long shards of pelvis protruded amongst a leather waistband that curled over the tip Goliath's boot.

The cavorting steps sounded in an outlandish pattern, almost like children skipping as the first voice giggled, "Yes, yes, they always arrive at this surreptitious place if they have the guile and means. Through bargain or blood, they turn up, where the sepulchers of the Sons of God are said to be, far under Nebo. All of them appear, seeking magnificent ascendancy from the lovely Sanrevelle sisters, offspring of father Nyarlathotep."

He banished images of an episode in this chamber from his youth. Goliath tried to formulate a back-up plan. His breath still, he stared into the busted face of the skull and at the sharp points of the ruined pelvis. In his mind, Goliath started to hear an answer.

The laughter resonated as the other accent said, "Our acolytes outside allow them in, so content they are to be drunk on our meager gifts. Who could discern that drink and virility would be so desired by the gentry upon their service?"

While Goliath picked up the waistband and stared at the remains of the dead seeker of power, the higher voice asked, "I wonder if they sing lovely songs about us in their smoke-filled taverns and palaces alike? Do we inspire or frighten drunkards, royalty, and feral children the same? Do the Dhol Chants chronicle us or forget our loving embrace?"

"This could be, sister. Daddy told us that this may be the truth."

Six fingers on the leathery band, Goliath hatched a fresh scheme and thought, *Keep talking, sisters.*

"And they never apprehend until too late the secret of the Sanrevelle, do they sister? They strut with great swords on their backs and grand weapons in their breeches, seeking to take our birthright ability of divination and control in the only way it can be attained."

Goliath saw the image of Sanrevelle slide past him several yards distant. Either Sanrevelle didn't spy him or categorized the Philistine of modest threat, but either way, she...they...passed him by. The idea that a giant's body didn't concern the sisters surprised him, but he accepted that one of his chief weapons, fear, was now worthless. He knelt and scooped out two jagged bones at his boots. A breath escaping hard, presuming the façade of Sanrevelle would soon fall, Goliath prayed to Ashtoreth for strength and then to Ba'al Zebul for true courage. He grinned at his own weakness as he tucked the bones up into the waistband he scavenged on the floor secured under his shaggy bangs. Goliath also prayed this dead man's skeleton still possessed a measure of dexterity.

"Sister, I tell you, this one has been here before, long ago," the deeper voice stated, steps still dancing away from Goliath.

"How so, sister?" the other voice replied as Goliath glanced back at the entrance to the chamber. Hundreds of candles, their flames unwavering, lined the walls and terminated at this gloomy foyer. Truly, the esoteric images engraved on the edges of that entryway, cupped with the glyphs and mosaics on the walls portraying funeral scenes and rising winged spirits, lent this locale an identity of a sacred burial place. He had no idea if any Nephilums or fallen angels really lay interned in the stones where the sisters dwelt. His mouth parched, Goliath hungered for the taste of the outside world beyond that opening. The urge to run surged in his hips, but he repressed it.

"No man has ever come unto us and lived," the higher voice reminded Goliath. "That's how we draw our great strength. Who knows, savage, your father may have made that first man to best us, in you." Again, the threat returned to the words as Goliath heard her say, "When our daddy returns, we will have a vast compliment of Earth's superlatives prepared for him, stored up and exceedingly vital."

"Yes, no man," the other voice drawled, threat growing stronger as she spoke. "But long ago, nearly twenty years I would mark it, a boy accompanied a barbarian combatant to this place. That youth watched his great hero take us on in a quest for immortality and endless riches."

When he peeked around the pillar, Goliath couldn't see where the voices originated, but he did spy a series of containers. These bottles, smoky green inside, sat out like a tavern of the gods, for their rows went on and on…emitting a yellowish radiance, rising and falling like breathing. Unsure of where this light came from, Goliath concentrated on his task.

"That event with the boy and the hero is dim in my mind," the second voice cackled. "The youngster then saw the demise of his champion? He understood that the idol of ruthless fighters wasn't man enough for us? Is this the youth grown up, fearless enough to journey back to Nebo and try this again, or just a donkey on two legs?"

His determination steeled, Goliath recalled the

man of which they spoke, the King of Gath's prime soldier, Hamilcar. Goliath remembered the burly Hamilcar swagger in to take on the challenge of Sanrevelle. Undeterred by the reality of what she was, his pride and manhood threatened, Hamilcar waded into the undertaking and failed. Goliath was but a boy of twelve when this happened, a Philistine child close to man making time. He saw his hero, the older man, so virile, take it to the eerie persona. Goliath observed as Hamilcar's backbones turned to light and his flesh metamorphosed into a gelatinous stew before being consumed by this unearthly creature. Hamilcar, turned inside out, was a grisly scene, enough to fracture the mind of a strong man, much less a boy. Young Goliath saw Hamilcar's bones start to fall like leaves before he fled.

They let him escape, probably to tell the lurid tale, spread the yarn and bring more victims to their ominous lair. Goliath never forgot it. Like most Philistines, he got over it, but wouldn't banish what he owed his friend and teacher. When he neared Nebo in the quest for the priest's daughter and sniffing out insurgent coalitions, he decided the time to act came nigh. Like all Philistines, aside from a fighter, Goliath learned a trade as a half-trained blacksmith. He meant to do right where Hamilcar failed, and though he had lost his metal shanks, Goliath prepared to fight on.

"I tire of your sport, Philistine," the deeper voice slaked at him. "Come unto us and seize the clout we have gained. You understand the way it can be had, so do it now and take it if you are man enough."

Deep in his arid throat, Goliath swallowed, turned his body from the pillar and faced Sanrevelle, the legendary vixens of power. The voices stopped, as Sanrevelle lay back on a cushioned gray mattress, near to the many shelves of bottles that still swelled with brightness. This bed struck Goliath as an altar, so stark ran the surroundings in the middle of the vast, mostly empty stone room. Heart punching his chest, he knew it would be an altar indeed if he failed in his mission.

Beyond her in the large collection of greenish bottles, the color, however, now pulsed orange.

"What's your name, Philistine?" Sanrevelle asked, sounding earnest in her simple request. "I love to know the names of my lovers before they breathe their last."

Eyes on Sanrevelle, seeing what so many hadn't comprehended, that she was a twin human fused in one body, the warrior said, "I am Goliath, son of no one." He gripped his sword pommel tight and stepped closer, his long locks splayed across his face in a mask. "I return in the name of Hamilcar, one you have prisoner on the shelves beyond."

"Hamilcar?" they said in unison, exchanging a glance, their deep dimples increasing on a pair of identical round faces. "It's a name like any other and can join our legion of souls as easy as one like, say... Goliath." Both waved a dismissive hand at the rows of bottles, still steadily throbbing luminously.

He tried not to tremble at the sight, of the twin sisters in one body, yet his blade wavered, betraying fear. Unsure if his strong sword would suffice, Goliath carried it to the enemy anyway, first. Recalling Hamilcar's final spit in the eye of fate, when his manly idol drew out two knives and tried to kill Sanrevelle, only to have them scrape and blunt on her skin, Goliath hoped his plot would work, even if he had lost his smithy-crafted needles.

Naked, Sanrevelle lay back, spreading her three large legs and ample hips. Just above her pubic ridge, Sanrevelle's midsection split in two, dividing into the two sisters that talked to him, making up dual entities in one body. Both sisters sported shiny, flowing almond colored hair that trailed over their shoulders and dangled in rivulets between their breasts. Eyes as green as emeralds, Goliath thought these optic centers protruded too far for his taste. Each pale-skinned sister looked like any other nude woman to Goliath, save that the arms that met in the middle held each other and were shorter than the exterior limbs. He couldn't comprehend the third leg, almost backwards and pointing the opposite direction, surely out of her rump. Goliath's eyes aimed at her sex, seeing it not unusual, really, save for the area hairless and bore a double, protruding clitoris, colored violet.

"Don't tell me you came here to kill us," the sister on the left said, teeth gnashed in wretched delight, no fear for the giant in her manner. Though her maw was rimmed by her ruby red lips, the teeth in that mouth bore too many canines for Goliath's heart to achieve arousal.

The one of the right grinned as well, then turned her scarlet lips into a juvenile pout, as if hurt. "You insult me, great warrior. The desire to conqueror me and take my abilities with your manhood is not on your mind? I've heard the warrior Goliath slays women when he covers them. What a man!"

As she ran a hand full of long nails across their flat belly, the other said, "Yes, with our power, you can find any treasure, take any silly woman, delude any man's mind with ease."

A roar in his throat building, Goliath charged, sword ready to strike her in half. He pulled a dirk for his left hand and swung his right with an overhand arc meant to split them apart. From the area of the bottle collection, the color showed burgundy and the pulses of light emitted faster.

A sigh escaped her mouths and Sanrevelle propelled herself off the mat with blinding speed. Her grip seized the sword by slapping her exterior set of hands flat on the coming blade. Her other tiny hands grabbed Goliath's left wrist and held it fast. Resisting his forward momentum, she fell back, but stayed close to Goliath, easily balancing his weight. The twins giggled in unison, two legs curling about his calves, knowing they had him. For all of his might, he was held fast by the twin sisters of ungodly potency.

"So sad, for a manly fighter," the one on the left smirked and kissed his mouth softly.

Goliath's eyes flared like a forge and he smiled.

Sanrevelle's grin faded at this unforeseen action. When Goliath's head slammed into her face, her mouths opened in a scream. This sound, one muffled against the beard and rough face of the savage, sounded a tone of alarm. Pulling away fast from Goliath, releasing him, Sanrevelle's left twin howled as she clutched at her eyes. Blood and gray glop poured from her eye sockets as the bones on Goliath's headband fell away from her eyes and down her cheeks. Goliath's dagger swiped at Sanrevelle's left head, at the throat, not ripping loose the jugular vein as he planned, but gouging open a thick wedge of skin in her neck. He darted close, flat of the sword pinning the other sister, his teeth clamped on the flap, tongue searching in the wound for a vein. Goliath found the slippery vein, feeling like a long bean and bit down. Immediately, the right twin pushed the weighty sword and the warrior away. Goliath staggered back several steps as the sister on the left screeched in agony, blood shooting from her neck.

He returned the dirk to his belt, spit out the vein in his teeth and screamed the name of Ba'al Zebul. He turned the sword upside down like a spear, and stabbed, nailing the left foot of the mystic being to the flooring. The sword tip passed through the appendage, but wouldn't cleave into the stone, so Sanrevelle yanked her limb back and limped away a few paces. Her blood, colored purple and pulpy in its texture, splattered on the floor. The light from around the bottles surged violet when she screamed. As Sanrevelle fell, the sister on the right tried to conjure a spell. Her sister still yelled. Goliath leapt on her, knocking Sanrevelle to her abundant backside with his thighs. Blade still pointed down, pommel held with both hands, he drove the sword into her injured neck, striking bone, twisting and stifling the screams forever.

He stepped back and watched as the wounded twin gagged, clutching at her throat before falling limp. The remaining twin sobbed with dysphonic grandeur and shook her sister, trying to invoke the proper spells. Goliath guessed them enchantments of healing, but they failed, as this sister cried, frazzled and unable to complete her sentences in a coherent manner.

Goliath faced the rows of bottles, which oozed a blackish light by then. Again, his guttural roar sounded and he powered into the collection of containers. Like a bull loosed in a refined banquet hall, the Philistine thrashed and stabbed, crashing his forearms through the shelves, sending the bottles to flight amongst the splintered wood. The bottles rolled away and his boots stomped them down, like a nest of baby rats running for freedom. Just like those tiny lives, Goliath crushed the small bottles, letting wisps of bubbly air out. No drama existed in the act as he destroyed them, save for the moaning voice of Sanrevelle. Unsure if he freed Hamilcar or the rest from a type of slavery to this entity, Goliath performed his duty thoroughly.

Face full of pain, voice bursting with tears, she snapped at Goliath, "Barbarian swine, my sister is dead. Our power from Nyarlathotep is fading fast from us, and now you can never have it. By destroying those soul jars..."

Goliath turned back to her, raging, "I didn't come

here to gain knowledge of divination or to find ways to ferret out damnable gold. I came for Hamilcar. I came for revenge. I came to see you die! Soon, I'll feed you to the sons of Ba'al Zebul."

A shrill in her voice, she proclaimed, "My sister's dead, you maniac! I can't live without her! Do you know what this means?"

"Yes," Goliath responded placidly as he dropped the sword. The clatter of the heavy weapon on the stone floor made Sanrevelle jump, catching her failing breath. She froze, helpless or at least too fatigued to do anything, Goliath thought, her power halved. He started to undo his midsection buckle and push down his pants, saying, "I guess I better hurry."

*****

Out from Nebo's underworld, Goliath stood over the tiny wizard he concussed earlier. The little man's eyes opened, and he looked across the ground, focusing on the form of his fellow mage, driven into mush under the shield resting in the hands of Abimelech. He then gaped up at the champion. Goliath dropped a corpse from off his shoulder, breaking both tiny legs of the wizard at once. The spellcaster screamed from the pain and then in realization as he saw the dead faces of Sanrevelle.

"Wait," the small one exclaimed. "Spare me and I'll tell you of great plots! They are all against you, the kings, the priests, Kmentosi in Ashdod, Eucimar in Ashkelon, Nekimai from Ekron with General Samien..."

"Men will beg for another moment this side of eternity, no matter what," Goliath barked with no humor. "Can you hear that, little worm?" He leaned over and then set his eyes toward the flat territories about Nebo. "Can you hear what rises off the plains to feed on your folk and off this thing you worshiped as a goddess?"

The priest turned his head. Terror in his face told the Philistines that he could hear the sound, like a sizzle of cooking meat. The noise grew loud in all their ears.

"Hear the children of Ba'al Zebul, coming to nourish on the dead." Goliath stretched and then reached for his body armor. "Join your goddess in Hell. She'll never shit light on you again."

Soon, a cloud of flies appeared in the vision of the tiny wizard, and started to blot out the sky.

Soon, flies filled the eyes and mouth of the wizard.

Soon, even his ears filled with the insects, thus shutting out the laughter of the Philistine.

CHAPTER TWO
FEAST OF ASHTORETH

O ut into an unrelenting noon sun, Goliath again carried the immobile twins over his right shoulder, but a smaller form over his other shoulder moved. He observed the land as it progressed from the base of Nebo, turning into foothills, crags and eventually, level ground.

From out of the Philistine factions emerged two men in green robes. Not hidden in the rear guard, blood spattered their gowns and they sucked air, exhausted from participation in the fight. Their hoods back, balding heads glistening in the day's light, these two took a knee to the champion and then bounced their fists together.

"Exaltations be to Dagon," the one on the right exclaimed. "Our god has delivered the daughter of our high priest Nekimai back to us at Ekron."

Goliath threw the girl down from his left shoulder and she screamed in distress. After the fall from a great height, her spinning feet hit the ground and she tried to run in the tall grasses. Goliath swatted at the crown of her head, barely touching the girl shy of twenty years, but causing her to somersault to the earth. The two priests grabbed her arms. She bit, kicked and spat at them.

Goliath said, bored, "Dagon didn't bring this little one back to you, no matter what you believe." His voice held a comedic lilt when he handed his sword to Abimelech to clean, "You know what her punishment will be." He then faced a sweaty General Samien, still on horseback. "It seems pointless to me to argue over where blood is spilled for which god."

The priests nodded to Goliath for his service and ignored the daggers Samien's eyes shot at the champion. Many soldiers stared at the twins over his shoulder and grinned to each other.

The girl in the grip of the priests kicked at Samien's skinny teamster, who fed the General's horse and the mount of Colonel Baldassare, then stared back at the giant. The girl screamed at Goliath, "To Hell with you, freak!"

Goliath's countenance went listless. "Go on, curse me. Kill me with your words if you can." He yawned and his voice carried tedium with every beat. "No weapon fashioned by men has any luck against me, and even one from the gods failed to strike me down when all else suffered peril years ago."

She kicked still, saying, "I heard about you from my father Nekimai, how you survived the plagues of the Hebrews' Ark." Her voice leveled out and turned snide. "Do you want a prize? Do you want respect?" She spat at him and missed.

Goliath winked at her, his huge face filling with jollity. "Show me a god or a man who can slay me and I'll bow before his might." His tone turned dismissive as Abimelech brought him a skin of wine. "You're a silly maiden, not happy with your designed lot in life... married to a sultan of the Amorites." He swigged the wine and tilted his head to the right. "Not bad work if you can stomach it, huh?"

She spat at Goliath again. "I'd rather die than be a

brood sow for their kind."

Goliath gave a slight nod. "You will get your wish. You father owes the Lady Bednukah of Moloch a boon. You shouldn't have run away. The black Sabbath is coming."

At the mention of Bednukah, her eyes widened and the shrieks turned shrill.

He turned from her, drank from the wineskin. "Abi, we need to get really drunk tonight. I have a feeling for it."

Abimelech scanned the area, at the bloody bodies of the cultists and the soldiers who looted them. "I enjoy your feelings, sire. Such a waste, all of those followers."

Goliath finished his drink, but came near to spitting at Abimelech's words. "Please don't tell me you're going to say it was a waste of human life. This day was great even if it only watered the grass with blood."

Head shaking, Abimelech replied, "No, it's a waste of manpower. Many of them fled off into the basin beyond."

The giant faced the wastelands to the east as the army gathered up its dead and the litter bearers tended to the wounded. "So many bands of the disaffected roam out there beyond Nebo and the edge of Israeli territory. Amalekite leftovers looking for a future, angry Assyrians, pissed off Edomites not wanting to suckle to their king, criminals the Moabites cannot get a handle on, and Hebrews heading the wrong way looking for Egypt."

Samien inserted himself, saying, "If they had a god to rally themselves under, they'd create their own nation."

Goliath coughed once. "If they had a competent leader, they'd have a damned army."

Philistine soldiers laid the dead cultists out, trying to count them. They soon, abandoned this action when

Samien ordered them heaped in mounds. Goliath unshouldered his burden but directed the men to keep the body of the twins.

Balzer instructed his men not to pour oil on the bodies to burn. "Let the vultures have their feast. They'll pass down into the soil for a supplication to Dagon and El Elyon. Let men pass by Nebo and see the might of the Philistines."

Goliath looked up at the birds circling in off the ranges of Nebo and then directed his words toward Samien. "Well, not exactly Targhizizi and Tharumagi, but it'll do, huh?"

The General never turned his look, but Colonel Baldassare placed a hand over his heart. "Your mirth at the expense of the sacred mountains that hold up heaven means little."

Ire raising slightly at the colonel, Goliath replied, "Who spoke to you, badger? If I wanted a pithoi jar opened, you'd be useful for your overbite."

Baldassare's face surged and his lips covered his protruding front teeth, yet he never retorted to the giant.

Samien said quickly to Goliath, "Are you that bored with men and whores that now you must stab at the gods?"

With a swipe at the hinderquarters of Samien's mount, Golaith sent the skinny teamster Yaggah running as he said, "You take stock in my words like a dupe, General. If I told you I loved you, would you accept that as fact as well? We stomped these pukes into the ground. Let's celebrate."

Samien's face bore no happiness at the idea of victory or the celebration. "How long until another great escapade is thought up by the brain trust at Ashkelon?"

Abimelech's eyes met those of his master as only they heard the General's words.

Samien then said, "Though you pledge loyalty to

all kings of the Philistine cities, Ashdod, Ashkelon, Ekron, Gath, and Gaza, it's the people that love their champion."

His feet planted, Goliath sighed. "What is it you have on your mind?"

Samien exchanged a glance with Baldassare. "Like I do, you follow the orders of the King of Ashkelon, Vyndekay. He has fashioned himself King of Kings with no battle, and yet..."

Goliath completed his thoughts. "We lose battles to the Israelites and others under his reign?"

Abimelech said, "Talk too much more, General, and you speak of sedition."

Samien's face hardened. "The people follow you, Goliath."

"But I have no desire to be a king or an object of worship."

Horse wheeled about, Samien asked, "How long before you tire of being the lackey to others?"

Face to face with the man on horseback, Goliath thought but a moment. "And you'd rather I be the lackey to, well, you?" Goliath threw back his head and laughed, then his face turned annoyed. "Do you really think I don't go where I choose? Be it the passions of men or what they perceive the desires of the gods must be..."

Samien leaned out and sniped, "Someday, night will fall and even the gods must all die." He then kicked his mount and trotted with Baldassare in tow toward the formation with the rest of the mounted troopers.

Abimelech said, "A mule on a horse, rather quaint, no?"

The anger in his face fading, Goliath replied, "Charming. The beaver at his side is very sweet, huh? I can smell the disdain the brown-haired General has for me."

His gaze following Samien, Abimelech mused, "Perhaps Samien's brown hair is just a chance, a folly of the gods, not a bad firing of his Canaanite lineage?"

Goliath winked, voice still low. "We jest, but this world is full of bastards. Yet, I oft wonder after that pissy General and his Canaanite leanings. Can one like him ever be a true Philistine, even if he's bred into us a few times?"

"Oh, forget him." Abimelech spoke up so all could hear. "There'll be a great feast tonight."

Goliath took long strides as the teamsters brought up the horses. "Oh? Where's this?" His voice louder as well. "I think Samien and I need to drink this talk out."

While Samien did smile at this, Abimelech went on to say, "It'll take us the rest of the day to reach the village on horseback."

Samien's skinny teamster spoke up. "Those worshiping in the Grotto of Ashtoreth at Oresel promised a victory party for your men."

Balzer checked the sun. "It's not far out of our journey, and I know the king of the city there, a man called Fittlea."

"Oresel?" Samien ruminated. "Isn't that the village with the last ogre alive, one Tallis Shuruppak?"

Abimelech scoffed, "Oh, he's probably just an ugly bastard, but if he really is an ogre, then he'll provide sport. It'll be a great time to supp and they have plenty of temple whores."

At this, the men cheered and started to fall into columns.

Goliath peered over at the priests of Dagon who bound up the daughter of their lord. As they gagged her, tears bathed her cheeks. Samien rode right past and never looked down at them.

Abimelech climbed on the back of the horse a teamster offered and settled himself on the blanket affixed there. "What is it, sire? I'm sure they'll sacrifice a temple whore for your pleasure tonight."

Goliath raised an eyebrow at his shield bearer. "Your concern for the heat in my groin is touching, Abi, but slaying a slut with my manhood this evening isn't really on my mind."

Once they started their journey, the horses at a trot and Goliath at an even gait, Abimelech quipped, "By Baal's balls, why not?"

Goliath took his jest with a chuckle. "Oh, the ways of the gods and men tend to bore me as much as I joked with that Canaanite dolt, Samien. I sport no pity for that little one back there as she goes to face Bednukah in the Domain of Moloch by Jericho, but another part of my life closed when I slew that twin."

Abimelech nodded as they traveled through the raw fields. "Great Nebo holds many secrets they say, aside from the ones Neurath holds on the other side."

"They? *They* should talk less and screw more. The world would sound better."

Two young soldiers jogged up from the marching infantry. Though they stared at the giant, they spoke to Abimelech. "That was incredible," one said. "Tell your master we were glad to fight alongside him today."

Abimelech never spoke as Goliath's voice thundered, "I can hear you." He peered down at the youths, both still jogging to keep pace as he walked. "You're green under Captain Balzer?"

The closest trooper nodded while the other beardless soldier turned his eyes to the earth, afraid to speak. "I'm Cairn from Sharuhen in the south. This is Sadik from Joppa."

Goliath faced the fields of swaying grasses. "Glad you're alive, the both of you. We'll have a good night in store." Both soldiers broke into smiles. "Pace your legs, young as they are. You'll need them for the temple prostitutes."

After a stern look from Abimelech, the two youths returned to the infantry ranks.

The Philistines traveled for an hour before Goliath glanced back at Nebo. "My hero Hamilcar oft spoke of mysteries on Nebo, of clashes with the gods and whatnot."

"Was Hamilcar a wise man?"

"Not really, but a fighter full of more piss and wine than you could shake your tool at. I have avenged him at last, but will shed tears no further, as he's honored in their deaths."

"Yeah."

Goliath cleared his throat. "Hamilcar was a good man for a Philistine. Some other cultures would give him trouble for his multiple wives, whoring and drunken debaucheries in Ashdod. All right, not everyone pissed outside on the narthex of the temple of Dagon and lived to tell about it, but Hamilcar oft ran wild. He told me tales of the higher ones, the angels, some call them, falling and fighting each other." Goliath turned back again. "On Nebo."

Abimelech even checked over his shoulder as if he'd see the scene. "They fell to earth on Nebo?"

Goliath touched one nostril and blew his nose. "Not all of them, but I heard that a few did. Something worth fighting for up there, I guess. I don't know. Perhaps a wise man will tell me that story over meat and wine this night. Are there wise men at Oresel?"

"Perhaps a few, sire," Abimelech speculated, stowed his reins on his belt and cracked his knuckles. "That skinny-assed teamster back there, Yaggah, the one who fed Samien's mount? He was the one who told us of the feast and of a boon for you."

Goliath never turned his head. "The tall one, losing his hair and he's not yet forty-five years old?"

"How could you guess that?"

With a rub of both his eyes, Goliath related, "I see inside men easily. Really, his teeth are dung. Like a horse, one can gauge their age. Go on, what of him?"

"He wasn't so bold as to approach you with this information, the boon, so he told me a while ago."

Goliath let his eyes wander over the vast fields, now churning to grain. "As is the way of weak men with small balls. Even those green troopers had guts enough to speak to me in time. Continue."

"Yaggah said there's a daughter of Ashtoreth at the city, not a literal sire of the goddess, but one of her courtesans. This woman has goodly hips and a rather big frame. He said this woman has heard of the champion of the Philistines and no man could ever satisfy her until now."

Goliath laughed once and then his face turned grim. "Pimping out his priestess, is he? How old-fashioned, that puppy, Yaggah. Like I need a common man from labor to get me women."

Abimelech frowned. "He was being kind, sire."

Others in the ranks watched the exchange intently, knowing the giant tolerated his lifelong friend and his words. They understood they couldn't debate the weather with the champion or dare tread on his words like Abimelech. Aware of their fear, Goliath never felt himself difficult to approach, but he let the illusion stand. This way, he ruminated, most would leave him alone.

Goliath pondered Abimelech's words and then his eyes intensified. "Kindness? What a wonderful man he is then. What else shall he do to make us happy? Bring us rare rings and flowers to gain time in the bed mat?" At these sarcastic words, the soldiers nearby broke into laughter. "Please. Kindness is but a word, and a tool to gain advantage of others. A gift of kindness is like a bequest called love. And like one supreme God, love doesn't exist."

A shake of his head later, Abimelech said, "You'd rather believe in a pantheon of gods and goddesses than a single supreme deity?"

Goliath shrugged and adjusted the javelin strap across his chest. "I think I'd rather have the heavens or the bowels of the earth filled with petty cretins, fighting like politicians over the scraps of humanity and mankind's souls than to think that one big bearded *god* controls all. That would be very scary indeed."

Balzer gazed over from his mount into Goliath's face and wondered, "You really don't believe in love?" Many men tittered in the ranks as they rode, for not many of them believed in it either.

Goliath said, "I have felt the fleeting pangs of what regular men call love, but it's a disease, something to be gotten rid of fast. It only makes you weak. If one gives into weakness, pain ensues." Some of his jolliness faded and his tone took a staid twist. "Life is all about pain, not love, my good men. God? Some say God is love. If he is, I don't want to believe in him, even if I see his cunning and deceit everywhere." His head turned and Goliath shot out a grunt. "Ah, Jericho," he spat at the massive ruined city in the distance. "Important place, but not so friendly to the seafaring Philistines."

Captain Balzer rode even with the giant on the side opposite Abimelech. "The hamlet of Oresel where we celebrate is near there."

A contemplative nod later, Goliath said, "I've heard of that village. Something about an ogre living there you all said?"

Abimelech shared, "Last one alive, but I saw him once. Tallis Shuruppak, the ogre, was passed out at the time, half in and out of a tavern."

Face taking on a sour look, Goliath asked, "Was he

really an ogre?"

Abimelech shrugged. "Tallis looks like a really big and ugly drunk to me. Tallis isn't the King of Oresel, just a drunken bully or oddity."

Goliath pondered that. "Each town has one. Anyways, Jericho is where my concern lies and where they will go unto for the black Sabbath. The old ruins over a portion of Jericho never rebuilt are where the Domain of Moloch resides."

No one responded to his words as many heard those tales as children. They understood the priests of Dagon would give the daughter of their priest over to the Lady of Moloch. None wanted to be present for such an exchange or at least to ponder on it for very long.

Goliath beheld the village of Oresel growing in size before them. The lush meadows started to fade behind them and more cultivated lands stretched on either side of the moderately elevated road. Though brush crowded the roadsides by the shallow ditches, the crops grew well out around the lands by Oresel. As the army crested a summit, Goliath saw many men in the fields stop to stare at the sight. Many wore scant trousers while they tilled up the weeds. They all soon took time to stare at the Philistine troopers and then him.

The cluster of huts that edged in the unwalled city started to empty of life. Many came out to see the army and the champion as they approached.

Goliath muttered, "As good a place as any for a feast."

*****

The Philistine army stripped naked and climbed into the river on the other side of Oresel. Long lines of the men splashed and tried their best to wash off the grime of the day. Goliath and Abimelech did likewise, though the officer class and many in the cavalry went with General Samien to meet the city king. In anticipation of the army's arrival at dusk, several serving girls waited on the banks. They brought them cups of wine and platters of sliced dates, along with drying cloths. Goliath winked at one girl as he undressed, and she flushed red before scampering away behind her friends.

Several girls that sorted pomegranates and fresh bandages pointed at the men. These weren't temple whores or servers, but children from the village performing their duty. The veteran Philistines paid their giggles and silliness little mind, but a few of the younger soldiers wiped themselves off fast before donning fresh gear.

A few servers and older women stood transfixed at Goliath, staring as he shook his mane off and then wiped off his hirsute chest. Abimelech dried himself and said, "The village teamsters say that dancers and the prime of whoredom has been brought in for us tonight."

"What a joy to be appreciated. Sounds like Fittlea knows how to feed his guests well."

"Did you hear tell that Eucimar from Ashkelon is coming here?"

Goliaths brows lowered as he rubbed a towel under his beard. "Really? The Arch Priest of Ba'al Zebul? I thought him busy with other matters, like exchanging letters with that Egyptian wizard Zorn or nailing willing acolytes."

"One would think."

"You'd think he'd have learned not to speak to Zorn since the tattooed wizard Paltibale never returned from the Egyptian's abode."

"Eucimar is a practical man, after all," Abimelech related, pulling a towel across his broad shoulders.

Philistine

"While distressed his partner in the priesthood Nekimai is losing a daughter to Moloch, he and the King of Ashkelon are coming here to endow us with fresh orders."

"Orders in person? I see." Goliath started the task of drying his manhood. One of the girls gaped, unable to look away. Goliath reached out his hand of six fingers. "I need another towel, maiden."

She turned and bolted away. An older serving woman, probably thirty years of age, threw Goliath a towel. Her eyes also watched his manhood, and the corners of her mouth dropped.

Goliath dried and mumbled, "Tell all of your grandchildren..."

Abimelech went on to say, "After their ceremony at the Domain of Moloch tomorrow, we'll head south, I hear, but they'll fill us in more later."

An irritated look spreading over his face, Goliath remarked, "South? What's south? To Edom?"

"The rising city of Relex."

Goliath rolled his eyes to the heavens. "Wonderful. More work for the goddamn priests. Samien will be impossible."

Abimelech shook out the curls in his long hair but never interrupted his master.

Goliath continued. "Priests are idiots, almost as much as kings or politicians. They all fight for the blood, lives and souls of men, scraping back and forth. No religion or king is different than another. They all do things in fear of a critic beyond the sky that uses rusty scales to judge."

They started out of the water and a girl just over ten years old fell to her knees before Goliath. Fairer haired than most Philistine children, he guessed her a crossbreed with another Canaanite bloodline like Samien. The girl asked, "Were you the one who captured the Ark of the Covenant?"

Goliath shot Abimelech a look and then took a knee, still looming over the girl. "Abi, children have no sense of nicety, she just asked what was on her mind. Would that all men and women had this girl's pluck. She approached the greatest living killer while he walked bare assed naked, and asked about a story. Huh!" His voice became imperious as he asked her, "You heard a story about me?"

The girl nodded, marvel in her eyes, but no fear. "I heard it was you that helped capture the Ark of the Hebrews long ago, before I was born."

As if seeing the incident in his mind, his eyes widened. "What else did you hear?"

"They say Great Goliath took it unto Ashdod, but the temple of Dagon was accursed by the Ark of the Israelite god."

In his mind's eye, Goliath recalled helping to lift the image of Dagon back into its place as it was found prostrate in front of the golden Ark. "That was a bad seven months for our folk."

"And the Ark even stopped where your mother resides at Gath. Were the people really smote in their private parts?"

Goliath rose up and she nearly fell down. "We gave the Ark back to the Hebrews. Their God can have it. It resides at Baal-Judah, or as some call it Kirjath-jearim now. They are welcome to it."

"Do you believe in their God?"

Goliath's eyes narrowed at her. "So many questions. Are you yet promised to a man?"

She nodded. "In a few years a Hittite soldier, Uriah."

"Then he'll teach you the ways of men and the importance of respecting other gods, even if you don't hold faith in them."

She blinked, confused but unwilling to ask again.

Philistine

"Well, little one, once you spend weeks getting boils from your groin with a knife, you respect the power of that god, even if his sense of humor is rotten."

When the giant moved away, she asked him, "Do you know the secret of life? Is there a hidden meaning? I hear whispers. You're not a common man and they say you're descended from the gods. I thought maybe you would know."

He faced her again without pausing to ponder her words. "Don't be a whore. Your back shouldn't ensure your comfort zone or your happiness. There can be a great future in whoredom, little girl, either as a man master or a woman to the bed mat. In the end, though, whoredom leads to emptiness. Be free. Run away from your future Hittite master. Cut his nuts off on your wedding night and offer them to the local deity for mercy. Then, learn to read."

Goliath then trudged up the shore and headed back toward the village. A few of the Philistine infantry performed a mocking round of applause to his words.

"Piss on all of you," Goliath said with a good-natured grunt. "I grow philosophical in my middle age. Would that there were enough whores to blot out my empty thoughts."

*****

That night, the feast of Fittlea proved a grand affair, spread out over an acre of property. Several awnings shielded in the portions of the yard in the rear of the stone buildings. The long tables full of food sat under the awnings manned by servers and presided over by the local king's portly wife. Though several tents and canvases provided a false ceiling to certain spots where many ate and reclined, most of the area remained open to the heavens.

Two different likeness of Ashtoreth, flanked by oil-burning torches, showed the outer boundaries of the party. One figure sported a set of feathered wings emerging from her back and swooping upwards. The other reproduction of the goddess stood rail thin and much older than the other, a more lifelike carving.

A hundred common Philistine soldiers reveled around the bonfires and tables, all carousing with the temple prostitutes and the common folks of the city. The soldiers showed restraint and good manners with the general populace, knowing offending their host with petty rape and brawling wouldn't be conducive to General Samien or Captain Balzer and their wrath or a possible doom meted out by the Philistine champion.

They all found Fittlea an amiable host. Most of Fittlea's hair had receded past the midpoint of his head, but a white beard hung over his chest like an apron. Abimelech exchanged niceties with the aged man before Goliath went to recline at the king's table.

Once Abimelech joined him, Goliath murmured, "Wasn't Fittlea a great warrior decades ago?" His voice stayed quiet, not wanting any to hear his words and disrespect their host.

Abimelech didn't eye the host as the old man embraced Balzer and others. "The years haven't dealt kindly to him. Too much sun and strong drink has made his face arid like the parched desert. Still, I think his wife's hand-stitched gown looks good on him."

Goliath shivered and he spoke softly still. "If my beard gets the color of a rabbit's pelt, spear me in my sleep."

"As you wish, sire," Abimelech promised as he took his first sip of wine. "You must try this. I'll fetch the choice stuff."

Philistine

Goliath reclined near one of the great tables occupied by Fittlea. Many others joined them as the huge roasted boar arrived on a litter. This brought applause from nearly all. While the women cut off the choicest cuts from the thighs, Goliath spied the wormy teamster Yaggah at the edge of the grounds. The only reason he noted the skinny man was what hung on his arm.

Yaggah led a rather tall woman into the party. Abimelech, carrying a large skin of wine over his shoulder plus three closed tankards by the handle, nearly walked into the pair. Not a small man by any means, Abimelech looked straight into the eyes of the rawboned woman. He nodded to Yaggah and glanced down at the flanky woman's frame.

Yaggah bowed and said to Abimelech, "This is Akisha, acolyte of Ashtoreth." He smiled and waved toward the small temple to the goddess as if the rough warrior missed the edifice nearby.

Abimelech's eyes took in the beauty on the arm of Yaggah. "I see," Abimelech said. "I'm astounded at how tall she is, barely an inch shorter than myself." Her bronze eyes set in fine over dimpled cheeks and a short chin. Akisha's hair ran out very long in streams away from the golden tiara the bunched up her topknot. Though the style of bending the hair into curls was unlike anything nearby, her painted eyes and lashes ran more akin to the fashions in Egypt than Judea.

Yaggah glowed, saying, "Do you think your master will find her comely?"

Goliath easily heard then and saw Abimelech admire her hips. Akisha had a thicker-set build than any of the dainty girls who starved themselves to be more attractive whores. "We shall see. He has not drank so much yet."

The shield bearer carrying booze left them and

returned to Goliath. Abimelech handed him the big skin of wine.

"Thanks, Abi."

"That painted tall one by the skinny teamster?"

"I see her and could hear you."

"That's the one they think can accommodate you."

Goliath uncapped the skin and drank deep. He sent her a penetrating look, up and down, then looked back at a platter of pigs snouts before saying, "Bless her then." He then nodded to the figure in the far left corner of the party. "Is that big pile of shit Tallis Shuruppak?"

Abimelech turned toward the huge individual, head obscured by a hood, drinking in the same posture as his master. "Yes. He looks docile for such a big thing, huh?"

"He sucks on the water pipe hose more than his wine skin," Goliath noted and leaned back. "Now, where's this woman again?"

Abimelech drank. "She's a big-boned girl."

With an abrupt exhale through his nose as he chewed, Goliath said, "The dragons and lake-dwelling Orms of Pictdom are big boned. That girl there is big assed, but a flat-tailed lass isn't what I need."

Once he'd chewed up a bite of pig snout, Abimelech said, "She's an acolyte of Ashtoreth."

Goliath drank again, wiped his mouth and saluted their host. "I don't care who she cries out to."

As the party around them laughed, many settled in to eat. The servants readily distributed sliced boar meat to the masses. They all ate and the wine flowed. Dancing girls soon stood on higher wooden platforms to perform.

One time, Tallis Shuruppak stood to go relieve himself outside. Goliath eyed the big figure and glanced at Abimelech.

"Is he really an ogre, sire?"

Goliath belched and replied, "How should I know?

I've never seen one." He then asked Abimelech, "I thought the King of Ashkelon and Eucimar would be here?"

"They are delayed, sire."

Goliath ate quietly as the men talked. He pretended to ignore them but did note Baldassare and Samien ate fast only to depart at a leisurely pace. Though most had shed their armor in favor of tighter garb, Baldassare still wore a dark under tunic and a mail vest.

The giant faced across the table toward Akisha. She sat, legs folded under herself, at a neighboring table not far from Yaggah. The giant leered at him and the emaciated man turned away. Goliath hid his amusement and set his eyes on her. She sent him a coy smile and fluttered her eyes, hands resting on her shiny knees. He returned appreciative looks, but never appeared enamored.

At the edges of the party, a ruckus kicked up. Several of the men from the village that stood as pickets for the grounds shouted. The beating of hooves and the yells of men became punctuated by the slick sound of metal leaving its scabbard. At this, the giant looked up, but made no move. Abimelech did rise up and stared across the grounds.

A Philistine soldier ran through the party and stopped at the head table. The giant recognized the youth with the droopy left eye as Cairn. The youth took a knee and said to Goliath, "Two men, sir, and they say they have came for your head."

Still chewing, Goliath chuckled. "Have they now?"

Cairn then gaped at Captain Balzer, then to Abimelech. "Forgive me, sirs."

Balzer waved this away and got up. "Who are they?"

"They claim to be Assyrian warriors," Cairn stated, getting his breath, wiping a smear of brine from his lips. "Two swordsman trained by Alkilyu of Tyre." At these words, Fittlea and others drew their breath in. "Ashur and Sargoth. They want revenge on Goliath for the loss of their sister, Lillita."

Goliath nodded, but never rose up. "I see."

Cairn added, "And their mother, Ansli."

Abimelech eyed Goliath and the Philistine shrugged. "I have no idea, really, and who cares if they have an authentic gripe." He relaxed back, took a drink and then started on a huge pork chop. "Go out, Abi, and bring me back their heads."

The crowd gasped as Abimelech turned from his master with no hesitation.

Goliath added, "Better yet, string their heads on bowstrings and hang them between the tits of Ashtoreth on each side here." He took another bite and ordered, "Get to it, now, be back in time for the raisin cakes. The ladies here worked all afternoon on them."

When Abimelech started across the party, Fittlea said with desperation, "Goliath, Lord, with respect, if I know who those men are, they are said to be the greatest swordsmen in Nineveh."

"That so?" Goliath belched as he raised his wineskin again. "Damn good thing we are in Jericho."

Fittlea took on a look of exasperation, looking down to see that Goliath's sheathed sword lay somewhat concealed between his legs. "But they were trained by Alkilyu..."

Goliath stated, "Who do you think trained Abi? I'm not a religious man, nor do I have faith in much. However, I'll bet my javelin I see the skulls of those assheads up on the idols in a few minutes' time."

*****

The two showed no fear of the hulking shield bearer

of Goliath. They took up defensive stances, their faces visibly angry at being dismissed by the champion of the Philistines. The man on the left stood a head and a half shorter than Abimelech and wore light armor of squared, unconnected bronze plates indigenous to the Assyrian military. Young, swaying like a panther, the dark-haired assassin's face shone clean in the moonlight.

The other, fairer haired one watched Abimelech carry out armor and weapons.

"I am Ashur and this is Sargoth, my brother."

Abimelech put on a wool undershirt, followed by his chain mail vest and then pulled his elbow spikes up his forearms. "I don't care."

"You send out a dog to fight us?" Sargoth shouted at the party, waving a falcata sword. The swordsman held a small triangular shield on his left forearm, swaying, ready.

The giant watched Akisha as she arose and dropped her woolen cloak. "A dog?" Goliath laughed, his voice booming across the party. "All the better to deal with bitches." He then drank again as Akisha started to rotate her hips. Those beating drums and strumming harps caught on to her moves. They began to play a rhythm for the tall woman. Goliath said to those at the table, "The young one against Abi, Sargoth, sweats too much. His fear gives him away. He also carries a sword that pitches toward the tip. A man who wants to carry a weapon like that is too weak to wield an axe. He has been killing puppies with it and that has given him courage. Abi is no mutt."

The warrior Ashur on Abimelech's right wore dark leathers with pointed metal spikes at the shoulders and elbows. Though he dressed like a Hittite soldier, Goliath guessed him half a Greek or some other mixed combination. The bonfires showed his stern eyes flicker wolfishly over his neatly trimmed beard. Feet set, solid and looking darker of skin than the other in Assyrian garb, Goliath doubted they were real brothers and wondered where he originated. Ashur knew how to hold the bastard sword in his hand, but Abimelech noted the spiked mace that dangled from his hip.

Abimelech donned his leggings, picked up Goliath's oversized shield. He balanced it on his thigh and drew out one of his short swords. A few guffawed at him in the party, drunk, but too stupid to hold back their impression that he looked silly carrying that huge shield forward.

Sargoth jumped back in the shadows with an elegant hop and prepared to slay Abimelech. He hid to conceal a coming move. Sargoth wore a determined look as he struck forth with the falcata. At first, he stabbed at Abimelech and moved past, executing a flèche move to perfection, but the blade never harmed the Philistine. The enormous shield of the giant deflected the shot, and Abimelech raised his sword to ward off a strike from Ashur's heavy bastard sword.

Again, the crowd laughed at Abimelech using the oversized shield, looking like someone stepping behind a wall or a barn door to hide.

Akisha gyrated, her hips in a wicked swivel, hands above her head, breasts bouncing. Goliath watched Akisha as the action cut loose behind her.

Abimelech exhaled, sounding almost bored. A great display of swordplay started, a fine exercise in slash, thrust, parry and counter thrust, to the point it appeared unfair to Abimelech. Though the two attacked with vigor, Abimelech blocked them repeatedly with the shield scissoring from the ground and his sword. Ashur would strike the shield as Abimelech slashed at Sargoth, then the action reversed, but Abimelech forced the big shield on Sargoth to tilt, making him take a self-protective posture.

Philistine

Sargoth started to breathe heavier, and Abimelech stepped out more to give him a target. The Assyrian stabbed, but the slender blade glanced off Abimelech's stomach plates. Abimelech then planted and rolled the great shield, causing the experienced warrior to step back.

Ashur went for the kill and Abimelech twirled, hands off the shield for a moment, and struck his head down on Ashur. The move made the crowd wheeze in shock, as it appeared he head-butted the assassin, cracking Ashur's forehead, but the foreign fighter failed to bounce off after the head-butt. The crowd applauded when it realized Abimelech's teeth sank into Ashur's cheek. Head snapping back a moment later, Abimelech spat a wad of flesh at Sargoth.

Abimelech transferred his blade to his left hand, lifted his arm, not only parrying the falcata of Sargoth, but also pinning it to the shield. Abimelech drew a dagger with his right hand and jammed it against the falcata, cutting the stylish blade in half.

Ashur held his wounded face as Abimelech shoved the heavy shield against him. Hand slick with blood, the wounded man struggled with the shield, its weight alien to him. After a shove on the shield from Abimelech, Ashur's left leg stretched behind him in the weeds and almost collapsed.

Fittlea observed, "Your shield bearer dances with that shield near to as good as Akisha in her all together."

Quickly, Abimelech's right fist struck Sargoth in the jaw. Hand still holding the dagger, Abimelech swiped fast, slicing off Sargoth's right eyebrow just as he stomped on the Assyrians' sandaled foot. While Sargoth convulsed from the heavy boot of Abimelech and the pain in his face, he warded off an attack from the Philistine's sword with his small shield.

Ashur took a knee, angled away from the shield with

a roll, and came up with a dirk. While the shield teetered and fell, he dived, his curved blade meant to hamstring Abimelech, but the blade struck lower. The greaves on Abimelech's calves proved well made for they deflected the shot. Ashur scrambled away on his all fours as Abimelech threw his dagger. The crawling man dropped flat to avoid the knife and rolled again. Abimelech then drew out the heavy sword from his back, and Sargoth struck at his solar plexus with his ruined hilt. The jagged edge of the busted sword didn't penetrate Abimelech's mail links, but crushed the armor in and bruised a rib.

Abimelech held his heavy sword high, unable to slash Sargoth as the Assyrian moved in close, so he boxed his enemies' ears with his elbows. The pointed guards on Abimelech's elbows pulverized Sargoth's ears, ripping each one away from his head as he stepped back from the Philistine. Sargoth dropped his ruined sword and clutched his head, screaming. Abimelech eyed Ashur, who started to choose his next move. Abimelech let his blade fall on Sargoth. Even though in agony, Sargoth used the small shield in defense. Abimelech's sword passed through the metallic safeguard, slicing into the man's forearm and cleaving into his jaw.

Akisha turned about, her rump hopping in tandem with the beats of the drums and the shouts of the combatants. Goliath's head made a slight move to stay with her movements. She kept dancing, the pads of her feet touching almost in rhythm with the blows of the fight behind her. The dark eyes of the dancer traveled up and down the sheath of Goliath's sword in an obvious addition to her dance.

Pulling back, ripping loose flesh, metal and teeth, Abimelech only regarded the ruined Assyrian face for a moment before a kick sent Sargoth bowling over a line of pithoi pots full of dried fruits. His bastard sword in hand, Ashur attacked anew. After clashing swords three times, Abimelech locked up blades and shoved Ashur back. Ashur stumbled, and flopped back on his buttocks. The Philistine glanced back at the Assyrian he mortally wounded.

Sargoth's dying face turned confused, gaping at the founts of blood, gray marrow gushing from his arm's stump. After a kick to the suffering man's chest landed right under the bronze chest plates sent him sprawling, Abimelech then looked to his right to check on his other opponent, still struggling on the ground. Sargoth became his focus and Abimelech grabbed up his other sword. He criss-crossed his blades, cleanly removing the fighter's gagging head, sending his stern face to the ground with a bewildered expression etched on it forever.

Akisha kept dancing. She turned to face Goliath and reached behind her neck. As Abimelech shook off the showers of blood bathing his left leg, Akisha undid the fixture at the back of her neck. Her ample bosom fell loose of its wrap and bounded as she danced. Several clapped their hands and cheered at all the action on display.

The blood stopped spurting from Sargoth's neck stump. Abimelech heard a rushing howl as Ashur came after him with full vigor. Though his blade blocked Ashur's kill shots, Abimelech got thrown back into the stone representation of Ashtoreth. The idol didn't move at his back as the foreign warrior tackled Abimelech again. By his maneuvers to quarter him off, Abimelech judged that Ashur indeed knew how to fight. This man's body stance showed he understood to keep Abi's dominant arm from striking. Ashur pinned one of Abimelech's arms down as he slammed a multi-pointed mace toward the Philistine's chest. Though his sword laid crossed over himself and his weight wedged to the goddess, Abimelech pushed away as the mace fell. The spikes didn't break skin, but tore away chain mail when Abimelech dropped down.

Stationing himself over the Philistine, Ashur kicked Abimelech, but blocked an attempt by the shield bearer to strike him using a short sword. Arms out, Abimelech pushed off the idol and tackled him. Amid the displaced guests, the two struggled, hitting the ground. Abimelech writhed on Ashur, trying to avoid the spikes on the fighter's body. Neither gained much advantage until Abimelech separated, arose, stayed low, and kicked the rising fighter in the groin. This action sent Ashur reeling back and the mace stuck to the ground. Climbing to his knees, Ashur struggled to get a grip on his aching manhood. A horse staggered into view, from the decorations on the mane, one of the assassins' mounts.

Akisha grabbed the edges of her string kilt as her breasts swung in the dance. At regular intervals, she lifted her covering, not giving a clear look at her sex, but every time she did lift, her dark eyes glared at Goliath, then looked away. She spun, gyrated her pelvis, and reached down at his sheathed sword that lay between his legs. She blew a gust of air his way as she clutched the hilt of the blade.

Abimelech sucked air and held his chest. He saw Ashur holding his crotch and struggling to rise. In moments, this fighter stood tall, trying to raise his weapon and shrug off the shot to his manhood. Abimelech gripped the pommel of his shorter sword \and swung upwards, striking the assassin between the legs before he could use the mace or take up the bastard sword to block him. The deep-voiced fighter growled, but his tone ran more in tune with a gelding than a manly shout of agony. The thick sword wilted and blood ran from his tongue. His blades at the ready, Abimelech stabbed one into his opponent's lower abdomen and sliced up, the motions raw.

"I like that," Goliath said as Akisha supplied a longer look at herself and curled her tongue out of her mouth, running it over thick lips. She turned, fingers fluttering, right hip cocked out, and let her hands join like a fan, soothing down the long sheath of his sword. She hopped forward, legs apart, straddling him but a few moments before gripping the pommel, and struggling to lift it. Goliath reached out and pushed it up, aiding in her intentions. She leapt back, still her legs swiveling, and drew the sword out of the scabbard.

When the Assyrian's guts started to unravel over his pelvis, Abimelech gave the horse an annoyed look, but a gleam lit in his eyes. Stabbing his weapons into the dirt, he grabbed a handful of intestines and looped them through the nearby horse's blanket strap. The dying assassin's eyes widened, knowing true terror as the stout Philistine slapped the horse on the rump. The roan galloped off, taking the guts of the fighter with it. Ashur stared on in horror as his insides unraveled. The horse ran on and there seemed little end to the intruder's insides. Even after he fell to his knees, he kept losing his guts.

The applause was deafening.

Abimelech took up a blade again and made a slight motion, cutting the man's head free, ending his suffering, just before the rest of his body jerked away, leaving a crimson trail at first, then vanishing from sight.

The giant's sword tip in the ground, Akisha slithered about it, careful not to touch the sharp sides. Her fingernails tapped on the edges and her tongue licked the pommel ball.

Goliath wiped his mouth, and then clapped his hands for the dance. He looked at Abimelech stringing up the heads on the two idols. "Now you see what it takes to be me." Goliath said as he gestured to Fittlea. "The burden of being *Goliath* is with me at all times."

"This happens a lot?" Fittlea stammered as the crowd, even Tallis Shuruppak, stood to applaud more.

Abimelech shrugged as he returned to the table, tearing off his ruined mail shirt. "It happens enough."

Eyes facing the heads of the dead men, Fittlea asked, "Was he a member of the famed guild of assassins from…"

Abimelech cut him off by coughing loudly. He bowed his head once to Goliath and replied, "No, just two damned idiots, trying to make a name for themselves by killing Goliath. Both were liars, today and before when they duped any around this area. They did make a name, though, and its *worm-food*."

Goliath smiled. "Assassins' guild? Can any of such an ilk have an organization? Such a group of backstabbers should be called community leaders, no?" As Akisha coasted to a stop and bowed her face to Goliath's feet, the giant rose up and said, "This is turning out to be a good night after all."

Akisha turned and started to walk out of the party.

Captain Balzer asked Goliath, "You wouldn't prefer one of the vestal virgins of the pure faiths I've heard of?"

Goliath followed Akisha, but paused to say, "Who'd want a virgin? It takes years for a virgin to learn to perform as good as a whore."

*****

Akisha led Goliath to a small grove of trees far from the village of Oresel. The night deepened as leafy trees caressed his arms. She dropped her hand from his, and in the darkness, Goliath came near to losing sight of her. From what he'd compared over the years with his abilities, his senses ran superior to most men. On scent alone, he'd not lose Akisha in the night. She wanted him, burned for him, and that fragrance he would follow to the edges of the ocean.

"You aren't afraid of an ambush?" she cooed in the night, reaching to grasp his hand again. His six digits dwarfed her hand, though for a woman, Goliath guessed her paw not so dainty. "I could be leading you astray."

"What do I have to fear in this world, even if you were trying to slay me? I can sense and smell the fear in you for me, but not hate nor malice."

"Really?" she half laughed, threw back her tresses so they slapped his chest.

"That smells different. And if you had a dozen little morons out here waiting to kill me, I'd have smelled them, too. When men are afraid, their balls sweat badly."

Akisha stopped, turned, then ran her hands up his stomach and touched his nipples. Though very tall for a woman, he still stood two feet over her. Akisha's eyes danced in the moonlight, and Goliath brushed an index finger up the side of her face.

"You're so unlike other men who ply me with words and flattery."

"I know what you want of me, and I'm not much of a poet. If you wanted romance you'd have chosen a man half my size, his balls in a harness and his heart outside his chest."

She dug her nails into his massive chest a little and he never reacted. Goliath did look at the distant ruins of Jericho's outskirts. Akisha turned to see as well, then reached back to fondle Goliath.

"Can you hear that, the rumble?"

"Yes," she answered. "What is it?"

As Akisha pulled his manhood free from his lower kilt, he frowned at the distant place. "What magic makes the ground echo like the sky?"

Her attention focused on his huge member. Akisha grabbed him with two hands and took a breath. "Who cares about that? It's probably Lady Bednukah and her familiar demon causing havoc in the Domain. It's naught for us to worry on." She grinned up at him and stroked his massive self, then stooped to slap her breasts with it. "You may kill me with this thing after all."

Eyes down at her, Goliath said ruefully, "You'd not be the first." His eyes then returned to face toward Jericho's ruined edge. "The temple of Moloch resides underground, yes?"

She sighed, her flesh warm and chest shaking. "Yes, yes, under portions of the fallen walls. So what?"

Goliath looked down at her again. "Do I feel very distracted to you?"

She blinked as he grabbed her shoulders. "No," was all she could reply.

"Good," Goliath picked Akisha up by her arms and then turned her around. His embrace around her breasts, he carried her further into the grove of trees and found an open place on the grasses. The giant lay down with her on his right side and ran fingers over her breasts, even down to her sex. His words, "I'll try not to slay you," were as gentle as his voice got as he started to probe her triangle of hair.

"Should I pray to Ashtoreth for her blessing?" Akisha cooed, her hips trembling at his touch.

"Pray all you want, call on the gods and all of their fornicating children," Goliath said with a blithe voice. The head of his member bounced on her labia and felt near to a fist on her. "I don't care."

And even amid her screams, Goliath could hear laughter. Hers, at first, like the banter of a person driven insane, and then a distant bit of mirth in the wind, as if Bednukah's familiar demon knew what the giant did in the trees.

Again, Goliath didn't care. Let the demon get his own woman.

Philistine

CHAPTER THREE
KINGS, PRIESTS, AND SACRIFICE

Akisha created more happiness and passion in Goliath's body than he'd care to admit. Too many times, he'd slain partners in the sexual act, so to find a woman able to take a goodly portion of his girth fostered an absurd excitement. The first time he took her, Goliath climbed atop and played his strokes carefully. Amazed at her abilities and feel, he arrived quicker than ever in his life. While he laughed at this, he buried his face in her breasts and then rolled onto his back.

She stroked him and her smile shone in the night. Her sultry voice went on for a while and he pretended to listen to the words. He did hear her say, "Truly, you're not like other men." She straddled his midsection and thrust herself back at his turgid member. It slapped between her buttocks and then he reached to maneuver himself. As his slick seed ran from her and Akisha thrust herself back to get more of him in, they heard horses in the distance. They soon ignored the sound of new arrivals.

Her hands flat on his chest, Akisha rode him partially and grunted deep in her throat. A few times, she coughed, causing her sex to flex about his manhood. Sweat ran down Akisha's face and breasts. Her fragrance increased, only fueling the giant's strokes to a greater speed. All the commotion of voices and horses over where the party still raged never stopped their actions.

"Damn you," she moaned, eyes shut tight, hands becoming fists in his mane of hair. "Sonofabitch…"

His senses afire, Goliath gritted his teeth as torrents of pleasure coursed through his frame. The heat built inside him and he prepared to arrive a second time. Her musky scent built up, stronger than before. As the point of no return arrived, his senses registered danger. No single woman could smell that potent nor so different at once.

"Yes, yes, oh, yes, now," she screamed, hands pounding on his chest.

For a moment, he thought her his slave, so enraptured by their mutual orgasm she'd reached a higher place of consciousness. Nonetheless, it was but a moment and Goliath had been covering women since his youth. In the same instance, he knew she faked her apex of pleasure and terror struck him. Suddenly, several womanly fragrances surrounded him. Akisha's grin of pleasure turned crooked and sly. The shrubbery around them moved as if the earth rejected their roots in unison.

Goliath sat up fast and threw her off himself as the whoosh of blades cut the air. Each arm that fell to the spot where he'd been lying was thin, female and sported a thick, two-edged dagger. Akisha tumbled off him as he swung an elbow back, inadvertently breaking the neck on the first encroaching body.

It registered fast that several women tried to kill him. He slammed his body back down and snapped arms like brittle branches. Saluting their pluck, if not their brains, Goliath rolled, swung wide and maimed another of the female assassins, but he'd missed several in his initial move. The voices nearby the party grew louder, and those women with their daggers paused but a moment before chaos reigned.

Up and looking about, Goliath saw bedlam erupt all over as a mounted group of new military arrivals joined the party. The remains of the band of armed women fled in all directions.

"Get them," Goliath shouted, commanding the notice of all in close proximity, swiping his arm across the field at the escaping figures.

The assassins fled like a disturbed rat's nest. One of the women planted her blade square in the chest of a Philistine guard. This new man on the scene wore fine linens and light armor. He guarded an individual Goliath recognized by his salt & pepper beard and iron headband as Vyndekay, the King of Ashkelon. The woman's blade penetrated this guard's breastplate and presumably, his heart, as the blood spouted in geyser spurts before he dropped to his knees.

From the darkness, a thuggish man in a glittering bronze helmet swung a blade and hit this killer with an overhand arc. The sword in his grip passed through her collarbone, lodging somewhere between her breasts and lungs. Another guard rushed forward, skewering her through the stomach with a lance, and another stabbed awkwardly at her left shoulder.

More figures emerged in the night to his vision. Goliath noted his old friend, the priest Eucimar, and an acolyte in a dark cloak. This acolyte of Ba'al Zebul soon revealed herself armed with a short sword. She stepped in front of Eucimar to cut down another assassin at the knees. Her obsidian hair flew free of the hood as this young lady rose, taking up a set stance before slicing the sword across the wounded assassin's throat.

Another hired killer fell to her backside and held

knives up in defense, trapped by the acolyte and the other men from the King. Two of her compatriots fled into the night.

"Alive! Take them alive!" The burly man in the bronze helm and regal armor shouted as he removed his sword from the woman near the King. "They are no good dead. We need their brains."

The King of Ashkelon agreed. "Listen to General Schlack."

On his knees, Goliath still towered above the common soldiers of the honor guard to King Vyndekay. Akisha then rolled from him toward the edge of the grove, not hiding her nakedness at all.

Goliath's eyes scanned the area as he stood and tried to size up the situation.

"Those women, they move like snakes. Are they hired killers?" a man on horseback wondered, his voice gruff and full of harsh tones.

"They desire my death?" Goliath asked, some perplexity in his words, but a trace of bemusement as well. He frowned at the men. "The King of Ashkelon and his General?" Goliath roared with laughter, enough to make the horses back up and the men uneasy. "What the fuck is it you want, ya perfumed pricks? My life, too? Get in line."

The moonlight shining off his helmet, General Schlack stepped toward Goliath and announced, "We saw them lurking near this grove and suspected mischief. How were we to know our champion covered a woman here?"

Some of the guards laughed and then kicked at the quivering assassins crippled by Goliaths swats, but the high priest of Ba'al Zebul stepped toward a woman still holding her daggers. "You came to kill someone here?"

The woman cried out loud and thrust her daggers into her own neck and wrenched them away from each other. More cries came out from the grove.

Goliath sighed and all eyes went to him.

"Where are my pants?" said the giant as Eucimar shook his head at the display of the dying woman. Goliath reached down, grabbed his kilt and donned it with no speed. His head did snap to attention as he looked around the grove at the scrambling men. "Where's Akisha?"

Eucimar wore a narrow look. "Who?"

"The one I did here with the hips like a wash tub."

The men exchanged glances but came up empty on her whereabouts.

Goliath strode out of the grove and blinked in the moonlight. "Gone. Hmm." Both eyebrows rose as it all dawned on him. "Aren't I the jackass." He then frowned at the arrivals and nodded at the King. "Vyndekay, so far from Ashkelon and your province. Why is that exactly? I heard you might be out this way."

A face full of scars and weather-beaten skin lost its color as General Schlack spoke up. "The King carries a great request from the united peoples and kings of Ashdod, Ekron, Gath and Gaza."

Goliath sent the stout general a sour look. "I didn't see the King's mouth move once." He gestured at Eucimar, who let the voluptuous acolyte amend the folds in the priest's cloak into a proper position. "And you sport the high priest, my favorite, in tow? This must be a special need."

King Vyndekay pulled his wrap nearer to his shoulders. "Let us retire indoors as one never knows what else lurks out here." His eyes focused on the distant ruins by Jericho. They heard the thudding laughs of the demon of the Lady, like thunder underground.

"Just a demon," Goliath said in passing. "Plenty in the world, just so few in a cage so close."

As the party started to depart the grove, Goliath

kept looking over the countryside. When Abimelech and other soldiers jogged up to them, no words were spoken. Abimelech fell in line to Goliath's right hand.

"They have caught one," came a cry from afar. "Over here by the river!"

Abimelech drew a short sword and the party gravitated toward the riverbank.

One of Fittlea's house guards lay on the bank, holding his groin, but two of the locals held one of the assassins. They stood soaking wet and flanked by two boys not yet ten years old.

The boy on the left spoke up, saying, "She became ensnared in my trout-lines. Imagine, sir, catching an assassin with a fishing line."

Hands on his hips, Goliath wondered, "Assassin? Why do you say that, child?"

The boy shrugged and pointed. "She wears pants like a man, carries two daggers and smells like hashish. Isn't that how they enchain these women?"

Goliath shot Abimelech and the General a look. "Bright boy. Many thanks." Goliath reached into a pouch on his belt. His huge hand held out something the moonlight made glisten.

The boy accepted the object and his face glowed. "A ring, with an emerald stone! Truly, will this lead me to more treasure?"

"Yes, and if you were older, that treasure would lie between a woman's legs. However, be wise and use it to feed your mother."

The boy grinned and stepped back.

"Always tend to you mother, boy. Slay any man or woman and all of their kin that threatens her." After the guards ushered the boys away, Goliath took a knee and faced the woman. "So, little one, you are undone here by a child's hobby. Your masters never taught you great caution?"

Philistine

She spat at the giant and hit his knee. "No man is my master."

Goliath smiled as the ground trembled from a minor earthquake. The men exchanged glances, but Goliath said, "Someone sent you to kill me, didn't they? Who was that? First, I get Assyrian swordsmen and now a gaggle of stoned bitches with knives. Who is it out there that waves their manhood at Goliath?"

The woman said nothing. Her dilated pupils danced in the moonlight.

Goliath eyed Eucimar for a moment. "Girl, shall I see if you could survive what Akisha did? With that little pelvis like a soup bowl, I doubt it. Tomorrow, the Lady will sacrifice for her demon in Jericho. One more life to her demon Amazarak wouldn't matter much."

Again, she spat, but her face filled with fear and faced Jericho. "I'll take my chances with you and your self."

Goliath laughed once more and the thunder around them chimed in, but no rain clouds gathered. "You let your mouth overload your vagina, woman."

Another time, the ground shook and a few of the men took on panicked looks.

Eucimar said, "There's great magick afoot, here and underground."

The two men from Fittlea's household looked at the woman's arms and suddenly released her.

She let out a sharp cry, one that grew faint fast and echoed like a fall into a well as her skin adopted a gray hue. In a moment, she stood taller, but rigid, and fell. The guards grabbed again, pulling at her arms. Each limb broke off as they gawked at what they held, transfixed.

Goliath kicked at her head and it burst into dust. The limbs the guards held fell apart into powder. "Stone. One doesn't see that every day." He faced Eucimar.

"Does Bednukah have that sort of power?"

Eucimar studied the stone body as it broke down into fine particles and even handed his acolyte a piece of the stone. "I've never heard of it as such. Keep that for later, Hasana. Goliath, why would she need to do this? Bednukah has a demon."

Goliath stalked across the lands and entered the village. There, most all of the inhabitants assembled and dropped to their knees, praising Goliath.

"Where is he?" Goliath snarled and grabbed Abimelech by the shoulder to turn him around.

"Who, sire?"

"That pricknose teamster who contacted you, Yaggah."

Abimelech glanced at a few soldiers, all arriving half clothed, roused from sexual revelries as well. These men started to search for the man in question. They sprinted into the huge open field where the troops bivouacked for the night. Each small tent only yielded up more men and temple workers.

Goliath released Abimelech and promised, "I'll get the truth out of Yaggah by reaching up his ass and pulling his tongue out."

Out of breath from searching the field, Sadik regarded the village and then murmured to Abimelech, "Why does the town fall so before Goliath? What's wrong with them?"

Goliath eyed the young solider, but turned away, his eyes scanning the crowd for Yaggah.

Abimelech explained, "Sadik, they're recalling the example of the village of Remhob."

Sadik blinked. "I've never been there."

"Nor will you ever," Abimelech said dryly. "A family of fighters sought to slay Goliath from that hamlet. They tried to kill him by poison and other means. The townsfolk claimed to be oblivious to it all and not hiding them."

"What did he do?" Sadik asked, but assumed the answer as his face reddened in the moonlight. "Kill them all?"

Abimelech nodded, "Every man, woman and child. These folk of Oresel don't want to be a part of a campfire tale."

Eucimar sipped from the ceramic cup provided to him by Hasana and said to Goliath, "I'd forget them for now."

Goliath gave him a frustrated look, "And you are here, why?"

"I'm here as I have to be present for the sacrifice at the Moloch temple. That and I'm going to siphon off some of that latent power of hers as I go unto Egypt to see Zorn."

Goliath's face brightened. "You're going to see Zorn, the greatest of all wizards? He takes so few visitors and I hear he slays anyone that dares approach his tower by the coast."

Eucimar nodded and avoided the folks begging for their lives. "He has contacted me in my dreams, and by a proxy, so I must go." His eyes met those of Hasana. Her stoic appearance broke, betraying worry for a moment. "It's a supreme honor to meet Zorn for any reason."

With a sharp clap of his hands, Goliath said, "I've heard he sends walking dead men to priests with messages. I guess they do as they are told."

"Quite."

"Has Paltibale ever returned?"

"No. My little spy in Paltibale's temple, Ahmee, wept so much that he went off to Zorn that she left to join the cult of Neurath at Nebo."

"That is sadness. Ahmee was once one of the ladies in waiting for my mother at Gath."

"Everyone grows up."

Hand to his chin, Goliath turned from them and thought aloud. "Paltibale was a good man, even if he showed that blue falcon he had tattooed on his thigh when he was drunk. I think it was his way of also showing his enormous manhood."

Eucimar smiled, still sipping his drink. "Probably."

"What a card. Still, I've heard that Zorn has lived for thousands of years. Good fortune with that trip, Eucimar." Goliath tussled the hair of a young villager in soiled trousers, crying for his life. "Bring me back a present."

"I hope to come back. My life of gathering knowledge and artifacts has come to this pinnacle so I relish the chance to discover more. But also, Zorn has revealed the truth of tales told to us about the arisen city down south."

"Relex?" Goliath gave the approaching King's party a sour look before saying to Eucimar, "They say it protrudes from the sea by the port city Ezion-geber. If it does, it does."

Eucimar drew back his tan hood and ran a hand over his bald head. "If what sleeps inside is true, then it should be of interest to you."

Goliath faced away from them again. "Are you going to say one of the sons of God sleeps there beyond eternity? They could've picked a better spot to arise than the backwash of the devil at Ezion-geber."

"Zorn has shown this to be so. It's true. He has given me a great vision, and I've even drawn a map and direction from my astral travels." Eucimar reached in his robes and produced a scroll on dried skin. "The great city houses a representation of Dagon himself."

Goliath turned back, bent down to study the map and then drummed fingers on his knees. "What value is that? What makes you think the representative of Dagon, or Dagon himself, wants to leave that city? If he wanted this, he would have left by now."

General Schlack, grasping a belt under his stomach, said in a deep voice, "You could beckon him unto us and bring him back unto Ashkelon."

Goliath leaned back, stood up in full, his eyes on villagers down the way, and then looked at the nearest dwelling. "You want bragging rights on the other shrines and cities of the Philistines? I see. This isn't a religious matter, I guess, or you'd send that god-lover Samien, but one of power. Figures." He turned and glanced about. "Where in Hell is Samien anyway?"

The King asked, "You object to the task set before you?"

Goliath lowered his head to face them all, one at a time. "I fear no commission, but thought myself of better use to the Kings of Philistia elsewhere. You're set to combat King Saul soon. Would I not be of better use there than on an errand for the gods?"

Arms folded, King Vyndekay said, "Eucimar sees this undertaking as true in his mind and the right operation to do. We have many men to fight the Hebrews. We have always appreciated your service and compliance with our orders. You ask for little for one so powerful."

Goliath shrugged. "You give me the things I like and I'm a simple man."

The King said, "Now with this city arisen, I can offer you something more than killing and whores. There's mystery here, adventure and a chance at solving an ambiguity in your own mind."

Goliath snapped his head toward Vyndekay and even the General held his breath.

The King maintained his cool manner. "Your melancholy speeches after a barrel of wine betray your yearning to ascertain certain details about your father. Your adoration for your mother at Gath is well known."

Goliath muttered, "I doubt a personage of Dagon

will solve any questions in my mind. If a son of a god truly slumbers there in the sea by Ezion-geber, well, who knows? I'd hate to think Neurath and myself are truly the only two left."

"Are you thinking about the possibilities that it would be so?"

Goliath fell silent for a time but then relented. "Of course. I'm no fool. I know the tales of the sons of God mating with women and how the great God of all flooded the world to destroy them in their human bodies and their offspring." He held up his right hand and fluttered his six fingers as if to add to the mocking nature of his voice. "Somehow, something like them survived and sired me. That isn't supposed to be possible, aye?" His fingers became still and curled into a fist. "However, I live."

The King never flinched. "Then you accept the task?"

Fists dropped to his sides, Goliath shrugged. "Your words twist me around. Sometimes it's better to not know all in life. Sometimes it's better to let an itch fester rather than scratch it raw."

General Schlack raised an eyebrow but Vyndekay's expression remained steady.

"Words, they cannot pierce my skin, but they can bruise my innards. Can they put out my eyes? No, but they can leave their footprints on my soul." With a low sigh, Goliath stood again, half smiling at himself. "Yes, I shall go see to this assignment if you think it is best I separate from the main army of Samien. Let Captain Balzer and several men come with us to Ezion-geber. I trust their timber."

The King nodded, but the General said, "The plans are in motion and Samien has other duties. A company would see to this city even if you never went along. Captain Balzer will lead our forces in this venture. You are a great promise of success better than a hundred virgins for sacrifice."

Goliath's hands flattened and then twelve fingers rested on his waist. "You're such fools with all of that talk of virgin sacrifice, like the gods give two turds for that little piece of flesh. It's all about souls. The only thing virgins are good for is if you get enough pure minds thinking on the same thing, they can distract one from what men really want. That is a pure form of mental magick, I hear. Men want to satisfy their flesh, be it between a woman's thighs or at the humiliation of a man in battle. Wizards? They confound me as they have little interest in women or war. There's something wrong with men who would rather cast spells and design games of the gods than get drunk and come."

Abimelech said to Goliath, "You're going unto the ruins at Jericho tomorrow?"

The giant's head tilted slightly to the left. "I shall see this thing they talk of in rare whispers, again." He stepped away from the rest with Abimelech in tow. "I see that Kmentosi from Ashdod has arrived over there. That wizard seldom leaves Ashdod unless he's going to the Madam Dralla Bojak. Watch him, Abi. Tend the preparations for our departure."

A frown on his stern face, Abimelech asked, "Shouldn't I go with you to the sacrifice in the Domain of Moloch?"

Goliath raised an eyebrow, never used to his words being questioned by Abimelech. "I tell you to tend the preparations because I trust you in that. You do trust me, Abi, that you really don't need to attend this rite of Moloch?"

A hurt look on his face for a moment, Abimelech read wisdom in Goliath's manner.

"I shall tend the duties for our exodus."

Goliath turned from him. "Get some sleep first. It'll

be a long day on the morrow."

Once Abimelech departed, General Schlack stepped closer and spoke loud. "I expected him to fall at your twelve toes, begging forgiveness for a slight of the tongue."

Goliath didn't look at the General as he said, "Abi isn't my slave, nor is he a dog. He doesn't always comprehend my wishes, but I cannot hold that against him. He's clever enough to see through my words and wants, in time. He has character and guts," Goliath paused, looked the General up and down. "Something many lack these days, but I feel you have guts, General."

His jaw locked, the grim, war tested eyes of General Schlack never wavered in the gaze of the giant.

Goliath smiled a little. "And you don't tout your exploits to impress me, good. You're wiser than I thought."

"A warrior knows when to stab and when to parry."

"Indeed. Be happy Abi serves me. If he were a regular soldier, you'd be his underling." He addressed one of the Philistine soldiers of lower ranks who guarded the door. "Sadik, is it? Go search for the teamster Yaggah. Break his nose but don't kill him. Yes, I know the others search for him. Bring him to me and find what happened to Akisha."

The young man Sadik bowed. "I shall try."

"Do it, don't try." Goliath towered over the youth. "You fear failure. Don't. Look for victory. It will give you courage."

*****

The Domain of Moloch could only be found in the mounds of rubble that was Jericho with proper direction

Philistine

from local priests. Daylight didn't give the grim locale of debris much splendor. Youthful acolytes in orange flaxen robes trimmed in red emerged from the disturbed blocks, crafty as ants and equally as thin. The acolytes watched their masters and the group of Philistine city fathers that came to the site. The hidden entrance proved a tight passage to enter the Domain.

Several who arrived with the Philistines stayed outside, among them, Kmentosi the wizard of Ashdod. He lowered his hood, but only Eucimar spoke to him.

Goliath hunched over and slid through the passageway in the stones. He paused to look at one of the Moloch youths. "Where is your soul, little one? Your eyes seem empty."

The acolyte neither moved nor replied.

Goliath glanced at the priest of Ba'al Zebul behind him. "Eucimar, I'm glad Kmentosi stayed behind."

"Now, now, just because he has a face even his mother couldn't abide by..."

"Like an enlarged skull barely holding skin, the ugly mutt."

"Kmentosi is a powerful mage, Goliath."

"Forget him. Your little girl stayed outside, too?"

Eucimar closed his eyes tight for a few moments. "Hasana doesn't need to see this."

"She's a fine girl, able with a blade, too."

Eucimar couldn't hide a grin in the dim light of torches. "Yes."

"Good work if one can get it, I suppose. But you need to see this before you journey for Zorn? That sounds as if you tip toe on the edge of madness."

His voice taut, Eucimar said, "I'd rather the Lady not know I was going to see Zorn, as it were, but there's naught to stop knowledge of my quest. Zorn beckons me and I will go to him. Lady Bednukah is doubtless annoyed that Zorn never called on her."

They stepped further down the hall and the ceiling climbed so Goliath straightened up. The temperature rose as they entered into the realm of Lady Bednukah, and Goliath said, "I wonder why he didn't call on her?"

Eucimar shrugged and swiped sweat from his forehead. "She never leaves this place or her creature, Amazarak." The party started down a series of steps barely lit by lanterns. A few times, Eucimar steadied himself on the champion's thigh. "I think she can, but doesn't, not much, truly not to sail to Egypt and see the greatest wizard in the world."

The steps ceased and Goliath grimaced. A small room immediately off the path opened into a cavernous chamber. Several braziers burned and their eyes soon adjusted to see the colossal image of Moloch to their far right. The stone likeness of the god reclined, across a placid stream, looking not unlike an upright bull, bovine in the face, and horns curled out. Plump in the middle, Moloch's representation held up its upper limbs, but the arms proved humanoid and terminated in splayed fingers. Down below, his huge belly spread out like a billowing skirt, open in the center, coals smoldering within. Above that spot, six other smaller slots burned on his chest.

Eucimar asked him, "To whom do you pray other than Ba'al Zebul? You don't believe in any of these gods, do you?"

Golden light making the sweat on his nose glisten, Goliath answered, "I talk to myself a lot." He squinted, perceiving just over a dozen sets of wooden stocks facing Moloch in front of the placid stream. His defenses went up and he touched the strap on his chest that secured his javelin. "I know something is out there, beyond night, outside our eyes that speaks as Baal, Dagon, and the rest...but they are not present at all times." As the others shrunk back behind the giant, Goliath gestured

Philistine

at the platform to their left that overlooked the lower region. There stood a slender female beside a billowing cloud. The woman's skin ran chalky all over and her blood red hair blew about as if all four winds struck her at once "But, look there if you want to see evidence of the supernatural, all of you. The Lady doesn't control a god, but a rather powerful dog, yes."

Lady Bednukah heard his words and opened her arms across her triple bosom. From this action, the cloud beside her flared bright crimson. A humanoid shape took hold and all but the giant shrunk back or fell to their knees. Goliath took a step forward, and his eyes were near to level with the feet of the pale woman and her demon. He looked up at them, regarding the demon first.

"It has been years," said Goliath, his manner unshaken.

The eyes of the red creature parted and no pupils dwelt in the slits, but yellow light foamed like bubbles in beer. In fact, these tiny suds sprang out in golden dots all over the thing, which sported a humanoid shape, but with skin more akin to reptiles than men. No children's jape, no horns or hooves, the demon did have lizard-like skin and the occupying creases around its eyes. The most bizarre feature was the fact it wore jewelry. Earrings dangled from his fin tipped ears, and a necklace of bullion links decorated his neck.

It spoke. "I notice you still dally with men, awaiting their wishes." His voice came from all around them and many who cowered checked behind themselves. They only saw grinning priests of Moloch, hands folded, waiting

Goliath raised an eyebrow. "I see you are still the bitch of a bitch, imprisoned by your own foolishness, Amazarak."

The demon almost shrugged. It then touched its

ears. "It's almost worth it, in the scope of eternity, to get these near and dear to me." Amazarak touched his earrings and a smile parted scaly lips.

Goliath looked closer and a scowl crept over his face. This made the demon Amazarak even more amused and the Lady smiled as well. "So she lured you in with two babies and trapped you?"

"They are perfect twins," the demon rhapsodized as in ecstasy. "You should hear them scream still!"

Goliath stepped back and only sent the Lady a passing look.

"What?" she snapped, scarlet lips peeled back. "No words for me, Champion of all men?"

"Fencing words isn't my thing. I fight."

Giggling, Bednukah's hands rested on her ivory-skinned waist. "You, one of the last of your kind, a simple fighter amongst a culture of death. You could be so much more."

Goliath walked back by Eucimar. "But I'm lazy and have not the ego to be worshipped. That'd require too much work. Killing the little fighters is simple." His eyes faced the demon. "Killing children is no challenge, and I see no need of magic in my life."

Green eyes sparking like candles, Lady Bednukah said, "If you did give in to sorcery, to learn the arts, what a powerful weapon you would be."

"I have my own life to think on, and I'm content or I'd not be here."

"All of the questions in your life are answered, giant?"

"Of course not. Wouldn't life be boring if they were?"

Bednukah's eyes glowed darker. He thought she conceded that point to him. "But you came along to watch?"

"Eucimar wanted me here. I don't care for ritual and sacrifice. It means nothing to me and lessons fall hard on my mind."

She grinned with shark-like teeth. "Then I will educate you, Goliath, son of goddess Orpah that resides in Gath. I shall give you a lesson even your mommy didn't tell you about."

Goliath folded his arms. "So far, you're merely talking me to death, and I've seen uncovered women before."

Her hands ran over her three supple breasts. "But none like me."

Goliath yawned. "I've seen witches with pneumonic teats before, to suckle their devils and feed a spirit. You don't impress me any more than the time I saw you skin a herd of goats by Sidon never using your hands."

The Lady kept smiling. "You will learn. I will teach you."

*****

Goliath took great strides, stomping the earth as if he held a grudge against the soil. He soon stopped and sat in the dirt not far from the edge of the village of Oresel. His shield bearer followed him close, eyed the sun overhead, but remained standing.

The soldier party packed up on camels. Captain Balzer eyed Abimelech and his master, but said nothing. Goliath figured his expression betrayed him and even spooked Balzer into silence. Abimelech, however, wasn't so easily dismayed.

"What did you see, sire?"

Goliath stared across the plains and never turned his face toward the ruins on the edge of Jericho. "There's a reason rituals are considered forbidden and feared by those not close to a sect. One might ask themselves what could be so bad, so degenerate that it would strike fear into a populace or have myths created about it."

Abimelech blinked. "The Lady Bednukah sacrificed several of the five city fathers and their offspring that fell into the cult. I assumed they passed through the fire of Moloch like the stories say."

Goliath waved for a crippled servant of Fittlea to bring him a drink. "For all I know, that happened in time."

"I heard the drums beating. They say they do that to drown out the cries of the babies."

Goliath nodded.

"Did the Lady use her familiar spirit to get rid of them?"

"Familiar, funny word for something that hates her so much."

"What?"

"The demon Amazarak is her prisoner and does her will, but he must. His power is increased by her methods and sacrifices, but ebbs away, drains to Bednukah for her own uses. That star about him keeps him honest and the constitution of the powders hemming him in lies out of my reach."

"Could you tell if she had three teats through her clothes? What does she look like?"

Goliath took the huge skin of wine from the servant and nodded at the cripple. "Clothes? Lady Bednukah isn't about clothes. Why would she care? When you have a seething demon as a slave next to you most of the time, such niceties as clothing are no longer important. She has dark red hair, but it turned bright orange when the ritual happened...stayed that way, too. Her eyes were green and her skin was almost pure white."

"Green like emeralds?"

With a frown, Goliath said, "Let me dispel any romantic lore trotted in your brain, Abi. Her eyes were green as a bad piss after drinking honey beer. Bednukah has a smile like she would sooner bite your pecker off as let you breathe again. The only thing I'd like to do to her with my penis is kill her with it." He drank once and added, "Through her brain."

Abimelech looked back toward Jericho. Goliath still stared away. "What did she do, sire?"

"Do you really want to know? There's a rationale to why I told you to stay outside. Those who did witness what I did will carry that image and tale to all for all time. Do you want to know or just wait for the fireside lie that others there will tell?"

Abimelech put his hands to his sides. "Tell me, sire, if you so wish."

Goliath took a long draw on the wineskin and then wiped his mouth with the back of his hand. "The fathers from the five major Philistine cities were stripped, then placed in stocks and kneeling benches. They faced the giant abomination of Moloch, as the Hebrews call it. It sits by a giant stone owl across a small subterranean river that runs through the Domain. Thirteen of them, the poor sots, thinking they would witness the fate of their daughters burning in the belly of the great idol. They were wrong. It was far worse than that."

Abimelech shook his head. "Sire, what could possibly be worse?"

Eyes closed as if witnessing the scene again, Goliath said, "Thirteen priests of Moloch emerged from under the citadel in the ruins, each in a robe, but this was soon shed. They stood behind each imprisoned father, waiting, working their manhood into a frenzy. I'd seen priests use their seed in ceremony, so that's no genuine surprise. However, when other servants brought in the daughters of these city fathers and placed them on beams under the faces of their fathers...they were nailed to these wooden cross bars, arms splayed out to the heavens."

Abimelech's mouth opened, but no words came out.

Goliath opened his eyes and stated in a matter of fact voice, "Each woman had a brace around her head and neck, the harnesses held their mouths open at an ample angle. Each lay under their fathers face at the opposite direction...so they could see each other. Then, the priests behind the fathers took to the men as one would take a woman. The act of defilement filled the hall with screams. The Lady looked rather excited."

"How did you know?"

Goliath shrugged. "All three of her nipples were hard. Never happened any other time while we stood there. The demon in the star that kept him prisoner just pulsed and seethed. He only seemed to have interest when the thirteen new priests of Moloch arrived and stood by each screaming father."

"What did they do?"

"When the acts reached a certain point, I'm not sure what, as many of the priests carried on their acts of sodomy even after this following...the new priests cut the throats of the fathers. It wasn't a clean cut, but a savage jab and removal. They knew what they were doing, though, as it was a slice for maximum effect. The consequence being, the gush of blood shot right into the open maws of their daughters."

"So they drowned on their own father's blood?"

"The demon glowed so brightly and the lady's alabaster skin shone like the stars. She screamed like a well-acting whore and vented her bowels as the power surge transferred from the demon to her. I left then with Eucimar."

"Why?"

Goliath faced Abimelech at last. "I was starting to get nauseated." He finished the skin of wine. "Aren't you glad I told you the tale?"

As he rubbed his eyes, Abimelech admitted, "No, but it'll be interesting to see what path the tale takes around the fires. Good night, to what end is that ceremony?"

Goliath stood and stretched. "Power, both from the demon due to the lives lost and the power set forth in the mind." Goliath stabbed his index finger at the side of his head. "It was meant to instill fear in the populace, to never cross the forces of Dagon, Baal, Ashtoreth, but mostly Moloch. Apparently, we have enough gods, or at least, for now. The new cults are a threat to the priests and the power base."

Abimelech nodded but said nothing more.

Goliath wasn't through, though. "We set about on this errand for the King of Kings at Ashkelon, but listen close to me, Abimelech."

The shield bearer harkened in, serious, as Goliath rarely used his full name.

"There are better things to be done with my time and our resources than to chase after a priest and his dreams of gods. He goes off to find Zorn in Egypt, while we go to see this arising city near Ezion-geber. Meanwhile, the army of Philistia battles the King of Israel at odd places. We should be more focused, shouldn't we?"

"What are you saying, sire?"

"I think our forces are being divided and manipulated. These voices and desires all seem to come from beyond or out of time as direction to our kings."

"I wondered why Samien departed with so many of us." Abimelech looked back toward Jericho. "Do you think this trouble is from Lady Bednukah or her demon?"

Goliath pondered that but kept his back to Jericho. "It doesn't feel right, but something is wrong, something is using the Philistines. I'll find it in time, but one cannot trap a wolf by chasing shadows."

"What do we do?"

"Go along for now, Abi. We will do as we can. You alone will I ever trust."

"Captain Balzer is a good man."

"He appears to be, but you have known me my entire life. Only you do I trust."

Abimelech nodded again, and Goliath understood that no more words were needed. Abimelech would die for his master, and Goliath held the shield bearer as just what he said, the only man on the earth he could rely on completely. With those words came a strong vow, one never to be sworn over an altar or a table full of drained tankards.

CHAPTER FOUR
JOURNEY AND SURPRISES

"I hate those damned things," said Goliath, one hand on the chest cinch of his javelin, the other scratching his beard. "Even if one of those gammalus can carry my big ass, I'd rather ride an elephant than something barely domesticated by the Assyrians."

Abimelech double-checked the packs on the humped beasts of burden, paying him little mind. The soldiers secured the materials packed on the camels and often sent Goliath obscene gestures as he gaped at the biggest beast of the group. He took the ribbing with good-natured gusto, returning their humor in kind.

Goliath then took a pitcher of water from a serving lady, who bowed profusely as she backed away. After he took a draw on the water, his steady voice asked Abimelech, "No sign of Yaggah, aye?"

"No, and rumor is General Samien and many more never showed at their destination."

"What? You talk like you eat manure. Speak plainly."

Wearing a half smile Abimelech stated, "Schlack doesn't want to say they are unaccounted for."

Contents of the pitcher sloshing around, Goliath pondered that.

"There's no sign of Akisha, either." Abimelech glanced over at the bustling people of the village. "The townsfolk are unquestionably happy to be alive."

Goliath took another drink and then spit the water into the dirt. "Damned if I understand it."

Abimelech remained silent and this caused Goliath to frown.

"You're a sharp man with a tongue like a knife, Abi. The whores in Gaza swear to it."

Not accepting the humor, Abimelech deadpanned, "Thanks."

"Tell me what you think."

Eyes on his master, Abimelech said progressively, "I think you're delusional if you think Yaggah kidnapped Akisha and forced her to leave with him."

"Do you now?" Goliath sipped more, his tone sardonic.

"Yes, sire. I find it awfully ironic that a group of assassins descend on you, both at the dinner and then as you copulate with Akisha. It was Yaggah that told us of Akisha and brought her unto you."

Tilting his head in reflection, Goliath said categorically, "That's what I get for believing the best in people. I should know better, huh?"

A moment passed as Abimelech let his master's sarcasm fester. "Your heart wants to believe different."

At this Goliath threw the pitcher and his rage boiled, "That's untrue. Just because she could survive me doesn't make her a resident in my heart. I'd never become a woman so fast."

Never did Abimelech get afraid or excited at his master's temper. "I'd say you are just being human, sire, but wouldn't I look like a rat-dick?"

Goliath wore a frustrated look. "So, Akisha was a ruse, a cipher or a whore meant to lure me to my doom?"

Hands out and then dropping to his sides, Abimelech

shrugged. "It nearly worked. What else would someone use for bait with you?"

Goliath's fury lessened and he tilted his head to the other side. "True. But to infiltrate our teamsters... what's known of Yaggah?"

"He was from the Pelethite tribe."

"A courier? Figures. He'd have access to many in that line. He was older, skinny, wormy even."

"Worms are not uncommon in this world."

At their words, the young soldier Cairn stared at them, then looked down, intent on securing water skins to the camel before him.

Goliath then folded his arms across his chest. "Damn him. It's a mystery for another day."

"Sire, you cannot believe any will give them safe harbor."

"Why not? I have never said they are guilty of anything yet. I'd be curious to know why they wanted me dead."

"I shall have the soldiers keep their eyes open for them."

Sadik emerged from the troopers, bowed toward Goliath and then faced Abimelech to say, "Sir, if I may?"

The shield bearer waved at him to speak.

Once he'd saluted them both, Sadik said, "Sirs, it is my understanding that Yaggah was related by blood to one of the Generals. I found that out in my searches last night."

Abimelech and Goliath exchanged glances. Goliath sounded surprised as he asked, "Schlack?"

"No, Samien."

Hands on his hips, Goliath threw back his mane of hair and laughed. When his head steadied again, no humor tainted his face. "That rotten prick! He whispers of sedition and of getting me on his side and then his blood kin tries to arrange my death? I'll see that

Samien's balls on my javelin and driven through his relative's heart."

"Sire..." Abimelech said, trying to calm Goliath.

Still in a rage, Goliath added, "Preferably his mother, but Yaggah will suffice."

"Thank you," Abimelech said to Sadik and returned the salute. "It's wise to share this with us."

Sadik turned and said no more.

Goliath let his hands drop and gave the double-humped camel a doubtful look. "It's a big animal, Abi, but..."

"It can carry you. It can carry more weight than you, or so they guess."

"My ass rests on a guess? Wonderful. Then let us all be gone from here. The regulars of the army march back to the sea and Philistia. Ba'al Zebul only knows where Samien departed for, aye? This path we take down near the Dead Sea and beyond will take a while before we reach the port city of Ezion-geber. I've had my belly full of this place here and its folk."

Goliath walked the perimeter of the grounds, as if making sure nothing hid from the eyes of the other soldiers. The group pronounced itself ready so the giant swung his leg over the huge camel and tried to get comfortable. He failed.

On horseback, Abimelech settled in beside Goliath and they departed the area.

*****

Goliath reclined in the evening, facing across the Dead Sea. His elbow resting on mounds of salt deposits, the giant peered into the waters and then at the crystallized shore nearby.

"The men would camp in the open farther south rather than here," Abimelech said to his master, and he shook off his head wrap. "There's plenty of daylight left and we can make a healthier spot. It would be better to be away from the lands of the Israelis even if we traveled into the night."

Goliath never replied, but kept looking at the spot where the water touched the shore.

"What ails you, sire?"

"Nothing, Abi. My heart is not heavy, but I look at this place with curiosity. You know where we are?"

Still expelling dust from his wrap, Abimelech nodded. "I know what the legends say, sire. The ruins of the cities are all but swallowed by the salt and waters. This land has shifted much over the centuries."

"Wiped clean by the hand of God himself." He seemed to find this funny, but never shared why. "I can see why the soldiers wouldn't want to sleep here. Try and find us a spot to rest where God hasn't pissed on his subjects, would you?"

"I will try, sire."

As his shield bearer turned, Goliath asked, "Do you think this venture wise, Abi?"

"Not specially. You were right in saying we could serve better in support of the army elsewhere. But this is the dance the priests and kings play. I have little say in the matter."

"But I could walk away at any time, correct?"

Abimelech said nothing.

Goliath said, "I go as my self leads. There's something in the south that gets my interest, so I favor the priests this time. Frankly, going back to Gath and seeing my mother is on my mind, but not important."

"Do you think it wise Eucimar goes to see Zorn?"

"Not really. If I had an inkling or an instinct, I'd say to stay away from that place. Few of the priests and priestesses have ever come back from there."

"None in fact, sire. What if they sent you to slay Zorn?"

Goliath raised an eyebrow at his shield bearer. "My, that would be interesting." Goliath leaned on the small tower of salt and looked down. The top of the pillar stood, globulous, melted from rain and the ages. He blinked and thought he saw what passed for teeth. He laughed with great mirth and moved away, pulling the pillar with him, sending it crashing to the lapping waves.

"I'm more curious about Samien and his ratty cousin, Yaggah."

*****

That night, Abimelech found himself fortunate enough to witness the surprise of Israelite soldiers when they raided the camp. He thought their action probably a first-class ambush move, to jump the largest of the tents in the night. Abimelech observed their stealth as he walked in the night, restless for sleep. The move these fighters deployed probably worked often. He guessed at these raiders confidence that many Philistines slept in such a long tent. He pondered, how could these Israelite soldiers know of the terror that slumbered beneath the canvas folds of the tent? Did the first sight greeting them of the torn tent of giant feet bearing six toes each make it real for them? Did they soil the sand when they discovered their gross error? How could they know that when they cut the material, they unleashed the champion of the Philistines from his slumber?

Though the Philistine mission didn't concern the Israelites, they soon found destiny at hand. From out of the hacked seams of the tent arose the champion. With but a waving of his arms, Goliath swept away a half-dozen men gripping short, slightly bent, swords. His forearm slapped the flats of the blades and the attackers fell together like so many cards in a game of chance.

Rolling into the sand, Goliath soon stood in moonlight. The invading soldiers that remained upright gaped at him, too stunned to move. They took the full brunt of the blow when he kicked two in the chest with a right to left motion. This rapid move cracked their ribcages. Abimelech thought Goliath certainly broke their hearts.

His mane of hair wild about him, Goliath scratched his heavy beard, eyes gleaming in the night. "Who disturbs my rest and doesn't bring a whore to ply me with?" he wondered aloud before leaning down into the folds of the ruined tent.

By then, the encampment grew alive with activity. The rest of the Philistine party flowed out of their tents and witnessed Goliath unsheathing his sword. He held it to the sky as the moonlight framed his colossal frame like a halo.

An Israelite soldier, surely in tune with his God, stood his ground and drew back the string of his bow. From the laughter abounding, this small man amused Goliath as he leveled the sword across his own midsection. The bowman let the arrow fly and Goliath's vast limbs twitched. Those of the tribe of Cherethim, soldiers of which the champion kept near to him, were familiar with great Goliath's lightning reflexes to deflect missiles, unlike the aliens to their camp. He moved swift, took but two strides, raised his weapon and dropped it onto the left shoulder of the Israelite archer. The blade soon connected with the sand, passing clean through the man's body and cleaving the small man in half at a diagonal angle.

The rest of the Israelite ambush party fled into the night.

After a single laugh, Goliath muttered, "Am I a bitch that they come in the night to attack me? What was this, Abimelech?"

"I think it was a further attempt by the tribes of Judah to expel us from this region," he explained as the Philistine soldiers gathered up the living raiders. "Though they give us great troubles, the Israelites cannot expel us from our native lands."

"Bah, let them try, Abi, most Cherethim tribe farmers could best their fighters," he snorted in disgust. "This mission doesn't involve them or their pretend king. Heh, a king for a race of slaves? That's a great amusement! They shall not stop our quest for Relex."

Captain Balzer lined up the prisoners and tried to question them in their tongue. Goliath reached down and took up a skin of wine as he watched this interrogation. With mild interest, he drained the wine and then said, "Balzer, you waste your time. It matters not if they know of our purpose in traveling to the port city. If you would like, we can make them a sacrifice to one of your gods and let the flies come for them in the morn."

Balzer nodded, knowing the intent of the mission. "Goliath, we shall construct an altar and sacrifice them for..."

"Nay," Goliath waved them off, sword's tip resting an inch in the ground. "There's no need. Here, let me save you the trouble. Perhaps the spirits beyond will favor me in our endeavor with such a sacrifice. Let them quit focusing their love on exquisite Akisha and focus on their true servants. You name the god of your choice, eh?"

Balzer stepped back as Goliath grabbed a bound up Israelite and body slammed him into the sand. He then seized another and performed the same task. A third and fourth time, he performed this function. A fifth body heaped on his Israelite brothers before Goliath held his sword aloft. Abimelech watched the cringing faces of the Israelites, all cross-wise on each other, hands & feet bound, unable to move. Goliath looked at Balzer and gestured at the bodies with his free left hand.

Balzer said, "Since we venerate Dagon all over our land and that is who is watching over poor fleeing Akisha, let us make this a sacrifice to Ba'al-Zebub. He shall preserve us."

Abimelech nodded in approval at the name that meant *Baal is Prince.*

"You soldiers are jokers," Goliath smirked at their pretended veneration of Akisha, as if it were all a grand joke. "Why not?" He then turned his sword over like a spear and stabbed down, impaling all five men at once. He ground the blade down to the earth and then released it. Blood flowed into the dirt as Goliath raised his arms and roared to the sky. "To you, Ba'al-Zebub. May you be the last of the gods venerated on this godforsaken plain." Hands back to his pommel, Goliath twisted and then released, almost playfully tweaking the weapon to see if it would stay rigid in the bodies. His voice calm, he wondered, "Is there any mutton left? I'm famished."

As Sadik searched for some food for their champion, Balzer turned from the sacrifice. "These Hebrews never could have known what we seek down south."

Tranquil as a sleeping child, Goliath replied, "Who knows? If our leaders at Ashkelon or Ekron think they can achieve idle power out of my self, they're badly mistaken."

Abimelech brought Goliath more wine as sand blew across the sacrifice. With a sigh, the shield bearer reminded him, "Rumor is the great Prophet of the Hebrews is near Ekron. It's strange that the priests keep track of him."

"They fear him. Hell, that's far from here. If I fear no God, his footman doesn't concern me. Perhaps after this venture, I shall go unto Ekron and see this Samuel myself."

Deciding not to question him further, Abimelech buried his fears. Having heard of the wonders of the Israelite God, and not believing most tales, he decided to trust the strength of his master. Few saw it, but Abimelech recognized an imperious serenity encased Goliath, masked by his muscled exterior. Though often cloaked in blood, he taught Abimelech that death was the only way to peace.

"Gods," he said with bile in his voice. "There are no gods, Abi, not anymore." Goliath looked to the stars.

"Your father won't return, will he?"

His look removed from the stars to Abimelech. "And well he shouldn't. I was made in his image, after his likeness unto my sainted mother, thus I live. I wonder after him, but I doubt he wonders after me. Truly, there should be more to parenting than dropping seed and moving on." He yawned and stretched, indicating he wanted to crawl into a tent and sleep. "Perhaps next spring we shall journey beyond the Pillars of Hercules again, eh? I love the environs in the great world beyond."

"Their timber is good, sire."

"I oft wonder if that bastard sea captain Weldon Yog still roams the waters for us of Philistia?"

"I've never heard otherwise and he's too mean to die."

*****

Two days later, many miles to the south, the party emerged from the twisted wilderness. They found themselves bored and surrounded by a vast plain of nothing. The winds soon came up limiting their visibility.

When the column of travelers stopped, Goliath shouted out from the rear, "What holds things up? There cannot be a crossroads in the wilds, even if the desert encroaches us."

Abimelech yelled back, "It's another caravan, traders mostly, bound for a nomadic oasis."

The wind coming off the desert striking his face, Goliath pondered that. "After that bog of inky muck we saw yesterday leaking from the earth, I no longer trust what lives under the desert." He paused, looked at the new caravan the Philistine troops encircled. "Do they have anything of value?"

Those travelers focused on the giant with horrific faces, but none cried out. All of them swathed in dirty robes, turbans and face guards, they couldn't help but try to communicate fear to their fellows in the caravan.

"They're reluctant of letting us near their long wagon with the tarps tied down."

"Is that so?" Goliath climbed off his mount, gave the beast a mock fist to the snout. "Well, in all of this emptiness, they run into us and choose to be difficult? Is it some treasure?"

Abimelech stated, "Their language is so crude, I cannot get my mind around it. I'd guess they warn us away more than anything."

Goliath walked to the bound up cart. The dozen nomads fell to their knees at the clearer sight and size of him. He produced a large dagger from his midriff belt and tapped at the cart's straps with the blade. "I can read the terror in their eyes. Fascinating, as it isn't for me."

The lead man from the caravan shook off dust from his faded robe before he screamed and jumped, near to putting his hands on the giant. A wry grin on his face,

Goliath cut the tarp strap. Just as he did so Goliath saw something out of the corner of his eye. The blowing sand flew so substantial he squinted and then pointed. "Abi? What is that in the brush?"

Abimelech and Balzer exchanged a glance and then struggled to see what the champion indicated. They took several steps into the strong winds, staggered, and then Abimelech turned to Goliath. "Just rocks."

Goliath holstered his knife and glared at a few of the Philistine soldiers. "Don't let these foreigners run off. They're mad enough." The giant then trudged into the winds toward Abi and Balzer, his face turned to combat the force of nature. He walked past them and knelt by the small mound in the shifting sands he pointed at.

Abimelech and Balzer flanked him as Goliath swept sands away.

Goliath cursed as if his words would banish the dust storm around them. He then nodded at the image on the ground. "He's staked down...no, forget that, crucified, see?" He reached for the lumpy figure. When the giant squeezed it, the surface gave. Not a rock formation, for once Goliath brushed away the accumulating dirt, the shape in the sand took on a human form. "I thought it a person staked out, but the staves through his ankles and wrists show a more sinister death."

Balzer yelled over the wind, "A worse one than being staked out in this storm for exposure?"

Goliath stood, kicked the body and searched around them. "He's been dead quite a while but the scavengers haven't had a chance to take him in this storm."

Abimelech rubbed at his eyes and glared at the dead man. "Why kill a man in such a fashion out here on this godless place?"

Goliath stomped away from them and they dutifully followed, afraid to be lost in the storm. Another form, partially buried, appeared before their eyes, identical to the last. Goliath mused, "There's a reason these wild lands are godforsaken."

This time Abimelech and Balzer knelt by the figure, also crucified to the dirt. They looked up at Goliath who shielded his eyes, then pointed to another figure in the distance. Again, they followed their champion to the next shape, dead.

Balzer admitted, "I don't like this."

Goliath said over the wind, "Doesn't get me randy, either. Look there. If my geometry is correct, there's a fifth man over there."

Abimelech drew his short sword and glanced around them. "We stopped these travelers in the middle of a five-pointed sacrifice?"

Goliath nodded. "Something like that. There was no way to know it, and I cannot tell why, but this all happened in the last couple days."

Balzer almost moaned in the wind, "I hope this venture isn't the death of us all."

Goliath's eyes cleared and he faced the caravan they stopped. "It may be the death of those bastards."

Again, the giant stomped his way through the storm to where the Philistines held the nomadic travelers. Once more, he produced the knife and the foreign men begged him to stay his blade from the large parcel's other straps. The dust covered cart shook in the wind and Goliath steadied it with his knee before cutting the main heavy cord that wrapped the wagon. He then cut the second line and the canvas blew away in the wind.

In the bed of the cart lay two cylindrical objects, also bound in cords. The cone-shaped objects resembled green-gray pods or stone eggs, but were also long like dates.

"This is what they hide and carry? Rocks?" Goliath chuckled as he ran a hand down them. "They feel like bone or stone, odd..." He poked at one of the knobby

protrusions and a slit appeared on the stone. Abimelech and Balzer froze, astonished as the slit widened and an eye appeared on the object. "Damn," was all Goliath had time to say as a high-pitched screech filled their ears.

Panic seized the Philistines and they drew their swords. Goliath took a step back, but never reached for the javelin at his back.

The snaps of the straps popping free sounded like arrows glancing off stone. They all took more steps back as the bound-up objects unfolded, emitting a high-pitched screech. As these things started to shake, folding out, transforming into a bat-like beast of reptilian origin, Goliath reached back and took a hold of his javelin.

The Bedouin nearest Goliath screamed, "Kongamato," just before the long beak of the creature opened, showing a rack of teeth any crocodile would adore. With a swift move, the creature's maw darted, snapping around the head of the Bedouin. The man's cry muffled and turned liquidy in their ears as the creature unfolded its triple-jointed leathery wings.

The Kongamato twisted and removed the head of the traveler. It pulled back with the head and with a single snap crushed the orb like a melon. No one paid much mind to the headless body as it stumbled a few steps and fell into the dust storm, jetting blood. While the creature chomped to accomplish its task of swallowing, Goliath drove the metal point of his javelin forward. With all of his weight behind the shot, the spearhead traveled through the Kongamato and out its back. Beak open and screaming, the jaw of the Bedouin hung off the Kongamato's maw like the worn underside of a horse's hoof. The long wings lashed out, slapping Goliath on each shoulder, nearly knocking him over, but he stayed firm afoot. His hands turned the javelin to tear loose a portion of the beast's side, but the creature still lived, its mouth closing, eyes staring at the giant, feet gripping the edge of the wagon like hands.

In full anticipation of the head's next strike, Goliath released the javelin and swung his arms together. The Kongamato snapped at Goliath, aiming for his face, but great hands stunted the strike. The giant held the Kongamato's mouth closed and wrenched to one side. The beast's neck wouldn't break. He cursed again, angry that the creature didn't die as easy as Egyptian crocs. Goliath inserted the long beak under his left arm and bore down with his body weight.

The other Kongamato in the cart started to unfold. Goliath still wrestled the first, seizing a wing and at last, snapping bones within the leathery skin. The bat-like legs flailed about Goliath's thighs. The clawed feet rested on his kneecaps and tore through the armored guards there.

Abimelech and Balzer swung their swords at the other Kongamato, but its flapping wings swatted them down. A Philistine bowman notched an arrow and let it fly. This missile glanced off the beast's armored head.

Goliath reached behind the Kongamato he grappled with, held the long bone extension from the rear of its head, and wrenched back. This bending of the creature's head proved fatal. A dry crack stabbed in their ears. The Kongamato's wings sagged limp and it twitched once. Goliath held the monster high before slamming it to the desert floor. He jumped on its back, trying to pulverize the bones of the beast. The other Kongamato took flight. Mouth open wide, its howl high in their ears, it vanished into the swirling winds above them.

"Curse them, sire," Abimelech yelled as the men drew near to their champion. "What were they?"

"They called them Kongamatos, bastard children of an Egyptian god, Seker," Goliath replied, kicking the head of the dead monster. "I've heard drunken tales, but never seen such a thing. Stay low, it may seek us again."

Abimelech blinked. "Seker? That's unlikely. Seker is a hawk."

Swinging his fists in the sandy air, Goliath raged, "Are you going to debate me now?"

All stood at the ready, prepared for a swooping strike. However, the screech of the creature faded above them. The lance in Sadik's hands shook, but Cairn remained steady. They waited for a few minutes before Goliath said, "I think it's a dumb beast and glad for its freedom."

Sadik offered, "Either that or it's lost in the storm."

The winds lessened as the Philistines meandered back to their formations. All waited on another attack, even if their champion didn't anticipate one coming.

Within an hour, the winds ceased. Goliath watched Balzer and his men set about torturing two of the Bedouins. As part of this act, they first executed the rest of the caravan members before the two captives, running a few through with lances. When this produced no new information, Cairn and Sadik set about to binding up one of the travelers and tearing him apart with horses.

Goliath pointed at something hidden in the dust a few yards off each of the crucified sacrifices.

"Idols?" Abimelech asked no one, looking at the stone figurines set on a pattern near the crucified men they'd found.

Goliath jeered his friend, saying, "Your grasp of the obvious stuns me. I shall buy you sweets at the port city."

"Buy them for your ass," Abimelech replied. "Look at them close."

After a few strides, Goliath did just that. "I thought them copies of bats, shielding themselves." Goliath touched the pointy tops of the idols. "Hardly a few feet tall and they're stone Kongamatos. Brilliant." He then tested the weight of one, found it wanting, picked it up over his head, carried it to the next statue and dropped it across the twin. His act of dual destruction and defilement caused the Philistines to cheer, as if his work made the Kongamato no longer a threat.

Goliath proceeded to repeat this action on the next idol about the time Cairn and Sadik yanked the limbs free of one of the travelers. This act loosed the tongue of the other, and he told Balzer that these traders simply were going to trade the Kongamatos to a menagerie in the port city of Ezion-geber.

Goliath sat in the sand by the last idol and nodded. "I wonder who would collect such things?"

They tossed the Bedouin at Goliath's feet, and the man sobbed in a tongue close to their own dialect, "The Alchemist at Owl-bear Creek."

An eyebrow raised, Goliath sighed. "Indeed?" He then picked up the last idol and crushed the head of the Bedouin.

When the idol crumbled to stone in the digits of the giant, a perplexed look spread on his face. He let the grains of sand and tiny bits of rock fall away, but held up several small bones for the others to see.

Balzer gripped the hilt of his sword. "What deviltry is this?"

"Let us go from here," Goliath said calmly, and let the bones fall to the dirt. "We won't make the port city today, but this place is making my ass hurt."

*****

General Samien arose from his bedroll and started to rub his lower back with both hands. His enjoyment of the setting sunlight in the cave's maw proved fleeting as

Philistine

Colonel Baldassare transfixed the opening.

"Sir, more men are arriving from across the Jordan valley."

"Good," Samien replied and twisted himself from right to left. "I trust they brought their own arms?"

"Several good bowmen from Sidon way have," the Colonel affirmed, hand resting over his heart for a moment. "But a company of Hittites from across the Transjordanian Highlands have brought a wagon full of spears."

His movements ceasing, Samien nodded appreciatively. "Good. Are they revels or warriors?"

Baldassare grinned a smile of yellowed teeth, "All of them are experienced men in the service."

"I prefer them that way," Samien commented and picked up his canteen. "They are better, not only in warfare, but they do as they are told from day to day, when there's no fight to be had."

Hands rubbing together, Baldassare said, "It's chilling in a way, sir. Her words are coming to pass."

Samien drank, eyes directed to the cave floor. "Did you have doubts?"

"We all have doubts, especially when faced with such amazing things."

Samien capped the container and faced his Colonel. "It's good you see past the reasoning that we may be her pawns, no?"

Baldassare's smile faded. "Sir, I have no qualms we are but pawns in this, for no one gives without expecting a payment. Her words, at what we desire, make it sound so easy."

Samien put down the canteen and stepped closer to the mouth of the cave. "Beware those that give too rosy of a forecast?"

"It's all coming to pass as she has promised."

"So far," Samien said quietly, hands to his sides.

Baldassare turned his head and nodded, hand again returning to his chest.

"What ails you, Colonel?"

"Age and worry, but don't fret on my account." From down the hill walked two young men, identical in appearance. "Here are the latest in her promises, made flesh."

"Twin killers. Amazing." A smile now formed on the General's face. "You two wear togs of sailors, yet, the ocean is so far away."

Both young men sported curly brown hair, unkempt beards and dark sun-tanned skin typical of sea life. The one on the left said, "Sir, we came, beckoned in our dreams to offer our support. I'm Barekbaal, and this is Darekbaal."

The other saluted at his name and picked up the conversation. "She has revealed much in our dreams, and we share the same want as you."

Samien stepped to the mouth of the cave and eyed each sailor closely. "Again, you're far from the sea. How do I know you aren't little piglets from the tit of Vyndekay?"

Barekbaal offered, "We are Philistines, usually residing in Ashdod, but our father holds a smithy shop in Baal-Hazor, south of Shiloh. Our presence away from the main lands isn't unusual."

Before Samien could speak, Darekbaal said, "Our father, Akalam, sends you this." The youth extended his hand, offering a bronze bracelet.

Samien took the object and turned it, then read the name, "Malak." His eyes again gave the twins a dressing down. "So he knows of her, too?"

Barekbaal nodded, but remained at attention. "Sir, he will offer his cache of weapons when the time comes. He regrets his injury forbids him from joining the fray."

Darekbaal added, "You know how our father

departed military service, sir?"

His eyes past them, focused on the setting sun, Samien said, "Akalam became maimed by Jonathan's band at the Michmash pass. The prince of the Hebrews ensured Akalam never would march into war again. He, too, comes from a line full of Canaanite blood."

Both youths wore looks of resentment, but neither let it boil over. Barekbaal said, "He still works in metals for their plows and implements, but they cannot watch him every moment in his weapon making."

Samien wondered, "And your loyalty to my cause is what? You'd be better served to stay at your posts in the navy, hoping to get a strike at the Hebrew king's son one day."

Head shaking, Darekbaal stated, "Our own leadership doomed our troops in those cases. I don't accept any god of slaves came to their aid. We don't want our father's sacrifice to go in vain."

A snide tone crept into the voice of Barekbaal as he asked, "Where was our champion and the brilliant generals? All playing games elsewhere."

Samien walked past them and looked into the highlands beyond the Jordan valley, where many men encamped in the wilderness. "And you bow your knees to Baal, per your names?" When he turned, both youths had bowed their knees to him. "Excellent," Samien replied. "It's time we had a spiritual resurgence anyway."

CHAPTER FIVE
ALCHEMIST AT EZION-GEBER

After roasting and feasting on several of the foreign caravan's horses, the Philistines set off again, descending down through the land of the Edomites for several days. To the east lay the regular lands of Edom, hemmed over by the Seir Mountains and to the west ranged the Desert of Arabah. Dust storms and high winds lashed at them, adding days to their journey. Although no haste to reach the port city of Ezion-geber ran in their veins, in time, the distant sight of it birthed happiness.

They stopped in smaller settlements near the final oasis before the city. Many living there came out to see them, having no quarrel with the Philistines, but for another purpose.

When a man rode away from them on a horse back into the city, Abimelech questioned Balzer, who had spoken to the rider. "Who was that? A soldier?"

"No," Balzer promised. "A representative of a certain locale brigade leader named Xylon. He's being quite pleasant."

Goliath splashed water on his face and shook his beard free under the thin shade of the palm trees. He grinned at the thong of children gathered there nearby.

"Children of Midian, folk of the Edomites," Goliath waved his hands, making sure to show all of his fingers. "Go your way."

The children persisted, wanting to hear a story.

Goliath told them about besting the towering monster made of living human bodies, and how the terrible wizard Enoicap created them to look like giants. They asked him of other worldly tales, and he regaled them of old stories he'd heard of the Philistine mythical homeland of Caphtorium. Soon, he tired of telling these tales of cyclopean cities and warrior schools.

Abimelech washed up, watched his master walk through the crowd and read the wonderment of the children in the wake of the giant. He joined Goliath at the mounts and said, "You're very entertaining. Perhaps the alchemist up the road will keep you for his collection of the bizarre."

Goliath shot him a dour look as he checked his canteens. "May the wasps take your sack, Abi. As a youth, I saw men of renown and supposed honor disregard the young ones. They thought themselves so much better than others. Even if such a thing is obvious in my case, I oft wonder if the tales these little ones spin to their grandchildren will be believed...if Goliath really existed, if he was that tall and had so many fingers. It's good to have that child-time, no?"

Abimelech shrugged as he turned his face from the children. "As you say, sire."

Goliath gazed to the south as the little ones dispersed, then back to the north. "For the times and chores of the mature can make the mind tired. Never get me wrong, Abi, I'd slay every one of these children and their fathers if their community rose up against me, but I sense a greater ill at work all over. Call it a hunch or a sensation, but I have the feeling of being played."

"Played, sire? Like a piece in a game?"

Philistine

Goliath looked down at Abimelech. "Yes, that's precisely my meaning. I knew I kept you around for more than carrying my shield and killing idiots I don't care to."

"Glad to serve. Ezion-geber will be a city full for our enjoyment. I'm sure Captain Balzer will want to adhere to the business for the King and Eucimar."

Goliath sighed as they mounted up again. "We cannot arrive and take off on just any ship for Relex. It'll take time. The men will need rest, wine and whores."

"We can only hope, sire."

"Ezion-geber deals with the Egyptians so much, they have a good quantity of such materials. You'll have time to clean yourself off and dirty up again. I'll seek this Alchemist before we set off for where Relex resides, if it still sits in the sea."

"Fine on the city, but why do you say that of Relex?"

Goliath straightened his head cover and cinched the mouthpiece across his face. "It has slumbered under the waves for centuries, no? I wonder how stable it is sticking out of the surf. Surely, we won't be the first to try to seek it out."

Abimelech sipped more water and conceded, "Unquestionably, corsairs have tried already."

Goliath brooded over this. "I wonder what they found. Abi, on your whoring trip in the city, find me that answer. The taverns will know sagas even if the magistrates of Ezion-geber tighten up their asses too much to tell us."

The group gathered up and set off again through the thickening wilderness unto the port city of Ezion-geber.

*****

Though a spread out spot and only partially walled,

Ezion-geber sat typical enough of a large port city to Goliath. Though not as outsized or modern as the seaport of Ashkelon, Ezion-geber sported similar architecture in its mud brick homes and stolen Egyptian styles for fences and gates. Since trade flowed free through this open city, the awnings and wares of the street shops greeted them as they entered the streets. Goliath noted the series of curtain walls about the outer edge of the city, abandoned in spots as if a change in power had stopped the importance of such a structure. He couldn't fathom who'd want to invade such an important setting.

Eyes on the street, Abimelech said, "I hear this city means 'backbone of the giant' because of that rock formation out beyond the fortifications."

Goliath turned, glanced at the distant hills that protruded out of the wilderness the closer they grew to the city. He scoffed, "Who knows? Those fortifications wouldn't stop a fart, anyways."

"Ezion-geber is an open city even if part of Edom and an Iduma city. Asiongaber, in proper Hebrew, means city of the rooster."

Left eyebrow raised at his shield bearer, Goliath spoke with deadpan words. "The city of cocks?" He studied the merchants and townsfolk, dressed in much drabber colored garments than the foreigners that frequented the streets. "By the looks of these people, I'd reckon they are known for their chickens."

The sun continued to sink and evening drew close around the city, so merchants started closing down their storefronts. Many lived in the rear sectors of their shops so their paths to get home ran short.

When the leader of the local militia arrived via horseback, dismounted and talked to Balzer, Abimelech said to the Philistines, "It'll be too late to start off for Relex tonight."

Goliath let go a sarcastic chuckle. "Praises be to,

well, think me up your favorite deity, Abi. I doubt Balzer has the balls to make the men run to a ship this night or even in the morn after that journey. Those extra days fighting the storms took weeks off their lives and inches off their peckers."

They dismounted and Abimelech retorted, "We shall endeavor to regain the latter this night, and tomorrow, sire. Hmm. Wonder if that man in the leathers is Xylon?"

The giant said nothing, unconcerned with anything so trivial.

Townsfolk and alien travelers alike gaped at Goliath as he brushed off the trail dust. Their astonishment at his size, then the recognition that the men wore Philistine arms and helms, told the tale to them. It was no time before the children of a shopkeeper said the name "Goliath" repeatedly.

The local magistrate, dressed in blue and white robes, approached Balzer and introduced himself as Solama Aggas. The Captain walked with Aggas and told him they'd traveled a long way. Aggas nodded his understanding while they moved further down the block.

Goliath said in a quiet voice, "He's talking about me as he figures I cannot hear him."

Abimelech never looked the way of Solama and Balzer. "What does he say? Play hard to get."

"Eat dung. He says he hears of me talking to children but curses me to Balzer for I don't speak to magistrates."

Abimelech shrugged. "The kids are less likely to stick a knife in your back."

Balzer talked with Aggas and then others in clean robes. He soon returned from farther in the city, rolling his eyes, well aware Goliath heard them at a distance. They could then smell the sea and feel the breeze of it, even if the bustling village obscured the waters for the time being.

"Damn docks," Balzer said. "Full of idiots. Some of our kinsman will be returning on the morrow, they tell me with split tongues. Curse it, I hate to wait longer."

Goliath stretched, eyed a turbaned man Sadik spoke with on the street corner and asked the Captain, "Are you in a hurry to see who really is god, Balzer? I give you no orders, but calm yourself and let the men recover."

Balzer nodded with a bitter look on his face. He had no angst for Goliath, only desperation to finish his duty. "The men do need rest."

Hands to his waist belt, Goliath corrected Balzer. "The men need to be properly whored up, Captain." The men let out a loud cheer. "And from the tales I overhear and the wares of the slut-monger on the corner there bullshitting Sadik, we came to the right place."

The man in the turban grinned and Sadik blushed.

Balzer spoke in strident words to them all, "Our funds are low and have to be managed."

Goliath said, "Sell these camels for the prostitutes or trade from for the temple whores. They stink anyways, the camels that is." He turned to the army, who chuckled hard at his words. "So do you lot as well."

The troopers took the taunt as good jest. Abimelech though rebuked him. "You're a hot roast yourself, sire."

Goliath smirked. "Then we all better get to a bath house or the goddamned ocean, no? I'd feel so bad if a tramp turned her nose up at my manhood due to road dust. It wouldn't stop me, but I'd feel bad about it."

Again, the men shared laughter as Goliath looked the city over.

*****

The men toweled off and dressed in fresher garments

furnished by the ladies of the square. Goliath eyed a tall man who entered. He noted him due to his skeletal thin body and superior height, near to that of Abimelech. The image of Yaggah flashed through his mind, but this man sported a long main of light brown hair and a heavy beard. He spoke to Balzer as Goliath approached him. The man then politely bowed to the champion.

Goliath said, "You wear the green tunic and emblems of a priest of Dagon, yet your head isn't cropped up tight. Why is that?"

"I'm Ahirom, and I'm from the country," his youthful eyes glowed.

Goliath saw then that while he bore tough skin burned often by the sun, the man was probably a hair over twenty years of age. "Awfully young to be a priest of Dagon."

"Alas, Champion of the Philistines, I'm but the oldest acolyte of my master, Lord Hevel."

"He sent you down here? Why? If he thinks himself too good to see us in person?"

Ahirom shook his head fast. "No. My master left for the city of Relex with a group of Philistines garrisoned here."

Goliath contemplated his words. "Hevel never returned, right?"

"You are correct."

"I'm getting tired of being right," Goliath muttered. "Do you want to come on our trip?"

Hesitant in his words, Ahirom said, "My Lord, my heart does so desire it, but my self must watch the temple here, small though it may be. We do serve a goodly purpose for our masters up north."

"I imagine you have acolytes to mind the temple and could come along. What's your purpose for those religious folks up north?"

Balzer spoke up. "He has made us a first-rate offer

that will make our selling of the camels a good option."

Curious as to why his question became missed, Goliath sighed. "We will steal more camels when we return if we have to. Piss on all these rules."

Balzer said, "Ahirom here has told us of a ceremony for his *collect*. It's important the temple vessels be copulated on this night or the morrow for the timing of a rite nine months hence."

"So, you will save the King some money by letting the men cover the breeders of the temple here?" Goliath applauded. "Do the men realize what they are being used for?"

Ahirom blinked. "You fear they have a care for such a duty?"

Goliath stretched and nearly put his head through the ceiling. "I'd want to know at least. Not every man wants to see what he has created used as a sacrifice nine months later. That isn't a matter of faith, but of the blood."

Ahirom wore a sly smile as he said softly, "A matter of the heart?"

Goliath glared at him. "The heart of an acolyte would appease Dagon about the same as a baby, in my opinion."

Angered, but playing it cool with the giant, Ahirom said, "You're not a scholar of the faith, in all respect."

"But," Goliath reached out, his hand encircling the head of the priest, leaving only his eyes to see out. "I'm bigger than you. It doesn't matter what you believe, little priest. Your ass on the altar may not please Dagon, even if he *is* in Hell, trying to find a way out, but it'll make my penis hard enough to forge copies." He released Ahirom. "I don't care where the men drop their seed. Tell me where the Alchemist of Owl-bear Creek is."

A look of shock emerged on Ahirom's face.

"Are you surprised to be alive or that I want to see

the Alchemist?"

Hand to his jaw as if to straighten it, the priest asked, "Why ever would you want to see that person? Do you want your future told? Surely, there is a lady in the market for that."

Goliath shrugged and pulled his javelin to his back. "Poly-patronage doesn't thrill me in what you have in mind for the soldiers this night, so I have other matters on my mind. Who is this Alchemist and where does he abide?"

Relaxing at last, Ahirom said, "The Alchemist is more of a *what* than a *he*, Lord. But he is called Coriander. He resides near the crypts and cemetery by the southeastern fortifications of the city. It's true he can see the present, far away as well as the future. But watch him, for he lies."

*****

Once them men stowed their gear and affirmed their quarters in a barracks behind Dagon's temple, their champion parted company with them. Goliath strode through the off sections of the town, away from the worship centers of Baal, and far from the poly-copulation center at the behest of the worshipers of Dagon. Though he garnered some attention as he passed through a quarter of dwellings set aside in a brick formation, Goliath kept moving. He surmised the regular populace of the city lived in the outlying parts, leaving the more transient merchants to occupy the standard stone dwellings closer to the middle. The better-kept places lay in the distance, his keen eyes took in, topped in a manner more akin to Egyptian architecture than that of Judea.

Egyptian influence ran rife in the city ancillary to Edomite, Goliath noted, down to the cartouches on the doorposts. The thin alliances with the Pharaoh kept the city open and well traveled. If the Edomites, or the Philistines, for that matter, decided to seize the city, fortify it and impose rules on any that passed through there, the Pharaoh might decide to crush Ezion-geber and take over the area. In time, Pharaoh Psusennes I could do it, he guessed. Though the Egyptians oft employed the Philistine warriors in their army or for missions of death on the seas, Goliath despised them. It was not for their learned ways or advancement in various arts, but something else burned in him for those on the neighboring continent. Egyptians were shallow, well, shallower than most, so obsessed with the gods that they built empty dwellings for them.

He drew closer to the place of the tombs and the Alchemist's place of collection, noting in the outlying suburbs open arenas and men of all lands crowding into them. By great torchlights, they wagered gold on the events. Women traded goods outside as men gambled over the actions within. Goliath stood on his toes to see what happened.

"Wrestling," he said with a nod and moved on. "How barbaric." He wondered if the mighty-thewed Grecian grappler would prevail over the slender fighter with obsidian-colored skin, but he only pondered it for a moment.

The land of the dead stretched out into the region beyond the city. Hills rose up in this southern sector. The bluffs trailing down these hills showed much alteration as boxy edges and angles testified to the presence of crypts. At the base of the hills, a crude cemetery stretched out, divided into orderly lines of the dead marked by weathered rocks.

Hands on his hips, Goliath saw a stone structure

terminate as if it led to an invisible building in the side of the hill. "Looks like an unfinished barn," Goliath mumbled as he looked the rectangular door sunken into the hillside. "A door to nowhere?"

A raspy voice said from within the structure, "One has to know where to look for a door."

"Show yourself, stranger. I do have all night but even I need my rest."

The stone door slid open a foot and a short man, hunched over, peered out. Goliath pulled the door open and saw the rest of the speaker. The figure leaned on the right side of the opening, hobbled by a lame leg. A huge hump on his right shoulder grew in Goliath's eyes as the man staggered into view. His long, greasy hair, hung over his face like a veil, but when he raised to look on Goliath, the Philistine saw slanted eyes on a round face.

"Not from around here, are you, little one?"

A liquidy tone gurgled from the humpback's throat as he said, "No, but that's no matter. I'm the servant of Coriander, the Alchemist. My name is..."

Nostrils flaring at the stench of the humpback, Goliath said, "I don't care what your name is. Tell your master I'm here to speak with him about his collection."

The humpback said, "He dwells below, but so does his menagerie and collection. You'll be impressed." Eyes widening, the small man said, "He'd love for you to be a part of his treasures."

Goliath wrinkled is nose at the idea and the man's odor. "He can collect me once I'm dead. Open the way or I shall just kill you and enter."

"Is your life one of answers or threats?"

"A little of both. Do it."

"You'd kill one such as me?"

"I killed a hunchback in Aphek years ago. Their bones break like straw. I didn't even mean to kill him, but I get clumsy when drunk."

The man turned and waddled further inside the alcove. He reached to one side of it and tripped a secret latch. The click in the air echoed loud and trickled across the land of the dead.

A torch flared in his hand and this made Goliath start a little. He hadn't seen the little man strike a flint or any such thing. Still, unimpressed by magick tricks, the giant squeezed down into the narrow path behind the humpback.

While they sank under the earth, the brick walls narrowed and cool air washed over them. Eyes keen in the dim light, Goliath paced their descent, mindful of a trap or trouble. He sensed no malice or grim tidings from the humpback. The path opened up and Goliath felt relieved to move out of close quarters. He registered surprise to see a huge realm underneath the earth before him. The chamber spread out, larger than the wrestling arena he'd just seen. Several small men shuffled between the defined stalls. All lame, some twisted, many deformed and freakish, but all careful in their intentions, as if performing scheduled tasks.

"You will see the collection? I...please, giant one, are you the champion of the Philistines, Goliath?"

"I doubt there's any other like me that you have ever seen."

"You're correct, sir. We have the pickled corpse of one near as tall as you, though. Come this way, please, call me by my name..."

Goliath's ire rose. "I'll call you Dungstain from now one, little turd, now show me this giant and then your master. I wonder if you have a humpback in your collection?"

"Your might and size has brought your ego to such heights," the small one said as they walked down the line of stalls.

Philistine

Goliath saw horses with six legs, two-headed cows, and stuffed bodies of pigs with more limbs than a centipede. "In this case, it'll suffice."

They stopped by a long line of tubular objects. The hunchback pulled the cover off of a few of them. The translucent tubes, like long bubbles in the water, lay before them. Filled with an amber-colored liquid, Goliath saw bodies floating inside each. One was of a child with three eyes and another held a gorgeous woman with her labia lips going the wrong direction. The hunchback stood by the longest tube, which held a black-skinned man near to the height of Goliath.

The Philistine knelt by the tube and said, "Impressive, Dungstain. If he had six fingers and toes, I'd really be curious."

"He came to us from beyond Stygian lands, beyond Kush from the south on the dark continent."

"I'll bet." Goliath stood. "Now he's a decoration for your master?"

The humpback shrugged, kind of.

"Do I need an engraved invite to see this donkey, or should I start to break things until he arrives? I was going to tell him one of his prizes won't be coming here."

The humpback turned and motioned for Goliath to follow. They passed by a few cages that held misfit children, almost knotted fists of flesh unable to speak, but able to shed tears. They stared at the Philistine as he passed.

"What does your master glean from this?" Goliath waved his hand at the children. "Those twins over there, the children joined at the head...and all of this nonsense. What's it for?"

A sly, almost girlish voice seemed to chime in from everywhere to say, "The magick of awareness, of their misery and uniqueness adds to my cerebral power. Their bile, their selves, their cries to their god in their suffering are as tasty as tears."

Hand to his javelin strap, Goliath said in a composed voice, "Show yourself, Coriander."

A slender man in a burgundy loincloth and a lavender vest emerged from a passageway opening. Though his hair ran white and nearly receded to the middle of his cranium, Goliath sensed no weakness in his flesh. Coriander's skin glowed a tan color, and the Philistine figured him an Egyptian. Still, Coriander smiled a grin that appeared rather catty in nature and entirely too white.

"Your collection will be missing a couple Kongamatos," Goliath told him in a matter of fact voice. He then saw an enormous woven basket like one pomegranates in a market place were sold from. His eyes squinted as he took in the odor of snakes. Gaze back to Coriander, who seemed to get closer to him without taking steps. "I killed one after it got free of the Bedouins transporting it."

Coriander raised his head a little, but didn't look sad. "A pity. Where are the rest?"

"Rest? There was but one with it."

Coriander then blinked several times but his face never changed its expression. "There were a half-dozen in the deal. Don't tell me those sand scum lied to me."

Goliath pondered the idols and told the alchemist of them. "When I broke one apart, there were bones inside. Any ideas on that one?"

Thin arms folded across his chest, hand soon up to his chin, Coriander thought for a few moments and said, "That's not a good precursor. You see, grand Goliath, I'm not the only one to use odd means to focus my power." Head bopping, he asked, "You come from Jericho way, have you not?"

"You can see that with your mind? Am I that easy to read?"

"No, but tales on the wind, words from couriers are, colossal one. Were you there to see Lady Bednukah?"

Brow furrowing, Goliath said flatly, "I saw her, but that isn't why I was there. Would she be the one turning things to stone? An assassin also had this affliction with stone."

Eyes rolling and the inane grin deepening, Coriander replied, "Her approach is more direct. Her ego is such she would want you to know she's the one stabbing at you."

"Typical, I suppose."

"True, mighty Goliath."

The way Coriander said *mighty Goliath* stung the Philistine like a cloying insult. "But you seem to get off on your own self, for selfish means. I don't see you attacking anyone, but sucking in oddities for use in your web here, like a deranged spider."

Coriander giggled like a girl and Goliath's skin crawled. He cursed himself that such a sound made him uneasy, but the eerie Alchemist wasn't like most men. His moves slinked like the mating of a cat and a dancer. The pores of his skin sprang up as ovals, not circles under Goliath's keen eyes, and Coriander smelt almost reptilian.

The alchemist said, "Spider? Well, you're correct in that I care little for the realms beyond or their silly power struggles. However, if you follow my words, it sounds like someone else is practicing such a trait. I wonder why these creatures were turned to stone. It seems so pointless."

"Maybe the point isn't evident."

Coriander grinned again. "Spiders...would you want to see an amazing thing I traded much dead in the crypts for?"

Goliath wondered why the dead were his to traffic in. "I don't care about such things. They say you can devise the future or see the present far away."

"Really you must see the spider."

Goliath growled. "You test my patience, little man. I may not be able to wring out of you what I want, but I can squeeze the life out of you and put an end to this collection of waste."

Coriander let his lips close over his teeth, but still a smile bled from his face. "I can show you my spider from Egypt, from the almighty Zorn himself, and then I can see if your questions will be answered."

"Zorn?" Goliath tried to hide his surprise. "He deals in spiders?"

Coriander motioned with his head and started to walk. "Well, not as such, but you will be flabbergasted at what you see."

Coriander took up the necklace from his chest and pressed it to a wall. The stone ground and a door swung in. The bizarre lighting struck Goliath first, as six stones glowed on the ceiling. At first, he thought they provided light into the room. Soon, he saw that while they did light things up and show the spider clearly, they emitted long beams of light, hair thin. Whatever lurked in the lines, it kept the spider at bay.

Though not a spider, Goliath saw lucidly enough, but a good reason existed as to why Coriander called it as such. The thing had eight legs, but they were human legs. Two chalk white, two were Nubian black, and the other four more tan in hue, all attached to a central body, one torso made up of buttocks and breasts. The bubbling body did sport a humanoid head, eyes wide apart, and a blank expression.

"Impressive, this Zorn," Goliath mused at the hideous creature, wanting to slice it in half to make it depart the planet. "He has made a thing of great mystery, or a freak commanded by a body all tits and ass. Amazing but..." Goliath voice trailed off as he saw that one of the tan legs pointed a mark, a tattoo...of a falcon, shaded blue. Rage filled Goliath, and he couldn't hide his emotion to the point his fists slammed his legs.

"What is it, Champion?" Coriander said smoothly, somewhat taken aback by Goliath's reaction. Still, the Alchemist persisted in his sarcastic manner. "See something you like?"

Barely audible, Goliath said, "Eucimar is indeed going to his doom, poor fool." Calmer, Goliath leered at Coriander. "I wanted to see what sort of man collected flying monsters, and I have that answered. The fools at the temple told Balzer you can see afar with your powers or have sight into the future."

After a slight bow, Coriander admitted, "I have this power. Come, into the land under that of the dead, great Champion, and you will see the future as well." When Coriander closed the spider in and set the wall back, Goliath shot the humpback a dirty look, causing the little one to shamble away. "They are all a part of me, well, for the most part," Coriander said as they delved deeper into the darker passageways. The tunnel slanted as they headed further down.

"I'd like to see what lies in wait for us at Relex, and why the priest of Dagon never returned." That image of the tattoo on the leg kept running across Goliath's mind, and the fact it belonged on the thigh of the wizard Paltibale.

They passed by several corpses in crypts, covered in webs and dust. Coriander stopped and faced the lurching giant. "Your confidence is not absolute?"

"I've lived a long time not being stupid, but my attitude over wizards is low."

"You trust my words?"

Eyes rolling but only seeing the porous ceiling of the tunnel, Goliath said, "Not really, but one can never be too careful. Besides, crossing me isn't wise. You may think to send me to my doom." The giant's tone turned dire. "May the gods protect your skinny ass if I survive the wrath of the evil you send me to, if you lie." A few moments passed before the Philistine promised, "I will return."

Coriander's teetering laughter filled the tunnel, almost making Goliath jump as it split the silence. "There's no need for confrontation, Champion. My self is seeded far and wide but I'm not immortal, not yet. The essence of Alchemy is different than common wizardry or that which Zorn has figured out."

"I really don't care," Goliath said with a bored voice, eyes scanning the stone shelves holding bodies. "Just tell me what I wish to know."

They walked for a long time before Coriander wondered, "How is the Lady Bednukah?"

"We never had cakes and wine."

Following more giggles that buzzed down the tunnel, he replied, "She owes me, the rotten woman. I sent her a special mother as a magickal gift once. It was said in some circles that the young woman was to have been impregnated by a Night Howler, as she was a virgin. Perhaps that's a tale and she presently fell for the talk of a flesh and bone traveler, but at any rate, the mother carried twins, perfect little babes." Coriander paused and looked back at Goliath. "What is it? You groaned?"

"Never mind. Just thinking of the Hebrew edict about not letting a witch or necromancer live. There are times I think their God or his mouthpiece got it right."

"How evil of you," Coriander purred. "Bednukah owes me for that gift of the babies."

"Don't you wizards ever just get drunk and pay for a night of whores? Why is it always blood, death, infants and grudges?"

Coriander turned away and started moving forward

Philistine

again. "That's life, no?"

"I suppose I'd enjoy it more if I had more power like you?"

"Would you now?" He then spoke up loud to inform Goliath, "We are under the cemetery on the plain."

"I figured that. Are you going to tell me you're a ghoul as well as a magic man?"

Again, the skittish laughter echoed in the tunnel. "Goodness no. That would be immoral. No, I sense a great mystery on your heart and mind."

Goliath grunted, tired of leaning over so much, so he took a knee and stopped. "I must be getting old if I give off such feelings. A man has to think, no?"

"Certainly, but you send off mixed signals from your mind and soul. You worry not much for your life or the future, but your anger boils at your honor being bruised."

Goliath grimaced that the alchemist kept walking. He proceeded after him, hunched over. "Any man would feel that way in if they felt used or played."

"You agonize over a slight to you, I can sense it, and that a vast unseen power manipulates you."

They moved forward several yards and then Coriander hopped down into a lower level. A room opened up before them like a mini crypt full of drawers, replete with several fresher bodies to sour the air. Coriander set about opening up each drawer, as if unsure of what he sought.

Goliath stood up in the chamber, but still couldn't reach his full height. He took a knee once more and rubbed his back. "Perhaps I see enemies where there are none. A tough life and an existence of war will do that to ya."

"But you fear no opponent of flesh," Coriander reminded him, face a-fire as he found the treasure he wanted. "True, you've had a harsh way, but made it smooth via your self. Now, you consider the gods are conspiring against you?"

Eyes never wavering off the alchemist, Goliath snapped back, "I'm sort of down on gods right now."

A corpse pulled from the drawer, Coriander asked, "Your mother is a venerated goddess at Gath, correct?"

"Leave my mother and the lauds the priests give her out of your filthy mouth, or I'll put part of you in every one of these damned graves."

Even though he held the dusty body, Coriander slapped hands together behind it. "Oh, don't fear me, great man of war. A wizard is harder to kill than most."

Although Goliath's thoughts drifted on the spider and Zorn, he replied, "Maybe for some, but I like my chances."

Coriander laid the corpse out on the center slab of stone and took a metal device from his belt. The device looked like a pinchers for turning food on a grill, but inverted. Coriander rolled the corpse over and inserted this device under its backside.

"What if I told you my seed lives on after I pass it, grows and lives like a swarm of insects?"

Goliath watched the Alchemist manipulate the body's limbs, breaking the corpse's hip. "I'd say you were talking out of your ass."

To his knees on the slab, Coriander started to pull up his long tunic. "You cannot understand the means of divination I deploy. You will soon observe why I subsist here and benefit from this place."

At last, Goliath comprehended in full the mage's intentions. "Leave me out of your silly games, ya puke."

Left hand pulling out his organ, Coriander asked, "You want to see what lies at Relex? You want to know what really stalks you in the ether realm?"

Goliath waved dismissively. "Do your magick, madman. Seeking to impress me is like trying to piss a canyon full."

With that, Coriander thrust himself down, penetrating the corpse, giving out a low whimper as he slammed into the body.

The necessity of the act ruminated in Goliath's mind and it all tweaked his disgust.

The wizard opened his eyes as his motions quickened. His eyes shone as white slits. "Yes, yes, I see the great city, arisen from the bottom of the city, Relex itself!"

The Philistine nearly slapped his hands together on the Alchemist's head for stating the obvious. "Say something so stupid again and I'll squeeze your head until shit comes out your ears."

Lips peeling back, glee running over his body, Coriander said, "Steam rises from the monoliths of Relex, and the slime moves all over it as if alive."

Goliath looked at the floor and then the ceiling. He saw a host of tiny insects scurry there and couldn't exactly identify them.

Coriander threw it down harder, saying, "Great perils lie there for you, mighty Goliath. Things unnamed from eons best forgotten lie in wait for you, wanting you as a part of their majesty."

"Where are the others, the Philistines that went on before our group?"

Coriander moaned in bliss. "They are still there... they will always be there..." Suddenly, Coriander's pupils reappeared. "I see what assails you! I see what is after the whole of your kindred."

Interest tickled, Goliath tried to stop staring at the bulb-headed insects and focus on Coriander. "Who is it or what is it?"

"Not Lady Bednukah nor her demon savant, but she uses this force after you. It uses Bednukah, too. I perceive that which this *one* is after, and I can glimpse her desires, creating a fresh god in the flesh and an offspring for the focus of a grand new Philistia!" Anguished cries rang out and Coriander arrived. "I know the name of the new goddess."

Goliath frowned. "To divine the future from necrophilia..."

Coriander didn't withdraw as he breathed heavily. "Who said I need to do that? I have that power without this copulation exercise."

Rage stoked, Goliath bellowed, "You little prick!" His voice grew so loud the insects scattered away from the noise. "I'll feed your balls to that spider!"

Coriander jumped back, avoiding Goliath's grab for his throat. His words came out smart and strong. "Careful, you have not met my seed."

From out of the stiff corpse crawled additional small insects, each sporting a yellowy hairy body, many legs, and a bulbous head. Goliath's wrathful eyes glared down at them for a moment, then locked in place. If he stared long enough, the insectoid heads resembled that of the mage before him.

Coriander's grin ebbed a little as if disappointed by Goliath's lack of horror at the revelation. "They are so many, you are one, Champion. Leave me to my glee and triumph and just go on." Saliva dripped from his lips as the insects chattered in agreement. "Know that in one part of the world, you are not the master."

"I don't care to lose games, even ones of the mind." Goliath moved closer and seized Coriander by the right shoulder and throat. "You're all alone, you bastard."

Smile gone, eyes bulging, the sudden realization that Goliath wasn't going to talk any more and crush his throat filled Coriander's rabid mind. He choked, vented his bowels and started to rasp, "Stop! This is madness! I know the name of the goddess that assails you. I recognize the new goddess being created!"

Philistine

All six fingers delving into the flesh of the wizard's shoulder blade and neck, Goliath said in a steady voice, "I'll choke the life out of them, too."

"Malak," Coriander pleaded, his arms not fighting Goliath but entreating him for mercy. "Your blood kindred is named Malak."

"I have no kin save for my mother," Goliath roared and felt the tissues of the wizard's throat crush under his grip. "The other one like me, Neurath, is of no matter, and only likened unto my father after a fashion." Goliath shook him and the teeth of the alchemist snapped together. "Spin a lie on your deathbed." The Philistine then closed his paw and the bones in his grip broke. He snapped Coriander down, making certain the connection to the spine busted. Goliath threw the corpse of the wizard on top of the old defiled body. The insects scattered and Goliath stared at Coriander.

The mouth of the wizard kept moving. No sounds came from his ruined throat, but his lips formed perfect words. Over and over, the alchemist said four words.

Goliath dropped to both knees, intertwined his fingers, formed a bludgeon, and said, "You lie after death, too." He raised his hands and brought them down. The blow caved in Coriander's face and the wizard stopped moving. The giant rose up to his feet again, hunched over and started to exit the room. Head twisting fast, he noted the great traffic of insects, all scurrying around the dead wizard. Suddenly, all of the creatures faced Goliath.

Instinct is a powerful thing and Goliath lived by listening to his keen wits. They screamed at him to run, that danger abounded, so he left the room, fast.

Down the hallway, he loped, making sure he followed the correct path, shoulders bouncing off the walls on occasion, knocking a body out of its eternal rest often. Coriander had tried to confuse Goliath when they went in, he'd noticed, but never counted on the ardent wits and sense of smell the giant possessed. All around him the crypts and dead bodies shook. At first, he feared an army of the undead arising to attack. Then, a worse scenario bubbled in his brain. Goliath wondered how many bodies the old rapist had laid with in such a way, and how many examples of his mobile seed ran loose. The idea that they seemed cognizant of their master's death bothered Goliath. The bother bordered on fear, something alien to him in the world, and he had to get in the open.

His movements restricted, Goliath moved on as best he could, hearing the swarm of insects arising behind him. Once, years ago, Abimelech and he journeyed in a place far beyond the Pillars of Hercules where they saw a countless number of red ants consume a warrior. That vision kept coming back to his mind. Of all of the ways Goliath thought he would die...in battle at the end of a hundred lances, pulled apart by teams of horses, burnt alive at a stake, or heart exploding covering a big-hipped whore, Goliath never wanted to be eaten alive by so many tiny enemies.

He ran into the door to the outer crypt area and bounced back. Anger broiling in his throat, Goliath dropped his shoulder and charged again. Since the door gave some, he knew a concentrated blow would send it asunder. The bar sealing the other side of the door splintered and Goliath tumbled into the edge of the menagerie. True, no army stood ready for him, so that was a plus.

The humpback staggered nearer to Goliath, but well out of arms reach.

"Well, Dungstain, your master is dead." Goliath shook off his arms of the grave dust and straightened his back before he promised; "I'll put you out of your fucking misery before I leave."

Philistine

Before Goliath could advance on the humpback, the small figure bent over to the floor. At first, Goliath thought him begging for his life, and that would be typical and didn't distress nor impede his moves. But when the fabric on Dungstain's tunic split, showing his hump coming apart, this did give Goliath pause. In a moment, the disfigurement burst completely, and a hundred tiny seeds of Coriander flew out. Several of the insect-like seeds landed on Goliath's left forearm.

Not waiting to see if they bit, Goliath crushed them, then swiped them off, afeared they'd drop into his flesh and run amok. His boots stomped, crushing many of the seeds as they scattered. He saw the other attendants gawking at him, wild, but never approaching him. Goliath backed up and rammed into the huge woven basket. He steadied himself and backed away. However, his initial impact and hold caused the basket to turn over. The fact that something serpentine tumbled out of the basket didn't shock Goliath, but the fact that two of the giant serpents were in there sort of surprised him. The snakes unfolded slowly and Goliath stepped back, over the body of Dungstain, and headed for the way out.

"Set us free," came the shouts from those in the cages. "Let us go from that evil mage!"

Goliath looked into the faces of the deformed children, the freaks and twisted members of the collection and thought of their lives if he indeed opened all the cages. It only took him a moment to decide on his course of action.

*****

"Sire, you'll want to see this," Abimelech said to Goliath as the giant reclined outside the crypt complex.

Goliath faced the sunrise and raised the skin of wine to his lips. "What is it now? I've seen all of the amazing things inside. You and the men have your orders."

Abimelech nodded vigorously. "And we carried out the commands, sire. Captain Balzer and the rest never batted at eye at your edict."

"We're Philistines," Goliath grunted and took another drink. "The populace would expect naught else."

"True, sire, but the men are wagering over something. You must come see!"

Goliath let out a deep sigh and followed Abimelech back down into the complex.

Torches and fires lit the spot well, and the devastation the small Philistine fighting force wrought rang absolute. Blood painted the walls, and several body parts littered the grounds. All around, death and destruction decorated the area. The crafts smoldered from the vats of boiling oil dumped down the stairway shaft and set ablaze after Abimelech led the men down. Once the oils had burnt out many of the insects, the Philistines executed Goliath's decree to the letter.

Goliath peered down at the middle of the ring of soldiers. They didn't need to part to allow him room to see what transpired.

The two giant snakes from the basket locked mouths in a kiss. The reality far more sinister, Goliath nodded as he saw what they fought over. He unslung his javelin and stabbed it through the serpent on the left, far down in its body. This didn't kill the snake, of course, but it drew back on its swallowed victim.

The two snakes had started to feed on the twins, joined at the head. Both serpents swallowing the bodies up to the conjoined spot.

Goliath turned and carried his javelin. "Now seal this place forever. Cave in the roof, whatever it takes."

Philistine

Abimelech nodded as he followed his master. "That was quite a story."

"I hate bad stories," Goliath answered as they headed up the steps.

Abimelech noted, "Malak? I've never heard of such a goddess. I will consult the acolyte Ahirom, though. Perhaps you misunderstood his final words, as he never said them outright."

Goliath shook his head hard from side to side as if trying to banish what he knew to be true. "I know what he said about the new goddess born. 'Her name is Akisha.' How about that?"

"I know a half-dozen Akisha's back in Gath alone, sire. For the record, there are hundreds of children named Goliath these days, too."

Goliath looked at sky. "No, I think it is her. Ever just have a feeling, Abi?"

"Many times. I try to reason and make sense of them."

"Feelings are for weak-minded men. It makes them think too much. Revelations are different. They make men die."

CHAPTER SIX
RELEX RISEN

Dawn rose over Ashkelon, but King Vyndekay hadn't yet slept. He planned to attempt slumber soon, but the night had required his attention. Never a strict advocate of the gods, that night he bestowed acknowledgements and held out hope in their powers.

Eucimar claimed that's why his prayers and sacrifices went for naught, that Vyndekay really didn't believe in the acts strongly enough. A man of action in his youth, a warrior turned politician, Vyndekay wondered after the departed priest's words.

On this night, the tenth anniversary of the death of his son, Kedvybaal, blood spilled. At the altar of El, and then at the temple of Dagon, Vyndekay pondered on the things his mind usually pushed out: The fact that his son died ill, not in battle, not poisoned, none of that. A promising fighter, a good talker, Kedvybaal died on his back, sweating and cold. A wily priest suggested the young man died after a trip to a whorehouse in Gibbethon. Vyndekay, a general at the time, burned the locale and slew all the whores, but it didn't bring his son back. Though he again honored Kedvybaal with the sacrifice of a boy stolen from his home in Ziph, he never believed his son would come home, nor was that the intention. Somehow, the blood and soul of this child would make the gods happy and Kedvybaal's trip through the afterlife better.

Walking to his home, flanked by guards and advisors, Vyndekay thought on the fruitlessness of that sacrifice, and the fact that he did have other sons with other women, but not for his favorite chosen mate. His son was gone, that was the way of the world, but he didn't have to like it.

Gods and goddesses held genuine power. For proof, he needed to look at his daughter Emana. She'd been returned to him from death's shadow, and for that, he respected the powers beyond.

He stopped on his walk and men with him came near to running into him. The King saw the lithe shape of his young daughter looking from open shutters in their home. He noticed his advisors suddenly fought down bouts of chills.

"She's just a little girl, you donkeys," he told them and waved at his daughter.

Her eyes never blinked, nor did her gaunt face show any emotion.

A horse thundered up to them and the soldiers grabbed for their blades. They soon relaxed. Half of the advisors said the name, "Hyrum," naming the courier famed for his fast horse, simple ways and lothario reputation.

"Sire," Hyrum saluted and bowed his head. "I bring news from General Schlack."

The King squared his shoulders to the rider and waited for the message.

Hyrum folded his hands and stated, "The stories are true. There's a movement among the troops to break away and follow a rebel faction."

"Led by?"

"General Samien, sir."

Vyndekay showed no surprise. "A pity. He's a fine warrior and planner."

One of the men behind the King said, "That's why men will follow him."

"But he's not the king of any city, and his opinion of policy isn't an issue." He faced his advisors and proclaimed, "He's a soldier. Samien needs to remember that soldiers take orders. His innovation on the battlefield is one thing. However, treason is another." He faced Hyrum and asked, "How many are with him?"

Hyrum quickly responded, "Schlack doesn't know, but he suggests the army and navy take a new oath unto the King of Kings."

Vyndekay smiled, and then buried this expression. "A good idea. Let the word go forth that all men on leave or off with their kindred must return unto the five cities. They will take an oath to our land, our gods and our kings."

Hyrum saluted and waited for the King to dismiss him. Vyndekay did so with a nod and turned from them all.

His eyes searched for the sunrise. The King then turned southeast, wondering after those sent on the errand for the priests. His head jerked, facing the shutters where his daughter stood.

Behind the slender girl stood a shape, one Vyndekay at first took for a spirit. However, in a moment's time, he saw it was the wizard, Kmentosi.

Eyes closed, he didn't have to ask himself why the arch-wizard from Ashdod was in his daughter's room.

He did have to ask himself if all of this would be worth it.

Steven Shrewsbury

*****

Little sleep came to the Philistines at the port city. Not long after the sunrise, Goliath strode behind Captain Balzer and the two dozen Philistine soldiers toward the docks of Ezion-geber. Two large crafts distinguished themselves from the other vessels by their somewhat bastardized mating of designs and galley holds structure. The ships' long bodies, swooping designs and sea bird-headed prows were unmatched by any other seafaring craft in the yard. The sun washed over the sails as grizzled sailors poured buckets of vinegar disinfectant on the decks.

Thumb tapping on the pommel of his sheathed short sword, Abimelech told Goliath, "They arrived in the night."

"Good for them," Goliath said as he closed his eyes and let the sun wash over his face.

"The crews went for rest save for those couple sailors, but the local Philistia populace set about the task of making the ships ready. Per Balzer's orders, they're being cleaned, disinfected and ready to sail."

Goliath peered over the docks at the stout men mopping the decks of the colossal canoe while others dumped refuse from out of the oar holes. A man on the dock pumped a handle on a series of pulleys, and a long tube shot water into the rowing galley of the vessel nearest them.

Abimelech watched Goliath as he then looked across the city. "Put your mind at ease, sire. There'll be plenty of time to discover the truth about Akisha when we return home."

Philistine

Goliath didn't look angry or upset. If anything, his placid nature made the other around him uneasy. "Whatever she and that wormy cunt Yaggah are about is of no matter to me, in the end. What Coriander said may also be nonsense. What? Did you think my heart grew found for Akisha's innards so that she seeped into my heart?" He sounded like he delivered a jovial jab, but menace lurked in his tone. "You need to drink more." The others shared a laugh at his rebuke of Abimelech. "Whatever their silly plans or wants, they are from a dog's ass to me. Why, that skinny woman you sent to my chamber this morn, what was her name?"

With diligence, Abimelech answered, "Trebluha, widowed daughter of master builder Ahkuh-Rhan of Gaza."

Goliath nodded heartily. "A talented lady for a seamstress. Her hands worked me as good as my own, damn 'neart, and yet, I feared no pangs of love nor did I hear the plucks of a lute in my ears when she smiled at me. Mind you, she did have magnificent brown eyes."

"That's why you let her live?" Abimelech asked as the men exchanged grins at the champion's words.

Suddenly aware of the looks, Goliath muttered, "Piss in your helmets, you rat bastards. Yes. She's a wonderful woman, full of kindness. I'd never disgrace her with death by me in that regard. I appreciate your choice. It was an awful night last night."

As the Philistine warriors spread into formation, waiting to take orders from Balzer on which vessel they'd ride on, Abimelech said to Goliath in a low voice, "All right, so your bluster for the men is done. If the wizards are seeing something dangerous in Akisha..."

"Wizards need to get laid more and cast spells less," Goliath grumbled, thumb through his javelin strap. "A wizard? That's a priest with no hard on. I'll deal with this if it's an issue." He set his eyes on his shield bearer.

"Abi, there may be no tomorrow to worry on. We're here to get a representation of Dagon for the priest back home. Nekimai the priest and Kmentosi the arch wizard of Dagon can fight over it."

"That'll be a fine battle."

"If this pup Ahirom can keep his guts together, we will see." Goliath's head turned, seeing the two members of the vessel approach. "Things are looking up. See who it is, Abi?" Goliath grinned and addressed the taller of the sailors. "You old fish-eating dog!"

The tall, skinny man with white hair stopped, hands on his hips. "I didn't know they made pricks to walk upright."

Goliath guffawed. "After the parade of them you saw dancing from the room of your sister?"

Hand slapping the knees of his shortened up breeks, the white haired sailor laughed. "They were headed to Gath to see your mother!"

Still laughing, Goliath held out his right hand. "Weldon Yog, you salty old sonofabitch, so glad to see you in service to the Kings of Philistia."

Weldon slapped Goliath's huge hand, his slender fingers lost in the mammoth grip. "King Achish owes me still, so I abide his coins. I heard tell you were in town." His voice, nasal, gravel-laced and raw, asked, "Staying in trouble, I hear?"

Goliath released his hand and gestured toward the city. "This town is minus an Alchemist and his collection."

Weldon made an obscene hand gesture in the direction of Coriander's crypts. "Good for the worms that eat his carcass. They can kill every one of those damned priests and wizards in my mind." He then let his eyes rest on Ahirom who settled in not far from Balzer and Sadik. "Great morning to meet a god, huh?" He then turned from the priest, rolled his eyes to heaven and nodded at the short man in the faded headscarf who stood next to him. "Can you believe this old sinner is still alive?"

Though he didn't shake the hand of the short man, Goliath named him. "Nopsik? By Ashtoreth's shaven ridge, you must be a hundred years old."

The short sailor shook his head, earrings wiggling and answered, "Half that, but feel all of it."

Abimelech slapped Nopsik on the back. "I thought you died after the Grecian whore bit off one of your boys."

Anyone in earshot took uneasy steps until Weldon said, "Well, the medicine men at Ugarit saved his ugly ass. Just think about an iron tool out of a forge applied to a wound? Yeah, it wasn't pretty."

Goliath and others wore tart expressions. "Guess that's why the gods gave you two. Sounds wonderful, but glad to see you walking, Nopsik."

The short man winked and took a hit from a small flask at his belt.

Weldon faced down the dock. "They have packed provisions, and we have new stout rowers from the reserves in town. Our men got in last night and that round are still resting. The alterative crew will be enough to give you a look at what you want."

Eyes focused on the horizon where the sky kissed the water, Goliath asked, "You've seen it, haven't you? Relex itself?"

Weldon shrugged, his face losing its humor. "Sure. What's to see? Big-assed thing sticking out of the water that was never there before."

Ahirom stepped forward and almost seethed in pride. "I knew you had. Are the tales true? Does it bear the geometry of the gods? Are there doors, windows and towers?"

Weldon hopped over onto the deck of his ship and

tested how dry the boards were with his boot. "Yeah, all that and more." His coarse voice lessened. "It's a weird thing, though."

"How so?"

"All sailors are full of tales, bad things or oddities they spot in the ocean."

"I imagine so," Goliath answered, glancing down the line at the sailors for a moment.

"I've seen the city a few times now, all on different days." He looked south into the sea. "It's still wet."

Goliath's eyes narrowed but Ahirom asked the Weldon, "What do you mean, still wet? From the waves and spray?"

"Any thing from the floor of the sea would be wet on its arising, you know?" Weldon fidgeted. "But so many weeks later, why would it keep bleeding water or glisten in the sunlight?"

Abimelech wondered, "Why is that?"

Arms folded, Weldon stared up at Goliath. "Why indeed. Get your big ass on my ship. I'll have a few less folks here to compensate."

Goliath eyed the breadth of the vessel. "Mighty fine of you."

Weldon quipped, "If we capsize, I reckon I can ride your giant butt to the shore."

A deep chuckle resonated from Goliath as he stepped over onto the ship. The large craft never reacted much as it was created to wrestle the sea. "I grow fatigued at so many riding my ass, Weldon Yog."

Weldon gave a quick nod, then pointed, directing which troops to go on the other vessel, but did allow Ahirom on their ship. "Ever think of seeing the rest of the world, big fellow?"

Goliath put his foot on the side of the ship and intertwined his fingers on his thigh. "Like the trip across the sea we took years ago?"

"All right, that wasn't such a good time, but there are so many other places to go."

Goliath searched the sky and the wispy clouds. "You're correct."

"You ever get the urge to travel far, let me know. There are lands of ice and snow, lands of deserts and dancers...hell, there's a place far from here where everyone has yellow skin and the women make ya come just to look at them."

Goliath smirked. "They must be comely, then."

"Oh, it isn't all honey and oral gratification, big guy. There are lands that smell like piss as ya pass by. There are places where the men aren't as hairy as the women and have bigger tits. They always blow on long reeds, too. But it's a fun time to see them all, a trifle better than...having *folks* ride your ass."

Suppressing a laugh, Goliath pondered this and understood Weldon copied his thoughts on the Philistine establishment. "I'm just a warrior, Weldon, naught else. I fight. It makes me happy."

"Piss fire, I can find men for ya to kill. What's your heart's desire? However, I don't know of any land where there are people like ya."

Head turning, Goliath sent him an indignant glare. "Why the hell would I want to be around others like me?"

His bloodshot eyes widening, Weldon shook his head. "Gotta point there. Suppose that would make the cheese less binding if there were a thousand of you gigantic penises in the room. But if ya ever grow tired of dominating these tiny assheads, I'm usually around a port city."

They all settled in the craft and Ahirom raised his arms to pray for a blessing from his god. Only a few of them really paid attention.

Steven Shrewsbury

"From the beams that give life unto this world;
shine down and show us the path, eternal Dagon!
Show us power, from you and your brothers
in endless night;
Take us into the chaos that is your bosom
And grant us rapture unto your home
Send the signs in heaven, let the
hammer of night fall, forever
Bless you children on earth
Who hope to go someday
Beyond the stars!"

Goliath looked at Weldon for a moment then back to the sea. "Is it too early to start drinking in earnest?" He almost missed Nopsik due to his short stature; Goliath drew back and noted the small sailor held a large skin of wine up toward the champion. "May the gods bless your happy ass."

*****

The two vessels sailed for hours until noon arrived. Most of the morning the sea ran reasonably calm and only a few of the soldiers threw up.

Ahirom scattered portions of flat bread into the sea. Many of the sea birds came in for the bread, but a hawk swooped in, attacking the seabirds.

Hands making prayers motions, Ahirom said, "A proper sacrifice to Seker."

From his position on his backside, resting against the main mast, Goliath asked, "Entreating Egyptian gods, are we?"

The rowers rested, letting the ship move on under the power of the wind and the current, and Weldon pointed at the sun. He then sliced the air downward. "One doesn't see that very often. Ahirom, what do you make of that?"

Though Ahirom planted his hands on the edge of the boat and focused on what arose in the sky, he wasn't alone. The rest of the crews didn't join the young priest at the edge, but the sight transfixed them as well.

"Stunning," Ahirom said, as if unable to fix words together.

Goliath remained reclined against the mast pole. "Smoke from the water that arises into the sun? Pretty, but naught that spectacular."

Ahirom's face flushed. "It is truly..."

Goliath mumbled the completion of Ahirom sentence at the same time, "...a sign from the gods, yeah, yeah, yeah."

Ahirom, enraptured, went on to say, "Any fool can read the portents from the sea on to where to go, and even the dim are guided by the sun itself, the eye of a god in the sky." His elation made Goliath smirk and Weldon shake his head. "The cloud in my mind is gone, and the messages hidden by my familiars become tangible!"

Goliath arose, stretched and noted Abimelech, who munched his lunch of jerky with several other soldiers. "I should've expected a religious experience from a priest." The men let out laughs amid their bites, but Goliath peered down into the waters. He did a double take and pointed. "Weldon, what sort of fish are those?"

Weldon joined Goliath and frowned at the shapes in the Red Sea. He spoke with no loud voice to startle anyone, but said, "The life in the sea is going bad the closer we get to the risen city or whatever it is. Look at it. What kind of fish are those ya ask me? The kind we'll never eat."

Though many of the sailors turned away, knowing what lurked in the sea, several of the Philistines gaped where Goliath indicated. They all saw living monsters, such as they had never beheld...things double-headed, triple tailed and covered with fins all about. They gazed on true horrors, black, shapeless things that turned to a liquid foulness when Abimelech stabbed his sword into the water. They saw headless, spongy things like bloated stars with green rays about them. Sadik joined Abimelech and did succeed in spearing a leprous-eyed thing, bearded with stiffly-oozing slime. He couldn't get this creature off his sword fast enough.

"You think that a miracle?" Goliath said to Ahirom, pointing in the water. "I hope this trip does not bode ill for us."

Ahirom beamed with confidence, more than any had seen since they'd met him. "Miracles abound, Champion, and the palace of the gods is nearby. I'm confident we shall have in our possession a child of Dagon himself."

A wind hitting his back from the north, Goliath brushed the long hair from his face and said, "I hope this makes the priests back home happy."

When Goliath returned to his seat, Abimelech whispered to him, "Little Ahirom has dreams of grandness."

Shifting on the deck, Goliath replied, "I suppose he does, but I never gave it much thought. What do you mean?"

"He's a young priest in a backwater port. If one did have ambition and was barely out of novice training, how better to push one's self further in the high priesthood than to get a living rep of Dagon in one's hands?"

"But that's the ambition of Nekimai and the priests back home."

Abimelech nodded. "But who will march with us back home and be seen with the god by the people first?"

That image played out in the giant's head. "Politics

in the priesthood," Goliath sighed. "Kill me now."

Ahirom went to his knees, not out of reverence but to keep from being pitched overboard. The sea rolled and Weldon sounded off commands to row anew and to adjust the sails to the winds. The priest pulled a small piece of parchment out from his robe and kept nodding as he read to himself.

Goliath wore a distasteful look. "Bitch, but that wind is cold."

Weldon shouted to him, "Yes, the waters run more frigid the closer we get to Relex or whatever."

Ahirom smiled. "You don't believe it is Relex?"

Weldon responded, "It's something, but there's no placard to indicate just what it is, son. I got a bad idea what it is, and I don't think it's Relex, the city of the ancient times where sons of god rest for eternity."

The priest glowered. "Then tell me your thoughts now."

"You'd still insist on going. Best ya see for yourself. But it's amazing, for sure."

The closer they drew to where the mists arose from the sea, the icier the gales grew around them. Though the sea remained choppy, it wasn't anything the experienced sailors couldn't handle.

Abimelech scanned the sky. "Not many birds around, even if we are far out."

Goliath shot him a look and then refocused on the destination, now starting to become visible in the sea. "Funny that you'd notice that."

All chatter ceased on both ships as the sea became serene. The water took on a foamy texture as the greenish hue of the sea blended with a milky-white current turning a bluish hue. The closer they sailed to the marvel from the depths, their hair raised as the winds continued to grow frigid.

Goliath stood as the distant object developed in

their sight. Once most of it became clear to him because of his superior vision, he broke the stony silence. "I'm impressed."

Weldon came down from the elevated forward sector of the settling ship and stood by Goliath. "I told ya, one doesn't see this every day."

For in the shifting sea protruded a multi-towered locale much like a child's sand castle. It presently spread out to fill their vision, and sheered up to a great height with piled escarpments. The tiered precipices and pinnacles hung like towers over the zenith of lower, boxier dwellings. Prickly and outrageous ran the buildings edges, full of twisted décor and bizarre molded angles.

A steam arose off the city and the breath of the Philistines became scarce. The green slime of the seabed that once coated this edifice had peeled back for the most part, exposing bricks and masonry running an alabaster color. The sun glinted off points in the grand structure, giving off the facade of crystalline spires.

The back of his hand slapping Goliath's thigh, Abimelech waved at the crew for his master to observe. Goliath saw what his shield bearer witnessed, the look of astonished awe in the roughest of the soldiers. Men adept at murder and rape let their jaws drop, their faces frozen in a mystical wonderment as if a childhood dream became realized before them.

Nostrils expanding, Goliath grimaced. He turned to Weldon. "You know what it is, too, don't you?"

Weldon rubbed his hands together. "I'd never gotten in this close yet, but it's obvious to the dumbest sea dog. It's ice."

"How in all of Hell isn't it melted? Such a thing cannot be here."

"Your priest is out of luck in his faith, as this damn thing never arose from the bed of this sea or I'll eat your javelin."

Forehead furrowed, eyes grim, Goliath said, "Where did it come from then? But it appears like a city, carved into the ice."

Abimelech jutted out his jaw at the cleric. "I wonder what the priest thinks of this revelation? Surely he sees what it really is."

Ahirom wasn't at a loss for words. On his feet, hands in the air, he declared, "The abode of the gods is here, preserved for those that breathe having passed through the endless void of space. Wisdom ineffable shall be ours and mastery beyond all thoughts of simple men."

Goliath winked at Weldon. "Well, there ya go."

A pinnacle of ice aped a tower made of blocks, right down to the seams, and rose unmeltable into the wan sun, beetling above all its fellows on the flat top of the great berg. An ebony spot formed on the high pinnacle. Like an eye it blinked, but like a spore, it burst forth, spewing a flood of liquid down the front of the city. This tide of ebony rushed down the many stairways like a cataract in a steep cavern. Steam arose from this ooze, boiling, bubbling; clutching at the stone steps like malignant hands. Still, the black liquid moved in a flood. The vapors rising from the ice features took on the forms of a myriad press of phantoms, wreathing obscurely together and dividing endlessly.

The berg shone in part with an eerie luminosity; and from its loftiest summit poured the inky torrent. All the cliffs and buttresses beneath ran with ebony rapids or cascades. The sheeted falls churned, fuming like boiling water as they plunged toward the ocean. The sea around the city clouded and streaked for a wide interval as forms writhed in the pitch-black spew.

Weldon barked out orders as the waters shifted beneath them. The sails of their craft billowed out. The vessel Weldon steered slanted, sending their aft portion closer toward the edge of the arisen city. He also called out to men to signal the other craft to not draw farther away but to come alongside them.

"It's alive," Goliath remarked as he stumbled on the deck due to the shift. Many men hit the boards as the boat careened. "There's something alive in the blackness."

The monstrous iceberg belched forth volleys of darkness into the air from its apexes and crags. At first, they appeared as giant globs of snot shot from the nostrils of a stygian giant. But these globes soon changed in the air, taking on the form of tentacled creatures, bound for the waters below.

More black ooze poured on like syrup from the upper chamber of the tower, shooting out over most of the slime-encrusted buildings clearly now made of ice that never melted.

Baffled, but still in a religious state, Ahirom held on and shouted, "Do you see them? The children of Dagon!"

Though he held to the mast rope tight, Nopsik sucked on his flask, then tumbled free to the deck and rolled before shouting, "Why doesn't it melt?"

The priest started to speak, Goliath cursed and fell to his all fours as the boat shifted again. "It's enchanted, not a random event, here for a reason."

Weldon ordered the sailors signal the fellow ship to draw back and they complied. As the oarsmen of their vessel tried to battle the drift from colliding with the edge of the floating metropolis, a deep rumble echoed out from within the edifice of Relex.

Abimelech pointed at the creatures. "They are backwards."

Goliath cursed and snapped, "What say you?"

"Dagon has a fishy bottom and a man's upper half.

Those things crawling all over from the tower are the opposite."

Weldon yelled across the bow, "We are hung up! Something has a hold of us."

Goliath glared at Ahirom and tried to rise. He failed, slamming back to the glossy deck. Convinced he must crawl to the rear of the vessel, Goliath yelled back, "Are we caught underneath on a crag from the city?"

Weldon already shook his head and stabbed over the edge with a long lance. "We aren't taking on water. This cursed black ooze has us. It's all over the surface of the sea."

A few of the oarsmen tried to reach out with their wooden tools and push against the city. Goliath saw the ooze that had slopped down formed a small bridge, enough to hold them up. More sailors jabbed down into the muck and had scant luck slicing the vessel free. They'd be liberated in time, but as he looked a farther up, another wave of ooze started to vomit from the upper tower. Goliath also saw that a dozen of the creatures slid closer to them. The beasts were no bigger than an average man, their lower portions scaly and flippered, yet, shaped like a human...but from the torso up they bore a striking resemblance to a squid. Inhuman eyes glared at him over wiggling black tentacles and knew no fear.

"Dammit," Goliath raged as he slipped on the water slopping over the deck. He grabbed the edge of the boat and bellowed at Weldon, "Move your sails and have the oarsmen give their damnedest." With that, he swung his legs over the side, his heavy boots slamming into the slime-covered side of the city of Relex. His huge feet sunk in the muck several inches, but soon held firm as Goliath angled himself between the boat and the city.

In a moment, Weldon read the plan the giant enacted and cried for his men to press on. The sails unfurled but still found themselves blunted by the blocking form of the city. The men rowed on as the creatures from the ooze came closer to the ship.

Back flat on the aft outside portion of the vessel, Goliath heaved strong. His legs strained against the slimy surface, but never slipped. A growl started deep in the Philistine's belly and he shouted his own name as the vessel inched away from the city.

"Lay on, you big cocksucker! You're doing it!" Weldon shouted. "The goo is straining. Press on harder, boys!"

Abimelech tried to stab at the connecting ooze bridge with his lance while Goliath's head slammed into the vessel. Looking up, he yelled, "Heads up, Abi!"

Eyes up, Abimelech stepped back and brought his spear to bear. He was hardly set as one of the squid-men impaled itself on his spearhead. Run completely through, a yellow film coated the spearhead on the other side of the creature. The tentacles of the being grappled over Abimelech's arms, and the toes of the monster pattered on his calves just before he cast it back into the murky drink.

More of the beings started to plop down on the deck of the ship and atop the various men in rowing stations. Though some of the humanoid squids bounced off the deck, a couple impacted directly on the rowers. One stunned sailor elbowed a beast back off the ship, but another rower got his neck broken and fell limp. The curved beak that hid in the tentacles tore into the fallen sailor.

As it rained Dagons, it didn't take any serious commands for the Philistines to be true to themselves. Swords left their scabbards and the warriors sliced through the creatures, no matter what they looked like. At first, Ahirom screamed, begging the men to stop. But after one of the Dagons bounced off him and drew blood on his shoulder, Ahirom's attitude changed.

Weldon drew his curved sword, buried it in the lower torso of the Dagon nearest him and called down to Goliath, "We're nearly free." He then locked eyes with the nearest creature and smashed his forehead into its face, pulping the nasal cavity between its inhuman eyes.

The giant said nothing as he elongated his legs. The craft lurched and came free, depositing Goliath in the sea. He swiped at the edge of the ship, yet couldn't keep a handhold. A cheer came up from the crew as they drew away and then one arose on the neighboring vessel...but this merriment lived a short life. One of the Dagons fell from a great height and crashed through the deck of Weldon's ship. The beast passed clear through to the sea.

Underwater, Goliath saw this thing emerge from under the vessel. Kicking his legs, pushing himself back to the surface, the giant grabbed for the icy blocks of Relex and hoisted himself out of the drink onto the city.

The sailors from the other Philistine vessel notched arrows and supported their brothers in peril. They picked off the creatures with their missiles and motioned for the rowers to get closer.

While Weldon used curse words even Goliath didn't know, the Philistine tried to get a firm foothold on the lip of the city. At his feet in the waves a set of yellowed eyes emerged. Goliath swiped a hand down, grabbed the beard full of tentacles on the face of the mini Dagon and lifted it from the water. With one motion he smashed the creature against the slimy rocks, causing a black and yellow stain to smear the surface as he brained the beast.

Goliath almost called out to Weldon to get his men to the other vessel, but the Captain was no fool. Already Yog started to get his men away from their posts. The vessel rode the waves, yet would not make it much longer. A few men panicked and jumped into the sea to swim the relatively short distance. Though Nopsik and Weldon shouted for them to wait, these men couldn't be swayed. Once in the water, they found they were not alone and were pulled under by the children of Dagon.

Weldon and his men fixed arrows, taking aim at the water. Goliath felt a cold sensation on his shoulders. He swung his arms up, thinking the creatures at his head. However, something worse than inky ooze covered his shoulders. All twelve fingers deep in the substance like a wet drapery, Goliath soon saw this thing, though covered in the black sticky goo, as like a carpet it unraveled from the top of the tower. Too late did the realization grip Goliath that what he held, and what held him, was alive and drawing him upwards.

He bounced off the slick but boxy stone surface of Relex, struggling all the while. A few times, his progress stopped as his legs caught a firm hold. Above his head he heard metallic clicks. Good old Abimelech, he pondered, faithful to the last, grabbing a bow, shooting his arrows up, trying to save him instead of jumping to the next ship for his own escape.

No longer concerned with the peril of the others, Goliath put all his strength into saving his own behind. Again, he found himself hoisted up and traveling several stories across the wet, yet frigid surface of the city. The symbols and bizarre faces in the ice looked familiar, like words on old lost cities the desert swallowed long ago and best left to the dirt.

He brained a few more of the Dagons, but different horrors awaited him. Goliath exploded a few nebulous jellyfish-like things as he rose higher. Naught could prepare Goliath for what awaited him at the pinnacle of the tower. He saw the truth, briefly, before the long tongue pulled him in fast. He beheld the thing inside the city, and that the icy container wasn't a city at all, filled with rooms and tombs of a forgotten realm, possibly full of sleeping gods & scrolls. No, Relex was but a facade of ice, a covered and black thing hideous to even the jaded eyes of the giant.

His gorge rose through an excess of loathing. In all the world naught could be likened to the foulness of it. Something in the creature had the semblance of a bloated ebony slug, but the bulk appeared beyond that of a whale. Down through the ice casing the body went on, with a half-coiled tail thick as the middle folds of his body turning back on itself. Where the tongue originated, a freakish maw curved uncleanly from side to side of the entire entrance. The mouth opened and shut incessantly on a pale and toothless orifice. Right before he vanished into the mouth, Goliath saw eye-sockets close together just above shallow nostrils. He figured the sockets eyeless, but in them appeared from moment to moment globules of a blood-colored matter having the form of eyeballs.

All around Goliath an ocher fluid rushed as a hundred tiny suckers brushed his body, pushing him down the gullet of the wormy thing. Breath held tight, understanding his fate completely, Goliath expanded his body, flaring out spread eagle like a starfish. He continued down for a long spell until he struck a bend in the tube. Unsure if he stuck in the creature's craw or not, Goliath resolved to make his stand here before the belly juices of the beast could eat him away. Javelin off his back, the giant made a swipe, easily cutting through the fibrous tissues around him. The being shook, thus driving Goliath on with the lance.

A series of wet tentacles started to embrace him, but when Goliath bit through the first snaky appendage that wrapped his mouth, more tremors vibrated the worm. Javelin slashing, Goliath near to abandoned the weapon in the muck as he drew his great sword.

He fanned both sharp objects, wanting free. His lungs hurting but not desperate just yet, Goliath avowed to get out of the creature and not have to leave by its ass.

The nose of his sword broke through and the giant pushed ahead, swimming in burning fluids. He worked toward the place where his sword broke free, flopping over rolls of slithering masses and a thousand fingertips with suckers on the ends of them.

As suddenly as he entered the mouth of the creature, Goliath rushed out of its body. Followed by a gush of greenish black bile, he slammed into the icy wall of the container for the great grub. His forehead bounced off the icy surface, and he felt his joints ripple as the force of the impact smashed him hard. Almost losing consciousness, fresh air in his lungs brought back to reality. He then fell several yards before he wedged between the ice and the worm's porous body. Goliath turned in the wedge, stunned to see himself pinned to the creature, which abruptly heaved away from its ice cocoon. He also became surprised that he still clutched his weapons. Again, he pressed his points home, inserting the javelin and sword deep. The worm reacted and drew farther away from the wall. When this happened, Goliath's weight began to fall. He created a double slit down the side of the beast, splitting it open, causing more guts and bile to eject out.

When Goliath had fallen far, still slitting open the creature, a dull whine thundered in the air and the worm thrashed. Flung against the wall of the icy city once more, Goliath thought his body broke on the wall at last. It took him a few minutes to realize the creature itself destroyed its icy cocoon, shattering the fake city of Relex into hundreds of icy hunks.

In moments, Goliath clung to what looked like a shingled roof as it bobbed in the ocean. His javelin caught in the gutter before he sheathed it behind his back. He kept his sword at the ready, fighting off a few stray sons of Dagon as the gigantic creature splashed into the sea. Free of its icy cell, the worm shone in the sun grayer than black, and sported a skin akin to a grub more than anything fishy.

Goliath stared at the countless hunks of the city as they sank or dropped from the creature, and how the worm continued to puke black ooze into the sea... but happiness came from watching tremors on the side of the creature. Where he earlier gouged a huge opening, the thing came undone. More and more of it kept pouring into the sea, and the giant shouted his own name at it, knowing he'd won. Even if he drowned now, he reasoned, it was worth it to kill this parody of the gods.

The thing from Relex started to recede and sink under the surface. Goliath scanned the waters all around. At first he didn't see the masts of the Philistine vessels. Then, and he rubbed his eyes, he beheld one of the sails. When the worm sank at last, the wake of the dying one sucked much under with it, but Goliath's ice flow flipped and flung itself in part of a vortex swirl. He then rode a wave farther out into the sea. Though tossed under the surface, Goliath held onto the mock shingle until it arose again to the air.

The sailors sounded their flutes, and he started to drift toward them. In an hour, Goliath climbed on the surviving vessel. He smiled, seeing Weldon, Nopsik, Abimelech, Cairn, Sadik and Balzer alive there.

"Glad you bastards can swim," Goliath breathed, exhausted as he put his hands on the shoulders of Abimelech and Weldon.

With a great laugh, Weldon said, "Yer gonna love this, big guy. The kid priest made it as well."

Rage stoked in Goliath again. "Speak to me no more of priests, Weldon. Those sons of bitches sent us down here to our deaths on a fool's errand, sent *me* to my death. Damned maggots. I'll see them all die."

Ahirom turned away from two masses of darkness on the deck. "It wasn't the priests who led us astray, great Goliath," Ahirom said, showing a great deal of respect. "Something is fogging our minds, a greater force at work than priest politics and petty one-upsmanship."

Still breathing hard, Goliath leered down at Ahirom and sneered, "You will have to convince me of that, little man. Blaming the demon in Jericho, are you?"

Ahirom turned away from him. "Something manipulated even that force, I can feel it. But I have a greater worry on my hands." He pointed to the two sons of Dagon on the deck, both bound up in rope and chains. "That Abi is a brute, near to killing each as he secured them."

Goliath shot Abimelech a look and said, "The cad. What will I ever do with him? Huh. So, what's the trouble?"

"I came here to get a representation of Dagon," Ahirom said, nostrils flaring. "I cannot go back this way. Which one is the real son of Dagon?"

Goliath drew out his javelin, took it with both hands and speared through the creature on the left. He then gestured at the one on the right and said, "That one there, he's god."

The champion of the Philistines ignored the cheers and laughs. He had just enough energy left to sit down against the mast, vomit and fall fast asleep.

CHAPTER SEVEN
PRICE OF PROPHESY

Ice-cold hands pulled Goliath from the bed mat. The champion understood he opened his eyes in a dream, for Weldon's ship existed no more and a desert surrounded him. A humanoid figure composed of billowing clouds yanked him to his feet. No wind swept the dreamscape of sandy planes, and the only sound was the thud of his heartbeat.

Unaccustomed to nightmares or fearful episodes, Goliath found himself amused by the vision. The sky churned dismal, violet and starless as the fluttering entity led him across the sands. At an impossible speed, they approached a stadium-sized locale. Though stone columns protruded from the dunes to indicate the corners of this edifice, enormous timbers made up the walls.

Goliath's heartbeat faded, replaced by the steady chants of a tongue seldom heard. His mind tried to wrap around the dialect and words, ones he hadn't picked up in years.

Outside the stadium stood dozens of spears with dead body parts on them, some aged and picked apart by unseen scavengers, others fresh heads and still wet with blood. One sported short gray hair and thin lips.

Goliath recognized her as his mother.

Orpah's eyes opened and she frowned.

Unable to speak in the dream, Goliath reached out, carefully held her chin and the back of her scalp. He pulled the head from the pike. Her eyes remained open and animated. Mouth moving, she tried to articulate something to her son. A stern look in her eyes, she looked at the stadium.

Goliath stepped forward and kicked the heavy wooden gates open. The doors moved slow, but allowed him access. All around young men in loincloths danced, reminding Goliath of ceremonies typical of novices to Ashtoreth. Far beyond these revelers stood many figures in white robes, all women, arms up, their voices chanted in high tones akin to flute solos.

Again, his mother's eyes persisted and the mouth jawed. A thought dawned on Goliath, as the dream dictated his actions. He placed his mother's head under his arm, reached out and seized one of the dancing youths. With not much effort, Goliath took a handful of hair and ripped the head from the young novice. He almost laughed as the jets of blood shot out, understanding this came as impossibility only a dream could accomplish. Besides, he usually had to twist a few times before a head came off.

He slammed down the head of his mother on the gushing stump of the boy's neck. Orpah's mouth gaped and gagged as blood spurted out of her lips. She coughed as crimson strained from her nose.

Then Orpah spoke.

"Glad you are quick on your feet. I haven't much time," she croaked. The arm of the youth waved up, limp and lifeless, but aimed at the chanting women. "I'm reaching out to you, my only son. Look on your aggressors."

He wanted to ask her if she was still alive, if this

came as a death warning, but he couldn't utter a sound. Goliath also knew he wasn't Orpah's only child...well, the only son with an unearthly father. This couldn't really be his mother talking to him, he reasoned. As always with his mother, though, the hard words became a lesson to be learned. He looked to where she indicated.

In the middle of the circle of chanting ladies in white arose another figure. It was a stony object like a phallic idol...no, a figure fashioned to appear as such, but having teats and hips, humanoid attributes...then it cracked down the middle and shattered its stony shell. Underneath stood a full-figured woman, beautiful and seductive, laughing...laughing at the world.

Laughing at Goliath.

Akisha.

He looked into his mother's eyes and saw them blank, listless. The body fell limp under his touch. Goliath grabbed another novice, pulled his head off like the top of a flower and jammed his mother's head on. Again, her eyes flickered, but blood streamed from the lids like tears.

"I'm not crying," she assured him. "It's the reaction of the blood from this little bitch." She spat more blood. "Think clear. Seek me out, the one balanced on six wings." She then fell silent as the second host body wilted.

A laugh split the air, not a female one. Goliath turned, holding his mother's head as the body dropped.

Over on a stone slab sat Yaggah, dressed in fine linens from Babylon, drinking from a golden goblet. He reclined on top of Goliath's mother's headless corpse.

The giant awoke howling when the boat nudged the edge of the dock. Several aboard and many on land jumped into the drink at the outburst.

Steven Shrewsbury

Kmentosi shoved the green sleeves of his robe up to the elbows, and thrust his hands into the open flap of the woman's tunic. Though she sported average breasts at best, he never touched them, running his long fingers across her belly instead. A look of mild annoyance spread on the skull-like face of the wizard of Ashdod. The look was directed not at the woman, but to the man wearing the pale flax robe of a male minister of Ashtoreth.

"She displeases you?"

Kmentosi slapped the stomach of the girl and shrugged. "She'll do for the task at hand. Keep in mind, Yaggah, I'm not a fine judge of women flesh any more than you are a priest of Ashtoreth." The wizard turned and indicated that they should follow him into the sanctuary.

Yaggah reached ahead and gave the woman a soft push in the middle of her back. She bopped along, hips shifting, tresses waving as they entered the main temple of Dagon. She paused and looked up at the huge depiction of Dagon illuminated by flickering censer fires, but again, Yaggah pushed her on.

"I'm used to getting vassals for men of the upper classes," Yaggah let him know.

Kmentosi kept walking and never turned as he said, "I wasn't specific. That is my failing, but it will do."

They passed through a green shimmering curtain and then paused as the wizard unlatched a lock. Stone ground on stone and Kmentosi disappeared through a dark rectangle in the dimly lit corridor.

The woman hesitated to tag along, but once more,

Philistine

Yaggah pushed her on.

Kmentosi bade them to follow, but the room proved small, dominated in the middle by a stone tub devoid of water. The wizard pointed at her, wagged his finger and then indicated she should get in the tub.

She glanced at Yaggah and gave the tub a doubtful look. Still, obedient to her profession, she undid the clasp at her neck and let the robe fall. Wearing only a thin gold chain about her abdomen, she climbed in the container.

Kmentosi walked around behind her and soothed his bony fingers down her shoulders. He clutched her wrists tight and guided them to the edges of the tub. She barely had time to try and look at the wizard before he snapped metallic clasps over her wrists.

When he moved around in front of her and bent into the tub, securing her ankles down low, she said seductively, "I adore it rough, man of the gods."

With a wry tint to his voice, Kmentosi stood and said, "You'll love this then." He turned away from her and cleared his throat. The dim lanterns danced as he pulled a lever, opening the roof to the chamber to the night. Moonlight spilled in and provided the room an ethereal glow.

Yaggah shifted from foot to foot, saying, "Can I have it so I can go now?"

Kmentosi nodded and turned about. In his left hand, he held out a ceramic vial toward Yaggah. In his right hand, he held a gleaming steel dagger. "That will make you hard enough to cover all the whores in the temple."

Terror filled the face of the woman as she understood her destiny.

The wizard frowned at her fright. "We have temple prostitutes here, child. Do you think I'd take in a common trollop for sex?"

Yaggah took the vial and stepped back. His rheumy eyes looked to her face.

She whimpered, lips quivering, and then they peeled back in a snarl. "You lying bastard! You killed me, dickless dog!"

Kmentosi blew on the tip of the blade and then raised his eyebrows to Yaggah. "At least you are easy to understand, doing everything for gold or glory, be it yours or that new goddess you cultivate." He sent the woman an acerbic look and snapped at her, "Do shut up, will you?"

She persisted at Yaggah, screaming, "You worthless rat! The gods will strike you down for this!"

Yaggah backed away, his face flushed, the vial held with both hands.

"Please," Kmentosi rolled his eyes and slammed his left hand flat to her sternum. "This is the least of the wrongs treading on his heart." Knife poised above her navel, he said to Yaggah, "Your blood kindred, Samien, well, he's a tougher egg to crack. He pretends to safeguard his motives for his actions, but he's a soldier, sooner done with gods than not. Most military men are that way." Kmentosi stabbed the knife in her just above where her pubic curls stopped. The woman screamed, eyes bulging, but it never stayed the hand of the wizard. He gutted her, striking up slowly to her breastbone.

"I must go," Yaggah said, and ran from the room.

She coughed, gagged and let out short squeals as the wizard gripped the decorative chain now shoved up between her breasts. Kmentosi stepped back, withdrew the knife and tore the chain free. He eyed the chain, kissed it, and then threw it on the floor. He placed the knife on the edge of the tub and reached both hands into the breach in the woman.

"Now," he said, pulling free her intestines. "Let us see what the future holds."

Philistine

It amazed Kmentosi how long she clung to life, but it made him happy. The visions for the future were clearer from the living.

"Yes, yes, good, Eucimar, I see your doom," Kmentosi grinned. "Excellent. Now, then, the army of Samien grows in the highlands, such a pretty little peacock he is, setting about his big boy games against Schlack." Head back, he looked to the moon and then back to the guts. "Yes, show me...so much blood about that giant... yet he still strides forth...damn him. We shall see what comes next for him." His smile so wide that saliva started to drip off his lips, Kmentosi thrashed his head several times and kissed the innards of the whore.

Abruptly, his face went blank. He rooted about in her further, as if searching for a lost coin, but came up with nothing.

A heavy sigh escaping him, Kmentosi stepped away from the tub and turned. He reached down beside the container and picked up a pitcher. He poured water over his left hand, then his right, and then upended the pitcher over his chin. The wizard washed the water about in his mouth and spat it in the tub.

Her jaw still shaking, the woman in the tub convulsed once.

Kmentosi pulled up another pitcher, this one made of metal, and poured it over her midsection, saying, "Die, already, won't you?" This liquid shown green in the moonlight and once this ran over her body, he again knelt. This time, he pulled out a flat metal tray from under the tub and sloshed around the contents. He left the room and traveled across the sanctuary of Dagon. Kmentosi paused, held the tray up toward the giant idol of his god, and then departed into a chamber behind the rear of the statue.

After he set the tray down, Kmentosi lit several candles. From a tall wooden cupboard, he removed a golden chalice. Once he had poured the contents of the tray into this cup, the wizard sat in his large chair. Adjusting the cushions, he reached and lit more lanterns, casting a great light on the image before his workbench.

His eyes glowed yellow as they studied the contours of the stone image, a hair shy of three feet tall, bearing flowing tresses, an innocent face locked forever in a gasp, hemmed by two thin arms, raised in protest. Kmentosi stroked the left cheek as if he consoled the rock icon, and then reached out and took hold of the statue's wrist. The rocky surface felt smooth, polished and tight. He pulled and busted it free from the stone image.

The wizard sat back and peered into the end of the stone forearm. Kmentosi broke off the hand at the wrist and probed the inside with his pinkie finger. The wizard drew out a thin bone. He blew on it, smiled and dropped the bone into his chalice.

Kmentosi brought the cup to his mouth, but sucked on the end of the bone to draw on the fluid within. He smacked his lips, nodded in approval and said, "Now, that is what real power feels like. Come unto me, Mistress of the dark. Anything for my goddess."

*****

Goliath reclined in a gigantic tub of soapy water. The huge basin, reserved mostly for communal orgies by the city magistrates, was discovered and commandeered by the Philistines to satisfy their champion. The master of the house rendered no overt objection, but his pursed lips fooled no one. He couldn't wait to see the giant out of his bath.

Philistine

The champion washed and soaked, aided only by the slender serving woman, Trebluha. Clad in a simple one-piece cloth garment, Trebluha stirred the waters and applied various salts to the mix as Goliath relaxed. Her deep brown eyes glanced at Goliath as he reached out, fiddling with the pins that bound up her reddish hair, and dropped back to the water.

The Captains Balzer and Weldon entered the room, giving the big man a nod at the same time.

"Glad to see you both so clean," Goliath remarked with a sarcastic voice. "I think it will be days before the stench of the sea and guts are off me."

Weldon gave the serving woman a wink, and she waved him off.

Hands on his hips, Balzer said, "I don't think the priest will allow that."

Goliath leaned his head back, allowing his long mane to sink in the waters again and said, "Who cares what he wants?"

The men exchanged glances.

"You wonder if I'm serious about killing the priests?" Goliath never looked up. "Yes, I am. I'm not without reason, though. If they can prove they aren't puppets and all out to kill me, I shall let them live." He suddenly broke into hilarity, mirth the woman Trebluha alone shared. Goliath playfully slapped her behind, nearly knocking her over. "I'm just lying. I'm going to kill every goddamn one of them I find."

As Balzer rolled his eyes heavenward, Weldon laughed. "Well, old sucker, good luck with that one. I have to get back at the sea and head up to Egypt. Story is there is some work for me over in the toilet bowl of Mare Nostrum, that's if Pharaoh Psusennes I doesn't kill me first." He extended his balled up fist.

Goliath slapped it and lay back into the tub.

"Fare you well, Weldon Yog. We'll meet again."

The sailor grinned. "Don't threaten me like that." He departed.

Balzer sent a sour expression to Trebluha and she glanced to Goliath.

"Wait outside," Goliath said softly to her. "Fetch me some fresh water to drink. The wine of this city starts to grate on me."

She turned, left and Balzer's jaw dropped.

"She never even bowed or nodded to you."

Goliath shrugged and closed his eyes. "She isn't my slave. Did you come here to lecture me on manners or to piss in your hat over the fear I'll throttle little Ahirom before we leave town?"

"None of us know if you're serious on the matter of the priests, nor does it concern us. The soldiers will follow you no matter what."

"I thought you were in charge," Goliath murmured, then said in a louder voice, "So if I get back home and start throttling priests, you don't care and the soldiery won't stop me?"

Balzer sat down, hands on his knees. "I can't see why the men at arms would bother. The priests have led us into bad battles as of late. Many may question your motives, but ultimately, they will follow a strong man rather than invisible gods."

"Ah, but Ahirom has a god for them, doesn't he?"

Frown spreading on his face, Balzer sighed. "That creature isn't god or Abi couldn't have hogtied it, no?"

"Good point."

"We lost a half-dozen soldiers out there on this venture. Those lives should be avenged and not only by killing the sea creatures."

Goliath sat up, rubbed his forehead and said, "I won't run back immediately, Balzer. I will rest here another day. My head is weary from the fight inside that ice city. I assume your men are ready to go back."

He nodded.

Goliath said, "Get your supplies together and ready our exit. I think we have lost popularity here due to the slaying of the Alchemist, Coriander and all the favors he entreated the city with." Forearms across his knees, all twelve fingers touching at the tips, Goliath added, "That magistrate, Solama Aggas, hasn't the balls to stand against us and will be glad when we just go."

Balzer corrected him, saying, "Actually, that turned out well. Folks here are glad Coriander is gone."

"Score one for us then. Well, you know the drill of supplies and carriers. We'll set off for home."

Captain Balzer rose up. "Have you considered what Ahirom said, that it is really a greater force manipulating the priests to kill you?"

"He talks out of his ass in order to save it," Goliath grumbled, then cupped water in his huge hands. "Still, it would take a mighty bit of magick to compel that worm in ice to us just to get after...what? Me?"

"Abimelech was trying to puzzle it all out, but seemed resigned to the whorehouse rather than contemplating it further."

Goliath chuckled and splashed the water into his face. "And you wonder why he carries my shield." Balzer saluted and turned toward the door, but then paused to hear Goliath say, "One last thing. Talk to the master of these grounds, I know he owns the rights to Trebluha there. She shall accompany us back to Gath."

Balzer blinked but quickly bowed to Goliath.

When the soldier had his back to the giant, Goliath's voice said calmly, "I never asked you to kill that perfumed prick in charge of this house, Balzer. I only asked you to show some diplomacy."

Trebluha returned and walked to the back of the tub. She ran a heavy comb through his wet hair, then stroked her fingers on his bruised forehead and hummed to him. In a minute's time, Goliath reached back and grabbed her waist. Gently, he pulled up her thin wrap and gestured for her to climb on him. His head remained on the edge of the tub as Trebluha lowered herself over his mouth.

*****

Abimelech and Balzer stood outside the alcove of the great home where Goliath bathed. The magistrate of the city and master of the home pointed in each Philistine's face.

The white-haired magistrate Solama Aggas showed little fear to the towering Abimelech and shouted, "You come to our city on your religious quest and cause a ruckus. We have good trade and relations with all of the countries thus; we stay out of your wars. Now, this indignity at the house of my brother, Zebedeo..."

Arms folded across his broad chest, Abimelech peered down at the man and then looked over at his brother to say, "You balk at giving up your servant woman, Zebedeo Aggas? She's past her prime for breeding or going through the motions."

When Zebedeo opened his mouth Solama Aggas spoke again. "You miss the point. You come and take what you want because of..." His voice trailed as he heard heavy footfalls.

Goliath emerged in the air, clad only in his midsection cover. "Is there a problem?" He sneered at the Aggas brothers, "Ah, how ungracious of me. I shouldn't have pissed in your larder."

Abimelech never unfolded his arms as he said, "These men don't seem to want to give up Trebluha on principle."

"Really?" Goliath looked down at Abimelech. "A man with principles? I'm touched." He then turned his head toward the brothers and grinned.

Though his teeth nearly ground together, Solama managed to reply, "You are only a few dozen men and one giant. A garrison of Egyptians arrived today, a hundred of them." The bile left his tone as he spoke gently. "They owe me greatly and so does the great Pharaoh of Egypt."

"Really?" Goliath eyed the magistrate keenly and Aggas' brother backed up a step. "Psusennes I is a sap in search of a tree."

Lips curling back, Solama said, "His men are here, well trained and armed. I suggest you gather yourselves and get out this very evening."

Goliath eyed the Aggas brothers and then threw back his head, laughing deep in his belly. "So, you prove me wrong. I'm glad I never bet on you having enough balls to stand up to us. I respect strength, if a lack of intelligence may be evident. We'll be gone soon enough and not stay another day. The men were hungry to leave anyway." Goliath turned, but paused, then said, "The lady comes with me though. I had Balzer ask you nicely and offer recompense. The time for niceties has past."

The magistrate cleared his throat and several men at arms stepped from across the street. Hidden in the passersby, the men all carried short swords and the harsh looks of men ready to deal death.

Goliath said, "You really don't want a bloodbath here with your own security force, do you?"

Zebedeo Aggas spoke up in simple tones. "You may slay many of us, you and your two fellows, but you cannot stand against us all."

Goliath's voice grew louder. "You overestimate my love of life."

Solama swallowed and took a breath. "You'd risk your existence over the life of a simple slave girl?"

"My life isn't the issue," Goliath reminded him. "Yours is. Is her life worth yours to you?"

"You arrogant bastard..." the magistrate spat, and then his face flushed, fear suddenly across his eyes. "You are but over a dozen men. Are you telling me you'd use a dozen Philistines to slay the garrison of a hundred Egyptians?"

Goliath squared his shoulders to him. "No, I'm going to use one Philistine warrior to slay a hundred Egyptians. Now, if you and your ladies with the short swords over there don't want to die as well, I suggest getting the hell out of the street and out of our way."

The magistrate and his men stayed in the street while Goliath, Abimelech and Balzer entered the house.

Once inside, Abimelech noted, "What a rude man."

Goliath ducked his head under the alcove entrance and said, "I'll go see Ahirom and his new prize pet Dagon. Here's what you both shall do."

Balzer said, "I thought you were going to kill the punk priest?"

"I haven't decided yet what I'll do with him. I had a bad dream a bit ago. I shall have him help me with it. We'll see what he knows about the nature of the universe."

Abimelech said, "That assface Solama Aggas will not molest us, not just yet. He will gather his guards and wag his tongue at the garrison."

"He's a rat," Goliath declared, hands on the side of the huge tub. "He'll never fight us in the open. He'll hide behind the skirts of the Egyptians or try to poison us, or cut our throats in our sleep. Now," he faced Abimelech. "Here's what you will do."

Philistine

Evening came and night soon fell. The commander of the Egyptian garrison walked into the street with the Aggas brothers. Fit, lean and hairless, the commander frowned at Solama Aggas. "You haul me out here and insist I take my men away from a feast to subdue a dozen or so Philistines, to discover them gone?"

The magistrate looked at the barracks that housed Balzer's men only hours before and then into the nearby bathhouses. Only a few serving girls wiped down the locale, but not a soldier strode among them.

"Nahur," Solama insisted as his brother receded. "They said they'd leave in due course, but Goliath made many braggadocios remarks..."

The Egyptian Commander Nahur frowned as his men filed in behind him. "We've come a long way for the exchange of the political prisoners tomorrow from the Quraysh clan from Mecca. Though the glory of killing Goliath would be an honor, better than raiding the Kaaba of its hundreds of idols, we are dead tired. We'll retire for this evening and then arise to see if anything has developed overnight. With any luck, they have gone from your city and spared us an ugly scene."

Nahur turned to go and Solama slammed his hands together, saying to his brother, "I doubt that the matter is that easily quelled."

Zebedeo shrugged. "Perhaps it's better this way."

Solama cocked his head to one side. "Is Ahirom still here or did he go with the Philistines?"

"That may be one method of knowing if they are truly gone. Isn't you daughter in with the acolytes of Ahirom?"

A bitter look flittered across the magistrate's face. "Don't remind me of her impractical games with those fools. Girls will do as they will, but my leash on her must be tight. Yes, send someone to see if Ahirom still attends the temple duties of Dagon."

*****

Clad in his full armor, Goliath passed through the outer courtyard of the temple of Dagon. The attendants at the gates only bowed and praised him as he entered. Never once did one of these commonly dressed folk or those attending the breeder mother sacrifice quarters next door question him. He was the champion of the Philistines, after all.

However, a dozen young men in plain, one-piece green frocks appeared from the shrubs that encompassed most of the inner entrance. Goliath paused, watching them pull their robes back together, then stopped and smiled as a single female emerged from the bushes, pulling on a dark cotton-weaved cloak. After this fast look, Goliath continued on.

"Stop," the female voice called out as the robed youths surrounded the big man.

Goliath did stop his stride and glared down at her. "Get along, little ones. I have business with Ahirom." He paused, drew in a breath and barked loud at the youths before him, "Now go!"

Two of them fell to their backsides, three others stumbled over each other and couldn't run away fast enough. One stood in Goliath's way, urine dribbling out on his sandals. He gawked up at the giant, lips quivering.

His voice calm, Goliath told him, "You better run along, too."

Philistine

The wet youth did as he was told, but the half-dozen that remained seemed made of sterner stuff. They already had their hands in the air trying to cast spells.

"Oh give it a rest," Goliath sighed and drew out his great sword.

Two of the novices backed away at the sound of the weapon clearing its scabbard, but the four who remained chanted louder.

The severe-faced girl stepped before them, folded her arms under her tiny breasts and scowled at the giant. "*You* better run along, big man, before the wrath of a god catches up to you."

Fingers gripping the pommel of his sword, Goliath roared with laughter. "I doubt you little shits could make the toe jam of the gods appear. Now, step back fast before you cast a spell that makes your balls fall off."

The girl stayed adamant. "Leave now, big mule."

Goliath's humor started to wane. "Seducing these punks that know nothing of women has made you brave."

"I know that you are outclassed before the realm of magic and all of its workings." Her look ran fearless as she declared, "You don't know who you are dealing with, Champion. Show some respect to Idra Aggas."

One of the chanting boys suddenly took on a look of terror, probably due to Goliath's chest shaking in laughter inside of his being. The young novice boy stood at the girl's left and said, "Forgive her. She's high-spirited."

"She has no brains, an Aggas or not, now leave me be." Goliath saw the boys put their arms down, and he asked, "What are you all, novices to Dagon?" When no one answered, he nodded. "I thought Ahirom was the novice, even for his age."

One of the boys volunteered, "He graduated to

assistant to the high priest Hevel some time ago. When master Hevel vanished at sea, we had no choice and Ahirom ascended."

"Did he now?" Goliath turned to the doors of the temple. When he pressed his hand on the doors, they failed to move. His hand flat on the door, it felt damp, covered in a skin of clear substance. Goliath wrenched the handle and the mass split around the locks. "Nice try, kids. With practice, you will become priests."

The girl Idra Aggas stepped forward, running around in front of Goliath, shouting, "You will be cursed for all time to defile the temple!"

He snatched Idra up and held her off the ground, nose to nose. She kicked him several times in the stomach until her air would no longer come due to his grip on her neck.

"And if ignorance could be sold by the pound, you could buy the universe." He dropped her and never looked back at Idra, but said, "And you'll be but a temple harlot or a brood mare for the sacrifices." He started down the aisle of the temple.

Goliath stalked into the foyer of the temple of Dagon. He stopped before a velvet drapery that cloaked the entryway to the main sanctuary. In his mind's eyes, Goliath saw the usual layout of the Dagon temples. They sported a large sanctuary with places for covering a temple prostitute or to bleed a sacrifice for the god...or bleed a temple whore if you had enough money. Before this would be the statue of Dagon and the place for burnings farther up the way. When he swept back the drape and ducked his head, the reality of his wonderings played out, on a somewhat smaller scale.

All of the stone slabs or cushioned areas for the prostitute offerings sat vacant. The few lanterns that flickered farther back in the sanctuary kept the simple mosaics on the walls faintly lit. Goliath saw that the images scribed in the stone surfaces were rough and incomplete. He couldn't recall hearing if this spot was a new locale for Dagon worship or not. So much had happened to him in the past few days, Goliath's mind burned to focus on the tasks at hand.

True to his memory of the temples, a stone representation of Dagon dominated the front of the room, somewhat recessed back behind a series of candles and torches. He tilted his head, seeing many of the braziers and sacrifice pits cluttered the left side of the idol. On the right side reclined a small bathing tub, much like the one at the Aggas home. The closer he stepped to the tub, Goliath beheld the water greenish, probably salty in composure. In this container, still bound up, lounged one of the sons of Dagon from Relex.

Most men would've jumped when the priest Ahirom appeared, scissoring out of the shadows behind the idol and setting his feet near the golden censer near his knees. Goliath's chin moved sharply, but his body kept stalking ahead. Ahirom looked down into the censer, that let mists drift up in a halo by the idol.

"So, you've come to kill me," Ahirom stated, not questioning Goliath's motives.

"Yes. But I'm not unmerciful. Tell me something great that will stay my hand, and I'll let you live this evening."

Ahirom peered up, his face awash in the golden glow from the censer. "You have me at a disadvantage, Champion." Ahirom's voice ran steady, clearly unafraid of his coming death. Goliath assumed his contentment originated in the appearance of the thing in the tub. "What have I to make my magick? There is no blood present or hereabouts. What have I to see the future or understand that which you desire?"

A small smile played on Goliath's lips as he sheathed his sword. "I comprehend blood is needed for sacrifice.

Look into your soul and open your mind to magick all around us in this city. Any moment now, you should have blood aplenty, nearby."

Ahirom closed his eyes and they popped open abruptly.

Goliath smiled in full and pulled out his javelin. "Do you feel them? Can you sense the souls departing their husks in close proximity? All of that blood gushes for you, priest." Goliath set the base of his javelin on the stone floor near the idol. "Feel it, celebrant. Quit fooling around and prophesy!"

Ahirom's hands spread out over the censer, his fingers quivering. "You are misguided in your hatred of the priesthood, it is not us that seek to slay you," Ahirom said, his voice becoming dry. "Dagon in the sea! I feel so many lives in the ether around me, ripped from their bodies, screaming for their stilled hearts!"

"Prophesy," Goliath ordered him and pointed at the censer. "Show me a vision, that will stop me from setting you amongst the others fleeing their flesh this night."

Ahirom chanted and his body shook. Soon, in the golden embers of the censer, forms cascaded, nebulous, but slowly taking on human forms. These figures, a large circle of women, wore white gowns, but suddenly switched in substance to glass. Their pure forms still moved and aimed their arms at a center point.

Eyes intent on the images, Goliath said, "Again, the wheel." The anger in his voice arose. "Tell me what assails me in my dreams. Tell me what this wheel is."

Ahirom said, "You see the paths from the crystal women to a central point? These beams may not be wood or stone, but they focus on a figure...this shape is the cause of your torment and what manipulates reality."

Just as the structure of this center female started to solidify, the entire image faded, replaced by the hideous realm of Moloch. The three-breasted sorceress

Philistine

Bednukah laughed, and her demon pulsed with power. All around them danced priests and children. This image of darkness overlaid the realm of crystal and light. Just as the hilarity of Bednukah began to fully annoy the giant, this illustration faded as well. The grim interior of the realm of Moloch dissipated into the greenery of the outdoors. This beautiful vista became punctuated by the huge semblance of fawning worshipers, common folk throwing down their cloaks and robes as a rather big-hipped woman walked over them. With her, adorned in fine clothes, strode a slender man in a golden crown and man sashes of shimmering fabric.

"Akisha," Goliath spat like a curse word. "You mean to tell me someone is worshiping that?" He leaned in to look closer. "Yaggah, looking rather fine in his raiment, I might say," Goliath mocked. "They won't be able to prophesy over the paper cut on a serving girl's thumb once I rip the heart out of that sissy."

The priest confessed, "I cannot understand it all, Champion. I don't know what this figure surrounded by crystal ladies is nor how she is the root of it all. I cannot say if Bednukah aids this force or sponsors the glorification or deification of Akisha..."

Goliath shook his head violently. "Why in all of Hell would they glorify Akisha? Why would they give such lauds to Yaggah and her?" Frustrated, he looked down at the priest. "All right then. You can live. Get your bearers and take up your god. We leave for Ashdod this moment."

Still shaken and weary from the experience, the priest asked, "Champion? Where did the so many souls come from for this vision?"

"I told the magistrate I'd use one Philistine to slay the garrison of Egyptians. I never told him which one." He paused, took up his javelin on both hands and said, "At least you didn't screw a corpse to tell me any of this."

Ahirom eyed him close. "What do you mean?"

"Forget it. I shall not kill you this day. We need to go now."

*****

Xylon, the Captain of the guard at Ezion-geber, returned from his late drinking with the Egyptian commander Nahur. They first noted a problem when no servants greeted them at the gates of the garrison's barracks. No wine bearers, guards, or men carrying food. Nahur drew a dagger as he smelled the air.

"Damn," Xylon said as he pulled out his short sword. He smelled what the Egyptian did: intestines.

When they stood at the doorway of the barracks, Nahur gagged, both on the wave of putrid air that slapped them in the face and from the utter revulsion at the site. Xylon held onto the doorframe with one hand and gripped the hilt of his sword fast. When he held the weapon, this imparted him little solace. A single sword couldn't stop whatever did this act of mass murder.

Nahur stumbled in for a few steps and then fell to his knees. "But Goliath was at the temple, correct? He was spotted by spies so our men stood down. There are no signs of..."

Xylon noted most of the Egyptians lay in bed, or seemed to die unarmed. The floor carried no set of giant prints in the spattered blood. Xylon placed his foot by the prints in the puddles on the floor and saw the shape of the killer's feet shaped into big boots, but not those of a giant.

"Most were speared," Nahur said as he pointed. "Look at the pattern, across the beds, one after another. The killer slew two dozen of my men before they knew what hit them. You see? It happened so fast. Many over here stood against him..."

Xylon nodded, seeing the dead men clutching their guts, and a spot where arms lay lopped off from their masters. Two men sat, back to back, propped up, headless.

After he regained his breath, Nahur said, "He wounded so many and then came back to kill them slowly. What sort of an animal does this?"

"Are all of your company gone?"

Nahur ran up and down the barracks several times before he swore and admitted, "To the last man. That bastard. I'll see that Goliath's balls on a stick!"

Xylon shook his head. "But he was at the temple, I saw him go in myself as the soldiers retired for the night."

His shoulders squared to Xylon, Nahur said, "Call out your guards. If the Philistines are still in this town, they shall all die!"

"Forgive me if I am not very apt for this mission. They wanted to go, and all they asked for was a serving girl for the giant. My magistrate Solama Aggas refused them, even threatened them with your military force."

"Damned fool! He doomed my men. I shall show Aggas and his brother!"

Nahur stomped out and passed through a dozen of the guards of Ezion-geber. Xylon motioned for them to follow him as the Egyptian stormed toward the temple of Dagon. He stopped at the inner gate and pointed.

The Egyptian wondered, "Do we need to go in to see what has happened?"

Xylon saw the wooden doors of the temple, well, barely...for the bodies of six novices hung from the overhead pikes, strung up with measures of rope. All of them had vented their sphincters on the steps of the temple...and in this morass of filth squirmed a single form…a nude female, struggling with her bounds. When she freed her hands, she tore off her gag and opened her mouth, but no sound came from lips crusty with dried blood.

"I must see to Solama Aggas," Xylon insisted and turned away. All followed him, unwilling to enter the temple of Dagon.

They found the magistrate at the home of his brother Zebedeo, arms and legs ripped from their sockets, but still attached by fleshy lengths. Solama lay under the form of his brother Zebedeo, who hung crucified to the doors of the manor. Zebedeo still lived when the men pulled the nails from his feet, a bit unwilling to open his hands as the nails came free of his wrists.

Nahur pointed at the right hand of the house owner. "They knew what they were doing, Xylon. The nails are through his wrists so as to keep him aloft. That there, the object nailed to the palm of his hand? That was done for another reason."

Swallowing hard, Xylon said, "They left him alive. They left him alive to suffer."

Nahur cursed and they looked down at the dead magistrate, then at the thing nailed to the palm of Zebedeo's right hand. "I wonder whose tongue that is?" he asked knowingly.

CHAPTER EIGHT
COMMUNION

The party of Philistines made good time for the first two days of their travel. On the third morning, they forked off to the west to take up a route back home nearer to the coastline.

"I'll get back to Jericho way in time," Goliath promised Abimelech as they traveled. "I have other matters to attend to back in Philistia."

Abimelech pulled a cover over his face to shield the wind. "There'll be plenty of time for that, sire. I want to put more distance between us and that city."

Goliath's face wore a mild look, focusing on the disappearing trail ahead of them. "What will the Egyptians do to us now? Throw rocks?" He lowered his voice and cursed the infrequently traveled route. "This damned wind is wicked."

After Abimelech turned to look at the wagon that sported Ahirom and his prize, he said, "I hate that damned thing."

Goliath never turned to see the carrier cart for the representation of Dagon when he said, "You heathen nutsack. Heh. Well, that's why we're upwind from it."

"Many have had to die because of this folly," Abimelech reminded Goliath. "I know that means little in the scheme of the universe, but..."

"Someone is up to no good and someone will pay," Goliath guaranteed. "Ahirom exists at my leisure."

"Do you still plan to kill every priest in Philistia? There's a small army of them training at Ekron alone."

At Abimelech's words, many men nearby stared at their champion. Goliath raised an eyebrow at the furtive gaze of Sadik. "And what if I did? We shall see." He then winked and said with a stern voice, "Perhaps we need to rethink our ideas of gods and blood for bread, aye?"

Abimelech read the men's faces. "Even your friend Eucimar? Would you kill him if he comes back from Zorn?"

"Yes. I'd feel bad for Eucimar."

"You could spare him," Abimelech offered with a wink.

Goliath declared, "I said I'd feel bad about it, but I'd still kill him. However, as I see more, the mummery of the priests isn't just focused on me. Something else beyond is my enemy. Yes, to the point of sending me on this silly venture, something wants me dead or out of the way."

"I think you're correct, after what you told me of the Dagon temple visions."

Goliath faced Abimelech, squinted through the sandstorm and said, "That means that worse things are in the offing, you read me?"

Captain Balzer held up his right arm and said in a loud voice, "There are some large stones over there. We'll pitch camp there. This storm is getting worse."

Once they reached the series of large rocks partially buried in sand. The troopers and those attending fell into formation and dismounted. They soon set their tents ready for the night.

Trebluha aided the other women brought along by the soldiers in setting up food and places to shield storage. Sandstorms blew common in the region, and they carried tarps to fend off the breath of the desert.

Balzer told Ahirom, "You're responsible for that, thing," his face twisted is disgust at the image of Dagon. "I saw you using part of your daily water ration to douse it."

Ahirom flared his nostrils. "It's not a thing, but a personage of god himself."

Goliath cupped a hand around his mouth and shouted over the wind, "Make sure god keeps to himself, then. God stinks worse than my ass."

With that, they settled in for the long night and proceeded to get drunk. Balzer warned them that the stores of wine and spirits they brought wouldn't last over time, but the men vowed to worry on that another time. Glad to be heading home after surviving the peril at sea, they wanted to drink and forget for the time being.

They regretted their choice to drink so much at first, for the blinding storm made them stay put for two more days. The liquor ran out early the second day, and Balzer started to figure up a rationing system for just the booze. At first, this panicked the younger soldiers, but Philistines prided themselves on being realists. Unafraid to die in battle, but unwilling to die stupidly, they complied with smaller rations. This made the slighter divisions of food and water easier to accept.

By the third day, all of the stories of battle and adventure gave way to yarns of history and scripture. Silence reigned in many tents, but a few soldiers still drew close to Abimelech and Goliath to hear more. Trebluha curled up near to Goliath, but never touched him. Many wanted to hear him expound on the hints he told the children at the oasis outside Ezion-geber.

Cairn begged Goliath, "Please, sire, do you really know of our homeland, of misty Caphtorium?"

The giant relaxed back and let his fingers walk over Trebluha's hip. "There are those that think our bloodline comes from the damned Grecians or some other folly beyond the Pillars of Hercules. Those men talk from their ass and never take care to clear their bowels before they spew." This earned a few laughs, but Goliath grimaced as a low squeal echoed outside. When the others heard this, they too lost their smiles. "There's a place called the Black Sea, and that's where Caphtorium lies."

Again, the shriek echoed outside and his story stopped.

The tenor of his voice muddy, Goliath said, "Even over the scream of the wind, I can hear that accursed thing sing."

Balzer stretched his arms out, looked in the direction of Ahirom's tent and remarked, "You call that singing?"

"Huh," Goliath grunted. "I call that thing a bipedal scallop lucky enough to look like the reverse of a Philistine god." He then cleared his throat and said, "There are always good tales to tell. Stories about me get dull after many tellings, and since I'm in the room, I tend to get taller in each one." He paused as the men laughed once more. "However, there are greater things to talk of than my own bad self."

With his fingers intertwined behind his head, Captain Balzer stated, "When I was a lad, we hunted in the edges of a land beyond the ruins of Irem."

Goliath turned his head toward the Captain. "The city of the pillars? Another legend swallowed by the sands."

Balzer agreed with a nod, "The old men with us said it was Irem, anyway. True enough, we couldn't see much of it all eaten up by the sand. At any rate, my father Itthobaal was a fantastic hunter and knew bad spots to stay away from. He was a live man, that Itthobaal for sure, and we hunted with a few feral men in the mountains nearby."

Goliath yawned. "I'm happy for you."

Balzer grimaced. "I'll get to the good part here in a moment. In the night, the barbarians celebrated the hunt, as even we do, of course. But they pulled a log from the forest. It had to be one uncut, sliced from the wood by a storm or some such thing. They burned this dead log and we all stood near the flames."

A smile spread on Goliath's face. "Did you see your complete shadow?"

"Ah, you know the story."

"I know the practice. Carry on."

Balzer said, "Well, the barbarians told us how the shadow cast that is headless? That man will surely die."

Sadik sat forward, face full of wonder. "What? If your shadow had no head, that was a sign of your coming death?"

Cairn asked eagerly, "What happened?"

Goliath interjected, "Balzer thrust his manhood up, and of course, it cast no reflection." Even Balzer laughed at his jest. "And yet, the bastard lives."

Once the laughter subsided, Balzer said, "They thought to spook us with the tale, of course. One of the men in our party, an excellent spearman named Sivad didn't cast the shadow for his head." The laughs faded as Balzer related the rest of the tale. "My father Itthobaal said he thought it all drivel as most of us do in terms of foreign beliefs."

The younger men asked at the same time, "Was Sivad dead in a year?"

Balzer nodded. "Yes. About ten months after, Sivad died, fighting the Hittites."

Goliath sighed. "Not an uncommon way to die."

Hands held out to concede that point, Balzer said,

"The moral of the tale is that Sivad started to drink more after this trip. Father said when the drink lay heavy on him, Sivad became obsessed with the ritual and tried to recreate it many times to invalidate the barbarian prophecy. He never succeeded in seeing what he wanted, and his drinking began to impede his abilities." Balzer folded his hands. "That's why he died in battle. Itthobaal said that he grew careless."

Goliath nodded. "Itthobaal was wise. Let that be a lesson to you all. Priests and even savages can tell you many wild things, and if you want to believe in them enough, you can fulfill that idea. A man's will to do what he wants or his fear can direct his existence."

Abimelech shuddered from the sudden cold. "Isn't that the essence of faith? Believing in things not seen?"

Goliath belched. "If this is going to turn into a religious discussion, go bunk with that smelly bastard over by the stone slabs...and his incarnation of Dagon." Again, the tent filled with mirth.

When the hilarity died down, Sadik asked Goliath, "Sir, you have seen one of the gods."

Silence reigned as Goliath stared into the face of the young soldier.

Sadik went further, saying, "We talk of gods and faith in them, surely you have seen one for real, not heard tales like us."

Goliath cleared his throat. "You can't believe every story you hear about me, youngster."

Balzer shot the soldier a harsh look, "Be quiet, Sadik."

Goliath shrugged. "I don't mind the young ones asking or wondering. If I choose to tell things depends on my mood. I'm a man of war, not an absolute asshole, contrary to some tales." Goliath smiled and it put them at ease. "Sadik, be careful what you believe in."

Abimelech volunteered, "I've seen an angel."

Goliath near to burst out laughing but suppressed it with some effort. "Are you going to tell them about the whore in Enkomi with no gag reflex?"

"I've seen Goliath's father," Abimelech explained and the tent grew deathly silent. Only the sounds of the wind outside could be heard as all held their breath. Abimelech sought to keep the younger ones from asking questions of Goliath, so he inserted himself in the conversation. However, all waited, unsure of the reaction of the champion.

Balzer looked from the giant to the shield bearer and said, "Was he from the country?"

"Not hardly," Goliath muttered. "I'd rather hear about the triplet trollops from the port of Tel Mor. I hear they came in order, eldest to youngest."

Abimelech ignored his master and said, "When we were both very young, I saw the father of the champion arrive in the night. Goliath slept on, as he could drowse through the end of time, but I habitually wandered the halls of the temple that housed his mother at Gath."

Sadik leaned in. "Was he a god?"

Never once did Abimelech look at his master as he said, "He looked like one, so very tall and powerful. He towered over Goliath's mother, Orpah. Not a god so much as an angel."

Sadik wondered, "Did he have wings?"

Abimelech said, "Six of them."

The soldiers exchanged glances and started to murmur amongst themselves.

After a sip of water Abimelech made motions with his hands, saying, "Two large ones on his back that carried him and remained out, two lower ones that unfurled about his legs, two more that covered over his shoulders. Four were smaller than the main two."

Balzer nodded. "A seraphim? No wonder Goliath is so tall."

Goliath coughed, bored. "I think Abi was into the wine that day. He was a bad drunk even as a boy. How he wields that sword amazes me."

While Abimelech made a filthy gesture at his master, Balzer's eyes narrowed at Goliath. "You don't believe his story?"

"I believe Abi saw what he thinks he saw. Any other man who said that of an angelic being near to my mother, I'd have gouged out his eyes and skull-screwed him."

Cairn pressed on, asking, "Doesn't that sound like your father?"

Goliath sighed. "I wouldn't know. I've never seen him." He then stretched out. "Isn't it time to sleep? Even that creature Ahirom worships isn't singing, so we better take our chances."

*****

General Schlack stood in his quarters, a series of modest rooms attached to the main garrison barracks at Ashkelon. He'd already been reminded it was time to go take the oath. Still, he lingered, looking at a clay tablet, reading a saying several times.

"Sir?" the cavalry commander at the door said, gently.

Schlack put on his helmet and read the tablet again. While the soldier never bade him to, the General told him what he read. "It's an old keepsake, a gift from a fellow soldier in the corps." His teeth grew tight and he raised the tablet only to dash it on the edge of a hardwood table. The object crumbled to pieces. "I've had that for twenty years. It is a personal thank you and a verse about loyalty."

Philistine

"Sir?"

"From General Samien."

The cavalryman stood up straighter and faced down the hallway.

"Never forget where you came from, young man, and I don't mean your hometown. That's why I room with my men, as they know I'm not greater than they. Once one thinks they are better than the army itself, it's time to move on." He saluted the younger man and smirked. "Perhaps Samien should have taken up politics, hmm?"

The soldier gave a polite smile but waited until his superior departed before he followed him.

Once they mounted up, Schlack said, "It's a terrible day when one must kill the ones you supped with."

They rode on to the front of the King's residence. Soldiers surrounded the home, a wonderful palace, but nothing as flashy as various in the region. Thousands of infantry, cavalry and sailors stood in imposing formations down the way and out of the city. Many passed by the doorway of King Vyndekay's yard, dropping a pinch of incense into a burning censer. With each soldier came the simple oath of loyalty to his homeland.

General Schlack rode in and his officers hung back. They let him have his moment to show the regular soldiers the edict excluded no man. Deliberate in his moves, even as he reined in his mount and slung himself down to his feet, Schlack carried himself with an air of power bordering on pomposity. His spine straight, chin up, eyes never making direct contact, a strut birds would envy...thus adding to his act of humility when he removed his helmet, took a knee and then deposited his pinch of incense into the censer. When he arose and saluted Vyndekay, many men in line repeated his action and let out a grunt in agreement for the act.

He led his horse over out of the way of the men until a servant of the King took the reins. Schlack then walked down the home and relieved himself at the latrine in back. In time, he joined Vyndekay at the front of the house. He stood at attention beside the King, who reclined on a small bench near his gates.

The King said quietly, "Do we have the arrival times of the other Kings?"

Schlack's eyes scanned the soldiers who repeated his act and moved on. "Achish of Gath sent word he'll be here by sunset. I trust you saw Bakara from Gaza here earlier?"

"He passed through."

"I saw him watering his horses."

Vyndekay maintained his serious façade but said, "As fat as he's gotten, his mounts will need plenty of water."

"King Ladral of Ekron will be here soon, if he can pry himself from the leg of the priest Nekimai."

"What of Dezmal of Ashdod?"

Schlack blinked. "I haven't heard from him, but he's frequently drunk."

"We'll give him more time."

The General nodded at a set of fair-haired twins wearing sailor's togs as they took their oath. "We have a fine set of men, sir."

"What can *he* hope to do? Can Samien truly expect to stand against a loyal force and attack us here at home?"

"There's only one reason to build an army, sir, to kill people and break things."

"We could send messengers to see what he desires, for certain."

Schlack showed no emotion. "His desires are easy to read. The exact time he chooses to act is the mystery. I say we gather up our forces and strike him down before he can enact his ideas."

The King leaned back, pondering the General's

words.

Schlack glanced over at the shutters of the house. His gaze stuck to the open window. He beheld the thin, pale daughter of the King. He would be ashamed to admit the sight made him shiver.

*****

Goliath seldom dreamt. This fact he oft told of at parties when men and kings waxed eloquent, telling of their faraway desires or dreams. Yes, he understood they meant waking plans, but actual dreams they related of ghosts, monsters and fears he scoffed at. Some speculated that he feared nothing, so his dreams came unto him empty. Others said every man dreamt, Goliath just forgot his nocturnal trips upon waking. This wasn't a real crime, and so he felt it better to disregard any terrors able to scare him.

That night Goliath fell out of his body and into the territory of dreams. He flew from the confining tent in the sandy desert into well-lighted gardens of greenery. Soon, the sky started to turn grim, dark as if a storm dangled nearby. Down on the ground he saw several bushes and lush fields. These transformed into mouths of many fangs, all uttering blasphemous words.

Comprehending it an illusion, Goliath thought, *Oh, that sort of dream, is it?*

The sky shifted in its colors, churning into billowing circles of things better left to sights glimpsed under the eyelids. On the ground the uncouth mouths screamed more, desiring blood, working on his mind to slay more and give the goddess what she wants. While Goliath pondered what goddess that was, he felt a hundred fingers on his body, yet no hands floated in the sky he flew across.

Strange walls made of bricks sporting more mouths stretched out beneath him, bisecting the fields of blasphemy. The walls shot across the lands, running incalculable distances. These green mouths parted and an ashen-colored soil formed. A perfect circle became visible. His focus remained on this spot, ignoring the words of death that the world screamed at him.

His nostrils puckered as a sulphurous odor that dominated the air. The ring in the dirt took on a more complex shape, like spokes in a wheel layered with colors of the rainbow. His body neared the ground but Goliath felt no land under his feet. A lump formed at each station on the wheel near the end of the spokes, a figure made of minerals like the salt pillars by the Dead Sea. Each of these figures glistened, akin to crystalline deposits, and formed into a humanoid silhouette. Never did they take on human flesh, but their bodies wore a feminine cast, though their breasts never took on great definition, content to be analogous in their figures. Their heads turned to Goliath, and each of them, twelve in number he counted, never birthed a mouth...but spoke in his mind all the same.

Kill them. Kill them all. Give her the blood sacrifice, and you will be free of it all.

Out of the focal point of the wheel arose a larger persona, covered in a long gown, set and sewn for royalty. Orpah. She didn't seem concerned at the grass made of serpents near her feet.

Goliath couldn't tear his eyes away from the image of his mother. Her hair, cut short and colored gray, looked just as it did the last time he saw her. Her stern jaw, piercing eyes and rueful expression not condemning him at all...then suddenly her dress spun in motion. Orpah's face never took on another emotion as her gown turned to a hundred writhing snakes, and covered her body. His first reaction was to save her but Goliath couldn't move. Orpah never fought the snakes. They all fell away or dissipated like smoke and a figure of stone stood in her place. Goliath felt himself start to rise up, and the cries of death and destruction were heady in his ears.

Just slay them all and it stops.

The vision faded and reality started to settle around his body. The vision dribbled away but not before another figure stood in the place of his mother. Goliath didn't recognize her, but he could distinguish a cruel look anywhere.

*****

Goliath awoke on the next day, still trembling from the nightmare. Only the serving lady Trebluha noted his tremors, and she only pressed a cheek to his forearm. She'd never tell, he mused, but that wasn't what weighed on his mind.

With no regard to those sleeping, Goliath arose, roused half the camp with his searches, but at last came up with a series of chains. Once he was satisfied they were strong, he promptly wrapped them on the feet, hands and upper body of Abimelech.

Though the shield bearer never questioned what happened, Captain Balzer asked, "Just what in the name of the almighty El are you doing?"

"The force that reaches out across the miles, that causes this storm that wants me dead, failed to do so in my dreams. It wanted me to try and strike at you, thus, making the company slay me in self-defense. This alien force is neither all-powerful nor all-knowing. I can sense it will next try to kill me through another venue."

Abimelech flexed against the chains and sighed. "Thank you for the warning."

Balzer and a few of the others exchanged looks. "You chain up Abimelech as you think him the most likely figure this entity will use on you? What about the rest of us?"

Goliath shot him a hard look. "I'm not as concerned for you runts."

The men exchanged glances, understanding that Goliath figured he could kill them easily enough, but not his shield bearer.

Goliath said, "In time, I'll figure out for certain how whatever it is knows where we camp. It's magick of some kind, and their rolling bones and blood rites give them a window to us. In time, these winds must cease."

Abimelech frowned at his chained state. "That must be a wonderful spell to turn the weather against us."

Laboring on the chains, Goliath nodded. "True."

Sadik said, "So you sit and wait for Abimelech to attack us?"

Goliath wrung his hands together once. "I wanted him taken care of with the chains first. There's far more to do."

Hands checking the secured points on the wrists of Abimelech, Balzer ordered the men in the tent, "Go see to the mounts and wagons."

Once the men filed out of the tent, Cairn stopped to ask, "Sir, is it true we may have to eat one of the humped mounts if this goes on longer?"

Though reclined, Balzer still held his military sternness to his body as he retorted, "That very well could be, but it beats starving."

Sadik joined Cairn, turned and departed. When the soldiers left, Trebluha pulled her cloak tight and exited the tent, too.

Goliath never faced Balzer as he wondered,

"Something on your mind, Captain?"

"Aside from the fact we might all be dead soon, but, that's the life of a solider."

"To die sitting in one place isn't." Eyes on Abimelech as the shield bearer submitted to the further chaining of his ankles, Goliath said, "Aren't you the fatalistic warrior, Balzer." Goliath's tone rose as he said, "You have readily accepted the fate any Philistine soldier might get if they travel close to me. Yes, you enjoy the lauds, gifts and whores lavished on those that are caught up in my path, but there's always death around me, one I might not taste and those near me aren't immune to." The giant faced the Captain. "I like you Balzer. You don't bitch too much and carry on until the sun dies."

"Thank you."

"Are you set to bitch and moan now?"

Balzer's stern front nearly cracked as he responded, "I hope not, but I wanted to speak away from the regulars."

Goliath studied his handiwork on Abimelech. "Then speak."

Abimelech lowered his chin and said, "I think my left wrist will come loose."

While Goliath set to securing the wrist closer, Balzer said, "I hear the things you and Abimelech speak of, that a great spiritual force reaches out to you."

"And you worry it will strike you down as well?"

"That's a given," Balzer said in a simple voice that made Abimelech and Goliath exchange a glance. "However, I'm unsure if you listen to the mutterings of the troops, not these men here but those in greater forces abroad."

Abimelech put forth, "Like those that clutch the leg of General Samien?"

His eyes alight, Balzer replied, "Precisely."

Goliath said, "Samien whispers of insurrection

against the Kings of Ashkelon, Ashdod, Ekron, Gath and Gaza. When he lays eyes on that tight-assed prick Vyndekay who fancies himself King of Kings, Samien gets a hard-on and it isn't for humping purposes. Not everyone can agree on every idea, Balzer. Not all military men appreciate being fodder for wrong-headed ideas."

Balzer said, "They court you often as the people adore you and the military follows your whims. However, bizarre defeats and strange happenings are making talk amongst the soldiery...happen."

Goliath asked in a bored voice, "Are the common troops rife with revolution?"

"Not badly, not quite yet," Balzer returned. "But there have been many desertions and strange talk."

Goliath relaxed back. "Samien is a religious sort so I cannot see him stabbing the priests in the back."

His gaze away from them at the flapping entranceway, Balzer mused, "But what if he thought those priests no longer valid?"

*****

Thunder rolled far to the southwest of their encampment, but Colonel Baldassare dismissed the noises. The Dead Sea carried various sounds over its waves, amplifying the simplest of echoes. Many wispy clouds knotted in the air, but no rains or harsh weather touched the grouping force in the Transjordanian Highlands.

General Samien talked with leaders of a deserting faction of Assyrian soldiers. Baldassare departed from the cave, confident the other Philistine defectors would watch over Samien as the Assyrians discussed matters with him.

The Colonel hated the Assyrians and didn't care

much for the hairy Edomites the rebels gave a spot in their army. Though accustomed to the smell of an army on the trail, the Edomites had a real odor unlike any he'd been near. Usually, such trivial things didn't concern him but he found it disturbing more each day. He walked away from the encampment, down the grade of the hill toward a small brook hidden in the forest. His mind wondered if he'd be able to create enough toleration in his heart for all the foreign forces joining their mantle. Most of them stood as good fighters and talked a great game, but couldn't hide their undisciplined nature. After all, he reasoned, they refused to serve their own homelands for a reason.

Baldassare couldn't let the fact that he'd rather see them as carrion for the crows cloud his judgment. He'd support his General and the goddess until the end.

The Amalekites bothered him more than the stinking Edomites. They bore no particular aroma, nor did they frighten away girls with their looks. The Amalekites were a broken people and far too eager to serve. They reminded him of a youth on his first man-making journey, far too fervent to have someone like them who's paid to spread their legs in the first place.

He checked both ways and found himself alone. A few men gathered up water far down to the south, but for the most part, he attained the privacy he sought. Baldassare undid his vest and then loosened his tunic. He shed his sandals and kilt before he again, looked both ways and removed his tunic. Once in the water, he took handfuls and splashed his face. Submerged, he found himself eye to eye with a youth carrying several canteens. The boy blinked at the Colonel, who sank into the water to his neck.

"Carry on down the way," Baldassare told him with enough menace that the child staggered backwards and ran away from the river.

His eyes to the sky, Baldassare understood his General hardly a slave to the existing religious folk of Philistia. In fact, he thought that a new regime of faith might be what the people needed. A shrewd tactician, Samien already took the greatest chance of all. If he so desired, the General could just keep going east and turn his back forever on his folk. But that wasn't Samien, Baldassare contemplated. Samien liked to fight and upheld what he thought was right.

The Colonel started to rise up, thinking of the trip he took to see Neurath on Nebo. The giant and his cult refused to throw in with Samien, unimpressed by all of the plans they had and the potential for fresh gods. Neurath's rejection surprised Samien, who also thought a chance existed Goliath may join to them as well.

If his leader had a flaw, Baldassare reasoned, it was he thought everyone would agree with his ideas immediately. Samien, jaded, sat up in his cave, throwing in his lots with an army of mongrels.

Baldassare let his hands swipe up his wet body. His right hand slowly traveled over his gut, then up to his heart. However, embedded in his flesh, his index finger traced the stone figure there. He then patted the stone and breathed in deep.

He couldn't feel his heart beat, but in the depths of his ear canals, he could hear it. In some ways, the droning thud sounded like a drum.

*****

Though the sun made the scene outside lighter, visibility remained only a few yards in any direction. From behind a cloth facemask, Captain Balzer asked Goliath, "We cannot hold out here forever."

Philistine

From behind his own cover, Goliath replied, "I have no intention of dying in the desert in the ass crack of humanity." He squinted through the dust storm. "These stones here where we bivouacked, there's no writing on them, correct?"

Balzer nodded. "Ahirom scanned them all and I was with him. That first night it was quieter and easy to see."

Goliath took a few steps and ran six-fingers across one of the slabs. He held his other hand up to shield his eyes. "Looks like there's no pattern to the slabs, but curiously they are all about the same size." His thumb tapped the stone, grinding in the dust accumulated from the storm. He cursed, made a fist and struck the stone lightly in frustration. Under his touch, a thin layer of rock crumbled from the slab. Goliath knelt by the slab and looked closer. He reached into his girth strap and grabbed a dagger. Goliath's fist around the handle, he slammed the flat of the pommel down onto the edge of the block.

"Damn," was all Captain Balzer could say as a thin coating on the slab cracked and fell away.

Goliath turned the blade around and started to jab at the place where the false skin ended on the rocks. "Look...sonofabitch..." He never waited for Balzer's opinion of the engraved markings on the stones. "Go get that damned Ahirom, drag his skinny ass out here." Goliath raised his right hand as quick as he stopped speaking. "No, wait. I'll do it myself."

Though the sand remained blinding, none of it impeded the giant from stomping to the tent of the priest of Dagon. He ripped open the tent, ducked and went in.

The tent was huge for the priest and his imitation god, Goliath mused, as big as the one for all the warriors. It stank worse than a port where the fecal bilge mixed with fish heads from a scaling. At the sudden intrusion,

Ahirom turned and held up a short sword.

"Priests of Dagon are never timid," Goliath said of the raised blade. "But you are pissing into the wind holding that to me."

Ahirom saw the giant unarmed, and still lowered the sword. "What is it you need?"

With a lightning fast grab, Goliath seized the tunic of the priest and hauled him to the door. He then noted the personage of Dagon, eyes blinking, still chained up but singing again. Ahirom's feet dangled as Goliath carried him with one hand to the rock hunk he disturbed. After he dropped the priest beside the slab, he barked out, "So tell me what that means."

Ahirom got up to his knees, rubbed his back and saw what Goliath meant. He took a minute to say at last, "This is old writing, from beyond the deluge itself. It's beyond my ability as a risen novice to translate."

Goliath shouted, "But I doubt it's friendly, aye?"

Bewildered, the priest confessed, "I cannot say."

"Bah, when did you little bastards in the cloister ever leave a message wishing good fortune on strangers?"

Once Goliath stalked off away from the stones, Balzer joined him and asked, "Are the stones the reason for the storm?"

"I'm not sure," Goliath confided in him. "Whatever reaches out to get me has tried to make me attack you all. It will then do likewise to you in your dreams on me. The stones? Are they a focal point? I just cannot say."

"We can have a go at destroying a few of the big stones, breaking the chain of power as it were?"

Eyebrows raised, Goliath said, "There's naught else to do, so give it a go. I'll help you."

"We'll break out the war hammers." Balzer leaned toward Goliath. "Did Ahirom know? Did he not warn us on purpose?"

"It won't matter, soon. I have another idea beyond

these stones. I think these slabs are cursed. The covering could be natural or perhaps coated down to deceive us. But if they wanted to strike at us in such a way, why not back in the city?"

"Solama Aggas grew a set of balls at the idea of exploiting the Egyptian archers. Maybe something inspired his manhood to go up?"

Glad to have something to do, the men relished the task. They took up the war hammers and made makeshift wedges out of helmets Goliath crushed for them. The champion pitched in and they destroyed several of the slabs.

That night, Abimelech rose up and tried to kill Goliath and many others. Still chained, Goliath held him down until the madness passed from him.

The next dawn, Balzer asked Goliath outside the tent where Abimelech rested, "Any more ideas?"

"Must I think of everything?"

"The men are talking of starving as the food is getting shy, even if they are still fit."

Goliath spat toward the rubble of the slabs. "Well, it isn't the stones. I wonder what else could bind this power to our company?" He turned his head and winced at the sound of the personage of Dagon, singing. "Captain?"

"Yes?"

"You and your men, do you like seafood?"

*****

That evening, Goliath slew and gutted the personage of Dagon. Consequently, they cooked and ate Ahirom's god, much to the priest's anger.

In the night, other Philistine warriors, heavy in the madness of the spell from afar, rose up to slay Goliath.

Three of the soldiers were lost, and the sandstorm never ceased.

The next morning Goliath slew and gutted Ahirom. After they cooked and heartily ate the priest of Dagon, the sandstorm stopped.

Philistine

CHAPTER NINE
GATH AND THE OGRE OF RANTIS

In time, the troops refreshed their stores at Beer-Sheba, and then crossed over into the friendlier environs of Philistia. The group traveled unmolested for the most part. Even bands of bandits refused to attack a military troop, especially one accompanied by a giant. After spending a day at Ziklag and changing mounts yet again, the Philistines set off north before daylight. Across fields of wheat and clover, the men set a fast pace toward their goal.

Though they couldn't see Gaza far off to the west, Goliath told Balzer, "The stories from the Philistines we've met are amusing, no?"

From atop his mount, Balzer scoffed, "Such silly tales. I was tempted to send Cairn off to King Bakara to confirm these stories of sedition and vows of loyalty."

At the name of the King of Gaza, Trebluha looked up at them, then to the west. *Of course*, Goliath reasoned, *she had no idea until then where they were exactly.*

Abimelech offered, "We'd better wait until we hear it from better sources than a few drunks and the folks of Ziklag. If they want our oaths, someone in authority will come ask for them."

The hour fell after noontime when Abimelech led the eighteen remaining Philistine soldiers into the middle of the city of Gath. Children avoided their thundering horses and heralded their arrival as the group approached, All turned out to see the one they'd seen before, the champion, walking in behind the troops. This time, though, they'd heard he'd come for a reason and it involved the priesthood. Tales from his rants and purchases at Ziklag flittered on the wind and rested on the tongues of all. Young and old alike peered from between their homes, smithies and shops. Even local King Achish came out to see them.

A few of the children threw crimson, violet and yellow flowers in their path. Soon, these same little ones yelled, but others giggled, saying, "Goliath brings monsters to Gath!"

Those that looked down the way wore stupefied expressions. They ran to Abimelech and asked, "What manner of creature does your master bring to us?"

As the thud of heavy footsteps stabbed at their ears, the Philistine populace of Gath gaped at what the teamsters led in behind Goliath.

"City of Gath," Abimelech shouted from atop his mount. "We have returned from the land of the Edomites. Sent on a wild chase by the priesthood, the champion of the Philistines was attacked, both in the flesh and in the ether realm. Conversely, we shall make an example of the priesthood and for all of those that walk in the force of darkness arisen against our champion."

The horses of the soldiers parted as Goliath made his way toward the center of the city. Four men entered the street from different angles toward Goliath. Each wore a priest's robe and vestments, but of a different ilk. Three of them fell at Goliath's feet, but one stayed standing, arms folded.

A stout man with flowing dark hair and clad in a

reddish colored robe begged Goliath from the dirt, "We have nothing to do with the attack on yourself, Lord Goliath! Spare us who worship Baal!"

Javelin butt grinding into the street, Goliath regarded the priest. "I'm down on all priests at the moment, but I'll not punish those in the house of Baal, for he watches over the earth and the harvest. Many years have I trod the ground. It supports me. Go your way."

Once the priest of Baal crawled away, the shaven-headed, clean-faced priest in a tan colored robe stood and spoke next. "And many times have you sought rest and food from the house of Ba'al Zebul. Though I fall on my knees before you, the lord of the flies will not beg for mercy."

Goliath nodded. "You have balls. You can keep them then. Ba'al Zebul guards the air and eats the flesh of the men I kill. I feed your god and give him a host to lay eggs in, and further a place for Ba'al-Zebub to strive. The sky stretches over me. Go your way."

On the ground cowered the green-robed priest of Dagon, his trimmed close beard at his jaw shaking as he looked back at the lone standing priest. "You spare her..." he stabbed a finger up from his green robe at the priestess standing, "Because your mother lives in Trazabaal's temple at Gath, the venerated goddess in the seat of Ashtoreth..."

"You aren't as stupid as you look," said Goliath, sarcasm flowing in his words as he eyed the high priestess of Ashtoreth for but a moment. "I come to kill you and your brothers here at Gath, Dagonite, and to destroy the dwelling place for your god. You will be an example to all of your brothers in that religion and to other faiths of our kind." He raised his javelin and the priest of Dagon covered his head, wailing. Goliath skewered the man through with the weapon, nailing him down to the street. The crowd gasped as Goliath lifted the weapon, held him up high on the javelin and let the priest slide down the shaft. Face to face with the giant, the priest said nothing. "Let it be this way unto your kindred, and sign unto all."

Trazabaal stroked her bare chin, her salt and pepper colored locks blowing in the breeze. She stepped aside. The people closest scattered, but many stayed at a distance to watch the eighteen soldiers surround the temple of Dagon and dismount. When a few of the priesthood ran to escape, arrows from Captain Balzer's men cut them down.

Many they hamstrung with lances and brought them to Goliath's feet. The giant took great pride in staking great shafts on side of the street and then the priest to them. These long items came from their weapons cart, meant as backups for Goliath in case he broke a javelin. Now, they served as a torturous slow death for the priesthood of Dagon, impaled from the rectum up their bodies for all to see.

An older man in the community shouted out to Goliath, "They will take hours to die!"

Goliath eyed the man, who ran away at the look. "If I am lucky."

The teamsters brought up the great beasts the townsfolk so feared. Giant, plodding, gray and heavy, the creatures usually quartered at Eglon, Lachish or Gerar in Philistia wore giant harnesses. These beasts turned, faces away from the temple. The teamsters ran chains from the harnesses into the temple and then affixed many to the pillars outside the main gates. As Goliath cheered them on, the creatures trumpeted and moved forward, easily pulling loose the pillars that held up the temple of Dagon.

Achish approached Goliath slowly. The graying King stayed a good distance away when he bowed his head to him. "You visit your vengeance upon us here at Gath, Champion. Why did you choose this city? Because your mother is here and you want fear to emanate out for your enemies from here?"

Huge hands to his hips, Goliath eyed the man clad in fine linens. "No, King Achish, because this place is closest to Jericho and the underground abode of Moloch. I have more business with Lady Bednukah."

At the name of the sorceress, the King Achish held his breath for a moment.

Goliath lowered his voice as the ceiling of the inner temple of Dagon crashed to the ground. "Fear not, for she'll be after me, not you in this regard."

Sadik ran to Balzer and saluted. "Sir, we have the priests and their acolytes all accounted for, I think."

Balzer nodded and climbed atop his mount again. "If a few escaped, that's fine. They'll carry the tale for us beyond."

Sadik said, "Sir, we spared the temple whores."

The Captain, King and Goliath all faced the youth. Goliath tilted his head a bit when he heard the distance laugh of the high priestess of Ashtoreth. Many older men stood afar watching the destruction, bemused both at the sight and now at the words of the youth.

The soldier blinked and said, "We received no order to slay them, sir."

Goliath laughed. "Pick out one each for your night of drunken bliss, slay the rest."

Sadik looked to Balzer, who nodded. Sadik then wondered, "Sir, what of the whores when we are done with them?"

Goliath said, "What do you think, young man? I'd hate to ask them to convert."

Abimelech approached Goliath, handed him a huge skin of wine. "A few more pulls and the entire structure will be down."

While Goliath drank deep from the skin, the forward porch of the temple collapsed. The beasts pulled more pillars down. Both big men ignored the wave of dust that shot around them, but King Achish drew back and covered his face.

Like nothing significant had happened behind them, Abimelech related, "When word spread we were returning to the land, sans the Dagon persona, a message came to us from King Vyndekay via General Schlack's men."

Goliath took another draw on the wine, his eyes east. "And so?"

"Our presence is requested in Ashkelon by the General."

"Yes? I'm all aflutter. It's for the oath?"

Abimelech took a few steps from the rising clouds of dust and thus, led Goliath from the spot. "They say it's a military matter, and they regret the trouble you've had with the priests."

Goliath raised an eyebrow. "That mutt must want something from me more than just a military stand."

"He didn't say, but suffice it to say, we are still part of the army."

"Yes, yes," Goliath said, bored. "I should give thanks, huh? Well, tell the messenger from Vyndekay that Goliath says thus: I'll soon make my way to Ashkelon." His tone then took on a sardonic lilt as he said to his shield bearer, "We're greatly weary from our trip and will arrive in two days' time."

Abimelech frowned, but nodded. He did a double take as Trazabaal walked closer to them.

Balzer said, "Do you think he will buy that?"

Goliath's ire rose. "Then tell him the Captain of our group strained his hip after he slipped in elephant crap and he must recover."

Balzer shook his head. "What?"

"Before you ask, it could happen at any time." He

then looked off to the east again. "I must go to Jericho."

Abimelech leaned on his spear. "How soon do we leave?"

The giant never turned his head. "I'll go alone, Abi. You take a whore and enjoy the evening. I don't want to give Lady Bednukah any angle on me."

The two stepped away, out of earshot of the King and others who watched. "You aim to slay her?"

"I aim to get answers. If she dies, she dies."

The priestess of Ashtoreth stepped up to their private conservation and asked Goliath, "Can I bear a message to your beloved mother?"

Goliath paused, thought a moment and answered, "I'll see her soon."

Trazabaal nodded and departed from them, her pale flaxen garments waving in the wind.

"An incredible ass for an older woman," Goliath noted of the priestess.

"True." Abimelech then spoke with a grave voice, saying, "You know I'd never tell you what to do, but let us just say I'm talking to the wind."

Goliath half smiled. "Go on."

"Pissing on those in the order of Dagon is one thing. They'll keep in line. However, making those of Moloch also against you, if you slay their leader..."

"Risky?"

"Stupid. Enflaming two faiths, well, I don't know. With such talk of disunity in the air, we may as well kill them all."

"We may well have to. I'd hate to give them a rallying cry."

But they soon learned that in their absence, a great rally had already happened, and it wasn't to the King of Kings, but indeed under the rebel banner of General Samien.

*****

His face illuminated by golden rays emitted from an iron bowl, Kmentosi rubbed his temples. Eyes seldom blinking, he then let his hands go flat on the sides of his face. "They keep coming, good." The wizard sat back, and the other two figures in the small room leaned in for a closer look at the vision. "This has gone on for days. Then again, nothing attained with ease is worth having."

The shifting lights from the bowl giving their faces a lurid quality, Akisha and Yaggah exchanged a look, and then stared back into the bowl.

Yaggah said softly, "The view isn't steady."

Kmentosi yawned. "The source isn't stable."

Her mouth opened, but whatever Akisha had to say stayed in her throat.

His head twisting from side to side, Yaggah said, "I'm having a difficult time, I mean, by the gods...the daughter of the King!"

A smile spreading, Kmentosi related, "It was only a logical step, really. Vyndekay owes me much, and this little deception on my part won't be frowned on by the gods."

Again, Akisha almost spoke, but her fascination by the view kept her lips tight. Every so often, the view shifted from the soldiers and sailors swearing allegiance and to the interior of a child's room.

Yaggah stepped back and faced the wizard. "You seem to know what the gods want."

Kmentosi arose wearing a catty grin. "Do I?" He then walked around them to a long cabinet. "I won't try to lie and say this all is for my own betterment, not furthering the bliss of gods. Dagon and his brothers endowed me with great power and ability or we'd not be able to see such things." He then opened the cabinet, reached in and took out a large jar. After a moment's work, he unsealed the lid and showed them what sloshed inside.

Akisha's hand went to her mouth and she backed up to the door. Yaggah looked in the jar and made a face.

His face blank, Kmentosi said, "She lets a giant mount her but fears a few extracted pieces of a human body?" He chuckled. "Relax. The King's daughter's eye isn't in this jar." He replaced the object in the cabinet and pointed at the iron bowl. "Emana's eye rests in a focal point in the depths of the bowl."

Yaggah turned paler than usual. "To think you replaced her eyes, good night."

Kmentosi shrugged mildly. "Her life isn't much these days, and no one will notice it." He gave Akisha a grave look. "I replaced her soul, months ago, so switching her eyeball with my plant was easy."

Her long tresses trembled while Akisha retched and pulled at the door. She continued to heave as the wizard walked over and unlocked the door.

Once she'd run out, the smiling wizard faced Yaggah.

Unamused, Yaggah asked him, "Goliath isn't dead, is he? Word is his party stopped at Ziklag."

Kmentosi swatted at Yaggah's arm as he returned to his chair. "Your voice shakes like a dancer, Yaggah. Calm yourself. What does he know? Does he suspect anything? For all he knows Akisha fled in terror that night. How could he know of the stratagem?"

Yaggah's terror made his voice shrill as he stammered, "But what if he does put it all together? He's not a stupid brute."

"There's no doubt he will hear of Akisha and her pregnancy, from the lauds of the priesthood and others. I wasn't counting on him living long enough to be a problem with all of that.”

“What will he do?”

The wizard rubbed his chin. “Maybe he will want her again.”

“What?”

“She took his manhood once. Perhaps he will set up housekeeping.”

Hands shaking wildly, Yaggah grabbed his greasy hair. “You’re fooling me, no?”

Kmentosi laughed. “Of course. I cannot see Goliath as the marrying kind or the stopping whoring kind.”

“What will he do?”

“Perhaps nothing.”

“Nothing?! She has his child in her body!”

“Maybe that isn’t as big a deal to him as you.”

Yaggah voice turned cold. “Damn you, wizard. I became a part of this to further a better program of my kinfolk, to help Samien and give the Philistines a better chance at godhood.”

“Don’t pull on my penis and tell me you are a whore, Yaggah. You did it for the gold I offered, the lauds and easy life the priesthood is giving you. They had a gaping need and you filled their grumbling ways.”

“Goliath will slay me if he finds out he was deceived into it all.”

“He’s not a god, my bad man. He cannot be all places at once.”

Yaggah took several shaky breaths. “Now must I run all over, a giant bogeyman on my shoulder?”

“His life may yet be ours. Calm yourself.” The wizard then looked at the door. “How is she on regular days?”

“Very well, but she wanted a better assurance of the plan.”

“Get her back to the abode,” the priest ordered. “If she’s lost or miscarries, the gods will not approve.”

Philistine

*****

In the dead of night, Goliath sat on a long bench in the village of Oresel. He was amused at himself that he couldn't recall exactly which fine home belonged to the king of that town, Fittlea. He'd sat there in the half moonlight for an hour before Fittlea walked to the giant, carrying a lantern and a large tankard.

"Ale?" the older man asked.

Goliath took it and thumbed open the top. "It's been a long day.

Fittlea sat by Goliath and nodded. "I've heard tell. You haven't come to slay me, have you?'

Goliath wiped his mouth with the back of his hand. "Not today, friend. No, I go unto the Domain of Moloch to confront the Lady herself."

"And you bringing her nothing to sacrifice?"

"No. She'll have to use me herself if she so chooses."

"She might."

Goliath scoffed. "The Lady's priests are mice. Let her use the priests as a sacrifice."

"You really think it's her that wants you dead?"

Goliath eyed him. "You only brought me one tankard?" He drank the rest and wondered, "How is it you know that someone wants me dead?"

"The tale of your revenge is vague, but on the winds. They say you blame the priests for your near death in the port city."

"I didn't nearly die," said Goliath, his voice defensive. "But the priests have a link to it. We were sent on a wild chase for the risen city of Relex on a priestly errand. Any real seer would've seen what it was, the frozen abode of a giant worm."

"Pardon me?"

"Never mind. It was a trap, or I don't have twelve fingers. The priests sent me on that venture, along with King Vyndekay and General Schlack. They claimed in the beginning the trip would appease the priesthood. I reckon those two are angry with me now as I didn't march up there immediately to declare my loyalty or whatever. I think after what I did in Gath, the priesthood will be in a different mood."

Fittlea looked off toward Jericho and said, "You trusted and liked Eucimar, yes?"

"You speak of him as if he's dead. He was the only one of the brethren I shared much with, over the years. I've liked many priests, but Eucimar was a real friend. I'm sorry no word has come back from Egypt concerning him."

"You blame the priesthood, but do others want you dead? If you recall those assassins associated with Akisha..."

"Don't remind me." Goliath's head jerked and he faced the King of Oresel. "Any word of that woman?"

"Akisha?" he answered, then his eyes widened. "You have been away several weeks, I wager."

Goliath's eyes narrowed. "What tell of her? Ahirom and others in visions saw her at the edges of the Philistine orbit, men venerating her. I could never understand why that would be."

"I don't think you need to ask the Lady in Moloch's domain about her. Well, I can tell you the answer to that one."

"I wasn't going to ask about Akisha in there. What is it you know?"

"There are whispers on the wind of her blessing." His voice turned droll. "She's endowed with a child of the gods, don't you know? Yes, many are excited in the priesthood, Goliath, because she carries the future of the Philistines in her belly."

A cold calm spread over him as he first joked, "I need to listen to that damned wind more." Soon, eyes burning in the night, Goliath growled, "Damn her eyes, damn me."

"And her nether regions, but you better hurry to damn her. I hear she carries the next form of the gods." He paused. "Your child."

"Donkey piss," Goliath said with a sigh and his voice turned light-hearted. "And the fools venerate Akisha because of her coupling with me? That's stupid."

Fittlea said gently, "How's your mother these days? Well taken care of by the priesthood?"

Rage in all of his limbs, Goliath sprang to his feet. "You're telling me that rat-dick Yaggah whored Akisha out to me, got a woman with a big enough slit to take me, just to get pregnant by me..."

"The last of your kind, or near to it..."

Hands becoming fists, Goliath yelled, "...to earn a life of adoration, veneration and luxury?"

The King shrugged. "I've seen people give up much for more."

Goliath faced the sky. "That's why they want me dead. Sonofabitch. The baby won't be that special if I'm still alive."

"It seems."

The giant walked in a circle. "I can see them duping me, getting me at a weak point, praying on my whims and lusts...but what force wants this also? Surely, Akisha and Yaggah aren't that important in the scheme of the universe? There has to be a greater answer. If whatever is after me has such power, why use assassins and not just strike me down?"

Hands up, Fittlea said, "It may be just a tale, Goliath. I've never seen her nor know of it as fact. But that's the saga on the breeze. The Lady of Moloch will know."

Anger quelled some, Goliath replied, "Most tales carry the germ of truth. Perhaps I'm being a fool, chasing my tail on this. I'm sure I'm not her only conquest, eh? Still," his body seethed, eyes toward Jericho, "I'd like to know what strikes at me in the supernatural realm."

"Yet still you go unto the Lady with no blood for her beast?"

Fingers drumming on his forearms, Goliath pondered this. "Any criminals hereabouts?"

"You know execution is swift and there are none kept in chains here."

"Damn. I figured maybe to just use her priests as the fodder for the demon."

"You would take on a second branch of the religions?"

"Now you sound like Abimelech." Goliath shook his head again. "Dammit. I hate to feed her appetite."

The King stared at him for a long time before saying, "You don't plan to kill her today, do you? Elsewise, you wouldn't care."

Goliath peered down at him and said with a grin, "Piss off." He never shared the fact that if he figured out how to kill her, Goliath would.

"There *is* the Ogre of Rantis, Tallis Shuruppak. Rather than grab a relatively innocent man, woman or their children, take her the ogre," he suggested. "She may value his bones over the soul or blood of an innocent, and who else could best him but you?"

"I sense you tire of Tallis or you wouldn't offer him up to me for such a thing."

"Do I strike you as a dense man?"

"No. You're astute in business. I wonder, would you know in what tavern at Rantis this Tallis holds court?"

Philistine

Goliath approached the tavern situated near the edge of the hamlet of Rantis. He stood so near to Jericho he could smell the Lady in the Domain of Moloch. The two men in uniforms denoting service in the Israelite guardsman corps stood outside. While they took note of Goliath, the door to the tavern opened and shut quickly, allowing a short woman to exit, a woman they immediately flanked. She carried a medium-sized tankard and did a double take at the looming champion.

Once they'd walked over to a wagon and horses, Goliath wondered after her stare. No fear of him lurked there and a dark, soulless pit existed in her eyes. The laughter from within the structure returned him to his task.

Impressed at the sheer size of the tavern, Goliath still wrinkled his nose at the odors emitted from the crude stone chute on the eastern side. From the mixture of mud bricks, slabs of older masonry and a hardened paste used to fix the cracks, this tavern had been constructed from Jericho's rubble plus a few fresh parts. Courtesy of his height, Goliath noted the builders took greater care on the roof, using long planks, pitch and Arabic gums to ensure waterproofing.

"I hope I don't have to pry him off a whore," he said to no one as he bent over and squinted at the shuttered window. An uneven glow seeped out of the latched window, and Goliath's ears picked up nothing usual about the conversations within. "If that's the case, he won't be in a mood for talking." He then cleared his throat and grinned, his rough smile appearing amidst a tangled beard. "Good steel will remove anything connecting a man and his harlot." He then thought of the Lady and a possible manipulation from the King of the village. While he tried to banish that idea, his thoughts ran wild. He didn't want to be ensnared in some eldritch trap. "Better to wait until he's stewed."

He opened the door and his nostrils flared at the scent of sweat mingled with stale ale. Goliath scanned the dim tavern, well populated with men and a couple women but faintly lit by candles, a few torches, and the churning hearth. Though he knew all would recognize him at once, he planned to make no great bones, just take some wine and relax on the floor in the corner.

"Let that mouthy-assed beast talk."

Once inside, the ogre of the town did just that.

"I am the strongest one in all of Canaan," the huge individual near the end of the bar blustered. He loomed larger than any in the mead hall. "None is tougher, nor a lover of greater capacity than I, Tallis Shuruppak."

Goliath ducked his head, closed the door, and moved away from the bragging creature. All of the patrons were shrouded in overcloaks due to the chilly wind that evening. As the litany of Tallis continued, many gaped at Goliath's huge self. Many elbows stabbed, as they alerted their brethren to the presence of the champion.

"I laugh at the shaking of spears," Tallis ranted, not taking a great note of the giant in his midst. "My manhood is longer than anyone's here. Stand up and I will buy drinks all night if you surpass me. What? No takers? Cowards and women you all are."

"But he's an ogre," a young man with his back to Goliath said, his voice buried in the other revelers of the bar. "Stands to reason he would be the toughest or biggest one around."

Many aged men nodded at the words of the young man, and they made Goliath grin. One older man looked the young speaker over and asked, "You're a stranger here, yes?"

The brown-haired youth nodded and said nothing more. He sipped a flagon and watched the ogre with irritation.

"He speaks the truth, outlanders," an elderly man said in a low voice, his face going flush as he noted the giant now kneeling by the bar. "But take care, all of you. Tallis would sooner torture a foreign-born youth than kill him."

"Yes," a rather portly man with a balding head agreed as he looked at the young outsider. "Have a care. We get all sorts in here, but sometimes one must tolerate depravity to drink in peace."

"I just came in to knock back ale, but I'm no foreigner," the youth said without lowering his voice. "I never wanted to hear the braggings of that freak of nature."

The young man had spoken during a brief lull in the bar conversation, and his words echoed dully through the crowded tavern. Conversations and games of chance ceased, and even young men discussing whorehouses held their breath. A pair of older gentlemen near the door walked out backwards, tripping over Goliath's extended calf, their faces masks of terror. Another old man with gray hair and a white beard let his ruby colored wine spill from his lips in astonishment.

Tallis swung his great girth around, facing the section of the bar where the young man sat. Adjusting the belt under his great belly, Tallis asked, "Who values their life no more than that?" The flames of the hearth cast additional light on the hideous features of the ogre, enticing a few to look away in disgust. Tallis' flesh, the color of deerskin, glowed purple in areas above his jaws. His jowls hung low on the cavernous skull, and his general facial appearance drew more kinship with a bulldog than any human. Tallis' face was longer than any dog, though, and his grinding maw crowned a tree trunk midsection.

Goliath wore a bemused look, wondering how this would play out.

As the old men scooted from the boy, one of them said, "We tried to warn you, puppy. He dislocated the limbs of the last man who crossed him, dragged him around town for hours, he did."

The clear eyes of the young man seemed to glow inside his hood. "How long did it take for this man to die?"

Tallis drank more, showing his lack of concern as the balding man said curtly, "We don't know, youngster. Tallis still feeds him and keeps him alive for taunting pleasure."

"Who are you, whelp?" the ogre inquired, the hoggish ears back of his oblong skull twitching. The enormous jaw of the creature ground away as his red eyes focused on the outlander.

"One who wants to drink in peace, ogre," the youth answered.

Goliath tried to hide his smile at the boy's pluck.

Squinting at the stranger, Tallis replied, "Who are you and where are you from, *auslander?* I generally like to know where men are from before I kill them." He looked right at Goliath and took no note of him, confusing the giant. "If I never ask, I can't incorporate it in my next sermon to the bar."

"The entire hall is exhausted at your mouth," the young man said and straightened out his body. No more than twenty winters, this youth was indeed quite tall, well over six feet, though still a foot shorter than the ogre. "Only a fighting man from Philistia would have the guts to say it."

"Guts can be ripped out and used to clean between

my teeth." Tallis clucked heavily in his throat, again looking at Goliath. *Maybe his eyes are bad,* the giant wondered. "Usually it's a matter of no brains, youngster. You're but a feral savage who walks upright on a junket away from the mountains...to die here? You are dense, boy. Who are you?"

Loosening his heavy facade, but not removing it, the boy responded, "I'm Qorus, a Philistine soldier born out of Ekron." Under his cover, Qorus wore a thick belt, showing the metallic tips of various objects. "I tell you so that when you fall into eternity, you will know who killed your ugly ass."

Goliath grinned at the boy's pluck. The patrons drew a collective breath, but Tallis laughed shallowly. He flexed his burly fingers. "Words from a seafaring savage? Are they your only weapons? How did you drag your self this far?"

Qorus said, "I'm a smith. I work in metals. I can find work anywhere and was following a foolish venture."

"No future in dying," Tallis grinned, his rack of shark-like teeth drooling over his hairy bottom lip.

"I'm not troubled by your fantasies," Qorus said plainly.

Tallis raised a curved eyebrow and started to reach for the sword slung to his hip. "There's a set of balls on you, that's for sure. Nevertheless, youth has clouded your judgment. That's a fatal error. Why, in the olden days..."

The youth dropped his cloak and bolted forward. Stunned at the move, the ogre still swung both his arms together to block Qorus's approach. Qorus ducked low. The immense, meaty thews of the ogre slapped only into each other. Qorus's hands then slammed into Tallis' face on either side of the huge maw. Blood spouted. When Qorus yanked and then released his hands, the onlookers could see he clasped curved blacksmith tools.

He abandoned his utensils in an instant once they inserted deep in either side of the ogre's face.

Balanced on Tallis voluminous belly, Qorus would have fallen off Tallis save for the fact the ogre flailed, embracing him slightly. Constricted for but a moment, Qorus leaned forward with an open mouth and bit into the ogre's nose. Not only did this move support the young man's heavy body, but also it provided him the moment he needed to pull another article from his cincture. Qorus used his weight to his advantage and pulled back against the crazed ogre. Tallis, screaming in agony, seized Qorus's arms. In all of his pain, Tallis clearly hadn't considered the youth's next act. Qorus had clamped a small set of iron tongs under the ogre's mouth. With Qorus repelling from him with all his might, Tallis pushed him away and inadvertently ripped his own jaw out of his skull.

His flailing paws slapped the boy down as the massive being stomped frantically in every direction. Goliath practically burst with laughter.

Qorus rolled on the floor. He drew no steel, but stayed out of the shambling path of the ogre. As Tallis moved, the first two implements, two pritchells, fell out of the hinge of his jaw.

Tallis howled and cursed, but the words were lost, for he could say little with no lower jaw. His agony made him stumble, incoherent, until at last his head cleared. The ogre drew steel and went after the youth.

"Tallis means wise or learned," Qorus taunted him, leaping onto the bar, avoiding the heavy blade of the ogre, which crashed into the floorboards. He squatted on his haunches like a cat. "Were your parents as stupid as you are homely, hanging such a name on a freak like yourself?"

Goliath moved away from the bar as Tallis swung his weapon and missed, smashing several tankards off the surface. The ogre then groaned in rage and swiped at Qorus with his left hand. The Philistine leapt over Tallis, grabbed his shoulders and flipped over his back.

The ogre spun fast, livened by his distress, and struck Qorus in the shoulder with his fist before the youth could set his feet. Qorus staggered, boots shifting, but did not fall as Tallis' huge frame shifted to face him. The ogre charged, arms outstretched, but Qorus slipped out of his way at the last moment. Tallis collided with a table and two wooden chairs, splintering them. He lost his blade in the debris, sliding on his own blood in the process. Tallis swung his head around to see where Qorus went, a long line of crimson gushing from his face.

Qorus laughed at the ogre, throwing a small table, and then a mug of mead at the bleeding beast. "Brag to me now, fat ass."

Tallis flung himself at Qorus, sent them both through tables and chairs. Before the youth could rise up, the ogre boxed his ears. From the ferocity of the slap, the onlookers expected the Philistine's head to burst. Qorus proved thickheaded and simply fell to the floor, limp.

Goliath came near to applauding, but held his hands down. Those huddled at the door of the tavern looked at Tallis rise up over Qorus, legs on either side of him. Many sighed, knowing this would be all for the youth. Still bleeding profusely, Tallis looked down and interlocked his thick fingers. Raising his fists to the ceiling, Tallis crashed the bony bludgeon toward the pit of Qorus's back.

The youth coiled to his right, curling his body around Tallis' shin as the blow hit the floor. With a thick forearm, Qorus struck the groin of the ogre. Tallis flinched, but never fell. His right swatted, clipping Qorus's scalp. The shot knocked the youth, head over heels, and set him upright on his buttocks, blood creeping from his scalp.

Tallis charged and Qorus bolted up towards the bar, evading him. Qorus then trekked down the bar, laughing as blood trickled into his facial features. He darted about the enclosed space, taunting the ogre.

With a liquid bellow, Tallis caught up to him at last. His huge hands enclosed Qorus's head. Going to his knees on top of the youth, Tallis roared and fell forward. Qorus gasped and suddenly, cried for help. The ogre lay motionless atop Qorus.

"Get this thing off me," Qorus said, but there wasn't great fright in his voice. "Tallis Shuruppak is dead."

Cautiously, a half-dozen men peeled themselves away from the exit. They eyed the immobile ogre.

"Are you going to help me or screw his corpse?" Qorus grunted and lifted the body partially off himself.

As if that was the sign that Tallis truly lay dead, the patrons of the bar pulled at Tallis' shoulder. With enough wriggle room, Qorus escaped the death embrace of the ogre. Stumbling backwards, Qorus hit the bar and stood up. He sucked air and let his hand rest on his thick belt.

Open-mouthed, Goliath stood tall, stepped forward and said, "Nergal be damned! The pup never even drew steel." Goliath slapped the youth on the back, and the Philistine boy jumped at the sight of the champion. "You bled him to death. Paint my ass red, that took brains."

The youth bowed his head and said, "Champion of all Philistines, what are you doing here?"

"Being entertained. Come, I'll drag this thing outside. We need to talk."

CHAPTER TEN
DOMAIN OF MOLOCH

General Samien returned from his night ride in the Transjordanian Highlands. His journey took him around the perimeter of his encampments. No one from neighboring lands paid them much mind as of yet. He'd heard from pickets that several Moabite spies lurked to the south. The Moabites under his command cursed their leaders and rules. Now, these warriors became content with a meal in their bellies.

"Wonderful," he said with a sardonic attitude as more grimy men came into their camp from the east. "More Ammonites." Samien watched the pickets frisk the incoming men, obviously of the Ammonite stripe by their style of helm and crooked swords. He didn't need to hear their words to know what transpired. Samien heard the Ammonites feared his new army, mainly because the Ammonite scouts sent to observe them defected and told Baldassare so. While he traveled back toward his cave, he ruminated aloud, "Not even their own folk want them. Now I must make fine clay pots from what most men throw into the streets."

Just as he was to dismount, a young soldier ran to the General, exclaiming, "Sir, Colonel Baldassare needs you badly."

Steven Shrewsbury

Samien put his heels to the horse and trotted down the lines of men encamped near under the tangles of the wilderness. He saw several small fires and other flames' flickers about, many with crude stone altars set up. Though many of the rocky altars held bloody splatters, the hungry soldiers had pulled back their sacrifices for dinner. While men of superstitions and some faith, their empty stomachs decided against giving the gods their burnt offering in full.

"Blood will be enough," Samien told himself as he stopped near a group of his officers. Once down from his horse, he studied the captains that surrounded Baldassare. One wore a look of fright, while the others seemed of sterner character, assuring the Colonel he would be fine.

Baldassare himself clutched his chest with his right hand. He leaned on one of the captains and shook his head violently, assuring them, "It'll pass. I think it was that damned goat the Hittite woman cooked."

One of the men offered, "Shall we have her flogged?"

Baldassare's eyes met Samien's. The Colonel's ire softened. "No. I'll recover." He raised his voice to the General. "I was sick, probably from the food."

"These conditions aren't for us well-bred men, not anymore. But men of war must remember where we came from.' The General turned from his ailing colleague and faced to the west. "I can feel something dire in the air, like a putrid wind from a battlefield's refuse."

One of the soldiers wondered, "The will of the gods?"

Samien shot the man a poisonous look and Baldassare said, "Curses on that idea, but there's some witchery in the air." The Colonel still held his chest. "I can feel it, deep in my heart."

"I feel no ill for us," Samien told them, eyes scanning the night. "Something wicked rides the winds, though." He then walked away from the others, never telling

222

Baldassare to follow, but the Colonel attended to him quickly. "Are you really all right?"

Baldassare nodded repeatedly. "Yes. Just a bout of the pukes."

"It's no sign of womanhood to have fears for the unknown, Colonel," Samien said lightly. "I just conceal it better."

The Colonel grinned. "That's why you are the General."

Samien turned and asked him, "Are you forming up the divisions properly?"

"The job will be done soon. They're starting to get into suitable units and drilled better than any land of their birth. We've woven our troops among them as best we can. Hell, we get more converts all the time. I'm angered that one of our best smiths, a young hungry killer, Qorus of Ekron, has decided to make his oath to Vyndekay."

His head back, Samien thought for a moment. "I remember him. That's a pity. Still, perhaps he'll stand with us again someday, once the army is defeated. He's a good man."

"He hated all the foreigners with us," Baldassare said quietly.

"There're simple things we're using as a means to an end," Samien reminded him, as the wind from the west grew stronger.

*****

Abimelech seldom disobeyed his master. In this regard to the temple prostitutes of Dagon, he overruled Captain Balzer. He ordered Balzer's men to slay all of the temple whores, not sparing any for later use. "We're setting an example," Abimelech insisted. He promised the men a better way and that the blood would ultimately please the gods. They wore long faces as they beheaded and vivisected the prostitutes in the ruins of the toppled temple. The pieces of the women were taken by the priests of Goliath's favored god, Ba'al Zebul, and deposited at their censers, downwind of Gath.

The Philistine troops grumbled and Captain Balzer took them first to drink their fill before visiting the temple of Ashtoreth. Invited there by Trazabaal in loyalty to Goliath, Balzer's men set up their actions in the outer courtyard, far from the main temple. The men took the temple prostitutes with great relish.

The likenesses of several other gods littered the edges of the outer sanctuary, being inclusive for practices to all gods. The eighteen soldiers shed their clothes and chose their partners. Abimelech saw that the younger troopers, so shy when they first did open copulations the night of the party in Oresel or in the port city, now more jaded did it like veterans. Abimelech himself was about to mount one of the lovely women who claimed to be from Nubia, and she had presented herself to him, oddly enough, doggy style on the altar of the Egyptian cat god Bastet.

As he dropped his underclothes and worked himself into the whore screaming to her goddess, Abimelech spotted the priestess Trazabaal in the shadows. Though he drove himself into the temple prostitute for the greater good of his own body, he stared at the lithe high priestess in dimness cast by the torches of the cat god.

Those violet eyes, they seemed to glow in the dark recesses of the temple. Abimelech gripped the hips of the moaning woman on the altar and could only watch Trazabaal...as she touched her small, pert breasts, and let her hands soothe over her body. Not a young lady, but surely one holding her beauty into her midlife, his attention fixated on Trazabaal.

The temple whore pulled away from him and flipped over. Abimelech climbed on her, never brushing the raven hair from her face and entered again. He nearly slipped on the cast aside samite robe, but held firm in his footing. The small woman cried out as the weight of his frame collapsed on her. His turgid member entered harsh as Abimelech used no romantic method. He grabbed the whore of Ashtoreth under the shoulders. Still, his eyes focused on the high priestess Trazabaal and her exploring hands. Trazabaal's tiny digits walked like graceful dancers all over her flesh.

Speeding up faster than he usually did in this position, Abimelech prepared to arrive. Abimelech surmised the temple prostitute an expert in her vocation by her gyrations and filthy talk. She tightened her slippery legs about him and demanded that he not spill his seed inside her. Confused by her words, Abimelech felt astonished at the Nubian pushing away and pulling him from her. She gripped the length of him and pulled, allowing his self to explode all over her stomach and heaving breasts. Braced on the sides of the stone altar, Abimelech mumbled, "Nisroch." He didn't care if she understood what that name meant or not.

Still sucking in air, the woman under him smiled and sighed, still working his member. The candles' light making her glisten, Abimelech then stared over at Trazabaal. The priestess quivered and gasped, her body trembling as she studied Abimelech bathing the whore in his semen.

Abimelech wanted Trazabaal, he could smell her, practically taste her...

Stepping off the altar and hearing the chants of the whores throughout the temple, Abimelech reached down for his underpants. Trazabaal slipped back further into the darkness as the shrine servant got off the altar as well.

The Nubian stumbled a bit like a new colt, then walked closer to the nearest burning censer before the mini version of the Sphinx. The high priestess materialized from about a pillar and reached out to the black girl. Wiping Abimelech's seed from the whore's belly, Trazabaal slapped it into the fire, chanting as she did so. The flames flashed. She howled and shook all over, as if an orgasm rippled through her body.

Cairn and Sadik approached Abimelech with the other men, all bare-assed and stunned at the behavior of the temple whores. Balzer said to him, "By Baal's ass, Abi, she placed it in her mouth once I arrived..."

"You need to travel more," Abimelech said blithely as he directed them out of the temple's outer yard. They grabbed their gear and heading out. "Though I'm sure you are no stranger to whorehouses, it seems they get more open the farther south one travels." He looked back and saw Trazabaal in the upper window of the outer temple ring. His gaze wandered to the distant towers of the temple where Orpah lived.

In the air of the night, he felt dizzy, though he didn't notice any of the others acting any different.

*****

Goliath walked with Qorus in the night toward the Domain of Moloch. Together, they dragged the corpse of Tallis behind them.

"Why is a young soldier like yourself out here in the night, killing ogres?"

"A decree went out from the five cities, to the five Kings of Philistia," Qorus explained. "Surely you received the call?"

"I've been away, but I've heard of a vow of loyalty required to fend off those who may join an uprising. Why are you out here alone? Were you looking for a greener pasture with General Samien?"

Qorus frowned and bowed his head. "There are no greener pastures, just more shit to be avoided."

"Better the turds you know?"

"Well, no one will know of my concerns. All troopers on the far frontiers or out freelancing must return home for a push."

"A trifle young to be freelancing."

Qorus patted his tool belt. "Smithing, sir, more than anything else. These idiots that aren't our blood kin know nothing of metals."

"True." Goliath scanned the country as if he could see every tribe or people Qorus deemed ignorant of metal work. "You can travel back with me to Gath, providing the Lady doesn't kill my ass once I get inside the Domain."

Qorus shuddered once at the mention of the Lady. "I can't see her doing that, sir."

"Why? I can die as easy as the next man."

Qorus smiled, shrugged and didn't accept this statement. "She wouldn't do that."

"Never can tell, and her being a sorceress has nothing to do with it. She's a woman and they're fickle. It's the demon beside her, the channel for her ability that ya gotta worry about."

"Have you ever fought a devil?"

Goliath's cheerfulness faded. "A few, long ago and far away. It's no fun. Never let one get inside you."

Qorus looked up at the rubble and the old wall that indicated the roof of the Domain of Moloch. "What's that like?"

"Ever had crabs?"

Qorus shrugged as they wove through the

treacherous terrain about the ruins in Jericho. "Most men have. It feels like that?"

"On the inside of your head," Goliath admitted. He stared down at the body of the ogre. "It may not look like it, but this is it. You better stay out here, though."

Qorus spat on the body. "You don't have to tell me twice. Going in there is suicide, sir. If you don't come out soon, I'll just go on back to Ashkelon, okay?"

After he stifled a laugh, Goliath took up the ogre's wrists alone and approached the door of the Domain. The skinny acolytes scurried around the stones, making Qorus draw his sword.

Stone ground on stone and a flickering torchlight broke the darkness. Qorus gripped his sword, ready to strike but Goliath never dropped the arms of the ogre. Two slender forms carrying torches stepped from the gap in the stone rubble.

Goliath heard Qorus say, "But there's no door there..."

Clad only in a red loincloth, the priest on the left sported yellow, catty eyes that blazed at his pale skin. The firelight served to make him appear even more eerie in the night.

"You are expected," this man rasped and stepped to Goliath's left.

"It figures your mistress knew I was on the way. I brought her a gift." He dropped the arms of the ogre.

The priests smiled.

While one priest departed, Goliath spoke to the other. "I figured she could put him to good use."

The man folded his arms and then turned his head as a half-dozen more priests emerged. Most were younger men, novices, and they soon set about arming up Tallis' body. "There's nothing good in the worldly sense to the uses we have for him."

Goliath sighed. "Give it a rest. You can't scare me."

Lips peeling back to show a snarl, the priest said, "You lie. I saw your face when we cured the thirteen city fathers."

Goliath stepped toward him, but the thin man never faltered in his stance. "Don't mistake disgust for fear, runt."

"And do not mistake murder for magick, Champion," the priest noted and turned from him.

Goliath let the novices drag the body of Tallis into the underground chamber before he started to walk in farther. Though he never brandished a weapon, all of his defenses were up. The ogre's corpse slid faster ahead of him and soon vanished in the lurid pulsing lights. Again, the scent of the chamber filled Goliath's senses.

*****

Abimelech walked outside of the temple of Ashtoreth and gazed into the starry sky. The sun soon started to break and interrupted his look. He felt very tired. True, the men were granted this leave by mutual agreement of Balzer and Goliath, contrary to the orders from Ashkelon that they should return in great haste.

A few others joined him as they headed to quarters, a long barracks the city of Gath erected long ago for visiting troops. With several of their home garrison either with the main army in Ashkelon or patrolling in the country for rebel factions, the soldiers had room to rest.

Just before they entered the barracks, Abimelech coughed badly and stopped. His hand on the doorframe, he coughed more. Sadik halted and showed concern. His eyes widened when Abimelech drew back a hand from his mouth, revealing he'd spat up blood.

"Damn," Abimelech remarked, half laughing it off, but his face turned serious when he touched his upper lip and found his nose ran with blood as well. Head shaking, he felt wetness in his ears.

Though blood flowed from his ears, Abimelech could hear a voice laughing in the night. His head shaking, he thought the tone belonged to Trazabaal.

He twisted about and faced the temple of Ashtoreth, but couldn't draw his sword.

*****

Goliath stood down in the domain of Moloch, at first looking toward the huge idol of the god across the river, the fire in its belly smoldering. He then turned over to his left at the form of the demon, still housed in the star shaped enchantment. The creature stood quite still, statuesque and stony in its ways. Near its cloven feet several of the priests of Moloch crawled, using long-handled tools to adjust and dress the edges of the star that kept the demon prisoner. One long implement dumped more of an ashen substance near the lines while the other brushed it closer in.

Bednukah stepped into Goliath's view from his far left, up on the riser. Her dismissive laughter went with her sour face, he thought, as Bednukah's three breasts moved in rhythm with her steps.

"I knew you were there before you came out."

"Can you sense my energy?" Bednukah asked, hands on her bare hips.

"No, I could smell you," Goliath replied, arms folded over his chest. "All of this heat doesn't do you any lauds, without many baths."

Philistine

Eyes wider, Bednukah snarled, "I can sense a star-child near to me, Champion." She bit the last word off like a dog fighting for meat.

"Do you want a prize for knowing such a fact?" Goliath shot back. "I walked up to your door, never riding in with an army. Do you think me so stupid as not to recognize his power?" His right index finger then stabbed toward the demon.

She quipped in a hot voice, "It's my power."

"Bullshit," Goliath dismissed her statement. "You're a clever jailer, nothing more. I didn't come here to ask about your power over him or anything like that."

Her dire snarl faded and a rather inquisitive look sank into her eyes. "You brought me the corpse of the ogre, Tallis. That was undeniably a fastidious gesture, one I'd pay for in bad magicks if I rejected his bones. Already, the priests strip away his flesh in the pot of wasting."

The demon suddenly jerked, as if awakened from its stiffened state. His voice sounded dry as he related, "They'll grind his bones to make my prison stronger." A dejected chuckle echoed and then Amazarak seethed with power, wide-awake.

Goliath wondered, "There's such an influence in bones?"

Bednukah giggled. "If you were on familiar terms with what the wizards of this earth would give for the bones of the lawgiver hidden on Mount Nebo, you'd understand how petty your troubles are. Many lives have been lost in search of *that* prize."

"What do you know of my troubles?" Goliath asked, hands falling to his sides.

She winked. "Only what my deary dear here tells me in visions. Oh yes, I keep track of you at times, Champion, but get not your ego in a cluster. You are not the only one."

"I'm underwhelmed. What do you know of my dreams?"

She frowned, all humor draining away. "What would I know of them?"

"I doubt you show up in them on accident."

Fingers drumming her buttocks, Bednukah's catty mouth purred, "Really? That's breathtaking. Perhaps you're more enamored of me than you let on. The power given to me isn't wasted on you, dear heart. Do you think I sit here in the ground and play with the priests? I'm traveling far in the ether realm, Goliath, so far beyond this miserable world into places the Elder Gods first came. Can you even dream what lives outside the world hung in the system here?"

"None of that concerns me," Goliath retorted. "You know of a sign, a wheel with women in white all around it?"

The demon looked at his mistress and Goliath's eyes narrowed at him.

Bednukah's head tilted and she reflected a moment before saying, "It sounds like a temple of vestal virgins, but there's no such use for them near me. Temple harlotry is good for my magick, not a practice of karmatic purity."

"I can believe that." Goliath stayed focused on the demon, knowing the creature understood what he'd spoke of, but his tongue held tight.

"You're a passing amusement, Champion," Bednukah said with humor again dancing in her voice. "An abnormality in this terrible world of blood and stupid, inbred people."

Goliath shook his head and started to take a step toward the door.

She added, "But you have blood in you from somewhere else, don't you? You're different from your five brothers, are you not?"

Right hand to his hip, Goliath said, "They have a different father than I."

"And are not giants," She noted, her humor lessening. "It isn't for their sakes Orpah is venerated by the priesthood. You're the last of your kind, fathered by one of the sons of god, and thus, that's why you don't take my utter dismissal seriously. You know you're not just a staggering freak or an abnormal man. You know you're something more."

"For all the good it does me." Goliath again started toward the door.

"Someone wants something more from you. Someone's got something more from you."

"Speak it plainly, you rotten bitch," Goliath roared back, and the demon laughed so much the infants hanging from his ears screamed anew. "Tell me a tale if you know a good one."

"They never told you of Akisha?"

Eyes rolling toward the ceiling, Goliath replied, "What of her? Is she still gaining fame as my lover? Is that maggot Yaggah whoring her out to men that want to cover one who survived my bed? Tell me the saga you know." His mind far away from the tale Fittlea told him, he desired the Lady to affirm the story.

"They never told you why she is so special now? Why would any backwater fool worship or think her special, just on word alone? No, she is now more to all." Bednukah ran her thin fingers over her flat, pale belly. "She carries inside her your offspring, the next in the line of the gods. That makes her extraordinary, no?"

Face transforming into a mask of burning hate, fists clenched, Goliath stormed back as the tale confirmed, "You lying bitch." He drew the heavy dagger from his belt. "That's a lie."

"Why would I lie? She carries your seed, no? She survived it, and thus, soon, will be venerated by all as the mother of a child of the gods. Why, in no time, she'll supplant some other pretty slut who survived sex with a fallen devil...oh, say, like the one who lives at Gath."

Goliath charged her, dagger in hand. Not three feet from the raised sector, he slammed into an invisible wall. Like he struck greased ice, Goliath slid down to the ground and gaped at the demon. The creature held up his finned hands, projecting the power to hold the giant back. On his all fours, Goliath was near to eye to eye with the priests molding the star in place around the demon. These men scurried back behind the devil, and Goliath looked up at Bednukah.

She waved a finger at him, saying, "Temper, temper, child."

On the floor, Goliath's mind reeled as the confirmation sank in. "That's really why they want me dead, but she could just as easily be with child by any swinging dick." He wiped his mouth with the back of his hand. "I wonder who *they* are, though."

She clapped her hands and mocked him. "You're bright, after a fashion, big boy. If there is a family of giants running around, how special are you? If she has the lone survivor of the Nephilum from her thighs, then she gets all the lauds. If you still live, well, not so much."

"And you are helping her?"

Bednukah threw back her red curls and laughed, all three breasts bouncing. "Why on earth or all of Hell would I care for her plight or glorification? I watch, I see, I laugh. My life is stimulating as I watch the entire world through my demon, and he gives me raptures undreamed of on earth. Akisha's tricks are amusing, and your reaction, priceless."

"Where is she?"

"What am I, your servant? You brought me an ogre's bones, not the hymen of a princess. Find her yourself."

Back on his haunches, Goliath coughed. "Piss on

her. Who'll care? I'm alive. Her tricks can only go so far. What wizard would follow her lead?"

Arms folded across her teats, Bednukah nodded, feigning reflection, and said, "There's a great revolution afoot, don't you know?"

"I've heard."

"Surely in the army of Samien there are religious zealots or scorned wizards, perhaps one with a grudge on you, one that would want to kill what you love."

"I don't love anything."

"You love your mother."

Goliath rose up and his face turned grim, but a grin played on his face. "She's protected in the temple by more enchantments than a carnival whore could pay to break."

"True, but who else could such a powerful hater strike at, if she had a mind to, that would hurt you to the quick?"

Goliath stood and wondered why the Lady used the word *She,* not referring to Akisha. "I care naught for my brothers..."

The demon grinned, salvia dripping from his fangs, droplets turning to tiny octopi creatures as he said, "What of your blood brother?"

Goliath's eyes widened. "Abimelech?"

The demon said, "It is a game, grandson of God. Like any woman, your adversary doesn't plan to kill you fast. She'd rather do it slowly, a tiny piece at a time."

The Lady laughed once and then her look transformed into hatred. She leered at him for a full minute. "Is your enormous ego bruised? Could you not face the fact that a woman bested you on the bed mat? Must there be a giant conspiracy to satisfy your self-esteem? Go and chew on that for a while."

Goliath noted the priests, all of them keeping away from the star and him, more gravitating toward the image of the smoldering Moloch.

His head jerked as several priests started to flow into the chamber from behind the image of Moloch. From the small river that snaked underground, the champion saw a slender raft emerge in the torchlight. Hidden behind the flaming likeness of Moloch stood the gargantuan owl, somewhat lost in the shadows. The flickering lights betrayed that this owl was empty, so when it spoke, Goliath felt no trepidation as to the mystery involved.

"The ferryman brings the effigy of Care," the deep voice intoned as the robed priests knelt across from the flaming belly of Moloch. The owl went on to say, "Take the one born in bitter tears and have it come to serve our great god."

The robed ferryman stopped by the edge of the small lake and two priests rose up. The ferryman reached down, picked up a bundle larger than Goliath expected. Infant sacrifice was nothing new to him, but this person offered up was larger, beyond toddler years.

Bednukah's voice came out cloying as it said, "Do I sense a twinge of sorrow in your breast, mighty one?"

Dismissive in his words, Goliath replied, "The child is a freak, I see by malformed spine and ruined mouth. Such are common for your practices, to kill the runts and the irregular."

She grinned and her watery skin grew whiter. "Blood is blood, Champion."

"You make me wonder if the blood of a bunch of priests would be more sufficient to the god."

The demon chuckled deep in his abdomen, but turned in a semi circle in its prison, leathery wings on its back curling around it. It was then Goliath noted the creature sported more than two wings, four by the look of him. Then again, its skin changed frequently, so the being was one of illusion and delusion to others.

"Did you steal that pathetic babe from its mother or did they give it up willingly?" Goliath asked her, eyes on the child the priests handled.

She said, "The child is a boon from a faithful follower for good affluence in the future. You know how things work in this world, Champion. If one has many children, it can really be a blessing, no? Oh, a son to farm, a son to fight, a son for the priesthood, but woe be to the extra daughter to marry off or the ugly one not fitting for slut service…or common labor. The deformed, well, what good are they but for me and my magicks?"

The demon snorted and his forked tongue slathered over his scaly lips before he said, "The General gave her up easily, well, after I blessed the baby as it formed."

Though he tried to hide his thoughts, Goliath blinked. "You cursed this baby on purpose?"

Bednukah said, "A common enough practice. They are seeded, cursed in the womb and thus, easier to send to me."

"Sonofabitch," Goliath mumbled.

"Now," she went on. "The General is beholden to me for taking this and gives his faith to the ether world. It provides me better focus."

Eyes closed, Goliath saw the crooked nose of General Schlack, one replicated on the face of the toddler now going unto the flaming altar of Moloch.

But just as Goliath turned to leave, she called after him, "When I travel in the ether realm, I hear the priests talk at times. It entertains me, even when the night howlers aren't suckling at my teats. When all of this talk of Akisha came up, they set their tongues to wagging."

"Priests are like kitchen girls with their talking," said Goliath, as his pace slowed to a stop.

She took a few steps to her left; palms now flat on her hips. "They talk of the veneration for your mother,

Orpah, and what the real fear is of anyone harming her, beyond the enchantments of the priests of course. Even Trazabaal fears her, though they've known each other in friendship for decades."

He never turned to face her. "You bore me with things already known."

"Any new goddess in flesh wouldn't have her obvious ties. For example, the priests concluded, the real power of Orpah isn't in the wizard's power or the threat of her looming son taking out reprisals, or even her other boys that are warriors. No, the real fear is far worse." Her voice dropped to a deeper, snaky tone. "They know she had the love of a fallen son of god, a six-winged Seraph. If she died, and the Seraph was so taken with her, then what if he returned to bring his wrath on the world?"

Goliath's face did turn and he frowned. "The priests talk from their asses and are fools. If my father were coming back, he'd have done it by now. I reckon he has bigger things on his mind."

"But it's all fear."

"Fear built on rotten stocks," Goliath said with a grunt. "I've spent enough time in here."

As he turned away again, she called out, "What would you ask your father if you ever saw him?"

Goliath never turned back as he said, "My mother was a comely woman once. Please don't confuse or try to outweigh the balance a grand romance on a stiff prick. I'm not an idiot."

"But surely you must have a question for him, a desire to understand that which burns inside you...an answer to your life?"

Goliath stopped, grew silent for several seconds before saying, "Don't bother with your words, Lady. If I had such a question, I wouldn't tell you."

To the sound of her echoing laughter, Goliath departed the Domain of Moloch. He walked down the long hallway, but then paused as he heard the low voices of men, unconcerned with him. A thought birthed in him that it may be priests deep in gossip. His morbid curiosity stoked, Goliath peered into the small chamber awash in yellow light of a series of glowing lamps.

"We make the great choice of the gods now which initiates will be given better grades, ascend, and which will go unto the belly of Moloch." The tallest of the priests said to his five brethren.

Goliath grew curious at what method they'd use to judge the new novices.

After making an incantation in a strange language the tall priest dipped his hand into a rough cloth sack. He squinted at the first small tablet in his hand and said, "Joaba moves up. I like him."

Goliath turned away and his laughter echoed for a time.

*****

At first, Goliath felt unsure if the Lady Bednukah or whoever would really strike at Abimelech or his mother, but Goliath decided that he had to get back to Gath, fast.

Sunlight bathed the exterior of the ruins that concealed the entrance to the Domain. A hundred yards away in a clearing, by the assembled stones of a well, Goliath spotted Qorus. The young warrior grunted and thrust his body down, obviously covering a woman who clung to the well's stonewall. With every stride Goliath took he saw more of the story unfold.

A headless body lay twisted in the dirt, hand still clinging to a dagger. Off to Goliath's right lay two more bodies, one missing an arm, but clutching the spot in his stomach where another bloody wound existed. The other man still lived, shuddering, but blood stained the back of his mailed shirt. A few horses wandered nearby, and one reared up and turned from the giant, but did not bolt.

Qorus looked over his shoulder as he grunted louder, at last.

"The water expensive here?"

The young warrior withdrew from the woman, still partially clothed in her worn cloak, and glanced at Goliath. He made no effort to hide his own nakedness. First, he took her down girth strap and swung it around the beam that extended over the well. Qorus then tied her wrists together as she struggled, but her efforts were weak.

"Don't pity her," Qorus warned. "Rotten woman, lured me to her thighs by the water so the men there could kill me."

Goliath glanced back at the dead men. "I'm low on pity right now. You took the bait, but survived, I see."

Qorus let loose a string of profanity and then said, "I took her anyway after. I leave her now for the priests of Moloch to find." He grabbed her by the scalp and shouted, "You'll wish I cut your throat after they are through with you!"

"Get a horse," Goliath said, dismissing it all with a wave, turning his face toward Gath. "I travel fast once I hit a rhythm."

Adjusting his kilt, Qorus looked back at the domain of Moloch. "Things go well?"

"Get a damned horse. I have to go."

With that, Goliath started his jog toward Gath. In time, Qorus, on horseback, caught up.

Philistine

*****

Akisha felt the babe move inside of her. This troubled her to a degree, as most midwives told her this action came early. Then again, she harbored a child of the gods, so who knew of their schedules?

Though the care she received came on par with nothing she'd ever experienced, the nagging fear that Goliath lived...and all that implied, made her nights sleepless. She wanted for nothing, save for rest, and the ladies refused her any potion to bring slumber due to her condition.

After a morning nap, she walked in the temple of Ashtoreth at Ashdod, a much smaller affair than the elaborate domain lavished on Orpah at Gath. Someday, Akisha ruminated, she'd have a place like that.

But the giant lives, her brain reminded her, and all fears returned to the surface. He was supposed to die that night...he was supposed to die in the port city...he was supposed to die on the return trip at the hand of an inspired Abimelech...

Her fists struck down on the window's edge, and her eyes searched the rear courtyard of the temple grounds, as if she'd find any answer or the frightening face of the giant waiting for her.

What would he do if he found her? Would he be pleased that she bore his offspring? Would he add up the series of mishaps and blame her? How could he know? Would he really accept her word or that she was a dupe of the priests? She could always fall back on that, she thought, but staying away from him, hoping for his demise gave her a better feeling than confronting the champion.

She'd fought hard to get where she was, and the scheme seemed flawless. "I need this, I deserve this," she pouted, no ears to hear her words. "This isn't a time to weaken." Akisha told herself this, her mantra reassuring her of her destiny. "I've wanted to be a goddess all my life, since the dreams of the night, I wanted this." Her aching belly betrayed her mental exercises of assurance, though. Comfort, stability and a chance at a better tomorrow, she understood her reasons for goddesshood weren't like those of Orpah.

Akisha reached out and closed the shutters. Her back to the window, she looked at her bed and sighed.

"The tales spun in my youth, Orpah, of your angelic lover, so sweet," her arms embraced her bosom as if an unearthly lover cradled her in his wings. "Your story made all little girls want to be goddesses. None ever came close to your life. So favored you were." Her arms dropped when she considered the romance of her own state, a much different eventuality than the yarn of Orpah's love life. "What stories will they tell of my life with Goliath?" she then half laughed. "Whatever General Samien wants them to know, is that it?"

Kmentosi's grinning maw entered her mind and her baby moved again. She tried to steal up her resolve, tried to banish all fears and place her trust on the men, and the far off female voice that guided all of this into fruition.

She faced a small stone fetish of Ashtoreth on her makeup table. She blinked hard, not believing at first that the head of the stone figure started to turn and face her. Terror gripped her body as the lips of the fetish moved.

"Calm yourself, daughter," the husky, but feminine voice told Akisha from the fetish. "Let not worry be your enemy."

Philistine

"Are you Malak?" Akisha whispered, eyes darting. "The wizard here plays so many tricks."

The stone face morphed into a smile. "Be of good cheer, daughter of the earth. All will come about in due course. You are bright to bear fear, but rest assured; all will be well. You shall be my true daughter and what lives within, shall be our new champion. Trust in Malak, daughter."

"I will," Akisha said, fighting back tears.

"Do you trust me?"

Akisha went to her knees and kissed the tiny feet of the stone figurine. "Yes, Malak. I love you."

"And I love you, little girl."

*****

The sun started to set when Goliath and Qorus arrived in Gath at the temple of Ashtoreth. By the actions of the Philistine warriors when they arrived in town, Goliath understood their panic. Soon, their words that Abimelech lay gravely ill sank into his ears. Quite winded, Goliath stopped at the rear courtyard of the temple, where many of the Philistines from their trip stood, spears in hand.

Two young ladies knelt nearby, but it was Trebluha, resplendent in her new clothing of a lady of the temple, who wiped the blood from Abimelech's face. Her wide eyes looked up at Goliath as the other girls fled.

The giant knelt and she said, "He's almost gone, but fights so for life."

Abimelech sucked air and mumbled unintelligible words through his sweaty lips.

Goliath faced out across the rear yard into the next lot. Captain Balzer and a few of the soldiers walked away from the thick fig tree and said, "Most all of the priests and wizards of Gath are in hiding."

"Oh?" Goliath stared at the figure on the tree. "Why is that? Your example nailed to the tree there?"

"No, they hide out of fear of you, because they cannot heal Abimelech. Trazabaal here, high priestess and leader of the temple whores, has received her just payment for services rendered. It was her that cursed Abimelech."

Shock struck Goliath's face. His jaw dropped and at first, no words emerged. He gathered his thoughts and fears, asking, "How are you so sure?"

Sadik stepped out from the men, shrugged and said, "Abi kept saying her name, but the rest was easy. She confessed under torture."

"Crucifixion will do that."

With confidence, Balzer said, "She's the instrument of the Lady of Moloch."

Goliath said softly, "Yes, well, I could've guessed that."

Trebluha's hand rested near to Goliath's, but she never reached out.

The giant stood and faced Balzer. "Tell me, Captain, does the Prophet of the Hebrew God still hold himself fast at Kiriath-Jearim?"

"Yes, but why? That spot is rumored as assailed by Amalekite commandos. Those sneaky scum trickle around the Hebrew army, otherwise engaged."

Brows furrowed, Goliath's anger grew. "Why would that King of Israel allow them there?"

Cairn volunteered, "He's busy. Frankly, by him blowing off his best prophet, I think he wants the Prophet dead."

Balzer concurred. "I don't think they are on the best of terms, but the Amalekites are drunken imbeciles. They have cut a drunken swathe through the lands, bragging that they will join up with General Samien."

Eyes on Abimelech, Goliath wondered, "How do you come by such knowledge?"

Balzer eyed Qorus. "There are many soldiers traveling around since the edict from King Vyndekay. We all drink, talk and..."

"Fine, fine..." Goliath shook his head.

Sadik said, "The Amalekites want the Prophet's head for Samien. They said it will give them better rank in the new army and nation he plans."

Goliath nodded and said, "Wonderful. Though Abi cannot travel, I must go to that place where they have him cornered."

Balzer informed him, "The first emissaries from Ashkelon are here, but the General is behind."

"I'll be with them shortly. My visit to the Prophet will not take long."

Philistine

CHAPTER ELEVEN
SAVING GRACE

Though a forward party arrived a Gath, General Schlack rode with a regiment farther behind. Mindful of an assassination attempt by the rebel factions of Samien, Schlack rode with the cavalry regulars.

When the men stopped to water their mounts and take a rest, a sergeant of the cavalry saluted the General and pointed east. "Sir, the forward party sends back a messenger."

"What is it, Sergeant Ninkory?" Schlack asked as he splashed water on his face. It only took a moment for him to smile, like the others wiping their faces at the well. "Such a messenger must bring important news," the General jeered and the others shared his mirth, for a skinny youth on a donkey arrived in their midst.

The boy swung his leg off his donkey and hopped to attention.

Schlack stepped forward and smartly saluted.

After returning the salute, the boy said, "I'm Melita, messenger from Gath, nephew of King Achish."

The men tried to stifle their giggles. Melita didn't notice or didn't care.

Schlack nodded. "I know your uncle well. He has trusted you with this message?"

Ninkory elbowed a fellow soldier, saying, "Melita is a girl's name."

The soldier whispered, "It means bitter."

Ninkory whispered, "Someone must have been bitter to hang that name on him."

"Enough," Schlack shot them angry looks, causing the men to all fall silent. His attention returned to the boy. "Say on, Melita."

"I'm here to tell you that your wife is dead."

Hand raised to his chin, the General nodded. "Which one?"

Melita held his eyes shut for a few moments, as if reading the message there before he faced Schlack and said, "Your second, who resided at Rantis, the Lady Talitha."

His head back, the General looked to the sky but didn't close his eyes. "I see. She was indeed my second wife of the lot, an older maiden when I took her on, a widow of my brother, Hayden, who perished fighting the Hebrews at Adullum. Poor lady, she wanted a child so badly, to care for her when she grew dry and I had no more use for her. I provided such a babe, but things aren't always as men wish them." He dropped his view to stare at the child messenger. "Sometimes, the gods will barren women that way for a reason, son."

Melita nodded once, his clear brown eyes shining in the day's light. "Would you like to know how she died?"

"No," the General answered him with a steady voice. He donned his bronze helmet and said, "Perhaps later."

The boy's bottom lip quivered for a moment, but his spine stiffened. "I am sorry for the tidings, sir."

"Death comes to all, son," Schlack told him and placed a hand on this left shoulder. "Go, water your donkey and yourself. I shall not slay you, neither will the men harm you."

Once the boy led his mount to the well and the

General walked away from the company of men, Ninkory joined him. "Sir, do you want to be alone?"

An acidic look on his face, Schlack snapped, "Don't be a pig's ass, Sergeant. What do you want?"

"That little performance with the kid, there..."

"It was no performance."

"But, why...?"

The General stared across the plains. "That's how one controls the weak. Take a lesson, Sergeant. One cannot always beat or screw courage into men."

"But how does one control the strong?" Ninkory wondered.

"By letting them think they always have more options than you. Come, let us go unto Gath. I rode out here to see more than our champion. I wanted to test the mettle of the common folk in our nation."

Soon, he discovered things in Gath weren't as he thought.

No messenger came to deliver a special note of what transpired at the outer court of the temple of Ashtoreth. Several citizens, some afraid, some angry with the champion and his group, and many priests shouted the story unto the General. In time, once he paused to stare at the ruins of the temple of Dagon, Schlack dismounted at the courtyard of Ashtoreth and walked to the tree still sporting the body of Trazabaal.

Ninkory approached the tree and backed away fast. "She's alive."

The General said, "She'll take a long time to die. That's the point of crucifixion."

Trazabaal's mouth jerked open, but her eyes remained swollen shut from the blows inflicted earlier. "Free me..."

Schlack's expression remained as sterile as ever. "Why would I do that?" At his words, the crowd gasped, but the General only stared at the dying priestess. "You pissed in the face of the reason you are afforded so much grace in this city, and besides, I don't believe in your goddess." At his words, she coughed but couldn't formulate words very well. He went on to say, "Am I to be angered the champion destroyed the temple of Dagon? Perhaps that'll dismay Kmentosi back in Ashdod, but to tell you the truth, I don't care for that jackass much, or his god, either." He took a step toward one of the soldiers and waved at the tree. "Give her some wine. I hate to talk to myself."

The soldier upended the flask on Trazabaal's lips, and she greedily sucked at the fluids. She snorted, coughed and regurgitated some of the liquid. She then said, "Cut me down, take out the staves..."

"You have naught to threaten nor bargain with now, woman," Schlack said with derision in his voice.

Trazabaal cackled. "You have given me the means to curse you all, piglets! You cannot begin to imagine what's coming to this land. Your own leader defies you, great General of the war."

He turned, eyebrow cocked comically at his men, who smiled at his humor. "Does he now?" Schlack mumbled and pulled his dirk from his belt. "I see I have erred in letting you yap again. Careless of the troopers to leave you in such a way."

When Schlack raised the blade to her, she started to chant, to recite incantations and curses...

But not for long.

*****

As usual, when clad in his armor and heading into battle, Goliath checked over his shoulder. This time, his shield bearer wasn't behind him. That made him want to keep checking over his shoulder, but he resisted. The company of Philistines also hung back. Their number grew by the minute as the emissaries from The King of Ashkelon, arrived in small groups. They stood with the others, having been told at Gath where the champion was off to as night fell. Surely flummoxed by the message about what Goliath intended, they came to see if a full-scale conflict would break out. Since he crossed into Israel territory proper, many thought a greater war would explode from his trip.

Goliath took a breath and prepared to walk toward the village. A sound cut the air, one that made him fail to take his first step. It was the arrival of a white horse, arriving at a great speed and stopping abruptly not ten yards from him. Goliath turned to face the man who dismounted, a lean but healthy soldier with a neat beard and a purple cowl around his face.

The man took a knee to the giant and removed the piece covering his mouth. "Champion of the Philistines, I'm Hyrum of the court of the King of Kings. I bring you word from the coast."

"It'll have to wait, Hyrum." Goliath twisted his head away from the kneeling messenger and again faced the village.

"There's great peril to our forces in the south," the messenger persisted. "The Egyptians have attacked our navy and forced them back to land. The King asks for your presence as this trial begins and the revolutionary forces of Samien gather far off."

Goliath never moved his eyes from the buildings beyond as he said, "I'll return to Ashkelon soon, as I have promised the others."

Hyrum took a breath and said, "Yes, sir, but another matter is seen by the wizards of Ba'al Zebul at Ekron."

"Another needs me worse than the wants of kings or the visions of priests."

"They say it's a message from Eucimar from Zorn, coming unto us all in Philistia. One wizard says it may be made manifest beyond the gates of Ekron itself."

When Goliath faced the messenger, the man fell to his backside and his horse retreated, spooked. "Clean the dung from your ears, boy, or I'll rip off your dick and do it for you. I'll return soon."

Then, he stepped forward.

With his usual boldness, Goliath stalked right up to the edge of the small town, where a dozen men in light armor rode out and dismounted. They looked dirty, haggard and their faces overgrown with hair. Unlike the usual reaction and that of many of the town who fled, these men brandished their weapons at Goliath.

"What have you against us Amalekites, Champion of the Philistines?" one of the bearded men shouted, his large curved blade swinging over his head. "You know what dwells in here in the city of the woods," the Amalekite sniggered. They all stabbed their weapon toward heaven, taunting the giant. "If you Philistines were any sort of men, you'd never have let the Ark come into the hamlet of Kiriath-Jearim."

Goliath's booming voice made them lower their weapons. "I didn't come here for the Ark, you mongrels. I never guessed there were any of you bastards left after the Hebrews defeated you. I'm surprised you'd have the guts to walk within a dozen miles of Jerusalem like this."

The Amalekites made obscene gestures and one even dropped his trousers toward Goliath. Their dogs of war barked, barely held in check by a stout master with heavy leashes and a whip. The loud leader yelled back, "We aren't here for the Ark, either, but the Prophet of Israel's God. The man who slew our King Agag is here. That man will die today."

"I'm here for him as well, but not to slay him." He briefly wondered what sort of a unit they ran in, back in the day when they attached themselves to an organized army. "After I speak with the man who abides this night in Abinadab's home you can speak with him. Kill him then if you can."

"You aren't a man to give orders," the nearest man shouted and spat toward the giant.

Goliath pulled his javelin from his back, held it to his right side. From his left hand dangled the great sword Abimelech usually carried for him. "I'm exactly the one to give orders. Stand aside."

They all shouted their displeasure and willingness not to obey.

"Select your greatest man and let him come forward to fight me. If I beat him, you all can depart. There's no point you all should die because of the tongues of a few idiots."

All twelve Amalekites fell out into a formation, many holding swords, others spears, a few small axes, and one sported a bow.

Goliath looked beyond at the brick dwelling of Abinadab where the Prophet of the Hebrews dwelt. The giant adjusted his helmet and started to walk forward.

Only a dozen in number, Goliath read their anger, determination and hatred. They wanted the Prophet dead. They lived on a blood vendetta, as the Hebrews slaughtered them down to the infants, Goliath heard tell, destroying most of their folk. Their grit and resentment blinded them to the threat before them. He understood that as their error.

One of the dozen brandished a long broadsword, not crafted in the region. Goliath believed them to be rare, but clumsy weapons in open warfare. This man sported wild eyes and a beard curlier at the sides than down below. He stayed near the back, shouting directions to others in his native tongue. Three men holding short swords took up positions to his far right, middle and left. Three others holding spears shadowed these Amalekites while an archer sporting a long bow took a knee between the swordsmen to his right. Another soldier stepped up in the gap on his left, holding what looked to be a metallic fan...no, it was an array of iron-headed hatchets.

Three more men hung back from the rest, one brandishing a huge single-headed axe, another a double-headed mace...the last man held a whip in one hand and the leashes for several great war dogs in his other.

The man with the broadsword said, "He's but a man, not a god. Cut him down and let us be done with it."

At the edges, the two men with swords started to close in. The bowman notched an arrow and let it fly. Just as he released, the hatchet man reared back to fling his projectile at the giant.

Goliath jerked his head to the left as the arrow broke against his helmet. His javelin brought up to bear, took the hatchet shot. A second hatchet soon followed, also sticking in the shaft of the great lance. With his sword, Goliath parried the attack of the swordsman to his left, and then jabbed out his javelin, fending off the attack of the man to his right. The attackers hesitated, exchanging looks.

The giant planted his feet and bellowed, "C'mon, you little shits. You wanted me. Kill me if you can."

As two of the spearmen let their weapons fly, Goliath felt another arrow bounce off his helm. He dropped down, rolled to his right, causing all of the attackers to freeze. Covering a great distance with the move, Goliath came up near the man he fended off. His sword flashing in an overhand arc, Goliath chopped the sword arm from the stunned attacker. The Amalekite's face, still wearing the shocked look doled from the javelin jab, shook and then gawked down at his missing limb. He blinked, watching his blood spray, as if confused over what to do next.

The two spearmen ran forward to retrieve their weapons. They prepared to strike Goliath in his crouching position. The giant laid both his weapons down and reached forward fast at his aggressors. Each huge hand grabbed the spears as the fighters drove in toward his gut. His weight pressing down, Goliath snapped the spears off just under the heads. With a fast move, he pulled the spearmen together, crashing their shoulders jointly. The blow didn't hurt them much more than it surprised them, save for the one on the left. The white of his right eye turned to blood, the force rattled him so much. Each released their ruined weapon and backpedaled out of the champion's grasp.

With a backhand swipe, Goliath dented the skull of the maimed swordsman, sending him to his death. The giant then grabbed up his sword and again blocked blows from the next attacking swordsman. When another arrow glanced from his helmet, Goliath rose up. All of them backed away from the champion. Goliath leered down at the bowman.

"You're starting to piss me off."

Before Goliath could move on the archer, the group shifted. A bunch used to fighting together, they knew when to work in tandem. The man brandishing the whip lashed out, snapping the long cord near Goliath beard, then released the dogs of war. The muscled hounds ran forward, hungry and snarling. Before they arrived, Goliath warded off further shots from the hatchet man with his javelin. He threw this weapon down before the dogs, which promptly leapt over the shaft peppered with hatchets. His sword sliced one of the leaping dogs clean in two at the midsection, but the other two were on him fast. Goliath dropped his sword and grabbed up the dogs off his thighs like they were clinging spiders. Their teeth met the links in his bronze armor as he pulled them from his person.

The lone spearman with a weapon came in low and thrust up, trying to strike Goliath with a shot to the heart. The giant pivoted, clamped his armpit down on the spearhead in a move that froze the attacker. Goliath threw the two dogs off, one on the hatchet man, the other onto the man with the whip. As each man wrestled with the confused, crazed dog, Goliath brought his head down, crashing skulls with the spearman, helmet to helmet. The spearman lost, crumpling to the ground.

The swordsman with the short blade attacked again, thinking he had Goliath dead to rights, weaponless. Goliath reached down and brought up the upper torso of the vivisected dog, blocking the stab. Down to a knee, Goliath scooped up his sword as the man drew back and drove his weapon home again. Still taller than his enemy, Goliath blocked the blow, and his attacker's blade disintegrated. The Amalekite knew his fate in a moment, yet had no time to contemplate it further than that. A backwards swipe later, Goliath removed the head of the swordsman above the jaw. Blood spouted from the ruined head of the Amalekite for a few seconds and the dead man stayed on his feet.

Goliath switched knees, but stayed low to avoid another arrow. He slung his sword like a disk. The huge blade spun across the yard, heading to the master of the dogs of war. This man still held a slobbering dog like a man would as he carried a bride. He died with the dog in his arms, as the blade struck him in the gut, slicing him clean in two pieces just above his waist belt.

As the torso and the dog dropped, one of the empty-handed spearman pulled a pair of knives from his girdle. He stepped up to attack Goliath but hesitated, unsure of where to stab him. Just as his confusion reigned, the concussed spearman pulled off his helmet and stumbled into his path. Goliath grabbed up his javelin and swung the bronze butt of it around, crushing the jawbone of the bloody-eyed man, sending him to the ground. While the other spearman stood, frozen, Goliath swung the javelin and drove the lance through his enemies' heart at a crooked ankle. He lifted the Amalekite in the air and threw his body toward the man waiting with the great axe. Still, this man did not enter the fray. This stout man watched the dying man roll to a stop at his sandals and said nothing.

Goliath pulled the hatchets off his javelin staff and threw them back at their owner. This move proved awkward, but sent the slinger scrambling. Goliath then spider crawled closer to his prey with the freed hatchets. The man with the broadsword and the final spearman came to action. The spearman stepped away, backing up so far he started to fall backwards. He fell, got up and ran for his life.

The man with the broadsword held his weapon with skill as Goliath pounced on the back of the hatchet man. Though the soldier held a hatchet in each hand, Goliath's weight crushed the air from his body. A knee guard delving deep in the soldier's belly, Goliath let the shocked man stab at his armor with the hatchets. Goliath intensely swatted his flattened hands together on either side of the Amalekite's head. The popping sound caused by this action made those near pause. The archer stared at the eyeball that jumped free from the hatchet man's head. His hands shook so that he couldn't get an arrow notched.

The grunt of the man swinging the broadsword gave Goliath the cue, and he twisted off the body of the hatchet man. Still in a crouch, the Philistine dipped lower, causing the overhand arc of the blade to fall across his back. The momentum off course, the blade hopped on his armor and never made a mark. Goliath grabbed the ankles of the swordsman, stood up and threw the Amalekite over his head.

Upright, Goliath turned, saw the man with the double-headed mace coming forward, but he looked down at the swordsman. Goliath tightened up his elbow and dropped. The huge bludgeon fell right on the skull of the man with the broadsword. Though the Amalekite's mouth opened and he tried to block the giant with his sword, no cry emerged before the full weight of the Philistine dropped through his head.

Wiping the brains from his elbow guard in the dirt, Goliath quickly rolled away from the swinging mace of the new attacker. He rolled up to his knees as the Amalekite swung the mace, connecting with the giant's head. The helmet flew off and Goliath reeled from the shot. Hands on the ground, Goliath shook his head fast. Slightly dazed, he rose up quick, and grabbed the middle of the mace as the next blow started.

The Amalekite he grappled with was no small man, nearly as tall as Abimelech. Still stunned a bit, Goliath blinked and let go of the mace, jabbing a thumb in the attacker's right eye. The Amalekite never released his weapon, but some of his fight waned, angered by the shot to the eye. Goliath grabbed the staff of the mace once again, and pushed all of his weight down. The staff of the weapon cracked, then split. Goliath roared as his arms came up, bringing both broken ends onto either side of the warrior. A brutal boxing of the ears with the points of his own mace compressed the skull of the Amalekite.

This man fell and his bowels let go. Goliath took a deep breath and started to step toward his sword.

The only man who remained was the hulk holding the great axe. Goliath picked up his sword as the last Amalekite surveyed the scene. The axeman turned and walked away into the fields. Goliath let him go.

"Now," said Goliath as he grabbed up his javelin. "Where was I?"

Though the house of Abinadab was made of bricks and quite large for the village, the outer porch held a small tent. From these flaps emerged a tall man clad in a dusty one-piece robe. One hand on the rope securing his waist, the other holding a walking staff, the man with flowing white hair eyed the champion of the Philistines.

"You must be the Prophet," said Goliath, and he placed his javelin between them.

The old one looked behind Goliath at the devastation wrought and then stared up into his face. "You have done much to see me, slaying my slayers."

Eyebrows raised, Goliath fished a cloth from his belt. "You don't sound surprised. You know that I could kill a dozen mutts with ease."

"No. I prayed for deliverance. God came to my aid. He always does."

Wiping the blood from his sword, Goliath laughed. "I like that, a man who knows what he is. I heard you slew their King, Agag."

"My king defied God's will. Agag had to die."

"You sound like a warrior."

The Prophet said, "I'm not a warrior. I'm no mage, magician or trickster."

"I've heard that you have spoken with God himself."

His voice even, the Prophet replied, "Since my youth."

"Which is why you don't fear me," Goliath nodded. "I reckon after speaking with God himself, anything on two or four legs would be a let down."

"You come to me at great jeopardy to yourself. Not just with these dozen, but with the politics of your own kind. Tell me why."

"I think you know but you want me to say it. You prophets are like wizards in that you see things around many corners. My shield bearer, Abimelech, is gravely ill. The wicked priestess of Moloch, to spite me, cursed him, via the temple whores of Ashtoreth and their high priestess. He bleeds from the inside out and will die soon."

The Prophet nodded. "Why does he survive so long? Her evil surely would have struck him down fast."

"Abimelech is my blood brother. His veins are tainted with my blood, something not common to this world. Also, my mother wet-nursed him with me. She's uncommonly blessed."

"So I have heard. Your priests and shamans cannot heal him?"

Goliath planted his sword in the ground and went to one knee. Many Hebrews watching gasped at this act of humility, but many Philistines argued that, perhaps, he knelt to see the Prophet eye to eye.

"I ask you that, by the power of your god, you would see him healed."

The Prophet stared into the Philistine's face for a long time. "You make no threats, no boasts, no promises, and ask for mercy from a god you do not believe in."

"I know he's there. I've seen his work." Goliath's voice rang with frankness. "He has power. You're his Prophet. I can but ask this boon." Goliath bowed his head and said quietly, "If you chose not to grant it, there's naught I can do."

"This man must mean a great deal to you."

Eyes up and on the Prophet, Goliath said, "There are so few I trust. You have to understand that. Great forces and evil men conspire against me. Some tramp seeks to gain fame from a child that may be fathered by me or a goat for all I know. Abimelech is…" his voice caught in his throat before his resolve stiffened. Goliath declared, "He's my shield bearer."

"Indeed. I can see where you'd need one of those.

You should stay away from these petty little gods. They are but quibbling demons, empty vessels owing nothing but hate to the Almighty. Do you know who my God is?"

"I've seen many small forces claiming to be gods. I know who God isn't."

"Do you want me come and see your shield bearer?"

Goliath shook his head. "Just say the word and it'll be so. I know what power is. I need no grand act on your part."

The Prophet closed his eyes but for a moment and then nodded. He then cleared his throat and said, "I wish many of my own tribe would have your courage and faith. Go and see, your servant is healed."

Goliath rose up and said, "Yes?"

"Go, Abimelech is well."

Goliath turned, head bowed. "I'd have killed all the Kings of Philistia for his one life, if you but asked me to. I'd have brought your their children's heads on a long string if you just said the word."

"God doesn't require such things. However, there are enough gods, are there not?" The Prophet turned away and went back into the house that held the Ark of the Covenant.

Goliath walked through the dead men outside the town and pondered the Prophet's words.

*****

The Philistine warriors that accompanied the party from Gath stayed quiet for the most part. At last, Sadik rode near Goliath and asked, "I thought you would bring the Prophet unto Gath, force his hand to heal Abimelech."

The giant never regarded the youth nor did he slacken his pace. "There's a time for force and a time to talk. I hate talking but the world is a wide-open place. One can only cut so many things. For all the blood and chants, prayers and goats, I really doubt a man can force the hand of God."

"What can force the hand of a god?" Sadik inquired.

Goliath walked for a full minute before he replied, "Nothing. A god's will goes as it must. The strangest things please gods. Some say our gods are happy by blood or the burning of crops. Some gods want you to dance like a puppet. Others make you and leave you alone. Still, some others, require humility and submission. That's an act far tougher than slaying a dozen well-trained fighters."

The hours passed and soon only the few soldiers on horseback stayed with the champion. When they neared Gath, a great roan thundered toward them. Astride it sat Qorus, a wide smile on his face.

"Goliath!" he shouted. "You'll not believe it."

Again, the pace never slackened. Goliath in no way waited for word, he just proceeded on past the soldier on horseback.

Qorus asked the others, "What is it? What ails the champion?"

Goliath heard the others admonish Qorus saying, "You've not known him for very long. It's best to give him space at times like this."

Goliath approached the edge of Gath, and it looked like half the city had turned out to the street in the dawn's light. They weren't there to welcome the champion. They seemed enthralled with each other, dancing, drinking and singing songs. From out of their number strode Abimelech, barely clothed save for his loincloth and a bloody wrap around his shoulders. Trebluha walked behind him trying to hide a large smile with her thin hand. Goliath glanced at her, still stunned at how different she looked in the finery of the priestesses of the temple.

"Good morning, sire," Abimelech said, voice clear and loud.

Goliath stopped a yard from Abimelech, at last. "It's been a long night, Abi. Get dressed, you look like you just stumbled out of a whorehouse."

As he took up a position walking beside Goliath, Abimelech said, "Very good, sire."

"All of these drunks out here and where's the wine?" Goliath asked as he watched the shopkeepers securing their storefronts more as the dancing started to get unruly. "My mouth is dryer than an eighty-year-old whore."

Abimelech slapped a large skin of wine into Goliath's stomach. The giant gripped the container, opened it and took a swig. He then eyed his shield bearer, and then Trebluha, who did her best to look innocent.

The crowd danced in the street and all business owners of the shops watched in contentment for a time. Goliath couldn't help but let a smirk creep onto his grim face.

In the middle of the revelers, a couple jumping children knocked over a large clay jar a shopkeeper hadn't pulled in just yet. This container smashed when it hit the ground, causing Goliath to stop for a moment. The keeper emerged from behind his closed up windows and grabbed each child by the hair.

"We can make a new pot, and a couple more just like you as well," he cursed the two and then boxed each child's ears. "Like the new container, you be good or you will pass through the fire as well."

Goliath bristled a tad at the admonishing to the children, more at the words, the veiled threat of Moloch sacrifice. The broken vessel was empty.

When they neared the temple of Ashtoreth, the messenger on the white horse reappeared. Hyrum rode across their path but never stopped. His eyes concerned and his worry went back to the road leading in from the other side of town. When the three looked to where the rider stared they beheld a group of riders also on white horses. All of them were soldiers and they even carried the standard for the king of Ashkelon.

Goliath sighed and mumbled, "This crap keeps getting better and better."

The stout man on the lead horse removed his mouth wrap and revealed the obvious… it was General Schlack.

"We'd stopped in here earlier, but there were matters nearby, conscripting a few more men who had avoided service," the General said in his booming voice, eyes level with the giant from his mount. "I thought we'd swing by to see if you abided here still."

Goliath raised his voice and the party on white horses stiffened. "After I get this accursed armor off, rinse off and dine, we will start back for Ashkelon."

"Our messenger said that…"

With a steady voice Goliath cut him off. "I met your messenger, Hyrum. You can fill me in on the details in time."

Schlack titled his head. "Why do you look at me so?"

Eyes focused on the crooked nose of the General, Goliath replied, "I didn't know I was."

With a scuffing cough, General Schlack said, "You look as if you've seen a ghost."

"Forget it."

"Here," the General called out and rode closer to the champion. "I saw your handiwork in the rear courtyard. One certainly cannot abide the behavior of Trazabaal."

"Get to the point. I'm weary."

Schlack motioned with his left hand over his shoulder and two horses trotted in close. The men near

Philistine

Goliath and Abimelech gasped as Schlack's horsemen threw down the Nubian prostitute of Ashtoreth. The General then nodded and the horsemen dismounted and started to tie up the ankles and wrists of the Nubian.

"While your band will be able to swear loyalty in person soon," Schlack said flippantly, "here's my bond to you and yours, in blood." He held out his right hand and opened it.

Although most stared at the soldiers tying the ends of the ropes that secured the Nubian to the girth straps of their mounts, Goliath and Abimelech peered into the hand of Schlack.

The General stated, "She could've still cast spells in the state you left her in."

Abimelech reached out and shook the General's hand. When he drew back, Abimelech took the tongue of Trazabaal from Schlack's palm.

Schlack never lowered his gaze as the terrified woman wailed and the soldiers mounted up. "Anything you want to ask her before she's rent asunder?"

"No," Abimelech said dryly. "I doubt your methods have wrung much out of her."

Schlack smiled and Sergeant Ninkory spoke up, saying, "We weren't about to rape her."

Goliath drank deep as Ninkory shouted the order for the horses to take off in opposite directions. Eyes closed, Goliath thought he heard Schlack whisper to his adjutant, "That's how one controls the strong."

CHAPTER TWELVE
PLANS, OLD FRIENDS, AND A MESSAGE FROM ZORN

"Get that sonofabitch out of my dreams," Samien barked at Baldassare's face, his hands gripping the Colonel's shoulders.

"General, please," Baldassare gasped, trying to keep his composure as they struggled in the cave.

His brown hair soaked with sweat, Samien rasped, "I've had priests come to me in dreams before, but get that wicked bastard Kmentosi out of my skull."

Baldassare patted his superior's elbows to calm him, and the General unhanded him roughly. "General, we consciously never retained a priest or shaman in our cause."

"Because we believed that we followed a new way, a righteous cause, unpolluted by the nonsense of the past." Hands becoming fists, Samien raged. "Now, what do I get? Petty bitching by a priest who is angry about some of his fellow enchanters getting butchered by the champion."

A step further away from Samien, Baldassare asked, "There's naught I can do to make your dreams pure."

"I'm not a stupid man, please don't treat me as

such. We have shared the visions from Malak and listened to her words. We have taken up the banner of a better Philistia, but if we cannot rely completely on those saying they support us back home..."

"There's no evidence Kmentosi doesn't stand with us."

"If he stood behind us," Samien said, the fury bubbling between his lips. "He wouldn't be terrorizing me in my dreams, wanting me to go end his squabble with the giant because of the slaughter in Gath."

Baldassare stood very still as he replied, "We're in no position to attack them."

Samien retorted in a mocking voice, "But the brilliant priest of Dagon says we are in the perfect position to do his will. His will? What a self-centered dog. Does he think the priests of Dagon that Goliath's troop butchered will be the last?"

"From what you told me of the dream, yes, the only positive of his desire would be striking out and killing General Schlack. We can't be obsessed with killing the champion. That is a task best left for open warfare. Schlack is away from his base at the moment, and that would be quite a strike, but again, we're in no arrangement to do it."

Samien drank from a metal cup and then threw it against the stonewall of the cave. "He speaks of revenge, his sense of self bruised by an unexpected turn of events. I will not be the puppet of priests anymore." Again, he focused on his colonel. "You see, he tempts me with a grain of truth, and yes, a dead Schlack would help our cause. However, if we uproot now and go unto the land before they return home, bah."

"It's possible..."

His words icy, Samien stated, "Many things are possible, Colonel. While Kmentosi can create a homunculus good enough to fool a king, he won't make a puppet out of me." After a few breaths, Samien said with confidence, "We'll continue to drill and grow our forces. Our time is coming soon."

"Agreed." The Colonel loitered for a few moments and then turned. Still, he waited, but the General had no further words. He departed the cave, giving poisonous glances at the guards outside. These younger men looked away from him and searched the horizon for the sun.

He glanced across the encampment and saw the mouths of several caves shimmer with orange light. From their inners came the clang of hammers on metal as the makeshift smithy works plied their trade. Across the camp women and men boiled food in pots suspended over fires, preparing a morning meal, and then giving thanks to their gods loudly.

Once the Colonel trekked out of the camp, he climbed into the crowded brush of the hills until he found a rock large enough to sit on. He rested, hands flat on the bolder, and faced to the south. Eyes closed, he envisioned blurry circles in his head, spinning blobs of color not alien to anyone who'd ever been stunned in their life. However, when the circles started to become solid and became bisected by thick lines, Baldassare felt trepidation.

He sweated and his breath sped up, but he couldn't feel his heart beat.

"Calm yourself," came the thick, deep, female voice unto his ear.

Terror boiling in his mind, his eyes opened.

Once Baldassare realized he no longer sat on the hillside in the wilderness, he tried to scream. He failed. His head jerked, seeing the images in white all about him in regular intervals, all standing at the end of long beams of wood. The Colonel's head twisted, and he faced the throaty-voiced speaker.

"Malak," he gasped.

"Be of good cheer, Colonel," she intoned, her looming form cloaked in a gray sheet. "There's naught to fear." Her features pronounced from the hood, her lips parted, revealing teeth like raw diamonds. "Not yet."

Again, he tried to scream.

She patiently waited for him to stop trying.

*****

Goliath saw the company of soldiers he'd been traveling with and those others that arrived with General Schlack assembling at the edge of Gath. Many in the town turned out to see them leave, but several had seen such actions before and lacked interest in the departure. They'd grown accustomed to the giant champion and oft regarded him with no fanfare. He glanced at the crowd by the temple of Ashtoreth and wore a wry smile, understanding this was precisely why he liked it in Gath.

The soldiers under Captain Balzer allowed the champion his privacy, and they all took the blessings of the priests as they went. Goliath stopped and regarded the slender woman Trebluha. She looked up at him with a stony expression. He guessed she fought back tears or emotion. She'd been so good to him that Goliath really believed her different than most women. But, alas, she proved human and that was all right with him. His huge right hand caressed her cheek.

Trebluha poised in a sassy way for a moment. "They have really outfitted me like a maiden, no?"

"I knew you would clean up well," Goliath assured her. "Serving in the house of the goddess isn't so bad, is it?"

She smiled. "It's wonderful, really. It's so clean

there."

"I hoped it'd be good. It'll be better once they sort out who's in charge, once Trazabaal dies."

The woman held back, but Goliath figured her about to blurt out how it was unreal that she'd be allowed to stay there, but again, as was her way, Trebluha held her tongue. "Even your mother has been, well, kind."

"Has she now?" This made Goliath smile. He gazed up into the higher tiers of the temple. A shadow moved there. He neither motioned for her or waved.

Trebluha shrugged. "She's what she is, but everyone has been kind to me. I guess they know better?"

"They ought to. I don't ask for many things and they know it. I wanted a better life for you than the port city. Any woman with your talent and the guts to call me by my name deserves that." He knelt to one knee and looked her in the eye. Her thin hand in his, he kissed her knuckles.

When he stood and started to walk away she turned her back to him. Goliath stopped.

He asked, "You never inquire when I'll return?"

Trebluha faced the temple. "You'll be back. Who or what can stop you?"

Goliath trod on to join the party. Once he walked next to the mounted Abimelech, he heard his shield bearer say, "Ready to pledge your undying loyalty to the King of Kings?"

Eyes forward to the west, Goliath wondered, "Why is it I keep you alive?"

*****

Kmentosi made certain the lock on his inner chamber held secure before he lay down on the bed mat. He tried to dispel images in his mind of the temple at Gath. Souls cried out to him for justice, and he tried not to mutter myriad spells as he retrieved a curled sheet of parchment from the lowest shelf of his office. Hidden in plain sight, no one could guess the enchantments held on this piece of unassuming papyrus. With great care, he folded the jagged bottom of the scroll and used a dagger to tear a small piece free on the new seam. After he replaced the parchment on the shelf, he made certain a ceramic jar lay near the head of his bunk.

"I wouldn't want nowhere to return to in case my body is destroyed in astral flight," he said aloud to himself, setting the soul jar back further. "And I have time before my audience with the King."

He then lay back and placed the tiny portion of paper on his tongue. Entranced, he soon detached from his mortal frame and flew. However, the journey ended quickly and he slammed into an invisible wall. Kmentosi could clearly see before him the elaborate realm of Malak. The complex series of columns and figurines changed in composition and turned from reality into blackness, outlined with hair-thin lines of yellow light. Accustomed to the ever-shifting reality of astral travel, the priest tried to concentrate, attempting to contact Malak.

Usually, during such travel, the awareness of one's own body lessened. What provided Kmentosi a start was how much of his flesh he felt, how much an emotion of terror lurked around his confident mind.

In the lighted outlines, he saw the great wheel and the thirteen forms of pure white radiance standing at each station. These pristine figures all flowed to the center; however their goddess did not stand at the spoke in the wheel. The priest tried to focus more, and the panic rose. A large shape, cloaked in something hardly giving off a hint of light, stood away from the wheel, near its northern edge. Beyond this thing that could only be Malak stood another shape, one not denoted by any special outline to let him understand its sex. However, what made his fear climb was that this being beyond Malak sported two heartbeats.

Kmentosi felt shoved away, pushed back, as if he wasn't allowed to see what transpired beyond. He slammed into his flesh and nearly let his sphincter go upon opening his eyes.

"What in Hades does she play at?" he mumbled as swung his legs to the floor. He took a few breaths before he turned, avowing to go to the outhouse soon.

Eyes narrowed, he gaped at his soul jar. Though the lanterns burned dimly, he could see something amiss. He reached out and touched the jar. When Kmentosi picked it up, he felt chills race over his flesh as the weight in the jar increased. Fears that some odd demon had been sent back to torment him fell away as his fingertips felt the composition of the jar. In another moment, it crumbled to dust.

"Stone," he said with a dry voice. "My soul jar turned to stone."

He didn't make it to the outhouse to relieve himself.

*****

Though not as big as Ashdod, Ashkelon was an enormous city situated on the edge of the sea. The smell of the ocean struck the travelers long before they spotted the buildings and spires of the temples. Expansive lands for cattle and grazing were set aside from the plentiful fields well irrigated by nearby rivers. A beautiful spot and a center of much commerce, even the walls of the city stood better crafted and maintained than elsewhere in Philistia.

Before they reached the city, they skirted the edges of a vast quarry. Along the tops of this stone trench lay a series of squared blocks denoting tombs for the rich or overly religious. The manmade canyon below came to be as the huge blocks of stone were cut for the walls of the city or temples elsewhere.

Evening drew nigh as they entered Ashkelon through the outer gates of the curtain wall. Many young ones ran to bring them jars of water and wine. A pair of boys brought Goliath a pitcher of wine and then climbed onto his feet as he walked. He strode on, not reprimanding them.

Along the outer fortification, many men hung crucified to poles, arms over their heads. Their hands nailed, legs bound up, but broken to make them suffocate.

Goliath observed, "Those with the legs broken in crurifragium look to be Egyptians."

Qorus rode next to him and nodded. "The guards on the wall say that this is the start of war between our nations. Things have been so quiet and amiable between us for years. We have enough dilemmas with the rebels, much less torment over an Egyptian invasion."

Abimelech dismissed this with a wave. "Crurifragium. That there is a warning to others, and this is the latest puddle in a long pissing match between our nations. If the Egyptians really wanted war, they'd land troops and lay siege to our cities. We're good enough to hire out for their ships. Let them come. They're a divided land these days, anyhow, and I hear the damned priests of Amun control the lower kingdom completely."

Several spits roasted mutton outside small domiciles attached to round buildings that sported chimneys. Goliath knew smith shops when he saw them, and watched as the hulking men stumbled from each place, stretched and sat down to be fed from the spits.

"They're overworking the blacksmiths," Goliath said to Abimelech as he tussled the hair of the youth riding on his left foot. "They're indeed preparing for war."

Abimelech spoke with no emotion. "We're always at war, sire."

"Life would be a boring string of whores if not for it, huh?"

They moved on and Balzer dismissed many of the regulars to the bathhouses. The local boys hopped off of the giant's feet and he made a mock attempt to chop them both down.

General Schlack dismounted, pulling his sword & scabbard with him and told the soldiers that lingered, "King Vyndekay doesn't care if you lot are clean or not."

"Praises be," said Qorus to the General with a spiteful tone in his voice.

The older soldier swung his scabbard up and connected with Qorus's groin. The young man froze, grabbed the sheath and then crumbled to the ground. None of them moved to help the young soldier who lay on the earth.

Schlack kicked Qorus in the ribs, rolling him over. Qorus still held his crotch and gasped for air. "You're still in the Philistine army, pup. I don't care for your strength, kills or association with the champion. You still live at my leisure. You need to be taught respect." The General stiffened up and looked to members of his honor guard. "Take this one out, scourge him with rods and bind him up for an hour. He's tough, he can take it. Make sure he can hear those crucified as they suffer."

Qorus gawked at Goliath who never lifted a finger to help him. The giant turned away and the group moved on to the courtyard of the King.

Abimelech, Goliath and Captain Balzer entered the

stone tunnel that passed under the lattice work of laths into Vyndekay's inner garden. After he straightened up from the low warren, Goliath stretched out his arms. He looked over the benches with wooden backs set up in the well-tended courtyard. While ferns and other plants grew in this rather boxy decorated area, no flowers thrived. Goliath hadn't expected any, but it was a contrast to places he'd visited in their own lands.

King Vyndekay sat with Schlack and a man clad in the green vestments of the temple of Dagon.

"Strange we call the head of each town a King," Goliath muttered to Abimelech. "You'd never know it to look at him, dressed down so in common togs."

Abimelech said, "I never expected to see Kmentosi here."

The giant concurred. "Yes, but he usually does travel with his head up Vyndekay's ass."

Balzer turned and whispered, "I'm amazed to see any man of Dagon trod near you these days."

Goliath tilted his head to the left and then righted it. "True."

Although Vyndekay never heard their words, he eyed Goliath, and probably read the boredom and contempt his face. This evident emotion from the champion didn't rattle Vyndekay. His poise and strength is what made him King, Goliath wagered. He also figured the King wasn't a man for the rear guard. He'd distinguished himself in battle, along with Schlack, many times long ago. Schlack was simply too old for the rigors of kingship and politics. For that, Goliath would respect the old General.

"You're all well aware of the maritime assault by the Egyptians," the King said to those as they reclined. "These attacks press on my mind as hard as the defections to Samien."

Goliath grunted as he sat on the stone tiles and put

an elbow in one of the finely crafted chairs. He stared at the priest. "Kmentosi is it?"

Eyes steady, the priest of Dagon nodded. "It has been a long time." The temperature in the garden remained warm, but rivulets of sweat ran from the priest's close-cropped hair.

Balzer said, "We heard tell of it on the wind and then in greater detail from General Schlack as we returned. The men will make their pledge in due time and are itching for a crack at those disloyal across the land."

"That may have to wait." Vyndekay went on to say, "While we regret the folly of your mission south, we need you with us now."

Goliath said, "There are greater evils afoot than Egyptian attacks. Your priest Kmentosi there can attest to the tribulations on the wind that led us south and that run amok in our land this day."

Vyndekay sighed and said, "Religious matters mingle too far in with matters of state, and I hate to be a slave to either. However, the guidance of our priesthood has oft aided our soldiers..."

Goliath interjected, "And hindered us. The truly good mages and priests seem to get sent to Zorn, and never return, like Eucimar."

Kmentosi sat forward, "That's another matter we need to address. The emissaries of Zorn have arrived. Our fishermen and naval vessels spotted them. The messenger will go to deliver his message in the tombs at sunset."

Abimelech said, "We won't want to miss that."

His hands clasping each other, Vyndekay stated, "As it was an assault on naval forces of our people by the Egyptians recently, we shall answer them in kind. The sitting pharaoh is a weak man, only testing us out of spite."

General Schlack grunted and agreed with the King.

"Psusennes I is a man with no real courage for war. If we strike down the Nile, as we have in the past, he will be surprised and never have the gall for a land war."

Goliath listened and said nothing as Balzer put forth, "I see that we must strike back, but I worry for a divided army. The raids down the Nile are a tested clout and will work of course, but what if the Egyptians learned from our incursions in the past? What if they now have a better defensive system for raiders, even if our vessels are superior to theirs?"

The King pondered this and said, "A raid down the Nile is but one option. If we engage their navy forces, they can be crushed with ease. That is but one thing, but this tale of a coming conflict with Samien and his irregulars troubles me. We need a bigger act to show *them* we mean victory."

Kmentosi flared his nostrils. "Those of Samien are but a ragtag lot of mongrels, nil to worry on."

Goliath cleared his throat and they all looked his way. "Why not burn Tanis to the ground? Why not crush and burn the libraries of Memphis? Why not send me into kill the royal family and rape his daughters?"

Vyndekay showed a brief moment of mirth as he half smiled. "Would the latter act be one of great warning?"

Goliath shrugged. "I just threw that in as it sounded like a good idea."

Once their laughter subsided, the King said, "Either way, we have a good leader for the attack." He turned to the inner garden and said, "Captain?"

From the inner yard emerged a tall, skinny man in worn, sun-bleached clothes. With him walked a short, stocky man in a headscarf.

Goliath climbed to his feet and exclaimed, "You old bastard!"

The white-haired Captain said, "I never knew assheads came in that size. Dagon screwed the Gorgon, glad to see you!"

"Weldon Yog and Nopsik," Goliath said and grabbed up both men in a hug. "You are the bastards who survived the Egyptian attack?"

Weldon whispered at close quarters to Goliath, "We hear back in Tanis they didn't take the slaughter of the garrison at the port city really well." The giant set them down and Weldon said, "Though the priests in the south disagree with their other brothers, that act pissed them off as well."

"Oh damn," Goliath said with a laugh. "Well, things are looking up."

Abimelech stood and said in a loud voice, "Maybe not."

They turned to face him and then faced to where he pointed.

Two figures in dark robes stood in the outer court doorway. Their heads hidden by hoods, their pale faces almost glowing, emotionless, they waved both hands indicating for them all to follow.

They all rose up and Vyndekay said, "Curse it, the men from Zorn. It is nearing sunset so we better follow them to the tombs."

Weldon wore a look of confusion. "What's going on?"

Hands folded over his chest, Goliath explained, "A powerful wizard in Egypt sends his messengers to us in this way."

"I've heard of Zorn, lots of scary tales," Nopsik spoke up and then asked meekly, "Why doesn't he just send a scroll with his seal?"

While they walked out the way they came in, Goliath said, "Come along and see. You'll never forget how he sends a seal."

Weldon grinned. "Is that what's going on around here? I've heard folks in the marketplace and the titty bar talking about this Zorn or some creepy message from him."

Abimelech said, "It's said the dead deliver messages from Zorn."

Weldon chewed on the inner portion of his cheek, and Nopsik made the sign for a broken head at his Captain. The smaller sailor then made a sign for 'drink' and headed away from the party following Zorn's messengers.

Goliath looked down at Weldon. "How do ya feel about that?"

Weldon confessed, "Like I shoulda gone to the bar with Nopsik. Where are we going?"

General Schlack said from behind them, "The tombs. The messenger will choose the vessel for which Zorn's communication is to be delivered."

The sailor rolled his eyes to heaven. "I've seen some secretive organizations before, big guy, but that takes the meat pie."

Keeping pace with his master, Abimelech said, "This is Zorn's way to make sure the memorandum is believed."

Weldon glanced up at Goliath. "I know of a land up north, lots of ice and snow, and the women are kinda furry, but they are tall and big boned. None of their dead bodies talk that I know of, and their priests get women all the time."

Goliath let out a deep chuckle. "You tempt me, Captain Yog." Suddenly, Goliath stopped and the party nearly overran him. He snapped his fingers and pointed at Abimelech's waist belt. "For the priest, Abi."

"Oh, I nearly forgot," Abimelech said and reached into a pouch on the left side of his belt. He pulled out two small bones and offered them to Kmentosi.

The priest gave him a doubtful look.

Goliath said, "They are what is left of your

representation of Dagon."

Face flushed, Kmentosi tried to hide his anger.

The giant turned, but first said, "He was delicious, if somewhat sweet, and not worth the men that died to get him."

They journeyed outside the curtain wall of Ashkelon. Goliath glanced down the line of the crucified, but never spotted Qorus being scourged. It took several minutes and many in the party doubted the remaining sunlight for the mission at hand. However, one of the robed figures went down the slope that led to the crypts and stopped at one of the first stone slabs.

Weldon watched the others as the messenger approached the slab. "I suppose that prick wants us to move the stone for him?"

Goliath shook his head and looped his thumb through the strap that held his javelin to his back. "That won't be necessary."

The robed messenger held out his arms and the slab shifted, popped free from the wall and fell to one side with jerky movements. The stone never elevated, but an unseen force pulled it free and cast it aside with ease.

Weldon chuckled. "This Zorn is a show off. Why didn't he just transmit his message in the mind of a priest or a crystal ball or something?"

The priest Kmentosi stepped forward and took a knee before them, saying, "As they said, this way, there is no doubt the message is from Zorn."

The rotten scent of mildewed flesh wafted out to them. They soon saw a figure move from within the chamber and pass the messenger. The servant of Zorn reached out and released the bindings on the arisen body, then took the covering from its face. The reanimated man was very old, though recently dead, suffering mild decomposition.

The priest of Dagon let his jaw drop and he gasped. "Zorn can be cruel, though."

Abimelech stepped back as did most save for the priest and Goliath. He then said, "What do you say that for?"

Kmentosi stepped backward and turned away. "It's my eldest brother just passed over." When the being started to rasp words, Kmentosi broke into a run.

Goliath stepped forward, yet Weldon and the rest receded further. The sailor said, "If the priest has no stomach for it, ya better watch yer ass, man."

The giant said to the arisen priest, "What do you have to say?"

The dry lips parted and the undead thing spat dust as it said, "Come to me, Champion of the Philistines, and I will give you answers."

Goliath made his fellows step back again in that he laughed in the face of the undead thing. "Oh yes? Should I come unto the place where no man returns? Why should I? Do you think I fear your magic from afar? Go ahead and kill me, end my miserable life. That way you get nothing."

"I have what you need, Champion," the corpse said.

"And what is that? You want to offer me eternal life? Piss off. Who wants to live forever? What can you give me that is worth risking my ass for?"

"Your one true love," the corpse said and a rattle echoed from inside of it.

Abimelech grabbed Weldon's elbow and exclaimed, "What the hell?"

Goliath frowned and he glanced back. "It's laughing at me." He folded his arms and faced the body yet again. "You have to do better, Zorn. I don't love anything or anyone."

"Yes, I jest. I can tell you the whereabouts of Akisha and of her scheme."

Goliath shot back fast, "I'll find her myself. This land is small and my legs are long. Try again."

"I know who your father is."

The giant spoke in a low voice, but one almost denoting humor as he said, "Do you now?"

"I know where your father is."

"So with this you seek to entice me enough to travel to Egypt and get my ass killed or enslaved by you?"

The dead thing said, "I am Zorn. I see what lies within, even in you, Champion."

"You need me there for a reason," Goliath snapped, all humor spent from his face. "Don't piss down my back and say that it's raining. I cannot accept that you want to have me travel to your citadel and just bless me with knowledge. What is it you want from me?"

"When you hear the answer I will give to your woes, all will be apparent. It will solve both of our desires once you hear of it."

"Go to Hell, Zorn. There's a place there waiting for all wizards. Maybe you will get a really good seat."

Again, the undead thing rattled as if amused. "My destiny is my own affair, Champion. What I desire is hidden on Mount Nebo, an artifact that can turn the heads of more to idolatry than you could guess. I ask a simple boon for your strong arms."

Goliath's right eyebrow arched. "Really?"

"Really," the dead thing replied. "What is a bag of bones to you? It would be so simple." The voice lowered, became coyer and rolled out, "I know you are soon bound for Egypt. Please stop by and see me."

Goliath looked over at the messenger, pallid and silent near to the dead thing. "No one ever comes back from seeing you, Zorn."

"But you will. Let that add to your mystique."

"Will Eucimar ever come back?"

The dead thing replied, "Perhaps he has chosen to

stay here with me."

Goliath still eyed the messenger, looking at the chalky white face, and then down at the hands clasped in front of it. He took a step forward, grabbed the sleeve of the robe and yanked up. The flesh under the robe was dark, sunburnt and ruddy, unlike the pallid face. Goliath tore the messenger's robe open and saw the tattoo on his heart, one mimicking the fetish of Ba'al Zebul... the same tat that Eucimar bore, yet, the person wasn't Eucimar...it was then Goliath saw the messenger's neck sported a thin red line. It wasn't sewn, but still, the line denoted when the bottom torso terminated. Goliath also noticed the messenger never drew a breath.

The giant spread out his arms as if to embrace the messenger and brought his hands together, both flat, against either side of its head. The loud pop sound the skull made as Goliath pulverized it made those nearby jump a little. The messenger's head, ruined, fell back, barely attached to the stump of a spinal cord. Goliath gave the messenger a slight tap on its chest and it flopped to the ground, dislocating its right shoulder on the stone slab from the tomb.

When the brother of Kmentosi convulsed and vomited out a stream of maggots, many of those in the party ran away. The dead man took a few steps and fell down into the stones by another tomb entrance. While many had seen plenty, Goliath stayed close. His eyes focused as the flies started to appear on the body.

Abimelech stood closest to Goliath and said, "The rest are heading back to better, uh, digest the comments." He stopped in his motions when he saw his master failed to budge. "What is it, sire?"

"I think another revelation is coming," Goliath muttered, eyes fixed on the spew from the man from the crypt. "The flies swarm the body like it is fresh again. That's unnatural and usually only seen at Ekron. Look."

Philistine

Abimelech stepped back as the flies started to increase in number, swarming over the acting oracle of Zorn. Soon, the flesh putrefied at a magnified pace and was no more. After the flies started to arise in a cloud over the bones of the oracle, Abimelech backpedaled away. Goliath, though, faced the form in front of him.

"How was that for you?" Goliath asked the shape in the air as it formed into an insectoid shape, but bearing a somewhat humanoid torso. Countless flies made of shimmering wings, reed-like limbs and the head, which resembled a gigantic fly.

From out of the swirling accumulation of insects came a grating voice, in a way like the scrape of steel on rock, but after a fashion, like a thousand voices all forming into one. "I've had better."

"You manifest to me, Ba'al Zebul, tasting the leavings of Zorn's great magic bridge?"

Ba'al Zebul hissed, "Fah, Zorn is no god, nor is he a negligible demon. The lowest malevolent sprite in the everlasting abyss pisses on him."

Goliath glanced back at the cowering men, Abimelech amongst them, and then said to the form, "He seems awfully interested in me."

"He enacts a drama with you," Ba'al Zebul stated. "But I can perceive a mode how all of his twaddle will profit me."

"There would be no other reason for you to be here."

"We have forever understood each other."

Goliath shrugged. "Yes, but do tell. What does Zorn plan for me?"

Ba'al Zebul admitted, "I do not know, as I cannot penetrate the magicks of his citadel. Yes, I thrive outside it."

Goliath's eyes narrowed at him. "How so?"

"You will soon see. After a fashion, it will aid me, too. Zorn does hold that answer you seek, one obscured to most of us."

"What makes you so certain I want the answer? If I wanted it bad enough, shouldn't I have asked you?"

"But I know not if the answer is so. I have a suspicion. I sense Zorn will lead you in a route that will find us both...fortunate."

"And that will be?"

The outline of Ba'al Zebul floated to the left slightly. "Back to the Domain of Moloch, another place forbidden to my form."

Goliath laughed. "Aren't you all brothers, you demons and fallen ones?"

"Moloch is a paltry cunt, a lesser entity propped up on the souls of infants, content to let women and a captured demon do his dirty work." Pride then dripped into his words as the god said, "My subjects are uncountable, like unto the host of heaven. I was there at the war in heaven. I fought. Moloch? Hah. He fell after us, he is a late comer to the party, not fit to lick the wastehole. He was not in the war against the angels. I fell like lightning." Bile grew in the voice as he said, "He was but a fart after the feast."

Hands to his hips, Goliath said, "You want to see ol' Moloch slighted, don't you?"

"It will entertain me to see him irritated, yes." The voice sounded stable then. "For that motivation alone, I will see if I can support you." The shape turned in a circle and then the voice came out drained. "Eternity is long, Philistine. I'm bored already. You, I like you." Ba'al Zebul sounded appreciative. "Someday I will relish consuming you unto myself, alone. I won't relegate the pawns or newborns for that, nay, I'll eat you myself."

"Thanks."

"Beware the god of the tunnels under the complex in Tanis," Ba'al Zebul told him. "It is not a god at all, but Seker can still kill you."

Philistine

Ba'al Zebul then dispersed and Goliath turned from the area of tombs.

Abimelech stood up by the still crouching Cairn, Sadik, and the few brave soldiers that dared to stay near after the manifestation of Ba'al Zebul. Behind these men stood Weldon Yog, hands always on his skinny hips, and Qorus, approaching at a staggered pace.

Goliath's eyes keyed in on Qorus. Partially dressed, exhausted, bloody and sore, looking mean as hell. "Still alive, I see."

"Yes, sir," Qorus said dryly as he passed Weldon.

"Good," Goliath affirmed. "I need men near me that can take an ass whipping."

Qorus stopped and puffed up his chest. "I never cried." He sounded like he was about to weep as he said, "No matter how much they taunted me or hit me, I never cried."

"Good," Goliath told him blithely. "Now stop talking. Do you think I was never beaten as a youth? It makes your body ready for the fight."

"You were scourged?" Disbelief dwelt in Qorus's words as the men encircled Goliath.

"I forget how many times, mostly by my mother. She can still hit hard."

Weldon stepped up and shook his head. "Well, did you get a blessing or a curse from Zorn or the fly god?" His cockeyed smile lit up his sunburnt face.

Goliath climbed up the slope and they followed him. He looked back at the tombs. "A little of both. However, Ba'al Zebul is of no concern to the kings or generals."

Weldon swiped his hand toward Ashkelon. "Like hell, big guy. They seemed awfully concerned when they ran like mice from him. I think it scares the piss out of them to see the real gods manifest."

Goliath started toward the city as the men flanked him. "Good. Keeps them from dreaming of killing me in my sleep." He checked back and saw a robed figure walk out to the area of the tombs where the messenger fell.

As Weldon laughed this off, Abimelech said, "Sire, they are only concerned with the politics and getting revenge on the Egyptians for what happened down south. There are greater matters afoot, your troubles not withstanding."

"I know," Goliath grumbled, and then watched as the robed figure in the tombs knelt over the bones of Eucimar's torso. The hood fell back, and Goliath saw Hasana clearly. She started to cry.

Abimelech continued. "Vyndekay really only is concerned with how he looks in this, and a strike at the hated Egyptians will do him well after strange losses to the Israelites. He thinks this will slap down Samien and the fostering rebellion without too much bloodshed."

"Why do you tell me all of this?"

Abimelech said, "You didn't see the look on the King's face when the oracle said it wanted you to meet with Zorn."

"He fears my own will may differ from what his balls want. Oh, killing Egyptians sounds like a good time, mainly because the leader of Egypt lacks stones and won't mount an invasion back at us."

Weldon put in, "Wonder why he attacked us in the first place?"

Goliath shrugged. "Maybe he has priests and politicians doubting his balls in Tanis. Who knows?"

Weldon said, "Thinking of my offer to go a-wandering yet?"

"More all the time. There are a few things left to do before I leave, though."

Weldon stopped and made sure only Abimelech and Qorus could hear him. "Then when we suit up and sail, let's keep going to the Pillars of Hercules. Piss on all of them, big guy. Let's just go."

Goliath looked to the sea and frowned. "You tempt me like the words of a pretty woman. I'm not so ready to be unfaithful to the one I brought to the party." He then looked down at Weldon and winked. "At least not yet. Many things vex my heart and I would see them resolved. My own folk are tormented by something and I aim to stop it...and what assails me."

Philistine

CHAPTER THIRTEEN
VETERAN SACRIFICE
AND THE SEA

Sleep eluded Akisha in large sequences for many days, so the attendants begged her to see an apothecary. Without proper rest, they reasoned, she'd lose her baby. While most priests performed this duty, she'd never seen fit to trust the powders and potions of the cleric class. Afraid for the life of the child and for her own skin when she heard Goliath returned from the south, Akisha tried praying to Malak for guidance. Although Malak's words and miraculous appearances in the strangest of places brought her heart ease, sleep eluded her. She decided to see a shaman anyhow.

Escorted by two guards from the temple of Dagon and Yaggah, Akisha walked to the abode the shaman deemed by Yaggah to be Ashdod's best.

"Vega will do you wonders," Yaggah promised, as the guards checked the small dwelling over. "I wish you'd relax."

Akisha shook her head violently. "The runners say Goliath is in Ashkelon. He has to know..." Her words halted as she glared at the guards.

Yaggah gestured for them to stand near the latrine

dug close to the small stable for Vega's horses. The guards rolled their eyes and stepped away. Yaggah drew close to her and hissed, "Be silent, Akisha! Those that know of your condition see it as a positive thing for their champion. They may even see a silly romance in it."

"I know, I know," she whispered hurriedly, her eyes scanning the shutters of the stone home.

Still in low tones, Yaggah said, "If they sense you fear their champion or want to run away from him, more tongues will wag."

Eyes to the sky, lost in thought for a few moments, Akisha let out a single chuckle. "I never considered the idea that the big fool would be overjoyed at the idea of my condition." She faced him and said emphatically, "He's supposed to be dead by now, remember?"

"Yes, yes," Yaggah mumbled and he pounded on the wooden door.

Hand to her stomach, Akisha said, "I'm not very special if he's still around."

"He's harder to kill than we anticipated."

Akisha swallowed and they waited for a few moments before she said, "He's harder to slay than even Malak first thought."

Yaggah frowned at her words as a husky female voice called out from inside the home, "Enter in."

He opened the door and Akisha glanced at the two guards once before following him. The guards loitered and took to wandering around the front of the shaman's house.

Unlike most homes in the region, Vega's abode held not a blank spot on its walls. Wooden racks and shelves, all containing ceramic jars and pots, covered each inch of wall space. The fireplace and single lantern gave a great illumination to the single room. A heavy drape sectioned off a smaller portion of the room to the east, barely camouflaging the foot of a sleeping mat. A spinning wheel, a loom, an anvil, a rack of metal tools, and two small tables occupied the western portion of the house.

Vega, a rather corpulent woman of countless years, turned on her seat away from a basin and cutting board. A pale, unformed blob lay in the middle of a patch of white powder.

"Greetings," Yaggah bowed a little. "I assume you received the word we were on our way."

Vega nodded twice, her tied back gray pigtails bopping off her shoulders. "Yes."

The silence became tense so Yaggah asked, "What are you creating?"

With no glance back to the table, Vega replied, "Bread."

Akisha wore a silly look and then became serious as she asked Vega, "Do you have something to help me sleep?"

Yaggah hurriedly offered, "She's pregnant."

Her rheumy eyes on Akisha's stomach, the shaman responded, "Good for her, then." Vega stood, shook off the seat that adhered briefly to her enormous behind, and then took a few steps to the northern wall. Though her hands were withered, Akisha thought them too thick to belong to a woman. One of these huge paws held up a small jar. "Sprinkle a lid full of this in your wine before retiring. I wouldn't advise taking more or drinking too much wine when in such a state. You'll give birth to a race of Edomites." After Vega smiled a mouthful of black teeth at her own joke, Akisha and Yaggah laughed politely.

"Thank you," Akisha said and took the jar. "The soldiers carried your price."

While Vega nodded and turned away, Yaggah asked, "Are you sure that is all you need? A few sacks of grain for the horses?"

"My life is simple," Vega replied as she sat back down and exhaled loudly. "My needs are just. That will give you deep sleep, girl, so do not exceed what I told you."

Yaggah asked, "What's in it?"

"It contains an Egyptian opiate, but the composition is bone meal. One can gain great power from bones, if one knows how to use them."

"Thank you, Vega," Akisha nodded and backed away.

Yaggah kept staring at her until Vega wondered, "Disappointed that I'm not in a state of agony for my craft? You have confused my profession with those of a dramatic sort. Now, feel free to let the door hit you on your way out."

As they walked back to the temple of Dagon, Yaggah muttered, "That was pleasant."

Akisha paid no attention to him as she closed her eyes, thinking of her previous night's visit to the realm of Malak. She adored her goddess, but seemed irritated that others dwelt on the edges of her wheel. The virginal power of those in the temple kept all out, but Akisha felt hurt. Of course, she reasoned, all folk think they are the most important to their god. She'd noted the shade of Kmentosi and that of another unfamiliar with her trying to gain audience to Malak.

What she found disturbing was that Ahkuh-Rhan, the master builder from Gaza, labored at polishing Malak's altars, seeming oblivious to the vestal virgins and the power of the wheel before him.

Maybe he couldn't see it, she reasoned.

When she considered the power Malak must possess to perform such a feat, Akisha shuddered and would soon pray for sleep. Nonetheless, Akisha wondered whom she should pray to.

Philistine

*****

Though most of the group that witnessed the spectacle at the tombs had trouble sleeping, Goliath slumbered like the dead. When he arose in the barracks and went down to the bathhouse to get a wash down by the attendants, he saw great activity in the city, even rivaling the war prep of the day before.

"What's the fuss, girl?" he asked the young woman using a long mop on his lower back.

"The story is the ships are loading for a great journey."

He pondered that and the supposed secret nature of his voyage. "Such tales they tell instead of the truth."

She threw a bucket of water on his backside. "There is no need to tell lies about what you all are doing. We all know about the attack on Egypt. It isn't like we can shout out and tell them we are coming from here."

He brooded over that thought as they wiped him down. He donned his clothes and stepped into the street. Goliath's eyes widened at a new prospect. Soldiers carried men on litters and headed toward the temple of Dagon, a few others toward the temple of Baal.

On horseback, General Schlack approached Goliath and said, "Come along, Champion. It's veteran sacrifice day. Since your groups will soon cast off for Egypt, it would be a fine day for such a thing, no?"

"I'd say," Goliath said in an uninterested voice as he followed the procession but made sure to go toward the temple of Baal.

Captain Balzer's brigade approached as a unit, and Abimelech broke off to join Goliath. Qorus followed

295

Abimelech and they met the giant at the double doors of the great temple.

Hands resting on the top of the stone wall before the gate, Goliath asked, "Is Weldon securing the ships?"

Abimelech nodded. "Yes, he had no use for this ceremony. I was surprised to see you walking up to see it."

He scanned the inner walls of the temple, drumming his fingers on the wall, and nodded to the temple prostitutes from various shrines that appeared for the ceremony. These women sported garments from assorted gods, but agreed to participate for the greater good of the Philistine folk.

Inside the main sanctuary, the temple women sat beside the twisted bodies on the litters and started to stroke the manhood of each injured veteran. The closer they came to their turn at the altar, the faster the motions went. One at a time, a litter was placed on the altar to the idol of Baal. Then a priest, a town leader, once even King Vyndekay, would raise a ceremonial dagger and plunge it into the heart of the crippled man. Each time, just before the deathblow came, the temple girls would lower their heads and start to bob on the victim's organ.

Goliath muttered to his fellows, "At least they are happy unto death."

His face amused and surprised, Qorus said, "I've heard of this practice, but never seen it."

Goliath said, "To serve as a soldier, one last time, they ask for the task. Better this fate and to be released from such a wounded carcass than suffer on, yes? I'd rather die this way and face eternity than live on as a crippled veteran of the wars." He then looked at Abimelech and said, "But I never have to worry on that, now do I?"

Abimelech nodded and Goliath walked closer to the altar. When he did, the giant heard Qorus ask Abimelech what his master meant. He also heard Abimelech tell the young man, "If he or I falls on the field of battle, it's promised between us to slay the other rather than to survive as an invalid or be taken prisoner."

Qorus whispered, "You'd kill your master rather than see him a prisoner?"

"Of course. I'd never let him have the dishonor of chains."

Goliath watched as warriors injured beyond repair were sacrificed to Baal. Once they'd been properly bled, their remains departed, off to a separate place for a communal pyre. He returned many salutes given by the crippled men, some who only had but one arm to salute, others, only the use of their chins to acknowledge the looming champion.

"Kill the Israelites," one man with half his face torn off and no legs begged him. "Make them all suffer, Goliath!"

"The Edomites as well," another voice chimed in.

The giant nodded and patted the bobbing head of the temple whore as he said, "Rest assured, I shall. Go forth into the great beyond and take the good fight unto their dead. See their women raped on the shores of their heaven and let the weeping of their children serve as the bawdy battle hymn."

The warrior with the torn face implored Goliath, "Kill me, great man of Gath. It would be an honor."

Goliath shrugged and looked to the priest, who willingly held out the bejeweled dagger to him. When Goliath took the knife, a chorus of cries arose from the litters, begging Goliath to kill them, too.

He looked over at Qorus and Abimelech. While his shield bearer turned to leave, he had to grab Qorus's arm to pull him along. Goliath heard Abimelech say to the younger man, "That's the price of fame and adoration."

Goliath had sacrificed three men, and stabbed

down the dagger in a fourth's heart, when he paused to laugh. Often, when they were killed as such while the temple whore performed her function, they exploded in orgasm involuntarily. Goliath started to make a game of how many whores could gag when the cut man under his touch rasped out the words, "Break the wheel."

A quizzical look on his face, Goliath asked him, "What?" He then felt silly as the dagger had destroyed the man's heart and the soldier was obviously dead.

Still, the dead fighter said, "Break the wheel, my boy. Destroy her that controls the wheel."

Goliath dropped the dagger and it clattered on the stone altar. He seized the body by the shoulders with bloody hands and demanded, "What are you saying? Who? Akisha?"

Blood bubbled from the man's lips and he muttered, "The sister..." and spoke no more.

"Sister who? What priestess?" Goliath let him go and the ruined soldier fell to the altar. Goliath grimaced at the prostitute who wiped her mouth on a prayer cloth, then folded it and placed it in her belt pouch. "Time I was going," he told the rest, disappointing other men that the priest would send them into the great beyond.

*****

King Vyndekay closed the shutters of the window that faced to the west. "I'll be glad when they are on their way," he said quietly, not expecting any to hear him in his private quarters.

"I cannot see why," boomed the rough voice of General Schlack.

Vyndekay jerked in his movements, shocked to find the old warrior in his home.

"The servant let me up," Schlack said, never taking his eyes from the King.

"What is it you want?"

Schlack wore an indignant look. "I never knew you'd become so unapproachable. I merely will restate that we should mount our offensive against the forces of Samien, sans this silly naval war."

"You don't think this will break the spirit of his men?"

"Fah! If their spirit weren't already limping like a broke-dicked dog, they wouldn't have joined up with a revolutionary."

Hands over his face for a moment, the King then took a deep breath and asked, "What would you have me do?"

"I know where the one encamps. The girls who wash the asses of my soldiers know Samien gathers beyond the Dead Sea."

Eyebrow raised, the King countered, "I thought a battle in the Transjordanian wilderness held no appeal to you."

"It doesn't," Schlack cleared his throat and they left the King's bedchamber. "You cannot swing a sword well in the trees."

"True."

"If it were late autumn, I'd burn the damned plain around them."

They headed down the stairs and Vyndekay asked, "What do you desire, Schlack? We've known each other too long to play at word games."

"I need to take a vast force, not the entire army, but one of substance, and stand against them. They are a rabble now. Give Samien time, and he'll turn them into a fighting force. Let me take a majority of the army, and we'll scare the mongrels out and perhaps send Samien into Babylon with his tail between his legs."

"Fascinating idea," the King said as they walked through the main floor of the house. "I shall sleep on it tonight."

Though Schlack made no attempt to hide his dislike of that delay, he remained silent.

The King stumbled as his foot struck a container on the rear pantry floor. Once he stood steady, both men stared down into a small wooden crate. They exchanged glances and then looked back at the crate.

"What are those? Rocks?" the General wondered.

Vyndekay took a knee and reached into the container. He pulled out a small, round stony object and said, "It's a head."

"Broken from an idol?"

"Apparently," the King said and let his hand drop down into the container again. "There are a dozen of them in here."

Schlack straightened out and coughed once. "Where did they come from?"

When the King stood, examining a small head in each hand, he soon started again. His daughter, Emana, appeared in the doorway that led out into the main living quarters.

"Dear," Vyndekay addressed his daughter, "did you do this?"

"Yes," Emana said in a soft, dry voice. "They were bad."

*****

Weldon Yog barked orders as Nopsik and the crew directed the large vessel away from the port of Ashkelon. The ship, though much larger than the one they piloted in Ezion-geber, maneuvered in the sea about the same.

Philistine

The wide sails and multiple rowers ground away, pushing them far into the choppy waves.

"This ship works better for you?" Goliath said as he glanced back at the docks and counted the vessels preparing to launch. He smiled at the number and wondered at the audacity of their mission.

Weldon grappled with the steering shaft and shrugged. He called out, "It's better for open sea travel, but about the same for speed. We can store more below as well."

Goliath needed no one to tell him that meant they could steal more.

The oarsmen here were great, stocky men from Philistia, bound up by muscle and rowing in shifts. The sails of the great vessel aided them so that there was little drudgery in their actions.

Goliath saw these sailors crisp in their motions and much tidier in their appearance, though still burnt and aged by the life of the sea. A couple, though very young, appeared the same way as hardened veterans. A reminder of how rugged sea life could age a youth came unto him as he noted two youthful sailors, twins, securing the rigging. They noted him with icy eyes of men ready to attack and wrestle a mighty ship assailed by the waves. He assumed them all well trained. Soldiers of the regular army shadowed every sailor. Goliath inhaled the sea air and turned his gaze. Down to their ramming prow, this vessel was made for war, and woe be unto whatever crossed their paths.

Goliath watched the easy swell of the open sea as they departed the harbor. Never an admirer of extended sea travel, the giant frowned at the broadening waters.

As the ship heaved, Weldon walked past, gave him a slap on the hip, and said, "Not gonna puke on me, are ya?"

Goliath sneered at him, "Only you, Weldon, so if I

turn green, come running fast."

The vessel, near to a couple hundred feet long, was the finest the Philistine craftsman made. Their Phoenician forefathers knew their craft, Goliath thought appreciatively, even if some of those below toiled as slaves to make it all happen. In time, they'd earn freedom if they performed well. He stepped to the hatch and opened up to the lower rowing quarters of the craft.

When Goliath twisted his face, Weldon grinned, hands on his hips, saying, "I'll see ya sick yet, Champion. The scent of a clean galley not to your liking?"

After taking a breath of the sea air and grimacing again at the scent from below, Goliath said, "Vinegar and water cannot cleanse the odor of pitch and bilge water, Captain." Goliath shot him a dirty look. "Don't you have something else better to do than make me tired?"

Weldon shrugged, "It's gonna be a long journey. We can hit a hundred miles a day, good wind and all, so that will make the King of Kings happy. We will hope the rest behind us makes as good time. "

Goliath muttered, "You said it," as he looked down into the rowing sections. He saw the many different men, mostly anchored by stout folks of the Philistine stripe, many who weren't much for the battlefield, deaf or blind, but powerful of limb. They were moored with hardened slaves filling out their time on Earth. It was more of an existence they toiled at than a life, he mused.

He closed the hatch and walked the deck, letting the air blow his hair back. In time he sat down near the mast and tried to adjust to the feel of the waves on his mind.

An hour into the trip, Qorus staggered near to him and flopped on the deck. Vomit in his beard, the young man glanced at Goliath, then bowed his head.

"Don't be ashamed," Goliath said and turned his face toward the sea. "Not all men are meant to be sailors."

"You must think me less of a man, after today and yesterday."

Never regarding him, Goliath said, "What I think matters nothing, soldier. You must be strong to yourself first, not to some god, ideal or champion."

"The General..." Qorus gritted his teeth, looking back towards Philistia as if he could see Schlack.

Goliath coughed and wiped his mouth with the back of his hand. "Piss on him. Son, you will always find an ass at the top you don't want to deal with, so you better get used to that. Besides, he did nothing wrong."

Qorus blinked at him and jerked his face away.

The giant said, "You need not like it, but you chose to be a soldier, not a wayfaring warrior. There's no fault in that, but if you place yourself under authority, then you will suffer the rod of discipline."

"I know," the youth said with bitterness.

"You chafe at the yoke, like those slaves rowing underneath us?"

Qorus nodded with vigor.

Goliath spat and said dismissively, "You're young yet. In time, my words will gain meaning to you. You can accept or reject them, it matters not to me."

Qorus carried a blank look and took deep breaths.

"You hide your emotions? Good. Learn that well. Bide your time if it is revenge or freedom you desire."

"It's easy for you..."

"Because I'm so large? Do you think I was born this size? I was a youth once, long ago. I trained as a warrior at a young age, too young in fact, but I have a tough mother. At any rate, I was the size of a regular man at ten years old. I hated the taskmasters and others set over me. They were told not to pull punches and they did as they were instructed. I learned hard lessons, but a certain sergeant, a real bastard, resented the hell out of me in their midst, blood of the gods in me or no. The priests gave me great blessings because of my parentage. The sergeant was a hard case and didn't believe."

"He was unfair to you?"

"Oh hell yes." Goliath held up his left arm and pointed at a diagonal scar near his elbow. "I never got that in a modern fight. That sergeant, Elren, slit me in a training exercise. He wanted me dead, but could find no way to do it without losing his own head. He oft promised me on the battlefield he'd slay me on accident. Elren, what a sonofabitch."

"Did you kill him in battle?"

"No," Goliath admitted and took a cup of water from Abimelech. "I was really no match for his skill at that time, so I kept my mouth shut, learned to hide my emotions, and waited. Well, we prepared to fight the Israelites and we bivouacked in the Esdraelon valley. I volunteered for a duty as a guard for the nights before the conflict. Often, Hebrew commandos would sneak in and slit a few throats, spear a few men in their sleep, a mind game. As luck would have it, one of these little men crept in and I was on him. I twisted his head, broke his neck and all, then an idea occurred to me."

Eyes flickering with humor, Abimelech asked, "Telling the Sergeant Elren tale again?"

Goliath ignored him and said, "I knew which tent the duty soldiers slept in and made sure which sleeping man was Sergeant Elren. I took the Israelite's lance and ran the mouthy prick Elren through. I then made great noise as I crushed the already dead Israelite man outside the tent."

Qorus smiled. "You got away with it?"

Goliath nodded. "Yes, got some award for it, in fact, slaying the killer of a superior. No one seemed to ask how he'd gotten so far into the camp with me on duty."

"You tell this story openly?"

"My days of spankings are over."

Philistine

Abimelech laughed as Captain Balzer joined them.

"Do I dwell on death? Of course, but it's a part of life. If one thinks on death they must face the paces of life. I'll die in battle some day and that's the way of the warrior. I'm not sad for this, but there are mysteries in life I wish to solve before I perish. If I do not, that's all right, but I must strive to discover that which vexes me."

Swaying with the waves, Captain Balzer said, "I see and understand all that."

Goliath replied, "Maybe you do, perhaps not. Death will come to me, violently, for where else is the destiny of a Philistine warrior? What else can I do with my life? Grow flowers and write poems for those with dung between their ears and no balls in their linens? No, war is for me. War is life, war is good, hell, war is a god. In that way, the Hebrews have it right, for God is all around us. I cannot take a piss without a fool wanting to see me dead, to place my pecker on their mantle and say, *I did it*. Bah. They are gnats, crawling up an elephant's leg with rape on their mind."

Many laughed at this expression.

*****

It was noon the next day when they saw the ship. In a matter of a few hours, with the sun overhead, most spotted the Assyrian vessel simultaneously.

Acting the part of a confused man, Goliath went to the front of the ship and scratched his beard.

Captain Balzer frowned. "I'm a fighting man, not a sailor." He turned to Weldon and shrugged. "I say we fight."

"There are close to a hundred slaves chained and rowing that beast," Goliath said as he gestured at the vessel. "There are but a few dozen Assyrian soldiers. They carry two older men in white robes, dignitaries I would guess."

Weldon said, "Good eyes, big guy. We could spend hours trying to avoid them, but in time they will catch us."

Qorus argued hotly, "What will they care for us? If they are carrying Assyrian politicians, why take time out for us? Who'd want to mess with us? There's no way they can know of our mission or all the vessels behind us."

Goliath folded his massive arms and stated, "True enough."

Abimelech shrugged. "A couple dozen Assyrians? Surely, in the open field, we could best them, but fighting on the open sea is another matter and the other ships are far behind us."

Those on the ship exchanged looks and pondered his words.

Impatient, Goliath stated, "We Philistines encourage fighting and creative acts of bravery. These groups the Assyrians fight in are orderly and take to combat as a single creature. They are boring, but hard to best. This will be a close-quartered brawl, and we will have the element of shock. They cannot fight as a unit in this place on the sea."

Goliath watched the Assyrian vessel growing larger and saw by the sailors' reactions that they saw their craft.

Weldon wore a grim look. "They will figure us for what we are in no time, but our complacency will make them wonder. Return to stations and continue about your business. You men, sit down and cover up, play sick." He faced his crew and grinned. "This won't take long."

The soldiers donned their cloaks and the sailors

tried to make themselves scarce. Time ground on as they all grew silent and still. The slim Assyrian vessel soon drew near and many times they shouted greetings. In time, the foreign sailors started to joke and laugh as Weldon pleaded dumb, trying to convey a message that they were all sick.

Goliath could see the Assyrians ignoring any warning and ready to throw grappling lines. Weldon hailed them again with friendly words, but the Assyrians made only vile, workman-like entreats, as if they were unworthy of attention. Their soldiers drew their swords at first, but most stowed them again, the closer they came.

A ratty cloak covered Goliath and he huddled low in close proximity to the side closest to the invaders. He let his long hair hang out of the cloak, but tried to hide his legs in the hold of the ship. His lance lay beside him, and the sword rested between his legs. Goliath's eyes focused on the young hothead before him. Qorus sat quietly and still, knees apart. With the intent of boarding the Assyrians, the Philistine crew was determined to appear calm.

The grapnels took hold and the ships soon became as one. When the first Assyrian leapt across the small gulf and boarded them, Goliath stifled a laugh. Another Assyrian jumped across, this time a sailor in filthy, damp garb. Both men had their hands on their hips, and the gait of roosters.

Never having to rise far to be of equal size with this invader, Goliath shoved this first man into Qorus with a meaty left hand. Qorus raised his cleft-headed smith's hammer, struck the Assyrian's chin, and split the bone in half. As Qorus swung back and drove the hammer down into the face of the Assyrian soldier, Goliath rammed his right shoulder into the other sailor, sending him into the cold waters of the sea.

Goliath held up his javelin and sword, then stepped

to the edge of the boat. The Assyrians drew a collective breath and let it out in the form of curses.

A third Assyrian, a soldier stunned by the sudden attack and emergence of the Philistines in mass, gripped his short sword by the handle. He unsheathed it, but quickly received the point of Goliath's javelin in his belly. Skewering the soldier, Goliath pulled out the lance and swung the weapon about, striking the impaled soldier with the brass ball on the butt of the spear. As this soldier fell over the lip of the vessel, headfirst into the sea, Goliath leapt across the expanse and let the cloak fall.

"Hold, savages!" one of the Assyrians cried as he drew his sword and ran amongst the ranks of confused oarsmen. Panic set upon the alien vessel as they beheld the giant in full. They all then saw the Philistine soldiers leap between the oarsmen and across the boat. Abimelech roared as he arose, then he jumped, swearing and then laughing.

Goliath drew his gleaming sword, shifted it to his left hand, and lifted the javelin. While the Philistines slashed hard and killed fast, Goliath reared back, flinging the spear over the charging Assyrian's head. The soldier ducked, but did not turn. Goliath stepped forward, seeing the spear impale a man wearing the red sash of the Assyrian leaders. This weapon pinned him to the small cabin near the rear of the vessel; his face expressed a doomed desperation. The spear passed through this Assyrian's body at the pelvis and affixed the Assyrian leader to the wall. He screamed, but didn't die.

Swinging the sword with both hands, Goliath's blade cut cleanly through the sword of an Assyrian soldier. He kicked the startled Assyrian back with his left boot as chaos reigned around him.

They knew surprise as their ally; so in an instant

Philistine

Qorus, Balzer and others leapt across the boat and began shoving startled sailors overboard. Abimelech roared laughter at the ease with which several well-placed kicks could so quickly clear so many from the decks. He grabbed his sword, and with a simple arcing motion, halved a sailor's skull. He smiled as Cairn, Sadik and the twin sailors from Weldon's new crew fought with no fear.

Qorus fought like a madman, Goliath noted, cleaving the skulls of two men by way of a huge sword he wielded. There wasn't as much fight in the Assyrians as Goliath had expected, for there were more wails of terror than shouts of combat from these men. If anything, the foreign crew became panic-stricken, stunned that anyone could attack them and reduce their numbers so swiftly.

A group of their sailors ran to one end of the boat and picked up bows. They released arrows, striking many of the Assyrian rowing slaves by accident.

Another soldier came at Goliath as he crushed the face of a sailor with his fist clenched around his stout sword handle. The massive Philistine's sword arced downward, dividing the helmet of the soldier and parting the skull as well. Lowering the blade, Goliath attacked the next man in line, slicing upwards, flailing open the abdomen of the Assyrian. This man fell, screaming, clutching the loops of his intestines as they spilled out.

Goliath looked away from his task of gutting a sailor for a moment, seeing Sadik swing a short sword, stab, parry, and slash like a veteran trooper. The youth slipped briefly in a smear of blood on the boards, but rapidly corrected his stance. He was a Philistine like his father, grandfather, and the endless line of his kin. Goliath expected no less.

The captain of the ship swung across the expanse on a sail rigging line and joined the fray. Weldon's lance snapped as he impaled one of the sailors, but he only laughed. He drove the remainder of the broken shaft into the heart of another sailor.

One of the twin sailors threw him a short sword.

Weldon caught it and yelled, "Thanks, Darekbaal."

Abimelech then took two sailors in headlocks and cracked their necks. His blades came out again and blood painted the edge of the ship.

While the sounds of fighting filled his ears, Goliath shouted at the two professional Assyrian soldiers in front of him. They turned to face him.

The one on the right spoke in the tongue of the Hebrews, which the giant understood. "Do you expect us to surrender?"

Goliath removed the left arm of the soldier on his right and then came back to gash the Assyrian's throat. With the action of his blade cutting the air, Goliath shouted to the last man, "No, I expect you to die."

All over the long boat, the sun glinted off of waving steel. The effect was muted by the crimson painted on the blades, and carried a sound of shouts and cries of death. Sweat mingled with blood as the swords struck the wood and leather of shields. The din was terrific and terrible, yet almost musical to the giant Philistine as he dealt death over and over.

Out of the corner of his eye, Goliath noted an Assyrian soldier cross into Weldon's ship near to where the squat man Nopsik held the helm. The motions of the small sailor were swift as he brought up the end of an oar into the groin of this unsuspecting invader. While he was stunned, Nopsik swiped his right hand across the tall man's neck. When the sailor turned to face Goliath, his cleanly slit throat gushed crimson.

The shields of the Assyrians were long and unwieldy in the close quarters setting. In an open field with many trained warriors, they could interlock these shields to

Philistine

form a wall or fort. The large armor proved the wrong thing to wrestle as the young ones clashed with their small, round shields and thrust upward.

A sailor fell under Abimelech's sword, but a husky Assyrian had the Philistine in his sights. His short sword shattered the iron helmet the Philistine wore, ruining the blade in the process. This gritty Assyrian was a cagey veteran; he quickly took up a fallen soldier's lance, and he thrust it up at Abimelech's heart. Abimelech roared as the blade slid past his side. Qorus arrived to help and slashed at the side of Abimelech's attacker, piercing the man's thin plate armor. The Assyrian stumbled and Abimelech bounced off of him, dancing badly, seizing the Assyrian by the throat with his right hand. As the powerful fingers buried in the neck of the Assyrian, Qorus ran the attacker through with his sword.

After only a few minutes, the Assyrian soldiers were all dead or cast overboard. While the Philistine warriors discarded dismembered limbs into the ocean, a few of the men shouted in joy.

Holding the gore-splattered javelin in his right hand, Goliath sheathed his sword as the two older Assyrians emerged from the back of the boat. Both men were much smaller than Goliath. Each man's face was lined and his manner refined. Neither man seemed overly terrified at the appearance of the giant warrior. One wore the insignia of a military man.

Qorus spouted in a voice that cracked, "By Baal, that was a killing! Praise be unto the gods."

"Is it the end for us, then?" the older Captain with a balding pate asked, leaning on the cabin wall, near the first impact point of the spear.

The other older man, stroking his full head of white hair back until it soothed down, stated, "We are both officers, and will fetch a good price in ransom."

Abimelech swiped his sword and sent this man's

head flying and into the drink.

Goliath grinned wolfishly as this spouting blood bathed the other proper man. He looked over Qorus and Abimelech. They were raw and covered in guts. Goliath said to the old men, "What do I care for your money?"

The Captain stepped forward and said, "Listen sir, we are of no good to you dead."

Abimelech shouted loud and proud, "Do not listen to those words, sire."

Goliath lowered the javelin and let the point rest on the Adam's apple of the captain of the vessel. "Even the buzzards must eat. Besides, you're not my people, nor do I care for your civilized ways of Assyrian or Athenian whoredom." Then, Goliath slit the Captain's throat with the tip of his javelin.

Goliath stabbed the butt of his javelin into the deck and said loudly, "I'm bound for the Citadel of Zorn. The sailors show us the way. You will not enter this place, for I must go to see him alone. Once there, you can all go your way and keep with General Schlack's plan of the strike down the Nile. Now let us get across this toilet of a sea."

*****

From the crow's nest of the main mast, Nopsik sounded out his high-pitched flute. When all looked up, he pointed, they saw the Citadel of Zorn.

Eyes shielded from the sun, Qorus said, "Hell, what is it on the ground around it? What is that, some elaborate ivory lattice?"

Weldon lowered his eye viewer and said, "No. Bones." He stared from the prow back to Goliath. "Lots of bones."

CHAPTER FOURTEEN
ZORN

Baldassare's eyes never blinked as he stared toward the setting sun.

"Colonel?" a voice called out.

He turned from his perch in the hills, seeing his General approaching him, calling out so as not to startle him. "Yes sir?"

Samien's steps fell slow as he approached him. "I'm impressed by the drills run by the foreign members of the infantry."

"Thank you."

Samien studied him and then faced where his Colonel looked. "I'm surprised that our folk have so easily accepted their shadows."

Baldassare stood and saluted. "Forgive me, sir."

His head shaking off the Colonel's momentary slight, Samien said, "It's nothing. Still, I like your plans for retraining and integrating the others with our people."

Baldassare stared past the General as if he could see the army and said, "Many bristled at taking an outlander under their wing, but they have learned to fight with a third arm...or an extra shield of flesh, as it were."

"I'm pleased with the force, but am worried on another matter."

Baldassare stretched and asked, "And that is?"

"Are you unwell? It is hard enough to coordinate all of this and gain a new ideal if I cannot count on my right hand."

"You can," the Colonel's words ran icy. "I am with you unto death."

"I don't doubt that, but it's natural for men to have a weakened resolve in such matters."

"Sir, never once have I doubted..."

"You misunderstand me. You've grown up in the army and are passionate. Tearing you out of a comfort zone and asking you to stand with me is a life-changing thing. If you are ill to your gut because of it, I understand. You should feel how awful my stomach is at night."

Baldassare turned a little and said, "I can rely on my own hand, my strength and the metal that turns men to gore. However, the spirits that assail us, those make me unsure."

"A man can break, he is but flesh. Metal bends or busts, it is a fashioned creation. I understand your worry on this new goddess nonsense."

At his final word, Baldassare's eyes riveted to the General.

Samien said, "I'd sooner be done with them all."

"But can we kill the gods?"

The General snorted. "Some are powerful only because we have given them breath. Take away their air, their sacrifice, and they will be no more."

"We are deep in it with this new goddess, sir."

"I know and I'm not saying that her power isn't right. I'm saying I'd rather worry about someone I can see at all times."

"I know."

"You really should turn in early after we eat. Some

deep sleep will do you good."

They walked down the side of the hill and Baldassare said, "It's the sleep I cannot get away from. I need rest, but rest brings dreams, and not all are pleasant."

"Perhaps we need to send for the whores. That usually clears my head."

"I'm unsure, sir." The Colonel brightened. "Maybe that will be a remedy, I don't know."

"You have bad dreams?"

Baldassare thought of his dreams, of the stone realm of Malak, the mirror image of the Dagon priest Kmentosi and the female form at the feet of the goddess. He swallowed hard, thinking of the tree of beating hearts concealed in Malak's chamber...and what dwelt beyond that closet...the stone figures of fighting men, poised all around, silent, dead, waiting.

"Just falling a lot," he lied to Samien. "Falling and falling."

*****

Goliath could swim very well. Aside from the looks he usually received in public or from any stranger, the sight of him taking to water gave those familiar with him pause. Abimelech even joined in to jeer his master, causing the others to exchange uneasy glances.

Fully armed and yet, still backstroking, Goliath called out to Weldon, "I'll travel on down the way towards Egypt proper after I see this great Zorn. Pick me up at a proper port."

The Captain of the vessel waved at him and smiled. "Go get 'im, ya big ugly bastard."

The giant swam across the expanse of sea with ease. He soon came unto the shore that stretched out by the Citadel of Zorn. He thought the sands of the new continent of a coarser variety than that of the beaches at home. After he shook off the water and checked his weapons, Goliath breathed several times as his eyes took in the locale before him.

The Citadel of Zorn reminded Goliath of a sagging tent he beheld once near Irem. The design of four stone pillars of the rectangular structure aped the sagging tent in that all of the corners connected to a main spire, and their connecting structures swooped low not unlike untaut tarps. However, it wasn't a fabric extended across the pillars. He couldn't comprehend how stone or materials could be manipulated in such a way.

The beach terminated and a stone walkway spread out, cut into tiles that looked to travel all about the location. Beyond this tiled walkway lay grasses far too yellow for the time of the year. All around the base of the stone structure lay mounds of bones. Like an exhaled breath, a wave of air swept across the bones. The buzz of flies became loud, yet soon, dissipated into nothingness. The countless numbers of bones spread out on these lifeless grasses.

Goliath set a single foot onto the grass. A grim smirk played on his great face as the bones started to shake and then slam into each other. Dust shot out at odd angles as the bones connected, restructuring them like a child reassembling a doll sporting connection joints. Goliath never drew his weapons at this incredible sight. No matter how great his courage, it was impossible to fight back feelings of trepidation as a small army of dead men soon stood before him.

Hands out in front of him, Goliath performed mock applause. He dropped his arms to his sides and quipped, "I bet he sets a mean table for supper."

All of these dead ones appeared as men, but a majority of them were skeletons. A few still sported rotted flesh or dust clogging their innards, but by and large, they stood as thin relics of life. But someone and some power endowed them with new life, a new lease to stand up, to pick up their rusty weapons and block Goliath's way into the citadel.

A few moments passed and the skeletons shuffled away from the pathway the giant faced. A trail parted and showed Goliath the way to an open doorway. A deep breath in his lungs, Goliath started forward. He eyed the dead men on either side of him, but none made a move toward him. However, their empty sockets stayed focused on him. Every dead figure faced him at all times.

The closer he drew to the citadel he noted the archaic carvings on the walls and the architecture of the building. "Not Egyptian," he said and got no reaction from the army of the undead staring him down. He stopped, leaned down, stared into the face of one of them and said, "Zorn isn't from around here, is he?"

Even before the mouth of the doorway, Goliath beheld the long tunnel disappearing on up into the configuration. Once inside the edge of the tunnel, the walls of the passageway shifted and smeared, making him pause. Beyond the tunnel lay another open courtyard partially illuminated by sunlight.

Hands flexing, he ducked his head a little and stepped further into the oblong hallway. He looked at the walls and saw bizarre images, but they weren't carved. Each image depicted a perfect representation of what one might see with the naked eye. Goliath saw that the images denoted a vast battlefield and two hills where the warring factions resided. Even he jumped when the images moved and started to show Goliath a moving detail of an event.

"You're a bastard," Goliath said to Zorn in his absence. "Making me see other men's memories."

Goliath took a knee and didn't advance any farther.

He watched the images and listened to voices in his head, transferring voices from the battlefield. However, a lone, deep tone resounded in his head.

"Look, Philistine, at the remembrance from the battle of Dohlram."

The giant blinked, well aware Dohlram fell centuries before his birth and hundreds of miles from Gath.

Well-armed forces placed themselves between a walled city and a distant set of rolling hills. Those Goliath assumed hailed from Dohlram walked with a swagger and oozed confidence. Not only did their well-seasoned troops, numbering in the thousands, give them assurance, but the fact that several practitioners of the mystic arts stood on their side. These men in robes chanted and waved their arms, ready for a coming fight.

Truly, without the aide of such magical forces, the voice in his head informed Goliath, *not many would enlist to fight a savage northern horde led by the fabled Zorn himself.*

Voices of the military sprang to his ears and Goliath stood fascinated by this moving painting on the wall. "One wouldn't think there were enough barbarians left in the hills after the slaughter in the past months," one of the cavalry captains commented, making sure his horse's armaments were secure. "Yet, look, Zorn has raised thousands to fight us."

"What an arrogant ass," a woman warrior commented as she secured the chain mail armor about her shoulders. Her eyes drank into the crazed barbarian horde flowing over the hills toward Dohlram. "Look at that big bastard leading them at us. He doesn't even wear armor."

After a man in flowing red robes moved his head to avoid her long brown hair, the spell caster gave a nod at the sight. The hirsute mass of seething warriors that came in over the hills in support of the gigantic legend Zorn jogged without care. Their metal weapons and heavy bludgeons held light in their grip. The distant troops moved with one purpose—the destruction of Dohlram.

Goliath admired their pluck.

The wizard observed, "Their guts are strong when backed by his power, Rani. 'Tis a shame he came down off the mountain from his fabled tower to confront us at last."

The woman Goliath assumed was named Rani gritted her teeth as she looked at their experienced lines of archers and cavalry that supported the troops. "Zorn came down from his great high mountain to see us in our defiance of him. Curses all fall to him. So many wizards in one place drew his attention. Would that we had the secret of his great power, aye, Dian?"

With a gesture to his fellow men of magic, Dian cracked his knuckles and assured her, "When this day is done, we shall see if the stories are true regarding Zorn."

"Indeed," she promised, eyes full of flames.

"A legend alive on the lips is only so strong. We'll see if he can stand against spell and iron this day."

Standing just behind the rows of men wielding long bows, one of the men commanding the pikemen stated, "Even the barbarians wear some light armor, yet Zorn is naked as the day he first saw the light of day."

Hair in the wind, the laughing Zorn let everything about himself be seen as he bounced in the saddle of his huge stallion.

Goliath nodded at the sight of Zorn, a man near to as large as himself, but of a darker skin tone and more supple of profile.

With a grunt, Rani said, "He has great pride, but I will make a sheath for my dagger from that fool's member!"

Dian grinned at the morning sky and added, "Better make that a short sword, Rani. Ready yourselves!"

"They're dead," one of the foot soldiers of the infantry shouted, lowering his scope. "The barbarian horde is dead!"

Confusion spread on Rani's face, but Dian and the wizards only exchanged looks of terror. Rani barked at the wizards, "What is that fool talking about?"

Dian closed his eyes as did several of the mystics. One at a time they opened their eyes and wore looks seldom seen on the faces of wizards—fear. "The soldier speaks the truth. Look in a viewer for yourself," Dian offered Rani a scope, and she snatched it from his withering hand. "The men charging us are dead already."

"Damn them all," Rani murmured, stunned at what she saw marching toward her. "Damn him!"

"Too late," Dian replied dryly.

The seething mass of hairy humanity reeked of menace, intimidation, and when the wind shifted, rotting flesh. Carrying their swords, axes and bludgeons, these men were as determined and intimidating as any group of charging barbarians, with the added element that they didn't breathe. The massive Zorn, alone, took air in his lungs as he rode above them, unable to contain his hilarity over the situation...that he'd raised an army, literally, from the marauding results of the fighters at Dohlram. Their skin pallor shone grayish in the noon day's light, and grave worms were airborne as they jogged toward a second date with destiny. Ratty, dirt-matted hair dangled from scalps and beards full of caked, dried blood. Some wore armor, some partially dressed in rotten furs or wild dog-gnawed cloaks, but many ran naked, uncaring and uninhibited.

Ripping the viewer from her eye, Rani shouted, "This changes nothing. Fix arrows and prepare yourselves! We'll kill them a second time, filthy bastards."

When the orders were barked out, the archers raised their weapons. Several of the fighter's arms trembled. Many gritted their teeth, determined to destroy these warriors from the hills, yet again.

Philistine

On cue, the charging undead savages brought up their round shields, never slackening their pace. The closer they came, the forces congregated around Dian and Rani could hear a strange cadence. No, not a marching call, but a song...a filthy ditty being sung by mighty Zorn himself.

Sheathing her long sword, Rani grabbed up an archer's long bow and notched an arrow. She stepped to the front of the throng of warriors and pulled back the string.

"Guide me, Dian," she requested of the man with the neat goatee. "Let me fell that mighty idiot and this will be over soon."

Hands waving, an orange glow emitted from his palms. When Rani released the arrow, it arched higher than human strength could carry such a missile. The projectile glowed orange and fell straight at Zorn's heaving, hairy chest.

Raising an eyebrow, Zorn raised his massive beard and held out his arms as if to embrace his coming death.

Excitement grew in her bosom and Rani's breasts heaved under the chainmail. Goliath thought the war would be over in an instant, for truly, the zombie barbarians would never fight if their Lord and master fell...would they? Conscripted from the earth to assail the congregation of wizards, what reason would they have to exist save for their master Zorn?

The arrow fell to Zorn's chest, and with it, all of Rani's hopes of an instant end to the war. When the arrow blunted and fell away from the hairy skin of the giant barbarian, panic gripped the thousands before Dohlram. Rani cursed but Dian and his fellow mages were dumbstruck.

"It's true then," one of the wizards said to Dian, trying to hide his emaciated face in the folds of a dark flaxen cloak. "Zorn can repel any weapon formed of magic."

The generals of the armies ordered the archers to fire their first volleys anyway. Some hesitated, but they did so in an uneven volley, filling the late morning air with arrows. This cascade was repelled for the most part by the barbarians with their shields. It was clear by the injuries suffered that Zorn's power against weapons didn't extend to his minions. Soon, it was clear that arrows wouldn't stop an army of the undead, for they forged on, wearing the arrows like spiked armor.

"He knows we're here," Dian fumed as the spell casters started up on a plan to turn the tide. "Damn Zorn, he came anyway, though he knew it would be a bloodbath."

Drawing her blade again, Rani climbed back onto her horse and shouted at Dian, "Divine the means of his power! We will not be made fools by this lout!" Kicking her horse in the ribs, she joined the cavalry charge at the coming barbarian horde.

Goliath shook his head, but remained enthralled by this replay of a battle long ago.

Rani knew their cause weakened as soon as the cavalry charge joined in front of the archers. After one volley, many of the archers broke ranks and started to flee. The hulking Zorn waved off many arrows, giggling deep in his belly at the attempt to kill him. The soldiers on horseback, however, fought on with great vigor. Many had scores to settle with the vagabond barbarian force, one they thought subdued in weeks past. Since some of their brethren, if not themselves in person, probably were among raiders on nearby lands, this was a perfect chance for another bloodletting vengeance on the savages who often raided their villages.

Even though many fled on the side of Dohlram, the clash of arms and flesh was great. The roar of war cries and shouts of the dying filled the air. Several of the undead barbarians dropped when their heads were swiped off their shoulders. However, many fought on even though their limbs or hands were hacked off. When the din of battle was at its highest, screams of terror filled the ranks...for dinner had begun.

Dian and his fellow wizards cast glowing orbs of power at Zorn, who flicked them away like a child in a bath at bubbles. When a majority of the armed forces turned to flee, Dian commented, "One can hardly blame them for fleeing. They are being eaten alive out there."

With the army of rotten savages in pursuit, the infantry turned and took flight, flowing around the group of two dozen wizards on the elevated portion of the hill. While a few wizards continued to send swarms of locusts and giant scorpions at the horde, the undead seemed not to care how much material they lost from their bodies. Still they pressed on, many stopping to dine on the innards of the broken legs from stunted cavalry horses.

Slaying the undead at each swing of her sword, Rani showed her determination to reach Zorn. Destroying the jaw of one undead barbarian, shoving it back into his skull with a kick from her armored boot, she saw Zorn and his mount loom. She hesitated but a moment when the zombie horde seemed to back away from her and head toward the hillock. She charged ahead, thrusting her sword at the thigh of Zorn.

Quicker than lightning, his huge paw grabbed the double-edged blade. No blood oozed from his fingers as he smiled.

"So angry for a girl of moderate beauty," Zorn chided her with a wink, his baritone voice rolling across the field like thunder, rattling down into her chest.

The image froze and Goliath frowned, indignant that the story stopped.

After he waited a few moments, he sighed and got up, deciding to head out of the tunnel. The deep chuckles in his mind told him he'd soon find out the rest of the tale.

Once out in of the tunnel, a large inner courtyard extended in an eight-walled sector. Though a roof was far above, it was uneven, poised on several pillars, and it allowed the sun to flow into the area. All around the walls a series of stone shelves made homes for small jars. These stood out to Goliath in their vast numbers and the colorful individuality of each jar.

A massive rectangular slab sat on a rather low mounted dais. From out of the shadows, using this slab as a place to rest his hands, stood Zorn.

Though Zorn looked near to the same age in the moving images Goliath just saw, he was now clad in a kilt about his waist and a sleeveless tunic. His expression wasn't one of shock, fear or arrogance at the sight of the giant in his courtyard. His beard hugged close to his face, not a hair out of place, helping to frame in impossibly blue eyes.

"I've been expecting you," Zorn said and reached down below the slab. "Come on ahead, fine sir. There is everything to fear, here."

Goliath stepped closer. "This is where all the wizards go and never return? An impressive building, Zorn."

Still bent over, half behind the slab, Zorn gave a mild shrug and said, "They are still here." He then stood up, hands holding the severed heads of four men. "Most of them, anyway."

Zorn let the long hair of each head go and the heads came to rest on the slab. All balanced upright, Goliath then noted all of them blinked and moved. At first, the giant felt Zorn manipulated him, playing a magic trick on his eyes like the moving pictures in the tunnel. The idea that the wizards' heads remained animated, sans their bodies, was preposterous. Yet, there they were, weeping, cursing and in shock.

Not Eucimar, though. His head knew precisely what to say.

"Run!" Eucimar rasped, eyes flaring wide. "Go away from here before it is too late!"

Zorn made a tsk tsk sound and placed Eucimar face down on the slab, muffling his voice. "Oh, it's already too late, but you have naught to fear from me, or at least in the manner that they do."

Though he stood in a defensive posture, Goliath still never drew a weapon. "Why is that and what do you want of me?"

Zorn's arrogance oozed from his pores with every move, but his shrug and expression proved genuine. "You are not a wizard, Philistine. Consuming you, Goliath, would essentially not transport me any closer to spiritual oneness. It would likely jostle me nearer to constipation."

"Thanks."

Zorn stood straight behind the slab, picked up an animated head beside Eucimar, one of a man with black skin and ivory hoops in his ears. "No, only a dunce doesn't utilize the offerings laid out before him. You are a means to a conclusion, and I would have us both satisfied. It makes living so much simpler."

While Zorn turned the living head in his hands, and even tossed it in the air once like a boy playing ball, Goliath tried to quell his rage. "You've mutilated my friend and now expect me to do you a boon? Balls you have, Zorn."

"It isn't a question of testicular strength or manly valor," Zorn chided him as he turned the head about, blew on an area behind the head's right ear and then took a bite. Jaw grinding, Zorn said, "You go as you must. I have gained your awareness with Eucimar and the information I can bestow. There is little in life you yearn for. I can decipher a few questions, but you know the method of life, don't you, Philistine? Nothing is free."

Goliath replied, "What do you have for me? The message from the corpse said you'd tell me of my one true love. That's only myself, foolish wizard, but you're not so thick. You mean to tell me of Akisha and her dull schemes? Bah, I will find her soon. The messenger said you could tell me who and where my father is?"

"That's the superlative mystery in your existence but to know of him? You fear little in this world, but you do fear what the revelation from him will bring."

Goliath rolled his eyes. "You sound like you know me so well. Endow me then. What will my fear be?"

Zorn smirked and then said, "Fatalism."

The Philistine chuckled and said, "Piss in your pants, wizard. I've had a downcast attitude for years."

"You weren't impressed with the army outside?"

"A half-assed resurrection? From what the wall shows me, you've done that trick before. If you want to impress me, put all the flesh back on their bones and have them crap me a vegetable salad."

Zorn comically grumbled, "I'm a magician, not a miracle worker."

"What's in the jars?" Goliath asked and waved at the courtyard, careful not to turn his back to Zorn.

"What do you think? What do you feel is inside them?"

Before Goliath could answer, Eucimar tilted on his ear and exclaimed, "Whatever is left of us! He keeps the rest of us nearby as a part of his karmatic magick."

Zorn winked. "It's all about bones, young sir. I have a great desire for a certain set of bones, ones I hinted at earlier, if you were bright enough to comprehend my words."

"What bones? You talk out your rectum." Goliath walked in a small circle, eyed the urns in the shelves and said, "So you let me depart from here and get these bones for you. In exchange I get enlightenment over my father and the answer to my heart's woes?"

Zorn chewed on the scalp of the screaming wizard,

pulling away skin like cheese from a baked platter and nodded. "You've killed more for less. I'm not asking you to kill anyone."

"Why are these bones so important? Why not just say the bones you have in the jars are that of whoever you wish them to be? I figure a powerful man like yourself could create an imp or monster with bizarre enough bones for you."

Zorn spat out a tick on the ground and then said, "I have my reasons. Besides, the bones of orcs, ogres and trolls are not like humans', more like sharks, but I digress."

Eucimar spewed out, "His name isn't Zorn! He's older than us all and not of any order of Melchezidek!"

Goliath's mind stuck on what Zorn said about the bones of extinct creatures and their bone composition, but he had scant time to ponder it. When Zorn reached out for the head of Eucimar, Goliath snatched it up first and stepped away from the slab. Eucimar swung by his hair from Goliath's fingers.

"Tell me more," said the giant to the head.

Eucimar was happy to volunteer more. "So many buy into his order of Melchezidek line as we hunger after the original priest of Salem, one thought to be Shem, the son of Noah himself."

For the first time, Zorn's face looked irritated.

Goliath kept walking and then said, "But he is not Shem, is he?"

"There is a reason he wants you to steal the bones of the Prophet," Eucimar said smartly. "He knows Michael and Lucifer already have fought over these bones. They were hidden so as an adulterous generation of a people couldn't fall into idolatry over the body of their leader. Zorn seeks the body of the Prophet Moses himself to corrupt the Israelites and many more."

Half smiling, Goliath blinked. "Is that all?"

Eucimar stammered, "All? Can you comprehend the power and change in history if he succeeds?"

"What do I care if they go back to the Earth in their worship?" Goliath said blithely. "Fools."

Zorn grinned. "If you do not care, then you should do the work that benefits your own soul."

A serious look taking hold on his face, and his mind wondering about the caging lines for Amazarak made from something other than real bones, Goliath sighed. *Surely, he thought, the lady would know that about the bones and not let such an error destroy her power over the demon. Surely...*

"You might be just jerking me around."

"Ashdod," Zorn said, still chewing, but taking time to put the gnawed-at head down before he folded his arms across his chest.

"What about Ashdod?"

Zorn said, "That's where Akisha is. She isn't out being worshiped in the hills territories or preparing herself for you on a wedding night. The high priest of Dagon, Kmentosi, shields her at Ashdod."

Mouth open, but words failed him for a moment. "That rat bastard...he was within my grasp..."

Zorn wore a friendly expression. "Don't be so fast to seek her demise, Goliath. It's a novel time in the world. It's a time to get rid of the aged ways men have trod in and bring on innovative ideas, new gods, new ways."

Goliath gave a disgusted grunt. "That bitch cannot live forever."

Zorn nodded and said, "True, but she doesn't have to. Just a little while can change history, no? One life can do so much. Your son or daughter can change all of Philistia, maybe for the better." The mage's tone ran coy. "Perhaps it's time for the city kingdoms to end and for there to be one King and Queen of Philistia."

"You are mad. I don't love her."

"What does love have to do with marriage to a monarch?"

Goliath looked back at the way he came, his mind full of images and fire. "I don't...I..."

Eucimar whispered to him, "Let's get out of here. He chafes at your soul. Don't listen to him."

Zorn said gently, "Find her, Champion, kill this Yaggah that props her up and consider my words."

Goliath saw it all in his mind, then he saw a wheel rotating on the horizon. Eyes open wide, he asked, "What images assail me from beyond? What is the woman and the wheel I cannot get free from my mind?"

Now Zorn rolled his eyes. "All of your answers lie with your father and your mother. You ask questions to the wrong people. The answer of your father lies in the Domain of Moloch."

Goliath thought of the things he avoided confronting his mother with and decided it was too late in the day to spare her any longer.

Zorn reached down low and gripped the sides of the stone slab. His shoulders jerked fast and when his hands came away from the rock surface, each hand held a slender sword.

The appearance of the weapons didn't make Goliath jump, but they did make him smile. "Typical of one such as you, Zorn. Why try to kill me now, once you know I will do your bidding to satisfy my own selfish wants?"

Zorn stepped out from behind the slab and eyed the blades in his hands. "If I wanted to kill you, you'd be dead already."

"So you think." Goliath backed up and set Eucimar's head down not far from the tunnel opening. "This won't take long."

Eucimar screamed, "He'll kill you! Run!"

Goliath shook his head. "He needs me alive."

As the giant turned away and drew out his great

sword, Eucimar howled, "Do you think you are the only one who can invade Nebo for the bones of Moses? He's fickle as flame!"

After he swung the heavy blade to the right, Goliath was met head on by Zorn's flashing blades. He swiftly slashed around the other way. Again, Zorn blocked him smartly.

"Nimble for an old cuss." Goliath chuckled, boots stabbing at the floor.

Zorn sized him up and they circled each other. "That armor is well-fashioned, but you have made a grave error." He made a bold thrust, aiming for Goliath's heart. The deathblow never arrived as Goliath slid to the left with the elegance of a dancer. However, he had no chance to drop his sword on the back of his attacker. This is what the Zorn assumed Goliath would do, for the death strike was a ruse. With great force, Zorn struck Goliath's jaw with his left elbow as he let the weight of the great sword drop against the scaled armor. Briefly, he hugged Goliath close. This move allowed Goliath to avoid the caress of the two swords. Zorn reached down fast to bring up a sword into Goliath's armpit. If he found a crease in the armor, Goliath's arm would be off.

Goliath saw the man face to face in the embrace and immediately slammed his head into the Zorn's face as he drew away. A wet pop echoed and Zorn's nose burst like rotten fruit. The sharp jolt of pain and spray of blood was enough to confound his plans against the Philistine. It also gave Goliath a moment to step away from him and attack anew.

The Philistine wasted no time. He slashed on either side of Zorn, but the wizard proved a dexterous fighter and warded off the attacks. When he staggered by the slab, two of the animated heads screamed their cheers for Goliath. Zorn gave one of them a disagreeable elbow, casting it rolling free, and squared up again against the giant.

Zorn stepped forward and stomped down, smashing on Goliath's right foot. When the giant staggered away from him, Zorn snapped his swords together at the handles and kicked at Goliath's shin. Stumbling badly, the giant regained his footing and saw Zorn standing with the joined swords. The wizard used moves like a man fighting with a quarterstaff. In a frenzy, Goliath swung his great sword in an overhand arc, connecting with the center of the false staff weapon. Too late, he read the eyes of Zorn, for this was exactly what the old one desired of him.

The handles of the blades disengaged their connection, but it was not via the blow of the broadsword. Zorn twisted in his wrists, taking the terrific impact of the sword in the middle of his chest. The two blades snapped up, connecting on either side of Goliath's chin. The momentum of the heavy strike carried both men down hard. It was Zorn who rolled on top and swung a roundhouse blow, smashing the two blades flat into the forehead of the giant.

Zorn was up and over him, grinning down, blood pouring from his chest. "I have blooded the mighty Goliath." He leaned down close to the bleeding face of the Philistine. "Isn't that wonderful? What do you say to that?"

Goliath's hands shot up and clutched the testicles of the wizard. Face a mask of blood that oozed from his forehead, Goliath hissed loudly, "I say that you won't be needing these." When Goliath yanked back, Zorn pitched forward, his voice howling and coughing, then falling to writhe on the grass of the courtyard.

"Run!" Eucimar shouted and pleaded.

Goliath grabbed up his sword and Eucimar's head before heading to the tunnel entrance.

"Oh, Philistine?" came an unconcerned voice from

the slab.

Goliath looked back and saw Zorn, sitting on the slab, his crotch bloody and ruined. However, the huge wizard munched on one of the final talking heads.

"Good show. And, consider my offer?"

Goliath didn't have much to say until he reached the outer courtyard. He stowed Eucimar's head in his side pouch and took out his javelin. He looked beyond the army of the undead and saw no ships in the sea.

The dead men started to move forward.

Goliath rushed headlong into the foes, burying his sword and swinging his javelin. He then swept the blade wildly to the left and to the right. Limbs were lopped as if disappearing in the metal flash. Goliath stabbed forward, sending bones flying, never once drawing blood.

The giant laughed as he swung his weapons, ruining the army of the undead, none strong enough to stand against him.

Pain struck the back of his head. A blunt object shook Goliath and made him stop in his frenzy. He staggered on, out of the area where the undead dwelt. He tried to make it to the beach, but his head was aching so. Down to his knees, he saw a line of men all dressed in military garb, but alive.

On his back trying to catch up with the spinning sky, Goliath saw a lone figure bisect his universe. Goliath swore and started to lose his grip on the conscious world just as the man spoke. He didn't speak Goliath's native tongue, but the Philistine understood him.

"I am General Sobek and you are the prisoner of Pharaoh Psusennes I, ruler of Egypt."

CHAPTER FIFTEEN
PRISONER

Akisha's head felt heavy once she swallowed Vega's concoction, so she retired immediately, fearful she'd fall after drinking the mixture in the wine.

At first, her dreams ran pleasant, for she ran as a girl again across the long grain fields of Philistia. She even recognized the simple stone altars outside the granaries of Timnah, just south east of Ekron, where she played long ago. This is where she first heard religious debates, as the old men of the gods resisted putting the altars indoors, insisting they be out in the air, closer to the gods.

Those were simple days, she recalled and that innocent happiness curled up inside of her mind, but soon, she felt her extremities turn icy. The perception no longer ran in the fields, but her self flew high above the lands. As if she jumped into a pool, Akisha fell to the ground and splashed into the stone columned realm of Malak.

She saw a sturdy man filing at various portions of Malak's inner dwelling place. When the robed figure of Malak sauntered past this carver, the man never made a big deal about her passing near. He worked on even as the goddess spoke to him. He wiped sweat from his brow and appeared proud in his countenance at his fine work. Malak's face, ever shrouded by her hood, seemed to radiate to the point Akisha make out her somber features. The goddess smiled.

Suddenly, Malak turned and walked from the worker. She passed by a figure robed in white linens and stepped onto the beam of her raised dais. The images all reverted to a black hue, only Malak appearing in the outline of wispy light. Akisha noted the figures in white now took on conical forms of yellow...but she had little time to focus on this sight as another shape appeared with the goddess. Terror struck Akisha as she thought it was the champion of the Philistines. In a moment, she beheld this man as another, though, lacking a shaggy beard and long hair, but a trim appearance, yet large and manly.

Malak said, "You have come unto me here in my place of power?"

The figure chuckled. "It is not so impossible, Lady Malak." A huge hand waved at the point Akisha observed them from. "Even those who dream can penetrate your domain."

Malak never noted Akisha but lashed out at the man, saying, "Only those I have promised to, and laid the pathway in their minds, can journey here, Zorn."

Akisha wanted to wake at the name of Zorn. Even she knew of the fatal tales concerning the all-powerful mage.

"There is naught to fear from me, dear lady. It was you who contacted me, long ago, remember?"

Anger bubbled from Malak as she sneered, "And it was you who promised me the Philistine dead and my desires foolish, no? He lives. I can see that from afar."

Zorn folded his arms, dripping with confidence. "I will slay him, in my own time."

"What do you play at?"

Philistine

"My own rules, my dear. I play for myself, not just your benefit. He will do my will, that which I require for my own means. When he returns to Egypt with his boon, I shall consume him unto myself, Malak. You shall see."

"Big promises, greedy man," she spat. "His ego rivals yours. How can you trust that he will do any windfall you ask?"

Zorn dropped his arms and shrugged. "I have no way to trust him in full, but I like his chances at fulfilling my will more than a host of others. If he decides not to follow me, I have laid my curse on his flesh. He cannot escape ruin now. I will have my prize or he shall die. At any case, it isn't the end of the universe."

Malak started to speak, but Zorn gave a dismissive wave and vanished from her wheel. The goddess spun around once, and screeched in anger, causing the darkness to fade and the ring of vestal virgins to kneel, hiding their heads.

The man holding a metal file stood, stretched and imparted a bored expression. "Bad news, ma'am?"

Malak took several breaths and then said lightly, "Not the best, Ahkuh-Rhan. Your work pleases me, though."

"Thanks," he replied and rubbed his lower back, oblivious to what just happened in the ether realm.

Akisha blinked and sat up in her bed, gasping for air.

*****

The days churned on, but Goliath remained certain less than a week had passed since his imprisonment by the Egyptians. Though no sunlight came unto his eyes, his system worked in regular intervals, so he understood the passing of days. However, in time, due to lack of good food, even this time keeping method slackened. Oh, they fed him. The slave girl often waved and smiled at him, but he would soon need more or his body would weaken.

Goliath also felt positive the cell he dwelt in wasn't meant to house feral men of battle but grain. He theorized the stone bin probably attached to a temple, as went the Egyptian tradition of hording food for their gods. Once more, he stretched out his arms again over his head. A smile danced on his face for a moment as he still found himself too short to reach the top. He looked down at the vents, knowing he could never pass through such a tiny spot. At times, he heard a scraping sound echoing under the stone floor. The first time he heard this noise he believed it a mechanism of some sort, perhaps for grinding the grain. However, in the night, he heard a screech and comprehended whatever made the sound probably breathed.

He didn't recall much about traveling to this place. The magic of Zorn and the shots he took made sure his memory remained a haze. He touched his wounded forehead and cursed the wizard. His foggy memory did recall being pulled on a cart and his feet dragging behind. The name *Tanis* kept coming up in his mind and Goliath figured that's where he resided. He'd heard of such a place with its great temple to three gods, and how it became Egypt's capital when the nation roughly divided. The citizenry of Tanis noticed the captive, his bubbling memory recalled. They cheered, a few spit, or heaped insults, but mostly he was a curiosity on his entrance. Many people lined the storefronts of various shops and waved.

Goliath recalled a long line of females standing with protectors. The women wore mantles of exotic bird feathers; some had their hair-died saffron and they wore little. He smelt them and declared them whores in his mind. Their guards seemed to safeguard their product well. These were not common trollops or temple servants. These creatures seemed of a different ilk.

The outer streets of Tanis smelt of stale wine, cooked food, and excrement. The breezes between the buildings slapped Goliath's bearded face and seemed to carry a scented taint not all unpleasing. Though already a mass of bobbing heads, more carts and people jammed the streets. As they trudged on with his form in the wagon, Goliath recalled voices talking, laughing, and coughing.

A few things burned in his mind. One, how long did they think they could weaken him here and two, why hadn't Abimelech made the Pharaoh sorry for his actions yet?

Goliath waved at a face that peered down at him. The countenance, surely that of a slave garnering a peek, smiled.

When an aged woman lowered down a decanter of water to him, he called out, "I wonder if you all are putting spirits in my drinks and soup? I'm thinking about careless things entirely too much."

She had nothing to say.

Goliath sat; eyes closed, and let his mind wander. He thought about Ashdod and the temples there. Yes, petty priests jerking the kings of the five cities around certainly brought hard times to the Sea Peoples. It had turned into a mess for their folk, and he was a sorry champion to let such things go on.

"Damn Zorn," Goliath cursed and then used greater words to cuss the sorcerer. "You're making me consider your words. That's evil." After he cleared his throat, Goliath said in a loud voice, "Makes you wonder how afraid I am of you little pricks. I'm contemplating overthrowing the value system of my own land while a prisoner of you all. Does that tell you assheads anything?"

Around the midsection of the stone bin, he could hear movement. He understood that someone could hear him. Unconcerned for the Egyptians for the moment, Goliath let his imagination play in his mind. He could see Akisha, great with child, being fawned over by the priests of varied religions. Oh, wormy Yaggah was there, the skinny assfaced man, ready to suckle at the teat of her grace.

"I won't be bested by a pimp," Goliath muttered, trying to bury the grin of Yaggah in his mind. He failed.

He thought long on the words of Zorn. The face of his own mother, gilded in her temple at Gath, came into his mind often. As much as he didn't want to face it, she held the answers. Eyes closed, he could smell the innards of the dreaded temple of Moloch. Answers...

One night (he assumed) when he slept, the images of the wheel and the laughing women came unto him. Goliath forced it all out as he felt it came near to his soul and close to resolution. Awake, he laughed.

He looked high above himself at the old men who threw down thin breads to him.

"Courteous bastards, you are," Goliath named them. He looked up at the crooked-nosed old man who threw down food. The servant...his scent and face...so familiar.

Stone ground on stone and a block of the bin moved out, breaking up the perfect symmetry of the blocks. Goliath never moved as he faced straight into the eyes of an elderly man, looking him over. Behind this clean-faced man torches danced and others peeped. The watcher waved these others away and got comfortable. Obviously, he sat to look in on the giant.

"I never believed the legend at first," the aged one said, his voice fatigued, yet one used to speaking and commanding respect. "I've heard many amazing yarns in my life, don't you know? The tales of the gods and the incredible deeds of their offspring on Earth are just that, stories, better suited for children ravenous for adventure or priests wanting to steal more gold for their personal use." The speaker adjusted himself a little and then said, "I've seen big men, fighters and thugs, even eight-foot-tall black warriors from far south of here. They are remarkable. You are indeed the one so many tales speak of, aren't you?"

Goliath put his twelve fingers out as he spread his arms. "My Egyptian is terrible. I am the one."

"Is your Greek better? They taught me many tongues when I was a youth."

Goliath switched to Greek. "It will do. So, now that you have seen me, what shall we talk about?"

The man wore a mild smile. "I am sorry you did not tour Tanis properly. It is a superior city, growing all the time."

"The finer women have hungry eyes, just like the whores in our temples back home."

"You are used to your self, Champion of the Sea Peoples, as I am used to the grandeur of Egypt. I wouldn't expect you to be easily impressed. However, I am surprised to see you taken so effortlessly."

"It wasn't my finest hour when that Sobek fellow arrived. Your name?"

"Hor-Pasebakhaenniut, but that is rather much for our simple conversation."

"I see. Did your troops see us sail near the shore by Zorn's dwelling? They seemed surprised to see me staggering out there. How many survivors ever come out of the Citadel of Zorn?"

At the name of the wizard, the old one's eyes opened wide. "None. Only his dead minions leave or dance as bones. I salute you for surviving his magicks and living to bring out that accursed monstrosity."

"Eucimar? Where is he?"

"The priests contemplate him, but he lives, such as his life is."

Goliath nodded thinking on the long name given to the man. "You're Pharaoh Psusennes I, correct?"

"I've heard you are wise as well as a great warrior. I am not disappointed."

"Well, I'm the one in the grain bin, King. Besides, the refined fingernails and rings of gold and lapis lazuli betray you."

"I am the third King of the twenty-first dynasty of Egypt. It is seldom I get to speak with a personage of history like you."

Goliath shook his head from side to side, trying to get his mind around the way the Pharaoh spoke. "Aren't Pharaohs living gods and makers of their own history? I'm surprised we can breathe the same air today."

Psusennes snorted and then replied in a brusque voice, "The victor of a war and the man in charge at the moment defines the past, Champion. Even those that fashion themselves as gods must expire in time."

Goliath rubbed his neck and said, "I'm glad for your practicality. What can I do for you, Pharaoh? Many of our folks have been employed by you or the priests that control the lower kingdom, so I assumed there was a general peace between us all. Why am I a prisoner?"

"I'm not sure you can *do* anything for anyone, young man. Matters of politics, well, that is another subject."

"Surely, you're here not just out of fascination but to ask a favor?"

Psusennes replied, "Our existence is fairly steady now, Champion. I have no great political fight on my hands, nor do I have a border problem easily solved by a giant in my employ."

"I see."

Philistine

"We are nearly complete in building the great temple here to Amun, Khonsu, and Mut. Aside from the aches in my joints and agony in my teeth, life is fine."

"You're blessed then."

"I admit, you fascinate the generals, but they'd sooner have you dead than free of this place. A mercenary army is one thing. A giant with good killing instincts, well, that is different."

Goliath thought of the archer garrison killed by Abimelech and wondered why the King never brought it up. "I see. What do the priests say?"

Psusennes glanced to his left as if the answer were scribed there. "Oh, they want you dead. They feel you are a curse from the terrible Zorn. Why else would you be allowed out alive?"

Hand up to his forehead, Goliath touched the scabbed over wound there. "Zorn showed me a great victory he once attained, centuries ago over many fighting men and dozens of wizards. He ate them all of course, and even took their toughest women warrior prisoner."

"Why do you share this with me?"

"Zorn never showed me what happened after he captured the women fighter, but in my dreams here, she has visited me and told me the truth."

Psusennes' brows arose as he said, "This must have some importance for me, no?"

Goliath stated, "Zorn offered her the flesh of her own friend, a wizard called Dian, still alive yet a torso, a bit bigger than my friend, Eucimar. He offered her to eat Dian's flesh and live forever like him. I suppose that is how he lives so long, on the bodies of wizards."

"Fascinating. Did she?"

"No. She drove a dagger into her own heart rather than do it. I have wondered if it mattered, for I think Zorn doesn't really get his age and power just from the act of cannibalism. He has years of magick to back him up and change himself. No, I'd bet it was a test. The result was the same no matter what."

"I don't understand you."

Goliath said, "Rani, the woman fighter, killed herself in my vision the other day. Zorn ate her. I truly think if she ate some of Dian, she'd have only proved Zorn's theory on the weakness of humanity and he'd have eaten her anyway."

The Pharaoh frowned. "You caution me in what way with this?"

Goliath cracked his knuckles and someone near the Pharaoh jumped. "Let me go. Nothing is worth what will come if you don't let me walk free."

"I'd like to know what you were doing there with Zorn, young man."

"Oh?"

The Pharaoh nodded with vigor. "I'm a practical man and my advisors have asked the prudent question. Even if Zorn summoned you, I would guess you never walked all that way from Canaan."

"Your point?"

"Philistines never travel unaccompanied. You are seldom hired as vagabond mercenaries unaccompanied. You fight much better amongst your own kindred. You wouldn't be here all alone."

"Yes? You have eyes, spies and priests to divine the future, Pharaoh. What do you need me for?"

"Perhaps nothing," Psusennes said with frankness. "Minor squabbles and rumblings are not worth full-scale wars. It has been decades since any of your kindred dared to raid down the Nile or attack us."

"Fear is a strange thing," Goliath shrugged, his voice even. "You have captured me, but fear the outcome if you slay me."

"I fear for the outcome if you never were here. This

way, you have tipped us off that something ghastly will come."

As the old man started to withdraw, Goliath called out, "Psusennes? I give you a chance, not as good as the one I gave earlier."

The old man smiled and shook his head, but returned to the slot. "You do amuse me, giant."

Goliath opened his waist kilt and let his manhood swing free.

Psusennes folded his arms and said, "All right, you greatly amuse me."

Never smiling, Goliath said, "Can you imagine what I can do to a woman?"

"I'd rather not."

Goliath dropped the tone of his voice. "Let me go now and I'll only slay your wife, not your daughters."

Anger lit in the Pharaoh's eyes and he twisted away from the stone bin.

Goliath called out, "Think on it, Psusennes. You can get a new woman anywhere in the world. Daughters and sons, well, they are of your own flesh. They are indeed harder to replace."

Psusennes started to walk away, and then Goliath's deep laughter filtered out the chamber. The stone was replaced in the side of the bin, but the Philistine's laughter echoed out of the top and all throughout the temple to the three gods.

*****

Weldon Yog climbed down from the crow's nest, dropped to the deck of the ship, slipped and nearly fell, but soon gained a strong foothold. He cussed and looked across the churning sea.

Abimelech saw the same thing the Captain beheld: nothing much. The gray waves of the sea rose like sharp mountain peaks, tall and imposing. Boiling clouds above were the same color as the cold, leaden sea. The sun had not shone its blazing white-orange face on the longship.

"Are we ready?" the shield bearer asked Weldon, eyes still on the water, but his hands turning to fists.

The Captain peered to his left and then his right. Though no land was evident, the sea certainly wasn't empty. "Yeah, pretty much. There will be plenty of killing had soon enough, so these boys and their randy pricks can be happy again."

Abimelech nodded and turned away. He took a knee and bowed his head.

Weldon turned toward him and asked, "Consulting your god? Who do you favor this week?"

"Your mother. She's always reliable," said Abimelech causing a great guffaw to escape from Cairn and Qorus.

Weldon grinned at the jab. They all moved in unison with the heavy waves and Abimelech made an obscene gesture to his brethren.

"Are ya that amazed he got a joke in? The big bastard is likely to get a good one in sooner or later." The Captain took a swig from a flask and then said, "From your name, I took you as a follower of Moloch, but by the way your master speaks of that god, that's kind of unlikely."

"Correct. My parents were followers of Moloch. The very tenants of that faith deem the congregation will never grow very large." He let a short grunt escape from him as if that was his ruling on that ideal. "No, I follow other gods and them only sparingly. I turn to pray and gain focus on what's to come."

Weldon said, "Good for you. I think about screwing, that gets me ready to fight."

"What do you think of while screwing?"

Yog winked. "Well, screwing, of course. Are ya weird or what?"

The odor of the men around him mingled with the scent of the sea. Near the boards, Abimelech could sense vinegar and pitch in the air. "If I die in battle, I shall meet my god. He must have a greater cause for me in mind."

Balzer stepped closer to them, shifting his weight from foot to foot as he couldn't hide his antsy nature. Weldon eyed him and grinned, yet made no disparaging remark beyond mimicking the man with no sea legs.

Sadik gestured at the waters. He filled his lungs with air, and then coughed badly. Weldon slapped him on the back.

"Careful on all that pure air, friend. You may disturb our brothers out on the waves."

Sadik nodded and said, "I'm thinkin' on what you said to the giant, a while back, you know?"

"And that was?"

"For him to pull up anchor and sail away to better waters."

"Ya listen too close on private words, kid," Weldon said. "And you're thinking we should do likewise before all of this starts?"

Sadik shrugged.

Weldon slapped him on the back again, but much harder this time. "Not a bad idea, but the coming day will be as satisfying as a block of whorehouses after payday. This day is going to be so great the Egyptians will never carve a goddamn line on their stone penis memorials about it."

Steven Shrewsbury

*****

Four guards walked with Psusennes as he crossed the temple courtyard. This spot sat vacant of many statues and obelisks, but still cut an impressive swathe in the landscape. He stopped and gazed about, then asked, "The other images will be moved here soon?"

Dropping to a full one-legged kneel, the man nearest the King nodded. "All is proceeding, Lord."

He nodded and patted the shoulder of his guard. "There is no rush. I'm getting to be older and thus, am inquisitive less often." He laughed to himself, thinking that a creative way of saying he was growing forgetful.

As they traveled into the vast inner temple, a trio of priests started across the shiny floor. Two knelt while the man in the middle bowed and spoke to the Pharaoh.

"Lord Psusennes, stars appearing to the city, I greet you! Now, I must ask you that the outsider be slain."

His right eyebrow raised, the Pharaoh said, "From the lack of venom in your words, Menkheperre, I take it this is not a passionate request?"

Menkheperre's bald head glowed as the burning censers reflected light from him. "Since his arrival, all of the priesthood here and at Thebes have been stricken with terrible visions and appalling nightmares. They are not of the behemoth in the grain bin, but some off-breed of his gods."

Psusennes leaned his elbow on a guard and then stood straight with folded his arms. "His gods are not our gods."

Nostrils flaring as if he smelled excrement, Menkheperre said, "Their gods are swill, my King. The

346

sooner he is dead and I am back at Thebes the better. They are a petty lot, reaching out to bring grime unto our wholesome gods. I would be done with them and their maddening visions"

The King gave an unconcerned shrug. "It is a simple matter. Still, I worry less on dreams and more on the might of a Philistine force lurking nearby."

Menkheperre admitted, "We have not been able to divine the whereabouts of any such force; however, the seas are rather vacant of merchant vessels."

"That is unusual for this time of year. You and your priests, what do you see in your vapid nightmares?" Once the Pharaoh spoke, the priests all waved him to walk closer to the altars and images of the gods.

The closer to the image of Amun they came, the louder the entreaties of a dry voice were to their ears. The high priest said, "With that head still talking over there, it is not a wonder some of the brothers are given to fearful nights."

"But you are made of sterner stuff, not afraid of a Philistine head, even if propped up by Zorn's power?"

They stopped and looked at the animated head on the altar. The thing chanted before Amun but not to Amun.

"It is called Eucimar," Menkheperre told his king. "He told me that among many curses and wishes of defilement to my wives."

The Pharaoh noted the head, folded his hands and said to the high priest, "What are your visions of?"

"I see pure women, virgins all set dancing about an evil temple, all focused and trying to drive me mad. They want the Philistine dead, too, yet I smell these women are of his own ilk."

"Terrible if one's own kin has no use for you. Why is the temple evil?"

"I know encroaching darkness when I see it. This

force uses the purity of vestal virgins as a focal point, but it practically reeks of malevolence."

Psusennes wrung his hands once, but let them go flat on his waist.

Menkheperre insisted, "Whatever the case, I think he should go, oddity or not. We can boil the flesh from him and make an exhibit of his bones or mummify him for display if you so choose."

"Perhaps the crocodiles are best for his dead flesh," Psusennes sighed, running his right hand over his bare scalp. "It is unfortunate this being has visited our doorstep." He paused, laughed a little and then shared, "He threatened my family if I didn't release him. Can you imagine that?"

Menkheperre faced his god and said, "Goliath is a savage and best left forgotten. The time for his barbaric ways is passing away. The mistakes of the gods and goddesses are few. Better he be forgotten than used to inspire others."

*****

As the servants let down food to Goliath on a tray, the giant said, "Life is so cheap to you all, isn't it?"

This time, the server was a younger woman and looked at the food like it was dreadful. Her eyes glared and Goliath read her thoughts.

In a few moments, one of the guards looked down at Goliath and cursed. "You didn't eat?"

"Not hungry, not for poisonous food, anyway," Goliath confessed, a wry look on his face. "You can throw me down that girl, though. I'm quite horny."

The guard shrugged. "So much for mercy." His arm shifted and suddenly, the bin started to flood with grain.

Philistine

Goliath floundered as the grain flowed like water over his feet. More vents opened higher above and he started to tread as more of the powdery seed fell all over the giant.

The server girl looked down in horror as Goliath started to sink in the grain. He stomped his feet, rising some but not so much. The guard left and she kept looking at Goliath.

"Help me, girl," Goliath called out, his huge hand up, floundering.

"I cannot lift you out."

"Give me your hand. You can help me."

She shook her head, confused, but reached down. Their hands were far apart. The guard behind her kicked her in the rump and other men laughed as she fell, screaming, atop Goliath's shoulders.

He held her in the falling grain, cradling her as if she were a child. She wept and said, "See? I cannot help you. Now we will both die."

Goliath stroked her cheek, wiped away her tears and kissed her forehead. "No, only one of us will."

When the block Psusennes used earlier sprang out of the side of the bin, causing a great vent of grain to spew out, the guards swore and went to see what caused the problem. They found something wedged in the open way. It was the serving girl's head.

From atop the bin, Goliath climbed out. "She served me well." The giant laughed as he swung his huge legs free. He dropped atop two of the guards, breaking their backs. "You gave me enough risen ground to leap up, thank you much." From out of their hands he plucked their outstretched swords. When he stepped off the crushed guards, Goliath looked at the blades he pinched between his index finger and thumb. These were short swords anyways and looked even smaller in his grip. With a casual flip, the blades twirled up until he held the handle of each weapon.

It only took a few steps before he encountered more guards and slaves. Though awkward in his motions, Goliath freed the heads of two of the guards with the tiny blades. The servants, doused in jets of blood, gaped at the giant as he strode past them, unconcerned with them.

"Goliath," a voice cried out in his native tongue from amongst the hiding servants. "This way!"

When the small man in slave robes stepped out, Goliath gave him a quizzical look. "Ba'al Zebul cried! Nopsik! How did your little ass get in here?"

The small sailor ran up next to Goliath and said, "I'm part Egyptian. What is one more slave to them? Let's go!"

When Goliath and Nopsik stepped out into a larger alcove, several robed priests saw him and scattered. However one never ran. A hulking man in a priest's garment, Goliath guessed him a warrior at one time adopted into the priesthood. Though being stalked by a giant, the big priest bestowed on them no sense that he was afraid. Powerful and brash, he stood firm before the Philistine. His courage made him race to an altar and seize up a metallic ankh.

"Good luck, you jackass," Goliath roared in challenge to him.

With the rough gait of a warrior heading into the lines of combat, the priest who lay down his sword for peace took up the ankh for war. Rushing ahead fast, the man in the robe dodged the swinging blades of the Philistine. He ducked low and swung the metal ankh up like an ax. Goliath criss-crossed the tiny blades down and blocked the move. The giant then lowered his head fast and knocked heads with the priest. Though the priest hit the floor, Goliath reared back, pain running through his forehead. He dropped one of the blades, hand across his forehead, stunned at the pain from the wound of Zorn.

Nopsik stood beside his champion, grinning in triumph.

Goliath stood over the priest, sword pointed downward and said, "This will hurt quite a bit."

The priest reached out, touched the altar and the floor beneath the giant & sailor gave way. Both men plummeted down and vanished from the temple.

*****

Outside the great temple, the Pharaoh and his high priest walked, but their tranquil talk soon ended. A messenger wearing the togs of the Egyptian's chariot class thundered up to them on horseback, dismounted, gave a quick kneel and bow before blurting out, "General Sobek sends word, Lord and master, that an attack is underway. There are many warships coming down the Nile."

"By the gods," Psusennes said with no shock. "It is what we feared."

The messenger replied, "They say the vessels are unknown, fast and new to our land. Many guess they are new models of the Sea Peoples."

"Proper defenses are being assembled, yes?"

The messenger nodded once. "As quickly as can be had, sire, but they are on us fast. They seem to travel at impossible speeds."

"I see."

"Surely the gods are with them."

While the King said nothing to this remark, the priest's face soured.

The priest said to his King, "Dead or alive, Goliath

will be trouble."

"Yes. He is a foul beast, by any measurement." He then turned away from the temple and walked several yards.

"Sire?" the priest questioned, confused as to his movements.

The Pharaoh looked to the sky. "He should be dead by now." He then faced the high priest again. "Correct?"

"If the gods are with us," the priest retorted, more to the soldier than to his King.

"Good," the Pharaoh said and started to wring his hands. "Very good."

"What is it you fear, sire?"

"Nothing. Just idle words. Make sure the troops are out and the proper sacrifices are made to aid in the battle."

Philistine

CHAPTER SIXTEEN
ESCAPE, RAID,
AND THE WAY HOME

Before the same dawn when Weldon Yog began his attack down the Nile River, General Samien smiled down from the bluffs at a thousand Philistine troopers. He doubted that General Schlack or anyone of real consequence led these men probing the edges of the Transjordanian wilderness, but he set Colonel Baldassare to work, nonetheless.

The Colonel's pickets spotted the large force of infantry and light cavalry probing the edges of the Dead Sea for the past days. This action caused Samien to abruptly call his forces to disengage their position in the wilderness and circle around. Since the troopers from Philistia crossed Israelite territory, their movements were swift. Samien wagered they only came to see and size up for themselves exactly what he had been building beyond the borders.

What the troopers found were women preparing food and no soldiers.

However, soldiers soon found the warriors. Some say what General Samien did was a military exercise. Others have said it was a calculated message. Many more said it was outright butchery.

First, Baldassare moved the Hittite archers in, launching volley after volley of missiles that landed in the center of the train of a thousand warriors. No sooner had confusion been born than the little Ammonites ran forward, gone to a kneeling position and deployed their slings. These diminutive men knew the craft of slings for their jagged stones caused confusion in the outer ranks.

Once the rocks landed, then the Edomite spearmen stepped forward, acting on a charge to the flanks of the troopers, but they halted and launched the first of two javelins into the midst of the force. They then charged headlong into the warriors with their long spears, supported at their hips by raging Moabite axemen and Assyrian & Philistine swordsmen.

Though they fought well and savagely to the incredible attack, the force sent from General Schlack was overwhelmed.

Not slain to the last man, the army was bound and put on their knees to General Samien, who rode his horse down into the morass of the battlefield in the morning light.

Colonel Baldassare saluted his superior from the field with a bloody hand. "Message sent, sir?"

Samien looked into the defiant faces of the officers captured on the ground.

He stared at the force of Moabites holding their axes nearby.

"Not quite."

*****

Goliath felt his body slump down and this snapped him back into reality. Confused over how far they fell, Goliath was more thrilled at the feeling of freedom in his legs. This feeling swiftly passed for the pain in his shoulders became the focus of his exhausted mind. Muscles flexed and he pulled himself toward the gelatinous bonds that bound him fast.

"Did I land in Moloch's snot rag?"

Looking down, he saw a tiny figure in the green glow. Unsure of the identity of this individual, his mind brought forth olden tales of dwarves, sprites and fairies in the Earth.

"Nopsik," Goliath said, a gush of laughter spewing from his bearded face. "My mind must be going."

"Glad you can laugh in the face of death, Goliath," Nopsik replied hurriedly. He held a small dirk in his hands. A blade of Egyptian origin, gilded with gold on the edges, it looked able enough in the dim light. "It took me an hour each to cut your feet loose of that goo you fell in."

Goliath stared down at him and said, "Then climb up me and cut my hands loose. What is this muck?"

Nopsik placed the dagger in his mouth and leapt up onto Goliath's leg. Balanced on Goliath's boot, Nopsik climbed the giant, reaching the thick belt, using his wiry muscles with his curved toes. When Nopsik balanced on the buckle and started to climb out onto one of his arms, he winked at Goliath.

"I'm not sure what this is. I'd rather not think on its waste properties or where it came from. It may be regurgitation, like from birds."

"Must be a big-assed bird. Hey, how the hell did you get in the temple?"

"Who am I, anyhow?" Nopsik was like a monkey in a tree as he slithered down Goliath's muscled right arm. Starting to saw on the gelatinous substance with the knife, he said, "The slave class knows where every gap is in this maze under the temple at Tanis. None of the cracks and vents are large enough for a man to fit down here. I took a chance. I made it. There is no way out for you that way, I fear."

"You should have run away, saved yourself," Goliath said bitterly.

"My life is yours, Goliath. If not for you, I would never be alive."

"I never wanted you to throw your existence away," Goliath remarked, trying to get his breath back. "Or I'd have never saved your ass when we sailed beyond the Pillars of Hercules."

"Perhaps there's a way out, sir. If there is indeed a beast down below, he must have a way out."

"Bah, it lives in the Earth. I can hear it scratching still, by the gods."

"It has to eat and get air from somewhere, Goliath. That and I have heard tales of tunnels one of the forefathers of Egypt installed when wanting to dupe his followers. He left himself a false route out to feign resurrection from the dead."

Looking around them, Goliath shook his head as if to clear his mind. "Did he escape?"

"Er, no, that's the drawback. Story was that his coffin was sealed and thus, the old magus couldn't escape his tomb."

His strength pressing on the bond, Goliath ripped the limb free with a grunt. Nopsik flew to the floor, but the nimble man flipped and landed like a cat.

Goliath extended his hand and demanded the blade. Nopsik gave it to him and watched Goliath free himself fast. Inserting the blade into the clear mass, Goliath muttered, "Some concoction of the King's priests?"

Nopsik said, "I think it came from that priestess of Bastet betrothed to the high priest of Amun. She makes odd traps and spells from her own body fluids." The boy grinned and said, "Goliath, a slave to pussy as always."

Philistine

At last, Goliath fell from the wall. Crouching, recoiling from being on a solid surface, Goliath gave the dagger back to Nopsik.

"Perhaps," Goliath ruminated. "If I go to where they just laid the bricks, I can push them back?"

Nopsik reminded him, "Into the face of guards? That tunnel will be guarded for some time. It terminated in an avenue of crypts. You would never get out that way. I think I can locate the gate to heaven itself."

Goliath stared at Nopsik indignantly. "Are you determined to get me eaten by that beast in the distance? What are you babbling about?"

Nopsik winked and motioned for the giant to follow him. "There's no obvious escape for one your size. However, I know of another spot where a tunnel passes close to the crypt of the magus."

"We are pinning our hopes on a dumbass wizard who cannot resurrect correctly? Outstanding. You can come to my house when I get home and mount my sister."

Nopsik grabbed his crotch at Goliath. "You don't have a sister. C'mon. There was a peculiar race of men that lived in this land even before the blacks the Egyptians rooted out."

They crept on, Goliath at a low bent but Nopsik walking upright. Goliath mumbled, "You seadogs and your tales."

"They built these tunnels and crypts, but Psusennes added to them and closed many exits. He could not destroy the mind of every slave who saw it happen. Perhaps there's something in that tomb to help us escape."

Hunching over further, Goliath swore as he followed the sailor through the glowing walls. "Why do the walls cast off light?"

"They're phosphorescent," Nopsik explained.

"What does that mean?"

"It means they cast off light."

Goliath groaned. "Why did I save your ass again?"

Nopsik giggled quietly as he sniffed the air. "It was an accident, remember?"

"There are no accidents," Goliath said, wishing he had a sword to face whatever horror screamed in the expanse. "Some wisdom saw to it you were saved years ago, elsewise I would have been trapped on the wall there forever."

"Life is full of lessons," Nopsik said, waving at many of the reliefs on the walls. "I think your weapons are behind the altar of Amun near Eucimar's head."

Goliath squinted, seeing abominable creatures carved in the rock, mating with humans. "God help us." He saw a rendering of a humanoid creature with a tentacle for a head and his memory burned of creatures he fought once, not long ago.

Nopsik smiled as he cocked his head to the right. Again, they heard a distant echo, like the scuff of metal on stone. "I think that's getting closer."

Impatiently, Goliath snapped, "You're full of great tidings, Nopsik. Is this place, the gate of heaven, any closer?"

"Yes," Nopsik nodded and jogged down the network of tunnels. Goliath reached out and took ahold of his left shoulder so he didn't lose Nopsik in the dim light. The sailor paused, looked down at Goliath's feet and said, "Your boots are making too much noise."

"So will you when I choke the life out of you, dammit!"

Nopsik stopped, glanced at the scraping sound, and then pressed on the wall. The place where the sailor ran his hand looked no different than the other walls. Then Nopsik said, "Throw your weight into this, Goliath."

Chewing his mustache, Goliath then said. "I will

have both shoulders on one side if I do that, Nopsik."

The screech of the creature sounded quite close, so Goliath braced himself and gave the wall a blocking blow with his right shoulder. The attempt was not his best, as he feared hitting a solid surface. However, Nopsik was correct in his search. The wall gave a little under Goliath's push. After a few more body blows, the wall cracked and Goliath saw that piece of slate, not a half-inch think, covered a wooden barrier. The wood was rotten and falling to pieces. He drew back, kicking a boot through it. This proved a bad idea for Goliath became stuck in the wall. Cursing, trying to pull back, Goliath hopped on one foot. Nopsik tried to help him balance as the wail and scrapes of the beast grew louder.

"By Baal, I need a drink," Goliath swore more.

"Me, too," Nopsik agreed, then suddenly pushed Goliath's buttocks.

Off balance, surprised, the Philistine fell forward. The weight shift sent him through the rotten wooden barrier and Goliath passed through the breech into the next chamber.

Using words Nopsik had never heard before, Goliath rolled over and half laughed. He then looked around the room, lit again by the green glow on the walls. As the big man struggled to his feet, Nopsik slipped into the opening. He looked back the way they came and then followed Goliath.

There wasn't far to go, for the room was a fifteen-by-twenty-foot box. The only thing in this small room was a rectangular container and a line of cylindrical clay urns.

Goliath looked at the doorway opposite the way they entered and said, "This is bricked shut."

Nose close to the bricked doorway, Nopsik frowned. "Yes. The priests sealed him in, thinking this persona dead." He pointed at the long box and then up at the ceiling. "I fear the tales are true and that he never escaped like he planned."

Goliath kicked at one of the long urns. It broke apart like glass and a roll of parchment fell out. Angrily, he stomped on it, fragmenting the stiff document.

He said ruefully, "Then there's no way out in here, dammit!" He peered at the remains of the roll of paper as the scream of the creature became deafening. Goliath couldn't decipher the characters. He faced Nopsik and said, "How is it the slaves knew of this spot?"

The sailor shrugged, wandering near the way they entered. "I think they robbed his sepulcher, Goliath. That's why his escape route is wooden. From the look of the sarcophagus, the old boy got nailed in there by his priests."

Goliath looked at the few urns left and grunted. "I guess they saw this stuff as pointless to steal?"

Suddenly, the scraping sound was on them and a large hunk of the thick wall gave way. Under the touch of pointed claws twice the size of a man's hands, the creature announced its presence.

Goliath grabbed Nopsik by his right arm and pulled him away from the opening as the shape blotted out the glowing walls. When two bird-like talons gripped the walls of the jagged opening, Nopsik murmured, "It's a hippogriffin?"

Stowing the sailor behind himself, backing away, looking desperately for a weapon of any sort, Goliath muttered, "I don't think so."

In the dim light, they could see the glittering talons, a sheen off many dark feathers and a slender head. The creature found them, yet did not reach out immediately, thus giving them scant hope.

His nostrils smelling the creature, Goliath reached down and grabbed one of the clay urns. These few objects interned with the unknown forefather of Kemet were his only projectiles.

When the creature opened is maw, looking rather pointed, Goliath thought it was indeed a Hippogriffin, the bizarre beast depicted on the reliefs as a combination of a lion, horse and eagle. However, the hooked beak, glowing eyes, and rustling wings that shown inky black from the glow of the walls made Goliath think it was more bird-like throughout its entire body. This fact never stopped him from heaving the urn at the open mouth of the giant beast.

Out of raw instinct, the beast snapped at the incoming shell, smashing the clay tube to bits. However, inside this urn there lay no parchment. These actions heartened Goliath. First, that the creature reacted in such a way, leading him to believe that it was nothing supernatural. Secondly, that out of the urn fell a long metallic object. Unsure if the article that clattered to the stone floor was a weapon or not, Goliath threw Nopsik on the other side of the coffin and started to kick at all of the lined up urns.

Recovering and staring at the squalling monster, Nopsik screamed, "Seker," before the creature extended its neck into the chamber. Nopsik flattened on the wall behind the coffin and Goliath did likewise as the beak of the creature, akin to that of a raven or hawk, smashed into the stone cover of the coffin. Taking a clean bite from the sarcophagus, the head of the beast arose. Its neck then stretched further, stabbing at Goliath, missing.

The Philistine, stunned at his latest discovery from the shattered urns...a bronze tomahawk...that he didn't notice the hawkish snout stab at his side. The blunt edge of the beak nailed him hard. Reeling and going to the floor, Goliath swiftly went to his all fours. Looking at the tomahawk like it were gold, he then leered at Nopsik, cowering against the wall and vulnerable.

"Seker," Goliath muttered as the creature thrashed

at the opening, unable to get in farther due to its wings. Seker, the god of the undead, Goliath ruminated. However, he saw the giant hawk writhe its tongue and breathe before it smashed into the coffin again. If it could breathe, it could die, he surmised.

Seizing a piece of the coffin lid in-between attacks, Goliath tipped it up and let the beak smash into it. As the beast struggled to get free of this mild annoyance, Goliath rolled across the coffin and dropped to where he smashed the urns earlier. The warrior gripped the tomahawk, briefly eying Nopsik as the sailor slithered closer to him beside the coffin.

Up on his haunches, Goliath tried to formulate a plan of attack.

Seker strained against the opening and Goliath guessed it would reach them in due course. The beast couldn't quite reach them, so it settled on destroying the rest of the coffin. In the dim light, Goliath could see a humanoid shape in the casket, and several small jars as well. The beak of the great hawk inserted into one of these jars and for a moment, was stuck. Just as it parted its beak and broke the jar, Goliath acted.

Forearm across the beak, Goliath reached back and swung the tomahawk down between Seker's eyes. Expecting a mighty crushing blow, but only managing to break the blade head off the old weapon, Goliath filled with anger.

Seker reared its head and connected with Goliath's sternum, throwing him back against the wall. The hawk screeched and then tried to reach in with one of its claws. Again, it failed to snatch them.

Nopsik looked up at Goliath, still covering his head and said, "A buried weapon would have been miraculous if it worked. It was meant to work in the next life."

"Piss on that," Goliath spat, looking at the handle of the tomahawk he still held. "There is no tomorrow."

Philistine

Though Goliath wrote off the dust in the air to the displacement of the raging beast, his eyes were soon drawn to the coffin. Truly, an ejecta of fine dust arose from the sarcophagus. Goliath thought it was blood pounding in his ears, causing him to experience strange things, but it proved to be truly emanating from the broken open coffin...a pulsing sound like a colossal heart beating. Even Seker paused and blinked his red eyes at this sound. Suddenly, a tall form unfolded itself from the coffin. Standing nearly a foot shorter than the giant, the occupant of the sarcophagus stretched and looked at its jet black hands. This being peered at Nopsik, then at Goliath.

"At last I am free," the arising man said in a bastardized Babylonian dialect. "Again, the great magician Ra-Horakhty, man-god of the rising sun, walks the Earth!"

Goliath and Nopsik exchanged a look.

The arisen magus went on to say, "At last I can facilitate the will of the Elder gods and call up the spirit of he who shall not be named!"

Goliath said grimly, "You're just what I need."

Fingers fluttering as if they were swimming in the powder cloud from the coffin, Ra-Horakhty blinked, squinted focusing eyes at him and said, "What?"

Goliath bellowed and kicked the arisen man-god in the belly, knocking him askew and back toward the twitching talons of Seker. With no hesitation, Seker snatched Ra-Horakhty by the left thigh, ripping corded muscle loose before burying its beak in the arisen mage's throat. Ra-Horakhty's mouth opened wide, but he could not scream, for his voice was robbed by the thrashing beast. The leg tumbled off and his head hit the floor as a spray of crimson spouted into the slick feathers over the head of Seker.

However, once Seker became occupied with ripping

the ebony mage to pieces, Goliath jumped. The bowed head of the blood-doused hawk, busy with splitting the rib-cage of Ra-Horakhty apart, never rose up as Goliath closed his left armpit over the beak...just before he drove the handle of the tomahawk deep into the left eye socket of Seker. The stunted weapon dug deep, causing the creature to explode in a new frenzy that sent Goliath flying against the far wall. This wrath made Seker drop the mage and bust through the walls further into the burial chamber. Head up and screaming, Seker's huge form shook. After a whiplash spasm that sent particles ejecting from its jaws, Goliath was splattered with grisly bits of Ra-Horakhty.

Wiping his eyes clear, Goliath scooped up Nopsik by the waist and looked at the widened doorway with hunger. When the enormous hawk tried to raise its head in another fit of anger, it connected with the low ceiling. Shocking Goliath, the head stuck there. Running across the room, Goliath pitched the sailor into the hallway, but reached down to grab a piece of the newly shattered ceiling. The jagged hunk of slim slate felt good in his hands. Dirt and further pieces of stone fell down from above, pouring over the creature.

Stepping on one of the hawk's claws, Goliath tried to plant his other foot on the floor to gain greater leverage to strike. Unfortunately, his right boot slipped in more gruel from Ra-Horakhty, and this action made the savage fighter miss his slashing blow. Trying to gain his footing, Goliath was wreathed in the wings of the beast as the head of Seker popped free of the ceiling. More dirt blinded the Philistine as his boots fumbled over the dead arms of Ra-Horakhty and the shifting claws of Seker. With a primal roar, Goliath slashed up, driving the jagged hunk into the main body of the hawk. Knowing he struck through the flesh, if not very deep, Goliath jumped up, tackling the right wing of Seker, and dropped all of his weight on it. When Seker extended the wing to shake off his aggressor, trying to bite at him as well, Goliath's legs intertwined through the long feathers and his body swung low like a hammock. The beak just missed him, but his weight, the move and the flail of the hawk's mass snapped the wing.

Sensing more ferocity and pain in the creature, Goliath twisted his limbs, trying to rip the wing loose. Seker, though, refused to be beaten and almost casually snapped Goliath's mane of hair in his beak and threw the man off himself. Back slamming into the far wall, Goliath knew his demise drew nigh. Getting to his feet, he shouted his own name and decided to charge into his death.

Before Goliath reached him, the ceiling caved in, covering Seker in immense amounts of dirt and rock. The thrashing creature fought, drowning in the debris, but alas, it fell under the weight of the dirt.

Legs partially buried as the room filled with a pyramid of dirt, Goliath still shouted his name as if he were heard. Not used to such an outcome once he prepared to die, Goliath stared, perplexed for a moment.

"Goliath?" the voice of Nopsik called into the burial chamber. "Can you get free?"

Looking up and feeling the cool air on his bearded face, Goliath chuckled in spite of his situation. "Yeah, I think we both can get free." Shifting his legs, Goliath thought he found a stone to balance on. Pulling his one boot up, his other leg shifted in the object. "Sonofabitch," he swore.

Crawling over the pyramid of dirt, Nopsik blinked and looked at Goliath's buried legs. "What is it?"

"I think it was the skull of that damned Ra-Horakhty I just slipped on. Damn, he ended up a gift of the gods when he showed up, but the old mage has been a pain in the ass ever since."

Nopsik looked up at the ceiling, saw the light and said, "That is quite a way up there, but I think even you can fit."

Goliath gave out a sharp laugh. "I sure as Hades hope so."

"Better let me go up there first, though," Nopsik told him as he scrambled up the debris toward the opening. "I'm just a slave. They won't think anything of me popping out of a hole in the ground."

"But you were my slave, or servant boy," Goliath reminded him as he pulled his legs up. "I'm shocked they just absorbed you into their culture."

Nopsik shrugged his better shoulder. "Oh yeah? What's one more slave to these people?"

The small sailor scurried up the opening, obscuring the light at times. Goliath cursed as he kicked more dirt down into his face, but didn't complain as he freed himself from the room. Not wanting to wait to see if Seker really happened to be crushed to death by the collapse, Goliath started up the tunnel.

His head above ground, Nopsik looked around and then down at Goliath. "It looks to be just after dawn. I thought as much. We can escape easily enough to the river, Goliath."

"Indeed," Goliath said, anger boiling in his words, his eyes looking back at the temple.

*****

Kmentosi turned his back to the risen sun and pounded his fists against the wooden door. He stepped back from the small set of servant's quarters, well made and attached to the stables near the temple of Ashtoreth in Ashdod. Frustrated at receiving no answer, the high priest of Dagon again went to the door and slammed his right fist on the boards, hard. Once more, he stepped back, fists clenched and surveyed the grounds. He turned around and froze, face to face with the man he came to see.

"There you are, Yaggah," Kmentosi snapped out his words fast, his eyes scanning the thin man up and down. "Aren't you doing well for yourself as of late?"

Dressed in new tunic and kilt, his shaggy hair shorter and tied back, Yaggah rubbed his thin beard and said, "Those of the temple of Ashtoreth felt Akisha would be more comfortable here than in the house of Dagon.

"Yes, and you get quality quarters here, even if they are next to the barn," Kmentosi sneered.

Confused, Yaggah asked, "What is it?"

His voice louder and redness filling his face, the priest shouted, "I went to warn Dezmal, the King of Ashdod, of an attack about to befall one of Schlack's armies out in the east. The servants refused to rouse him, can you believe that? They were told by Dezmal that I'm not to be received for just any reason."

Yaggah stepped in closer and whispered, "Would such a minor defeat be all bad for our cause?"

Voice quieter, but his vitriol running high, Kmentosi shot back, "Our cause? I was in from the beginning, body and soul, yet now I seem to be regulated to the sidelines." He held up a long index finger and pointed at Yaggah's nose. "Don't think of shutting me out of matters as they grow nigh."

Yaggah waited for the priest to take several breaths before he said, "Your contribution to the design is invaluable. Please don't take such a silly slight as a condemning act."

Turning in a circle, Kmentosi raged, "She has shut me out, do you hear me? I have been slapped back by her as if I were an accidental visitor to her private realm."

"It's a complex time."

His ire again focused on Yaggah, Kmentosi glared and said, "You have drawn me away from my true calling into this folly, and I will not be a fool for it, do you hear me?"

Yaggah shook his head and smiled. "Why are you so upset? We have been at this for a long time. Nothing with these powerful beings is as easy as you and I speaking. Calm yourself. You look so rattled."

Hands to his sides, Kmentosi stepped closer and said silently, "It isn't just this, you, tramp. I took the bones that Abimelech gave me, the ones taken from the representation of my god Dagon himself. I prayed over them, and then ground the bones to dust. Can you guess what I saw when I drank them and entered my ether realm?"

Again, Yaggah shrugged, confused.

His voice quite measured, the priest said, "Jilted by Malak, I went back to consult the god of my youth, my life, my vocation." His eyes closed and his voice deepened becoming a hiss, "I heard my god say unto me, *'Who are you to now seek after my consul? Why did you go a-whoring after another god more so than me? Where was she when we spat at the foundations of heaven? Go, little priest, and suckle at the goddess of want. I shall see you soon in the abyss.'*" Eyes open, he took a few breaths and said with a cruel voice, "Doesn't that beat childish rejections from whorish girls?"

"Kmentosi..."

Hand clasping Yaggah's sleeves at the elbows, the priest again frothed as he said, "Can you imagine how many lives I've sent unto Dagon? Can you imagine the way I feel now? Can I ever get in his good graces again?"

"Our gods are many and not as jealous as some, "Yaggah replied, pulling from his grip. "Calm down. Not many in the priesthood ever get a personal relationship with their gods. You are fortunate."

"Yes, and I squandered that by being greedy," he said with bitterness, turning from him.

"What is it you want?"

Kmentosi swirled, facing him again. "I want reassurance this will be as it is supposed to be."

Yaggah smiled and Kmentosi's mood darkened, though he was certain the former teamster turned goddess pimp mean to unruffle him. While they'd polished up Yaggah, his teeth still looked stained with dung. "There is naught to worry after, Kmentosi. We need your help. You know that the giant is doomed in Egypt. Things will come to past our way very soon."

"How do you know for sure?"

"I have faith," Yaggah gave him a wink. "In my goddess upstairs and the one afar off. Never have I been so elated. I'm at peace at last."

The priest turned and walked away from the temple of Ashtoreth. Hood over his face, Kmentosi trudged back toward his sanctuary, thinking of how good and special he felt the first time Dagon smiled on him. It seemed so long ago...

*****

Though the Pharaoh beefed up the military might around Tanis at the word of Goliath's capture, the Philistine forces never attacked where the army was heavily quartered. Reports came in to the Pharaoh and his generals that the port city of Lamenish burned and much of the adjoining city of Ahken had been set alight.

The audacity of the Philistines stunned the Egyptians by attacking the heart of their naval vessels the King brought up river in case of such an attack. Faster and commanding so many ships, the Philistines attacked the Egyptian naval forces still moored to the docks, leaving them crippled at their ports.

When Psusennes ordered his generals to call out the main forces to defend the temple and city, some of these commands went on empty ears. It only took an hour to realize a force of Philistines had come ashore long before the river assault. They'd infiltrated behind the lines of the military and slain them in their quarters. True to their nature, it wasn't just the Sea Peoples of Philistia that attacked. These men came from other islands, cousins of the Philistines, but ready to go to war against a foe they needed to settle a score with. Word that bands from the tribes of Karkisha, Pitasha, and the Tjekker folk stood with the Philistines roughnecks spread fast. These others, distinguished by their pale hue of skin and blonde or snowy white hair, fought well beside their cousins.

Kindred not withstanding, these tribes also wanted to loot the Egyptian cities.

"Savages," the Pharaoh declared at the news and the heated reports of the alien fighters. "Of course they will not engage us on the open battlefield. It isn't their way at all."

From their position high on the temple, they witnessed the slaughter of the forces that did clash in the areas outside the nearby city.

The Pharaoh was unnerved at how many Philistines and Sea Peoples attacked the Egyptian military. The berserk ground force advanced around the marketplace of Tanis and threw themselves into the rear of the army. Swarms of the screaming men brandished metal axes, swords and clubs, attacking the hastily assembled units of pikemen, infantry and archers. Usually, a charging foe was softened up by the military with artillery and projectiles from archers or the longbow classes. Few arrows were loosed before this barbarian force of berserk killers attacked.

The manner of the Philistines ran vile and unpredictable. Solid units of well trained pikemen, skilled in fighting with long pikes or spears, met this initial force. They divided their ranks to separate parts of the army as one force of pikemen stood, supported by many regular infantry fighters with crude bronze short swords and long shields. Archers tried to get ready, but only a few dozen managed to loose arrows as the Philistines' first thrust hit.

The heavy slaughter ensued, destroying pikemen and dozens in the infantry in an instant. The King tried to look for hope, for Philistines falling, but really never noted any doing as such. Their insane push was irresistible. The on-sweeping hordes attacked with communal entreaties to their champion, over and over, he heard his name chanted. Their push caused a few hundred in the cavalry to retreat and take up a different position. With great valor, the pikemen and infantry fought. They met the attack, and struggled, and died hard. The invading force was only stopped by the armored legion, a thousand elite men in stern body armor. However, the Philistines never decided to engage these men. They peeled off and went around the temple, confounding the forces getting ready to stand before them.

"The river," the Pharaoh gasped, seeing the plot play out like on a map. "The maniacs are going to reunite with their vessels!"

Menkheperre shook his head. "They came to free their champion or to just slaughter and burn in general?"

The King frowned. "While from what the slaves say, Goliath is in the walls feeding Seker as we speak, they are doing a wonderful job of wanton destruction."

General Sobek clenched his fists and said, "I must call up the auxiliaries and take the fight to them myself." He glared at the Pharaoh. "I'd return to the safety of your family quarters for now, my King."

Psusennes took his military escort and was led back into the chambers hidden near the rear of the temple. The guards and King alike stood stupefied at the scene: the house guards and military men all laying splayed, blood still wet on their tunics.

One of the King's guards held his short sword tight to his face and said, "They must've rampaged through here before?"

Psusennes shook his head slowly. "But they never came near here."

One of the guards emerged from the abode and took a knee. Tears streamed from his eyes, and he feared what would happen at the announcement he was forced to make. "The Queen, Pharaoh..."

"Curse to them all," Psusennes said, but never moved forward. "Tell me for true: she is dead?"

The guard nodded, looked up and said, "Torn apart," he reached down to his crotch and sliced as if to show how she was wounded. "It is safer in the main temple, my Lord."

The King nodded and turned. Two of the guards that brought him lay dead, their heads pulverized together into one mess. He saw no attacker, nor did the other guards, but they ran back for the temple all the same.

Joints aching, body screaming for relief, mind afire with the loss of his Queen and heaven knew who else, Psusennes staggered into the main temple altar room to Amun.

He fell flat, exhausted, and then realized no guards were with him. He was alone.

Well, not quite.

"I lied to you, Psusennes," the booming voice echoed

out into the chamber.

Eyes darted back and forth, the Pharaoh tried to find the originator of the voice in the flickering light.

The voice went on. "Philistines will do that, lie, don't you know? Our gods don't take such minor things as deception to an enemy personally."

"You will die for this," the Pharaoh promised. "All of your rabble. My sons will destroy every one of you for this."

"Oh, I don't think so. That would be the right thing to do, if you were all really men and true to your manly code. However, you are whores to politics and the wants of other lands. Such things will make doing what is right and natural, well, difficult."

A few footsteps echoed in the chamber as the Pharaoh crawled toward the image of Amun. Figures sat around the altar, smaller ones, girls...the head of Eucimar was gone.

Goliath went on to say, "I did lie to you, King of all Egypt."

Suddenly, the giant straddled Psusennes and forced him flat to the floor.

Mouth close to the King's ear, Goliath said, "I was freed, but never stopped at your wife." Goliath placed a knee in the Pharaoh's back, then grabbed the elbow and shoulder of Psusennes. With a savage pull, he dislocated the left arm of the Pharaoh. In another moment, he performed the same action of the King's other shoulder. After he dislocated the King's legs, Goliath departed the temple, leaving him alone with the bodies of his dead daughters, arranged as if having a drinking party by the altar of Amun, but all dead.

Steven Shrewsbury

*****

Though a war raged around him, it felt good to be near to the water again. Goliath held up the head of his friend and even Eucimar laughed at their escape. The giant stowed the head in his pouch and swung his weapons into the air, screaming his own name as he joined the Philistines battling as they retreated toward the river.

When Weldon Yog shouted for the giant to get his big ass back in the vessel so they could get going, all the giant could do was laugh.

Philistine

CHAPTER SEVENTEEN
ASSASSINS, REUNIONS, AND TO GATH

Kmentosi drew back his green hood and reined in his mount. Soldiers approaching him on the road flanked the horse-drawn wagon, openly bitched about the daylong ride. These men gave the priest a simple regard, never fully recognizing him, but never caring if he rode up next to them as they paused to rest. The hillock the band stopped at crested near Ashdod, but these men favored the road stretching farther south toward Ashkelon.

The Philistine soldier wearing a sergeant's insignia looked bitter as he waved at the tarp-covered wagon. "Do you want to have a look?"

Tired and empty, Kmentosi couldn't summon his usual commanding way to even agree. From the odor wafting off the wagon, the priest had little desire to view what lay within.

Nevertheless, the soldier in the cart pulled back the tarp. A few of the horsemen near the cart let their horses move away and shook their heads, a few half smiling in a sense of stupefied shock, the priest guessed. The rider of the cart never looked back, but the soldier beside him sat, head down, and breathing shallow.

Kmentosi couldn't count how many heads occupied the wagon. He could tell that they were Philistines by the noses and brows.

"Dreadful," the driver said, eyes on the valley ahead.

The priest eyed the other rider, seeing that mud and blood spattered his sandals and tunic. He also took note that the distant soldier was unarmed.

After a wave to make sure the tarp returned to its fitted spot, the horseman announced, "Proceed on. Hyrum has said that the General will meet us between Ashdod and Ashkelon."

Kmentosi pulled back and let the wagon carry on. Their grim mission and message to Schlack clear, they moved out. He watched them go, his mind turning over the idea that Samien would indeed follow through with his side of the idea and via Malak's blessings, may just triumph over Schlack on the battlefield.

It then struck Kmentosi that Malak's triumph and the new age would mean his downfall if he broke now. Wallowing in pity wasn't his way, he ruminated, though rejection by his god and goddess seemed unflattering, he had another card to play. He thought of Akisha, soon a living goddess to the folk, and her coming offspring. For the first time in days, Kmentosi smiled. He thought of puffed up Yaggah, his ego rampant and his station advanced as the herald of the goddess.

"I'll need to get strong again," he said aloud to no one. He pondered his old supplier of materials and her house of pleasures, Madam Dralla Bojak. At full strength, his magicks at the ready, Malak may not be impressed, but Akisha may just be in the market for a new prophet.

Philistine

Goliath let the sea air wash over his face as the ship's medic dapped a poultice on his forehead. He closed his eyes and recalled the first missions he experienced out of Gath, after he'd been trained and abused by the commanders. While at times it frightened him, other adventures it felt like sunshine on his face.

He recognized Qorus's voice inserted in the heated conversation on the deck. "It was great to slay the Egyptians. They live on their damned reputations and aren't immortal."

Cairn added, "They die like rats just like Assyrians."

Sadik chimed in to say, "I'm elated that our brothers on the islands saw fit to join us."

Weldon nodded. "Their words about General Samien trying to rally them to his cause as a naval force is also telling."

Others grunted in agreement, but the boyish voice of Sadik gushed, "What were those metal feathered birds called again?"

The acidic voice of Weldon Yog croaked out, "Stymphalian Cranes. They are tests of the gods, and still sport thin feathers that look like bronze. See? Captain Balzer uses the ones stuck in the mast from the birds' attack to torture that fool assassin."

Eyes open, Goliath waved off the medic and stared at the young sailor before him on the deck, spread eagle and making the boards wet with blood. Though his arms were tied at the wrists and secured to either side of the heaving ship, the youth's feet never moved as they'd been nailed in place. Captain Balzer poised on the sailor's knees, inserting a metallic thin object under the collarbone of the screaming man.

Nopsik asked from behind Goliath, "Barekbaal and his brother Darekbaal were such good sailors. Why did they try to kill the champion in his sleep after such a fine slaughter?"

"Indeed, why?" Goliath muttered and never rose up, save for raising his chin to look over the edge of the vessel. "Why would Darekbaal choose the waves and certain death rather than face the consequences?"

The question fell flat and no one tried to answer. Anyone who could hear the cries, smell the blood, urine and feces of the torture session, and hear the words of Eucimar as the disembodied head ranted in Barekbaal's ear, understood that oblivion was better. A few looked to the sea but none saw Darekbaal. None really expected to.

Goliath recalled the night, how sleep came to him at last, along with assassins' blades. Four of them, in fact, as the twin youths tried to slay the giant in his sleep, hands full of knives. One succeeded in pinning his beard to the rear deck while the other knife glanced off one of his ribs.

In a panic at his failure to sink the knives, Barekbaal froze. This is why Goliath reached out and twisted his knees, crippling him as the joints snapped in his grip. The would-be killer's brother Darekbaal stabbed down lower, trying to cleave into the giant's groin and belly. He never counted on Goliath sleeping in an armored codpiece that night.

"The ship and the waves' motion are bad on my balls," was all Goliath said to the jeering sailors, but he never had a chance to cripple Darekbaal. The young man jumped into the deep, swam for his life and vanished. They were in the open sea and Darekbaal chose his doom.

Philistine

Nopsik shook his head and looked down at the young sailor. "To think they lurked here with us as assassins, all this time."

Goliath sighed and all eyes focused on Barekbaal. The words of Eucimar and the questions of Captain Balzer ceased. The giant stood up, steadied his feet from the rocking of the sea, and drew out his sword. "Someone wants me dead. It's an old story, but one I grow weary of as of late." Eyes focused down at the prone man, Goliath set his sword tip between the man's legs.

Captain Balzer wore a grim look. "He'll talk. They all do in time."

Goliath's eyes focused on Barekbaal's eyes. "I don't think this one will." He leaned over and said, "You're already hers, aren't you?"

Eucimar eyes glanced up from his low position. "What do you mean?"

"Give it time," Goliath said, sword turning a bit on the boards. "Me alive is no good for whatever these traitorous bastards have in mind. Me dead, that will work it all out better, be it on the battlefield or in their temples, right?"

Barekbaal cried out, his voice scratchy and dry, then he froze in position. Captain Balzer backed up as the young sailor's skin took on the pallor of ash. Soon, the sailor went rigid and never moved again.

Balzer kicked Barekbaal's leg and he said what they all suspected. "He's stone."

The heaving of the ship put pressure on the restraints at the sailor's arms and the left one snapped off.

Abimelech stared for a few moments and then said, "Just like the assassin in the village."

Eucimar said to Goliath, "You seemed to have incurred the wrath of someone very powerful."

Goliath sat down again as the sailors cleared off the stone body and threw it into the sea. "But not one powerful enough to kill me from a distance. Curious." He reached out, picked up his bronze helmet and turned it over in his hands. "Still, it sends its acolytes and dreams to terrorize me."

Eucimar's face turned reflective as Abimelech set him closer to Goliath. "I wonder if this persona would know if you were dead or not."

"What?"

"Yes, maybe it would be better if she thinks you slain."

"I doubt that fact can be fabricated. Don't you maniacs of magick travel in the air, out of your bodies?" Goliath fluttered his twelve fingers in the air, imitating a wizard in the ether realm, causing the men to smile. "Whoever it is would know, I reckon."

Eucimar rolled his eyes. "Perhaps not to the force, the one that opposes you, but to others."

Goliath nodded, his eyes cast down on his helm.

Captain Balzer shook his head, saying, "What do you mean by all that?"

The giant replied, "Someone let those twins on here with Weldon. I doubt they used magic to get them time in the Philistine navy." He faced Weldon. "Where did this batch of sailors come from?"

Weldon blinked and then said, "Well, those two young ones weren't of my old crew from down south."

Abimelech nodded. "I didn't recognize them from before."

Weldon continued, "They were part of the assigned crews made back at Ashkelon."

Eucimar wore a snide look as he offered, "By whom?"

Weldon's usually boisterous look faded. "General Schlack."

Philistine

Goliath broke the uneasy silence by saying, "I figured I'd have to kill that prick in time, just not so soon. So much for his loyalty to me, aye men?"

While the men grumbled, clearly upset at the implication of their leader being against the champion, Abimelech lowered his voice and asked, "The General himself is corrupt?"

Qorus seethed with anger. "Imagine that."

Weldon thought out loud, "And the King at Ashkelon?"

Fingers gripping the sides of his helmet, Goliath snorted and said, "He and Schlack are joined at the penis. Always have been, and here they mount us up against General Samien and the priests. Perhaps we should become revolutionaries, huh?"

Eucimar grinned at the giant darkly. "I sense a great plan churning."

Goliath said, "Shut up or the young ones will play catch with you. I propose a deception."

Fists in the air, Qorus raved, "But the powerful ones will know you are not dead. It'll never work."

Goliath gritted his teeth. "Calm down, boy. You need to listen more. You'll get your chance at revenge, I promise. No, they want me out of the way? They want to install a new goddess and her bastard companion as an advisor or a bubo polisher? Good. What would piss in their soup on this social matter?"

Hands to his waist, Weldon grinned. "Yer killing me, ya ugly bastard, go ahead."

Goliath arose, tossed his helm to Sadik and put his hands over his heart. "I announce my undying love for Akisha, the one who carries my seed, the one who I will make my Queen." His voice, mimicking a romantic reader, made the men explode with laughter. Again, his tone went grim. "That'll piss off all the five Kings, but I'll find out who is my friend and who wants me dead. The deception need not last long. My religious advisor here, Eucimar the animated head? That'll scare the spirit out of anyone who thinks twice that's of normal timber, much less a dirty traitor."

Abimelech nodded along with his words, but Captain Balzer spat on the deck. "You dare not conflict with your master, but care to let us all in on this? You propose to disrupt Philistia tradition and power structure to find your enemies?"

Qorus injected, "If Goliath said he would take this woman, this new goddess heavy with his child, as his wife and declare himself King of all Philistia, wouldn't nations about us tremble? Wouldn't Samien think twice about his rebellion?"

Several soldiers and sailors grunted their agreement.

Eucimar said, "Many regular folks of the Philistines grow weary of their sons dying for foolish wars by the current rulers, hence Samien is followed to a degree. Samien commands too many mongrels and outsiders and no true Philistine wants to fight beside such scum. A central King, a man of divine blood, would give them peace in their hearts and truly a reason to follow such a person."

Goliath sighed. "God kill me now. But I have no such ambition."

Weldon offered, "But they don't know that. The military would follow you, and the other Kings would be pissing snow showers at the idea of crossing us."

Abimelech pondered, "Someone had the balls to oppose him already, though. Maybe Samien is the fingers of this alien force? Who can tell? They must have faith in something to protect them."

Goliath grinned. "I'm prepared to show them the error of their religion, then." Smile fading, he faced his shield bearer. "If we do this thing, I have something I must do that will help show the hand of the force we fight, a force wishing ill on all of our folk, not just us. The pieces will start to fall. I have a duty for you to perform."

"At your command, sire."

Goliath turned to Qorus. "If I send Abimelech off on a sacred obligation, you must stand in his stead. I'll need you with me until he returns."

Qorus blinked, stunned but soon enough screwed down his courage. "My life is yours, sire."

"Besides, you're bigger than the rest of these soldiers. You'll fit in Abi's armor." Goliath then looked to the ships' Captain. "Weldon, I may have need of some drunken sailors."

"Now where in Hades am I supposed to find any of those?"

Goliath turned to Sadik. "Take my helmet to Kikron, he's a blacksmith in Gath. The finest. Tell him to place an application on my helm to cover the bridge of my nose angled down, all right?"

Sadik nodded, proud to be given such a simple task.

*****

General Schlack stared down into the bed of the cart and frowned. He soon motioned the tarp to be returned and said, "Take this cart and burn the lot of it. We shall inform most of their families quietly of their demise, when we are more certain of it all."

The driver of the wagon dismounted and glanced at the bloody soldier on the wagon before saying to the General, "But we know what he said."

Schlack glared at him and replied, "Do you want me to announce the rebels slew our force down to the last man?"

The man shrugged, but tried to stay at attention. "It may be better than admitting several joined Samien rather than be slain."

"Good riddance to them, then," Schlack retorted coldly. His eyes then rested on the lone soldier sent back to tell them of the slaughter. "And why did they select you to bring this message?"

"I...I...wouldn't join them..." the soldier said quietly.

Schlack grabbed him by the ear and pulled him from the wagon. The youth screamed as he hit the ground. The General kicked him in the face and the youth flopped to his back. Schlack bent over and studied him. The general soon stood, chin up and said, "You are not bruised nor scratched. You didn't fight much, did you?"

The soldier remained silent, save for his weeping.

"Samien thought you unworthy of killing so he sent you as his piss pot boy," Schlack said and let out a disgusted chuckle. He then drew out his short sword and let the sunshine glint off the blade. "However, rest easy, boy. I don't share his sense of mercy."

Once the General had cleansed his sword and walked back to his horse, he said to the soldiers nearby, "I shall go unto Ashkelon. Tell all the men to be at the ready." He mounted up and declared, "Let it be known plans are afoot for a major engagement."

"But to where?" one of the mounted soldiers asked.

Schlack winked. "I will soon decide."

*****

Charged with the duty from his master, Abimelech broke off from the others who returned. He never landed with Weldon's ship, but with another that went off in a northern path for an obscure port. Since not all warships moored at Ashkelon, this wasn't unusual. Although the others cleaned and readied for the meeting with Vyndekay in Ashkelon, Abimelech changed and readied himself for his new tasks.

Once in the country, Abimelech took time to dismount and make a small sacrifice to his god. Though his parents worshiped Moloch and he openly paid lip service to Baal, the image Abimelech had tattooed on his inner thigh was that of Assyrian god Nisroch.

As he settled out in the open field and cleared a spot in the earth, Abimelech smirked at his own little secret. Not even his master knew he worshiped Nisroch but was positive the giant would be amused as to why. After Abimelech bled himself from his left forearm onto the cleared earth, he said a small prayer to his god and then rubbed the mud and blood created from the bleeding onto this tattoo.

Though no major religious conversion took place, nor did he owe Nisroch anything, Abimelech focused his tasks in life on the image and that was helpful. Why did he choose this god of a foreign land? He stared at the winged, eagle-headed god on his thigh and smiled. Nisroch looked very mighty and valiant. That was all. When he saw his own reflection in the waters or on polished surfaces, Abimelech tried to be that excellent.

Abimelech arose and remained mindful of his assignment. He mounted up and rode fast toward Ashdod. However, per Eucimar's spells and astral travels, Abimelech knew he wouldn't find the high priest of Ashdod in that town. His first target that day was Kmentosi. The priest of Dagon reeked of corruption and no words need be spoken or extorted from him.

"He has to die," Eucimar had assured Abimelech earlier in the day. "Yaggah and the rest will know you are onto them a score of miles off unless he falls. I cannot hinder the mysterious force that guides them with my power, but I can blunt the senses of the priest Goliath sends you to. Slay this priest and you will corner your prey. Be steadfast, though, for all of my warnings will not help you slay the victim if you are dense."

Abimelech thought of visiting the temple whores of a town as he passed, but since his last encounter with such women, he decided to wait.

*****

King Vyndekay of Ashkelon sat on a cushion in his palace. He shifted in his position at the end of the long room and listened. He looked over the other men also seated down the walls of the room and still paid attention, probably well aware of the gossip the drunken sailors had already spread about Goliath's nuptial plans. He noted the words of Captain Balzer's report, then of Captain Weldon Yog as they explained the exploits of the past days. The King nodded at the words of Weldon, how they rendezvoused with many other vessels out in the sea and attacked many ports, filling cargo ships with supplies and then turning their attentions south to Egypt. Every so often the two Captains would differ from each other and then from one of the warriors with them. These men filled in the blanks and the King nodded dutifully, somewhat quiet.

General Schlack sat near to the King's right hand and leered down the line of men and nobles assembled. His eyes rested on Goliath and then on his King.

Every so often Weldon's steely eyes met with those of the champion, but his expression never changed.

Vyndekay declared, "A wonderful success. Not only

are the supplies attained, but a message sent unto the weak Egyptians not to touch us."

Schlack peered down his crooked nose at the procession of men. "I question the ruthless nature our champion dispatching the females of the Pharaoh's family, but the meaning is certainly conveyed forever in that culture's mind now."

Goliath said slowly, "You're against raping and wanton destruction, General?"

"Of course not, but I wonder if that was a bit extreme and won't lead them to mount an attack on our homeland."

Goliath sighed. "I left their damned King alive, what more do you want? The priests of the lower kingdom may seize this and rise against him. Priests are wont to do bad things, are they not? The game I played with his mind will suffice. That Pharaoh will never attack us."

Vyndekay muttered, "Hope he lives forever then." He then spoke up louder and said, "The adventures certainly will fill the hearts of our folk with courage, and the return of Eucimar..." his voice trailed off as he looked at Goliath's left side where a mound of pillows propped up the head of the wizard. "...will lend new mystery to the world." He then stood and made a dismissal motion with his arms. After this action, all departed the chamber save for Vyndekay, Schlack, Balzer, Weldon, Eucimar, Qorus and Goliath.

Schlack wore a distasteful look. "You all can go."

Weldon gave a salute and departed with Balzer.

The General's eyes flared at Qorus. "Why do you abide, boy? Depart now."

Goliath said, "He bears my shield this day and acts as my second. One never knows where a knife waits for the champion of the Philistines."

Schlack's face reddened. "Where's Abimelech?"

Goliath looked down on him and said, "I don't recall

saying." He let several moments pass before he said, "As always, he attends to my will."

His cool maintained, Vyndekay said, "While my appreciation overflows at the acts described, I cannot abide your declaration before this meeting."

Fingers drumming on his knees a few times, Goliath stated with innocence in his voice, "I think when I announce my intention to be singular King of all of Philistia, it will be a galvanizing idea, drawing us all together under the canvas of our folk."

Schlack sneered, "I doubt the kings of the five cities will appreciate your sweet words."

"We're all Philistines." His tone shifted, grim. "Each city needs a leader, but deference to a single monarch wouldn't be difficult, and well, it would look better for other nations, no? Some already look to one or another as King of Kings, while it's not on parchment or a real title. We wouldn't be just a band of savage Sea Peoples, but a single nation with a ruling monarchy."

Clearly rattled by the giant's words, Vyndekay said, "This is a great deal to digest at once."

Fists on the table, Schlack raged openly, "The others will never go by this new ruling. You're not a god nor do you have that sort of power." Anger never ebbing, but his voice running colder, Schlack snapped, "Not all of Philistia loves you. Most just fear you."

Goliath tilted his head to the right. His voice remained calm. "Perhaps that'll be enough. I don't want them to go down on me, I want their loyalty as a monarch. I'm not asking for tribute or taxes to increase, just a stop to the foolish practices gleaned from current mass misrule."

"You *are* but one big man," Schlack retorted, glancing at his shifting King for a moment. "The army is many."

"I have brothers, though not giants," Goliath said

in a matter of fact voice. "Half-brothers, really. Each one is in a different city."

Vyndekay shook his head slightly and glared into Goliath's eyes. "You are so convinced another way is better for our people?"

Contempt dripping from his words, Goliath bent down to face the King of Ashkelon and said, "*You* are so convinced another way is better for our people? Don't throw me a bushel of fish and tell me it's pussy, King Vyndekay. I'm a fighter, not a politician, but I'm wise in the ways of men. I think you have been sold on a bill of goods, untested, rather than trusting the champion you know."

The King sweated as Schlack puffed up his chest. "Mind your tone. You speak of revolution and making order, but to accuse your King of…"

Goliath never looked at Schlack but kept his gaze riveted to the King. "I know, don't I? You have listened to a voice, gone a-whoring after another way. What has she promised you?"

At the gender being named, the King's eyes widened.

Goliath went on, saying, "She's no goddess, but has done what? Preached certainty? A pure way? Based on what? She hasn't granted us victory yet or you my death. Every so often, we win, but often the Hebrew King sends us back on our shields. Silly really. Who is it that drives this treasonous thought in *you*, King?"

Vyndekay shot back, "You think I talk of a whore with the capacity to take on a giant? You are a fool then."

His voice still tense, Goliath replied, "I know what you hear. She isn't Akisha, but far worse. She and her pure ones reside on a wheel, do they not?"

The King tore his gaze from the giant. Fists to his face, Vyndekay almost sobbed as he said, "You don't know what has been granted to me." He turned, pointed at Goliath and said, "You, alone, follow me."

Goliath nodded to Qorus and departed behind the King. They walked with no words out of the meeting spot in the main palace hall of Ashkelon and down into the King's house. While several children ran and played, the King pointed to a slender girl over in the corner of the courtyard. Dark-haired, pale, blank of eyes, the girl worked a sewing kit in her lap.

Vyndekay said, "My daughter Emana died months ago. She was consumed by fever."

"She sews well for a dead girl."

The King whispered, "The one you talk of, the one you seek to find, the one who seeks your death, has raised her to life."

Goliath folded his arms. "I see. You're beholden to this force because of that?'

The King turned away.

Goliath started to go but saw the girl look up. Many of the playing children called to him and he waved back. The cold eyes of the resurrected girl made Goliath shiver.

"Do not ask me who and where she is," Vyndekay said as they walked. "I will not tell you. You can slay me if you wish, but my daughter must live."

"Children are such a hindrance, no? It stops you from doing what you want and they make you compromise your ways."

"You make it sound evil."

"I never said it was, just an observation. However, you're wrong about your daughter."

"How so?"

Goliath stopped walking in the hall leading up to the conference chamber. "Everything must die, King. You, me, even little girls must breathe their last."

The King faced away from him and said, "The one you seek, she knows you are alive and coming for her."

Goliath laughed. "Fat lot of good it does me if I don't know where she abides." The giant then placed his hand on the doorway before the King walked through.

Vyndekay hissed, "You will not kill the King of Ashkelon, for all of Philistia will rise up."

"What is to stop me, fear of dying?"

"Doesn't the idea that Akisha bears your offspring interest you? The idea of holding your son or daughter? Of training up a warrior or, well, a female warrior as well?"

Goliath paused for a while before he said, "My heart and mind don't long for the same things ordinary men yearn for. You tempt me and try to cloud my mind. I'm the last of my kind."

"What of Neurath?" Vyndekay asked with a coy voice. "Isn't he like unto yourself?"

Again, Goliath chuckled, eyes scanning the area. "Neurath spends his time buried in scrolls and tablets, begging the gods for answers. Far from a man, he's hardly one of my own."

"Perhaps his counsel would be beneficial."

Goliath dropped his hand to the King's shoulder. "If you are leading me to a trap, I'll have you know that my brothers and my men will slay your family first. They will then kill you and you will spend eternity as the seat cover for my chair in Hell."

*****

As unlikely as it sounds, Abimelech found the wizard of Ashdod on top of a girl. He wasn't cursing her, getting ready to sacrifice her, or even talking her to death. No, when Abimelech thrust his spear into the wizard's back, Kmentosi was knee deep in flesh, as the saucy Philistine youths would say, or screwing the whore silly, in simple terms.

The priest's thrusting motions ceased abruptly when Abimelech penetrated Kmentosi's back with a lance, driving the foot-long blade through the sorcerer's ribs, heart and yes, into the sternum of the whore. Both gasped, and froze in a moment of astonishment.

Boot on the wizard's buttock, Abimelech roared the name of Nisroch, and yanked the spear out of Kmentosi's back. When Abimelech pulled the spear out of Kmentosi, the necromancer's body flew off the hooker, manhood swinging out. Still incredibly hard, Kmentosi's member spewed a long stream of milky semen, clotted with blood. By the mage's exalted mannerisms, Abimelech wondered if it was the best orgasm the cretin ever had. Perhaps it was the great rush of blood, or the shock, or maybe Abimelech just arrived at the exact moment Kmentosi also arrived. At any rate, the magus stumbled, breathless. The whore also gave a single gasp, legs spread, convulsing, covered in the blast of semen across her body as Kmentosi fell back and dropped dead from the lance's cruel blow.

Abimelech saw the flap that separated the rooms tear wide and the plump woman in scarlet standing there, starting to shout. "I'd have never let you through if I knew you'd deprive me of my wares." The Madam raged. "How will you make this up to me? Dralla Bojak demands repayment!"

"What's the price of a filthy whore that screws a magus sporting a deadly sickness?" Abimelech shrugged, impressed with the pluck of the Madam. "It's rumored that he has an illness that is passed on through his manhood and thus, to all others he touches with it, and those who later lie with his conquests."

Dralla chuckled, arms folded under her ample bosom. "A sickness transmitted by way of copulation? I've heard of such a thing at Aijalon, Eshtaol and Sochoh, but not in Philistia proper. Aren't you a damned fool and a funny one at that. The most we have to fear is pregnancy from all this screwing, tall warrior. Will you compensate me for her earning life?"

Abimelech looked around the seedy whorehouse and sighed. Sweeping his mane of hair back, he considered killing the Madam and the other half-dozen women in her stable. He decided not to, as the wizard had to die per Goliath's orders, and Abimelech remained grateful he got that much done.

"I suggest you take the wizard for his wealth. He's liable to be holding some gold or jewels. That should make you able to buy better girls and move out to Irem."

Jowls flapping, Dralla Bojak persisted, "No, you shitheel. The magus did good business with us. We gave him what he needed for his magic operations and he paid us back in other ways."

Wiping the gore from the spear on the soiled bed sheet, Abimelech wondered, "How did you supply him, Madam? Tell me. What could only you furnish a man such as Kmentosi?"

She motioned for Abimelech to follow her as she twisted a finger in the tight curls of her scalp. The woman opened a long cabinet in the room next to the one Abimelech had just entered. Bringing a large candle close, the Madam illuminated the content of the cupboard.

At first, Abimelech thought it a canning shelter, where vegetables were preserved for the winter months. Well, he was partially right.

Various jars held many odd shapes and bizarre figures. Some containers held many tiny ghastly silhouettes, others, only a larger one.

"You know what they are, Philistine?"

Abimelech nodded as he wiped the blood from the heron feathers of his spear on the hem of her gown. "Yes, babies that are lost. I've seen what falls from a woman before her time with child is ready. Why in the name of the gods hold them here?" Suddenly, it dawned on Abimelech. His voice lowered and he said, "You and your whores keep these for the wizard when he comes for his magick processes?"

Dralla shrugged with great effort, somewhat angered when she noticed Abimelech had finished cleaning his spear on her dress. "Beats having him steal live babies for his ceremonies, no?"

Abimelech appreciated the logic of Dralla Bojak. However, he changed his mind and slew every whore in the rickety house with his broadsword. After that, he burned the place to the ground. Once he was certain the building would be consumed, he got drunk with the money he stole from the wizard's body.

Then, he mounted up and headed toward Ashdod. His appointment with Akisha and Yaggah drew nigh.

*****

Goliath missed many things when traveling abroad. The sea air was all right, but he hated the sensation of no land under his feet. It amazed him how much he missed the lips of Trebluha.

He lay back and let her work her magic, for it seemed unearthly just how good she was at her craft. As her lips and teeth nibbled on his left nipple, Goliath recalled the look in her face as he returned to Gath. Oh, she loved him, loved him bad and there was no denying it. True to her nature, she never made a loud declaration of such feelings, but heaped on soft praises as she made love to him. He knew the difference. She didn't perform sex on him. Trebluha made love to him.

While he enjoyed her as much as he could, it was

obvious to two people why he was in Gath. Trebluha wasn't one of them. Goliath saw the outline of his mother in the temple tower when he arrived. Orpah understood why he was there.

She'd keep.

For now, Goliath enjoyed the slender woman who loved him to tears. His fingers ran down her sandy-colored hair as she ran her tongue over the length of him. He certainly didn't love her, but enjoyed the way she made the jagged edges of his heart, the places where most men let love in, feel.

CHAPTER EIGHTEEN
MOTHER

Akisha shook so her teeth rattled against each other, even in her astral body, she felt the sensation. She soon experienced the soothing words of Malak, a tone so gentle it flowed like butter over her head and down her shoulders.

"Calm yourself, dear heart."

"But he's back! He's returned to Philistia!"

"Apparently," Her words, while still tender and caressing in the light-kissed realm of the wheel, took on a terse quality.

"He was supposed to die."

"I know."

Akisha choked and then cried out, "So many times."

"Yes, yes, but be of fine cheer, dear heart. He has shone no malicious thoughts toward you, has he?"

"No."

"Has he sent words of anger or threatened you in court where our eyes and ears lurk?"

"No."

"Why do you worry for yourself?"

"I cannot help but feel worried that he will hate me for this."

Malak's voice lowered and became sweeter still.

"Goliath knows the ways of this world and has never worried on creating a bastard before…"

"Whoever lived through his actions before?!"

"Be that as it may, he knows the customs of a warrior. This world is full of bastards. He is one himself of a different fashion. I doubt he will be emotional over the life of another baby."

"But, won't he be jealous of the adoration given to me?"

"His mother might, but she'd have made a move by now. No, she cares only for herself, like any gilded lily of the gods should. I will never fault her for minding her own business, that one."

"Can you read his intentions?"

"No. He has a shielded mind and what he does speak, I see no idea for you in it other than silly things about an arranged marriage."

"What?!"

"Surely you hear these yarns on the wind with your ladies in waiting?"

"Yes, but I thought them nonsense."

Malak paused and then said with a stern voice, "He plays politics with the kings, naught for you to worry on."

"Perhaps I should ask Kmentosi to have a further reading, to look into it more?"

"Speak not to me of that one again."

"Kmentosi?"

"Yes."

Akisha gaped at the image of Malak on the wheel. "Has he fallen from your favor?"

Malak fell silent for a long time. "I sense he's fallen from favor in many ways. He is no longer important for our cause."

"But I thought him necessary to give me guidance as the revolution comes?"

"He was, yes," Malak replied smartly. "But he's so far away from me, I fear him a maggot back to his old gods. Bah, let him go into their slimy embrace. I shall find another to stand in his stead. The old ways are waning, dear heart. You are the future. All will be well soon."

"If you say."

"Yes, I do. Go bathe, relax and nap. All will soon be well. I haven't played out all of my moves against the nation or their champion."

Akisha's image faded from the ether realm in Malak's inner chamber and she opened her eyes to the place of the wheel. Malak took but one step away from the lines of vestal virgins, all steady at their posts, and even started to speak to the stone artisan Ahkuh-Rhan, wonderfully oblivious to her recent conversation…when she blinked and the darkness of the spirit sphere fell back on her. Malak's defenses went up and she heard the gurgling rumble in her ears, a beat she could easily translate as laughter.

"Show yourself," she ordered. "Your magick is no match for my focus."

Amidst the laughter, words formed, hardly recognizable, but she understood them to say, "You speak of magick. Who are you, little one, to spit at the toenails of those that battled God himself?"

Her anger white hot Malak stepped back on to the wheel and her power surged. "Begone from my realm, Dagon. I know your smell."

Suddenly frozen in place on her spot, she felt a wet tickle at her right ear. The voice was distant, but still audible, saying, "Not so kind to be immobile, is it, little one? I cannot hold here, but thank you for amusing me with this tale of magick."

"Where is Kmentosi?"

The voice gurgled in laughter again. "In here,

with us. You greatly amuse us beyond, little one. Your attempts at the Philistine give us great giggles." The voice faded more, but she heard it say, "Like a tyke trying the bow for the first time, you just cannot hit the target."

Her eyes opened and all was as it should be in her abode.

The vestal virgins, quivering, fell to their knees, breathing hard.

"You have done well," she told them, her right hand going to her forehead.

Ahkuh-Rhan stepped away from a pillar, his chisel dangling beside him. "Mistress? Are you all right?"

She took several breaths and didn't answer him.

*****

Abimelech never would deny he enjoyed his time in Goliath's shadow. Everyone knew who he was and in turn, the superior treatment commenced. This recognition brought out fear, respect, oral gratification and at times, blind hatred. As he rode closer to Ashdod, Abimelech pondered that was always a given and he readily accepted the rough with the smooth in serving his master.

One of the rough things was when not with his master, and out of his armor, Abimelech stood out in the minds of many. He, too, was a bigger man than a common Philistine soldier. However, many recognized him and would know who this unknown man riding was in time. He comprehended a secret mission would be fast. Goliath understood the view of the situation when he made the request. So far he made his trip and killings with little trouble.

Did he feel more confident when abiding with his

master? Of course. He felt better in the company of the military, but he was too well-trained to be skittish amongst the populace of Philistia. He didn't want to believe a conspiracy against his master and the others in the nation festered everywhere.

"That's the problem," he ruminated as he approached the edge of Ashdod. "One would have to hate all of us to direct the kings and generals to so many defeats by the Hebrews. Aside from killing Goliath, the Philistines seem a damned pawn for someone...something." He smiled, knowing Kmentosi usually was the closest advisor to King Vyndekay.

Abimelech rode around the back of the temple of Dagon and then dismounted fast. The stable area there welcomed him in, and they took him as a military man worthy of stabling his mount. He shushed the servants as it would quickly spread who he was if so announced. After all, Abimelech carried the seal of the high priest Kmentosi and all bowed at this emblem.

"Is she here now, the lady Akisha?"

The servant of the stables bowed and nodded. "Yes sir. She'd taken up time over at the temple of Ashtoreth, but returned here seeking our high priest. She relaxes this afternoon here with her ladies. Would you like me to procure one of them for you?"

"Not at present," he smiled. "Perhaps later. Is the one named Yaggah here as well?"

The stable servant turned his head and nodded toward the slender man who talked with a few other temple attendants. The skinny man spoke leisurely with these robed men before heading back into the temple. Yaggah, his own self, all resplendent in new clothes and jewels, oblivious to the presence of Goliath's shield bearer.

"Well, sonofabitch," Abimelech muttered and then handed the servant the emblem along with a few coins.

"Many thanks. I carry a message for him."

"Do you need to be announced? I shall call an acolyte."

"No need. I can announce myself just fine."

Focused on the amazingly ornate emblem of Kmentosi now in his possession, the servant nodded and turned away from Abimelech.

As Abimelech headed toward the temple, he thought of how much he loved his life. He'd kill to keep it, too. Yes, there was a wistful part of him that longed to see what was over the next hill, over the crest of waves with Weldon. First thing's first, though...

*****

Goliath waved at the boorish man who emerged from the smithy shop in Gath. "Kikron! They are still feeding you well, you ugly bastard."

The blacksmith's bulk came more from his mass of muscle shoved into a squat body, but the smith took the poke with good humor. "Still talking from your rectum, I see." He lifted up the huge bronze helmet of the champion. "Here. I put the application on that you requested."

The giant's eyes blinked, but his look of amazement held no wrath. "That was fast." He took the helm and turned it over in his hands. He nodded appreciatively as the blacksmith talked.

"The messenger got me the helmet and I set to work on it with haste. That addition on the forehead extends down over the bridge of your nose now."

"I see," Goliath said, nodding.

"It'll hold. It may take some getting used to, looking past it, but it will serve its purpose."

"Many thanks."

"My thanks came in the gold Sadik brought when he delivered it. A good kid, that one."

"He seems to be." Goliath looked at the smithy shop. "Why do you have those heads on your door post? That can't be good for business."

Kikron ran a hand over his balding scalp, but never turned to look at the shrunken heads Goliath referred to. "Those belong to a couple wayfaring travelers who tried to rob my shop in the night."

Goliath put back his head and roared with laughter. "They tried to steal from a maker of weapons?"

"Dumber than owlshit," Kikron pronounced, spat, and then said, "They serve as a warning, all shrunken up like that. By the way, I have a gift for you kind of like that."

Smile fading, Goliath wondered, "Oh?"

Kikron turned and shouted, "Anata? Bring out the twins."

Though confusion reigned on Goliath's face, his furrowed brow flattened when the stout teenaged girl brought out a pair of shrunken heads. Strung together with a cord through their ears, the pair of identical faces seemed to amuse the chubby girl, Anata. With a face as brutal as her father's, the girl said, "Here, sir. Daddy says you may want them."

"Oh?" Goliath said, taking the cord and raising the dangling heads to his eyes. "Does he now?"

Arms folded, Kikron said flatly, "If you don't want them, that's all right. Some guards brought them here, bought them at Rantis, they claim."

"Huh," Goliath said, eyes on the stitched up mouths of the twin faces.

Anata volunteered, "They were guards for one of General Schlack's wives. They wondered if a mage might want these for a spell."

Kikron asked, "Do you recognize them?"

"Yes. They are Sanrevelle, daughters of a god, I suppose." He let the heads dangle at his side. "Isn't fate a cocksucker?"

Anata shrugged. "Do you like them."

Goliath smirked at the girl. "Yes, I like them. I'll send you more gold for them."

Kikron shrugged and turned, "Whatever you see best. Try not to get yourself killed."

Goliath turned toward the temple of Ashtoreth and saw Trebluha awaiting him there. "I'll try not to."

Though she frowned at the heads in his hand, she smiled up at him before opening the gate.

Goliath put down his weapons, helmet and the heads in the inner court of the temple of Ashtoreth. The ladies that attended to him promised to keep them and clean them off. He then asked Trebluha, "They treat you well, still, I trust?"

She nodded as they walked and wore a playful smile. "It's a quiet, clean life, yes, they are kind to me."

Goliath gazed across the courtyard and to a set of stone steps the wound up to the southern tower. "Your days of filth and labor are over." He never looked back as he walked across the yard, alone, ducked his head and started up the steps.

The scent of flowers, probably cut fresh from the gardens, struck him. His mother enjoyed them and even used to like him to prune her flower garden as a boy. When he ascended into the upper level of the tower, he saw a spread-out loft section. Goliath then saw many bunches of flowers in bowls and vases.

Though sparsely decorated, the dwelling room appeared immaculate. A sleeping mat, several chairs, napping couches, a place to write or read, a reclining area for taking meals, everything a would-be goddess could want.

Philistine

By the main window's shutters stood his mother, Orpah, tall for a woman, but not egregiously so, and full of grace as she turned to see her son. Her face, plain, aging, but not full of lines nor sagging, and gladly not overdone with makeup. She still stared at him with icy green eyes that seemed to come from so far away. Orpah moved with the grace of a dancer, but never took an abundance of steps, and her gown swept silently across the floor. Her hair, trimmed up more than Goliath recalled, was short, mostly white and hemmed in with streaks of gray in a circle of black. Orpah always seemed to be looking down on him...

"No cause to kneel," she said and walked to her desk.

Goliath looked down at himself on one knee and then the ceiling. He moved forward and stood up a little. "The overhang is low."

She glanced at the rounded top of the door as if she'd never considered such a thing. "You look well."

"I am," he assured her, sweeping back his locks over his shoulder.

Her look intensified. "You have a fading bruise on your face."

"Several other places, too."

Her jaw tight, Orpah nodded and looked at the desk.

"How does the season find you, mother?"

Her eyes focused up at him. "Concerned, but that is my way." Orpah then stared down at her table again. "I heard tell of the escapade in Egypt."

"Word travels quickly nowadays."

"Priests talk so much, and so do the little girls who bow to them while they are naked. They then serve me as immaculates, thinking they deceive me...and yet, I hear their words and tawdry whispers." She glanced up at him. "You'd be surprised."

"Probably."

"They say you were prisoner of the Pharaoh?"

"Yes, for a time."

She nodded reflectively, eyes to the window. "I heard tell of the incursion down the Nile and that a slave set you at liberty."

"In a manner of speaking."

"And I heard tell of Psusennes I." Her thin fingers folded over each other as she spoke.

"Yeah," Goliath nodded, his hair brushing her ceiling.

"I hear he is still alive."

Goliath wore a wicked smile as he professed, "I slew his wife and his daughters, and left him alive, limbs dislocated in front of his god."

Orpah did not look at him as she let her hands drop. "That was careless of you."

His cocky smile faded. Words failed him.

She added, "Why would you do such a thing?"

"Because I left him alive to suffer, not only the pain of his wounds but the mental torment of knowing what happened to his daughters."

"That sounds like something a woman would do, to torment one long after the fact, in the mind." Orpah again looked up at her son and asked, "Are you fighting like a woman now? No wonder so many plot against you."

His jaw fell open but again no words came out.

Orpah said, "If you'd have slain him, he'd be suffering beyond eternity now. All of these mind games, they are best left for women."

Goliath said gently, "You're a woman, Mother."

Her eyes deepening in color, she affirmed. "Yes, I know." Orpah turned and walked back to the window. "And in your ways in life, in the middle of wars, death and besting of trollops and devils, you have come to see your mother to quell your heart." Orpah sighed. "You worry me, Son. Greatly"

Uncomfortable, he again returned to his knee. "You may have the answers I seek, ones you've chosen to hide from me in my life."

She turned and now wore a sly grin. "So many words, no questions, though."

*****

Akisha sank into her bath, enjoying the hot water. The serving girls added in vials of scented oils that made her nose expand. They'd soothed her down with oils and even drew shaving apparati only familiar in Egypt across her body. Akisha, slick and smooth, relished her drink, even if it was early in the day.

Hands across her belly, she patted it and felt what lived inside move. Always careful in the bath, she dared not take a chance. One fall, one misstep and she might lose the reason for her opulent treatment.

Akisha's smile, whiter these days due to the treatments of the girls, widened as she thought of her good fortune. Hands between her legs, she put her head back and said, "Come to me, Kmentosi, like in the night before I ever carried this. What a devious man serving a greater good." She picked up her cup of water and toasted the ceiling. "To Yaggah, best brother in my family."

The girls gathered her old clothes and started to lay out new items. They talked amongst themselves as they did so, saying, "Did you see the size of the visitor from Ashkelon?"

"Why do you assume he was from there?"

"His mount wore the insignia of General Schlack's

brand and they are quartered there."

"His overcloak looked like a priest's vestment."

The taller of the two girls laughed. "You ever see a priest *that* size?"

They giggled and the shorter one said, "No, I suppose not. He was a handsome man, that one."

More laughter ensued as the one dropped her voice to a throaty tone and said, "I'd love to bathe Abimelech any time."

Akisha dropped her cup in the bath water and sat forward. "What did you say?"

Both of the young women jumped and then faced their mistress. The taller one said, "Ma'am?"

"What did you call the one you are drooling over?"

"Who? Um, Abimelech?"

At first, her mind raced and thought it a common enough name. Then, she said, "Get me dry. I would see this man myself."

"I can say you want to meet him."

"No!" Akisha shouted. "Please, get me dry and we will look together."

Her heart couldn't be quelled as the young ladies helped her to stand.

*****

Fingertips together like identical spiders, Orpah said, "At times I pity you having to be out there amongst such fools. I try not to get attached to the girls who serve me. They grow, they mature and are no more."

Goliath then sat back on the floor to look her in the face better. "One gets used to the world, mother. If I tried to journey to lands where they claim to be learned and of such higher classes, that'd bore me to tears."

Philistine

Orpah walked across the room, smelled her flowers and then said, "But amongst these Philistines, you are indeed a champion. You were endowed with great strength and a life envied amongst men."

Goliath nodded but never said a word.

Orpah stated, "I've heard the girls say I am a slave to this temple and the priests, but that is imprudent talk from maids who don't think an old lady has good ears."

Goliath smirked but remained silent.

"I miss that round hipped girl who served me for years, Ahmee. She kept her tongue in my presence, but I heard she was all lips and ears for Eucimar."

"Ahmee? She now serves Neurath at Nebo, I hear."

At that name, she rolled her eyes, then sighed before saying, "Look, what I've been given in this existence, a life of comfort, esteem and rest. It is better than dirt and toil, no? It is a life in these parts that so many would kill for." Orpah paused and now she wore a catty smile, her eyes resting on her son. "Or so I hear."

"Lucky I'm so strong, hmm?"

"Luck has nothing to do with it," she said shortly, humor fading from her face. "It wasn't just the blood of your father I passed on in your flesh. My capacity to handle a god like him is not evidence of adulation or appreciation. No, if I was a gutter tramp or a bar whore, you could just as easily be that fat pig Neurath hiding on Nebo, fretting over his place in the universe."

Goliath said, "My father created me, but you made me champion of the Philistines. We both know this, mother."

Orpah shook her head. "Which is why it baffles me why some are so ready to embrace a slut who couldn't train a puppy to piss in the weeds much less a son to be admired."

Goliath thought of his youth, of the scourgings and

strict rules of his mother. There were so many joyful times, and he understood her vigilance. Neurath was the lesson, a Nephilum with a whore for a mother, and one who let him grow up free of the lash.

"True," was all Goliath said.

"Not everyone is suited to be a goddess."

Goliath agreed with a nod. He then related to his mother the words of Zorn and his troubles as of late. He told her of the wheel, the form after him and Zorn's implications of finding the answer in the Domain of Moloch to cure his thoughts of his father. He also confided the words of Ba'al Zebul to her.

"You need new friends," said Orpah as she pondered his words. Orpah sat on her napping couch, hands folded in her lap. "Zorn is a wise individual, but his wisdom is only for himself. He seeks a boon from you, the bones of Moses, to destroy the Israelites. If I were you, I wouldn't give a toss about a wizard's vendetta against a tribe of slaves."

"I have no intention of returning to Zorn."

"Good. That is the smartest thing you've said today. The bones of this prophet, they probably do hold good karmatic magic." She contemplated that a few moments and then said. "You need not return to him if you are that vexed over the astral images and about your father."

Hands on his knees, Goliath raised an eyebrow. "Oh?"

She nodded. "I shall tell you what attacks in the spirit. The method in which she has been revealed to you is fascinating, and clearly, not all of her doing. You see, you are meant to think Bednukah and her demon are the source of this attack. There is a good reason. Someone there is trying to tell you the truth and cannot."

"Bednukah is on my side? That's hard to grasp."

"Of course she isn't. I never said that."

Someone there...

Philistine

Her voice ran bitter but soon returned to a steady tone. "Zorn is correct that the answer for you lies in that Domain of Moloch, in one regard. But be careful what you desire to know, son. You are strong and can handle reality well. Bednukah and her dire realm blocks that which reaches out to destroy you and all Philistines."

"Who is it?"

Orpah said in a polite voice, "There are thought to be only two of you left on this world, many say one in you, as Neurath is a pathetic soul praying to gods for answers on Nebo. However, there is another."

"Who is he?"

"Not a he. She." Orpah did not smile as she said, "Your sister."

*****

Yaggah stood outside the stables of the temple, passing water by the high bushes, humming a bawdy ditty.

"I hear a wedding is on the way," a deep voice said to him and Yaggah nearly jumped. "Sorry. I didn't mean to frighten you."

Yaggah gave the speaker a brief glance, seeing only the tunic of the priests of Ashkelon. "Oh, that's dense talk. I'll believe the champion marries Akisha when I see it." He then turned to face the speaker and his smile faded.

Abimelech said, "Put it away or die with your dick in your hand, I don't care."

Yaggah nearly cried out as he reached for his belt and the short sword slung there. Abimelech proved faster, his right hand on Yaggah's wrist so he couldn't draw steel, his left backhanding the skinny man across the face. Blood arching from Yaggah's nose, the man slipped from Abimelech's grasp, rolling with the blow, and wrestled the bushes more than anything as he went to the ground. Again, Yaggah struggled to draw a weapon, but Abimelech stomped a foot into the pit of his back. The wind left Yaggah and tears sprang to his eyes.

Abimelech said nothing as he unsheathed the great sword from his back, invisible in the folds of the robe.

Yaggah's breath returned to him and he gasped, "I'll tell you...where she is...just..."

"I'll find her without your help. What a fool to conspire against the champion."

Blood smearing his lips, Yaggah floundered and snapped, "He never came here himself, did he?"

Abimelech took his foot from his back and kicked Yaggah in the kidneys so he'd roll over. "Your blood isn't worth it. I wouldn't have my master sully his blade with your black little heart."

"Listen to me!" Yaggah tried to push away with his heels. "I know who his father is! I know where he is! I know who his sister is!"

Abimelech held his sword down like a spear and drove it into Yaggah's heart. Hands up, he tried to stave off the blade, but failed. A look of astonishment spread over the pallid face of Yaggah as the shield bearer of Goliath said, "Good. So do I." He then shoved down farther, certain the blade was in the dirt beyond Yaggah. Abimelech then twisted the blade in a circle, making sure he obliterated Yaggah's heart.

All pretense dropped, Abimelech put his foot on Yaggah's jaw, pulled out the blade and stepped away from the body. He faced two of the temple guards as they approached. They sported short blades and even carried shields.

They'd need them, Abimelech thought.

"Stop!" one of them cried out. "What have you

brought unto the house of our god?"

Abimelech brought his sword around and stepped forward. With a great overhand swing, his blade crashed into the short sword of the guard nearest to him, breaking the weapon and driving into the guard's thigh. The upswing clipped the guard through his jaw and up unto his forehead.

When the other guard saw the brains of his partner spilling down his nose, he stepped back and exclaimed, "There's no need for bloodshed."

"You are wrong," Abimelech informed him as he turned, and chopped Yaggah's head free of his corpse. He kicked the body for spite and struck down again, the skull breaking open.

*****

When Akisha saw Abimelech stalking a urinating Yaggah, she retreated to the rear of the temple and approached the priests acting in Kmentosi's stead. She blurted out how they had to protect her and get her free.

While confused at her terror, they tried to tell her, "Rumor is that our master, High Priest Kmentosi is dead. We can feel it in the air."

Hysterical she pleaded with them, "The shield bearer of the champion is in the stables. We don't have much time."

Two of the younger priests exchanged glances. One stepped forward and said, "I was to meet with a great Prophet of the Hebrew God in Beth-horon today. You can come along with me and we will keep to the wilds. We must hurry, though."

Akisha was heading toward the main entrance to the temple when the call to arms for the guards sounded out.

Later that day, while sleeping on the ground guarded by priests, she heard tell from a messenger that Abimelech slew every last person in the temple of Dagon at Ashdod, even the serving girls.

*****

"Sister?" Goliath let the word hang like a strung-up deer.

Neatly crossing her legs and adjusting her long gown, Orpah replied, "Glad you are so curious about family bloodlines now?"

"Why keep such a thing from me?"

Her look ever steady, Orpah said, "What did it matter? She held your ankle as you were born from another sack. Yes, your paternal twin, as it were, but she didn't live long."

"Oh?'

"Or so I was told."

"I don't follow your words, mother."

"You have heard tales of the sired children of the angels or fallen ones and they are always great fighting men of renown, correct?"

"Yes, who hasn't?"

"Ever ask yourself why they were all boys?"

Goliath gaped at the flowers and admitted, "I never pondered such a thing."

"Of course, because you think through your manhood. You may be half god, but you are still half man."

"Thanks. If she were a fighting woman, a giant as well..."

"Again, get your brain out from behind your balls,"

Philistine

she said bitterly. "The seed that comes out woman is tainted, defiled and wrong. In the few cases it has happened, it is always so. She wasn't hideous by any means, but different and unlike any other woman."

"How so?"

"I never saw such a perfect face." Orpah's eyes glazed, as if trapped in a memory. Her face returned to a serious façade as she related, "Yet, I saw her fall into a deep sleep and turn to stone. Yes, heavy as an anvil. Ironic, as a female Nephilum are where the legends of the gorgon originate."

"Amazing. You mean the snake body and hair of serpents?"

"Please don't be such a savage. Men tell insane tales. A yarn is probably called a yarn because it spins, weaves and creates something broader than intended. Your sister was humanoid, but gorgeous, serene even. I wouldn't hazard a guess at her appearance now. It sounds like this is who is tormenting you."

"But you said she died, turned to stone?"

Orpah frowned. "Your father took her body away. He was known for having a big heart when it came to certain things. Isn't that astonishing? A god on earth, randy one moment, a pup of a father the next, but I suppose he had a weakness for his children. Perhaps he reanimated her in some way or she really wasn't dead. I do not know, but I know what I feel in the dreamlands and it smells like her."

"How can you be so sure it is her?"

She took a few moments and then said, "A mother knows. I can feel it. I feel her like I can feel you when you are in distress. There is a deeper soul connection between us. I never mentioned her or my thoughts that she lived as it never was very important. However, if she wishes you or our folk ill, then she must be dealt with."

"You make it sound so easy."

"You took care of me and made certain I was cared for. Who is she but a usurper to anything? Who is this piglet she has at our gates, and why has she decided to make her into a goddess? As I said before, not everyone is suited for divinity."

"But what does she want? Why inspire the leaders, lead them to wars and get them killed? What sort of game is that?"

"Sounds rather childish, doesn't it? Perhaps that is all it is, spite and pure evil desire for death. You are her focus and in her way if she is playing with power. Like all children when their toy soldiers no longer amuse them, they crush them."

Goliath fell silent for a time before saying, "I've always wondered if you were truly happy here with this life."

"Please stop your words of weakness." Orpah's words fell acidic. "You distress me. Your father gave me an envied life. After him, no other man compared. That is why you have only four brothers. I'd rather have no men in my life than a succession of little dopes. What is it you crave?"

Goliath took to his knees before her. Hands flat to the floor, head to her lap, he never faced her as he said, "I know who I am. I know I am the one, the last one. I am Goliath."

Her eyes on his scalp, she wondered, "You still seek an audience with your father? Acknowledgement or closure? Well, good luck, as the gamblers say. He is no longer what he once was, so be careful when you find him. Go see Neurath, he will convince you of your task. Go and see if my girl Ahmee is there with him and bring her back. That is as good an excuse as any to visit Nebo. Or, tell him the truth and kill his disgraceful ass. None of that matters to me." She then let her right hand rest on the crown of his head. The think fingers stroked his mane of hair twice and then, the hand dropped to her side.

"Neurath?"

He faced her as Orpah said, "I hear talk of what you plan, to become King and take this tramp great with your child as your consort Queen." She reached forth her right hand again, her fingertips touching the skin above his beard on the left side of his face. "Visit Neurath at Nebo. It will convince you such thinking is a folly."

She knows something, he thought, but wants me to see for myself.

Goliath let her index finger run up his nose and stop at the bruise on his forehead. He took her hand and kissed the palm of it. "I shall go unto Nebo and get my answers. Then, I shall seek out those who wish to destroy me."

"Good. Go to it."

His eyes focused in on hers. "They shall surely die."

Orpah stared into his face. "I expect no less than their deaths." He bowed his head again and was about to withdraw from her room when she said, "Show no mercy. That is an emotion for simple men. You are something far greater. You are the One. You are the last one. You are my first-born son. You are Goliath the Philistine. Now, go crush them to pulp and tell me about it later. It is time for my nap."

CHAPTER NINETEEN
ABODE OF THE GODS

General Samien awoke with a start, mind afire from his dream. Never a man to nap, he'd been so exhausted, he needed rest.

By the time Samien donned his clothes and reached the cave entrance, a company of his soldiers met him. All of their faces wore the identical shocked expression.

Samien scanned their faces and then settled on Baldassare. "You slept too, didn't you all?"

A few swallowed, ashamed to admit they slumbered at their posts or had indeed crept away for a snooze. But the Colonel, he joined several in nodding. "Yes. You heard the words and the warning?"

"Yes," Samien said, but suddenly realized over a hundred soldiers were saying the word with him. "I see." He smiled and then rubbed his eyes. "We shall all eat the punishment for dereliction of duty, my good fellows." They shared an uncomfortable laugh as the General waved to them, and several more standing near. "She has warned us of Schlack's coming attack."

Baldassare wore a humorless look. "We did send him an invitation."

"By design, he's coming at us, his manhood challenged," Samien explained, arms folded over his half-open tunic. "That arrogant fool will tred on a battlefield of her choosing..." he paused, all eyes on him, "...of my choosing. When the time is nigh and we meet him--you saw the dream and felt her power--her focus will give us victory."

While the men cheered and Samien gave instructions to start gearing up for the coming fight, Baldassare slowly slipped into the cave behind him. The General turned to move and faced his Colonel. He waited until they were alone before asking, "What is it?"

"Schlack will bring thousands of men, all of his best."

Samien nodded with vigor. "Yes."

"And the champion."

"Possibly. But with her focus on us, a thousand will fight like ten thousand."

Baldassare frowned. "But if Goliath is on the field..."

"You're closer to the goddess than me. I'm surprised I was deemed worthy of a dream."

"It moved you to action, didn't it?"

Samien now wore a sour look. "I see. Nonetheless, we have trained for this moment. I'd rather it's later, but this confederation may not hold for long. Probably better to strike now. But as I was to say, do you think she can slay the champion before our war?"

"It is my hope, but he seems resilient, no?"

"Quite, but I cannot center on that." Samien twisted around fast, looking at the massive encampment that stretched far into the oblivion of the Transjordanian wilderness. "Get them ready, Colonel."

Hand to his heart, Baldassare then saluted.

*****

Goliath departed from Gath and traveled only a few miles

outside of town when he met a small force of two dozen men. Captain Balzer led their ranks, and among them were the usual brand of men from the trips in the past weeks. Qorus, back in his usual Philistine armor, and Abimelech as well, all greeted him. He singled out Sadik and playfully boxed his ears, then the giant showed him the modified helmet from the blacksmith.

He noted a new addition to the band of troopers, a woman clad in leathers not unlike the soldiers. However, Goliath recognized her as the pale, voluptuous Hasana, acolyte of Ba'al Zebul. He opened his mouth to ask what she was doing with the group, but saw she carried the head of Eucimar on a cushioned seat aboard her horse.

"They sent you a handler?" he asked the wizard.

Eucimar rolled his eyes. "I'd have one if I weren't as such. Besides, she serves a singular function to keep me well."

On cue, Hasana undid a clasp near her throat and her tunic fell open. Her ample breasts hung lower, and Goliath took note of her large, dark areolas. When she raised Eucimar to suckle at her left breast, he understood that the girl must still have milk and volunteered to serve her master, again.

After they brought each other up to speed, Goliath gave Abimelech a joking jab. "Something told me Akisha would slip through your fingers, but it pleases me the wizard, Yaggah and the rest are done. Her escape is of no concern right now. I have a greater issue to deal with. I need to go to Nebo and speak with Neurath."

Balzer told the men to go into Gath for more road supplies as Abimelech handed Goliath a small bundle. The cloths soon fell away in the champion's palm and he held up a human hand. He laughed, nodded to his shield bearer and tossed the hand of Yaggah to the wild dogs trailing the troops.

The troopers dismounted and Blazer took a knee.

The Captain said, "A confederation of Samien's troops grows and that force draws together not far from Jericho. Through the wastelands, they will come and invade our land across Israel. Many think they are after the main body of the Philistine army. All of the oracles of Philistia see it and the news flows on the wind. We were allowed out by Schlack to warn you and escort you to a forward position as his ranks take shape."

Goliath laughed once. "So we could die first. Wonderful of that asshole."

Balzer added, "A great force will come in behind us led by Schlack himself, all of them."

Abimelech offered, "We could be set for an unfortunate accident, sire, out there alone."

Goliath thought but for a moment. "That may be and any of you can go when you so please. Join the ranks or fart in their direction as you run to Babylon. I won't think any less of you for escaping today. However, I'll have need of some of you when I return to the Domain of Moloch. Yes, I must go there after I see Neurath, no matter if Samien holds his balls near Jericho or not."

Balzer said, "You have our respect and our allegiance forever, Goliath."

"You allegiance may cost you forever."

Qorus said loudly, "Better dead with you than living under the bridle of these mad men."

As they set off Goliath heard Cairn say, "Neurath? Isn't he the one like the champion?"

Sadik answered, "But he's a fat joke, I think. None are really like our champion."

Goliath strode near the horse of Hasana and waited until Eucimar faced forward again. "You need mother's milk to protract you now?"

Eucimar glanced up at Goliath, and then looked at the road ahead. "Yes. That sounds good. We'll go with that."

Philistine

The giant stifled his hilarity, knowing Eucimar was probably sustained by the magick of Zorn forever.

Thumb over his shoulder, Balzer said to Goliath, "Our men are strong, Champion, but the care and feeding of a reanimated head, well, that'd be trying their mettle. Although no woman is welcome in our ranks, we'll tolerate Hasana. She seems ready to defend herself."

Goliath eyed her, clad in light armor plates, sporting daggers at her waist and twin short swords on her back.

Abimelech rode near his master and asked, "Did you get the answers you wanted in Gath?"

They moved away from the rest a bit as Goliath replied, "More of a confirmation really, between us, Abi. At the least, she has directed me unto the Abode of the Gods where Neurath and his cult abide."

Eyes rolling to heaven, Abimelech replied, "Is that the final location of all of those like your father and Neurath's as well? I thought we'd finished with Nebo."

Pulling his covering tighter about himself, Goliath shuddered from the chilly wind. He didn't care for the idea of Neurath's father, or any of the other patrons, making an appearance.

"We don't share the same father."

"I know, but many say they all once lived where Neurath resides."

"Some say that's where they landed, or fell," Goliath muttered.

Slowly, Balzer segued back toward Goliath and said, "These men truly have pledged you their lives. Any other man they would have skinned alive by now."

Looking at the approaching mountain range, Goliath said calmly, "They would have tried."

"You see, they think if one legend is so, then the rest must be true."

Goliath exhaled as if to show the hairy man just how bored he was with his words. "I'm more lucky than blessed. That's what you can build a fetish to—luck and chance. The older one gets, the wiser one becomes, as a rule."

The clear eyes of Qorus looked at Goliath and he said, "The oracles, they say we are all going to die, all of us Philistines."

"That's just preposterous," Goliath snorted in a deadpan manner, never looking away from the direction of Nebo.

"They say that you talk to angels, sir."

Goliath glanced at him and then forward again. "Who are *they* anyway? Some people talk too much. Listen more and don't ask stupid questions. That comes with youth, I know."

Abimelech tried to get the younger man to recede, but Goliath spoke to him again.

"Some of these folks who talk need to listen to songs about someone else," Goliath declared in a fatigued voice. "Sounds like many seek out a hero with a death wish, if you listen to those ballads about me. Who is the fool now, the hired man or his boss? All of that's a load of hokum. I'm a soldier. We all want to die fighting, no? It just doesn't matter to me where I happen to fall fighting. I just want it to be worth it."

*****

General Schlack stood on the roof of the temple of Dagon at Ashkelon. The fine smoke of incense provided him a lurid halo as the King joined him. Together they watched the formations of Philistine troops start to fall in at the edge of the community.

Schlack never looked at him as he asked, "Did you hear what has happened at the temple in Ashdod?"

"Yes," Vyndekay replied, also focusing on the troops.

"I guess the champion grew tired of being played, no?"

The King fell silent.

"I suppose we should feel lucky."

"His man struck down those unlikely to provide much of a fight."

Schlack's ire rose as he retorted, "Like hell. Those were calculated executions, gleaning a clearer message than a hundred speeches or boasts. People understand blood and loss. When a wizard dies, someone they walk in fear of, a man who kept you up at night, that means something. When the mighty are felled so easily, it gets one's attention."

"Then perhaps Samien and this war is what we need."

At the front of the massive formation, a riderless horse stood in place. An attendant held the reins, ready for the General to lead the assembling masses. The rest of the cavalry trotted in, not yet clad in their chainmail armor. They quickly dressed the lines. Most of the Philistines were younger men, probably aged twenty to thirty years if a day, dark haired or shaven of head.

Vyndekay grumbled, "They are a fine force sent to confront a bunch of mutts." The perverts of Ammon and Moab have bitten off more than they can chew, to fight us here in our own yard."

"The distant pretenders to the thrones of Assyria have thrown in with the confederation of our enemies. By the edges of the forward infantry spies have spotted the standard of the archers of the Amorites and the leftovers of Amalekite forces. They've came a long way to piss on our breakfast plate."

"They assemble in the wastes beyond the Dead Sea? That is a certainty?"

Schlack nodded. "Every bastard who can work or pull his pecker is taking up a spear against us for some reason. They will fold against a drilled army."

The King ruminated for a minute before he said, "You'd think they'd attack Israel first."

"We're as much mongrels to those joining Samien as the Hebrews," Schlack reminded him, thumb flicking the pommel of the short sword on his belt.

"True."

The General scanned his lines of spearmen, divisions of archers and regular infantry. "Once the forces come to join us from Ashdod, Ekron, Gath and Gaza, we will make a mighty force and crush out enemy. Who knows? On the way home we may burn Jerusalem for jollies."

The King bade him farewell and Schlack descended to join his men.

Atop his mount, he assessed things anew. His horse stayed with serried lines of cavalry and ranks of berserkers, regular infantry and bowmen in leather jerkins stepped forward, bows in their left hands, ready to strike as if the enemy lurked nearby. Pikeman secured their basinets and gripped their long lances to show their unity.

Sword drawn, the General declared, "For Philistia, we march!"

The men shouted their allegiance and the columns started to move eastward.

*****

Malak arose from her bathing pool and dried herself. Her mind felt cold and her innards ached, so hungry. She donned no garment save for her hooded robe that she tied over her waist. Never to be mistaken for a petite girl, Malak adjusted the opening, almost laughing at her hiding the nakedness no one would notice.

Well, nearly no one.

After she departed her sleeping room, she turned to admire the newly refurbished tiny pillars at the door and the swirled inlays down the hall provided by the hands of Ahkuh-Rhan. "A wizard with a chisel for a wand," she said, appreciation in her voice.

Malak walked down to the next room, and noted her vestal virgins all deep in slumber.

"Rest well, ladies," she wished them. "Tomorrow will be a tiring day."

She traveled down to another door, this one only opened by the insertion of her index finger in a lock. Malak peered into the chamber, illuminated only by the scant light allowed by the hallway lanterns. She took a breath, seeing lines of stone figures, all gazing back at her.

Once Malak locked this door again, she moved to the next door and unlocked it in a similar fashion. Within this room, though, no outside light was needed to show anything. A pyramid of red, glowing orbs pulsed, formed the shape of a peculiar tree. All of the orbs pulsed at regular intervals, but not at the same time.

She reached out and caressed one of the orbs and the red glow inside never reacted. "You gave your heart unto me, yet don't really love me that much, Baldassare," she said and giggled in spite of herself.

Malak entered into the main chamber of the wheel and glanced across the empty expanse. Her eyes focused on the jewel on the ceiling that stood over the center of the wheel below. She then faced Ahkuh-Rhan, rubbing his hands together, admiring his own craftsmanship on the nearby seating stations he'd engraved into the outer ring of the wall.

When she applauded, Ahkuh-Rhan smiled and

bowed deep. He arose and said, "It is a pleasure to do such fine work for you, Malak."

"It is I who must give great thanks. How can I ever pay you for such a service?"

"The agreed price is enough. I must confess, working on it is a pleasure to me. I've worked in the craft all of my life. Allowing me to make this location a fancy place, well, that was gravy."

She smiled and walked around the wheel, eyes scanning all of the added quirks of the craftsman. "You have created a wonderful place people will fawn over in a thousand years."

He laughed and shook his head. "As long as you are happy with it, Malak, I don't care about posterity."

"Your woman must be a happy lady."

Ahkuh-Rhan confessed, "I'm a widower. My wife passed years ago, giving birth to our daughter. I never saw fit to get more wives, really. Besides, I'm getting old and my ability is what it is, if I must confess. I do stone work better than anyone, so there's my pride."

"You are a wonderful man, Ahkuh-Rhan. Would you allow me to give you a warrior's price to show my appreciation?"

He stared at her, mouth open for a moment before saying, "That isn't necessary, Malak, but I sure am flattered."

She soothed her right hand across her robe and let it fall open. "Please, I really have a need within me. It will be fine."

His eyes on her breasts and then going lower, he said, "I really don't know if I can. You are a beautiful woman and I'm just a worker, mistress."

Hands on her hips, revealing her hairless body to him, she said, "I'm not about lords, sires and glory hounds, Ahkuh-Rhan. You are a fine man. Making you perform properly is an easy serum for one such as I."

Philistine

Although he tried to ward her off, Ahkuh-Rhan's affable nature took over. Like the good man he was, he accompanied her to the bedchamber and even bathed before sipping a green drink she prepared for him. He joked that he hadn't been so randy or stiff since a teenager.

Malak lay back and let him explore her body. A tall, big-boned woman, Ahkuh-Rhan took to her well and proved a strong, sensitive lover at times. The fingers of the craftsman made her squeal, showing his craft at creating an orgasm nearly as adept as his ability to hone swirls in a doorframe.

Although intimidated by her, clearly, she put him at ease after their first time. Malak wanted his seed inside of her and he gladly gave it, quicker than he used to, Ahkuh-Rhan promised.

When he mounted her a second time, she read the amazement in his face, the fact that he grew so hard, so fast...that his member felt harder than it'd ever been... but soon, his look of shock and pleasure turned curious, as the sensation of hardness spread...all over his body.

*****

In the dead of night, Goliath suited up and headed out of the small camp of the Philistines. No subterfuge was involved, for everyone understood this as a part of the plan. They camped just below the plain of the great high mountain of Nebo. The soldiers slept poorly, well aware that tomorrow was the day for confrontations. Many remained too giddy to sleep and honed their weapons as best they could.

Goliath looked over his shoulder at the hidden camp almost eclipsed by boulders. He gripped the handle of the broadsword and then his javelin. As he walked, Goliath muttered, "It hasn't changed in decades." Indeed, this side of the peculiar great mountain signaling the lip of the Nebo range still loomed exactly as he remembered it—like a toothless, open-mouthed and mangled skull. Somewhere in that monstrosity Neurath and his cult of women lived. From everything Goliath had heard, there was somewhere between a hundred and two hundred of them.

The warrior smirked at the words of Cairn to Balzer before he departed. "Does he plan to walk right in there before us and do this work?"

"Yeah, pretty much."

The Philistine approached the mouth of the mountain as the sun broke through the peaks. Time was of the essence and Goliath jogged on fast, not really knowing what to expect, only single-minded in his duty.

"Hold, traveler!" a deep voice called from above him.

Goliath stared up at the nasal cavity in the face of the sheer mountain. A lone figure loomed above him and Goliath guessed by the voice it belonged to Neurath. While awaiting a visual conformation, sunlight spilled into the mouth of the cavern. Though the maw narrowed considerably, there was a crude wooden barrier like a gate quite a ways in front of him.

"Neurath? Where are you?" Goliath called out. "We may as well get this over with. You have something that I need."

A deep thudding sound echoed out in the cavern. Goliath figured it laughter.

"What further jests will God send down onto me?" the baritone voice said, half-singing the words. "My life swells with tragedy and you come to provoke me?"

Goliath shrugged as his cloak blew out behind him. "Not necessarily, but it may not have to come to that."

Above, the large figure stepped further into the

light. Goliath frowned, knowing that this was indeed the persona he'd seen before. Neurath, undeniably a giant, a few feet taller than even most men, had gained so much weigh Goliath doubted his identity. Though he couldn't see his entire form, Goliath saw the dusky-skinned giant clad only in a dark kilt wrapped around his waist.

"So you want to see the girls? How droll, Goliath."

"You know me?" Goliath asked, feeling somewhat inane for saying it.

The laughter returned. "Aye, of course I do. I wagered you long dead, though, from the reports from down south and then the Egyptian way. Unlike these impractical mortals, I care little if you could massacre a dragon or ravish five whores in one night."

"It was seven, but who is counting?"

Neurath chuckled again. "My father came from beyond the stars, Goliath. I am half of what he was—and you know of my kindred on this benighted planet."

"Yeah, we all are famous one way or another."

"In any instance, you cannot slay me," Neurath bragged and soothed his six-fingered hands across his flabby abdomen. "Good luck trying to eradicate me, even if your life has been the way of the warrior. I sense that such a duty is not paramount in your mind, though."

"Not really."

"You care not why I am here?"

"Should I?"

"You know what is beyond the Nebo Mountains?"

Goliath shrugged. "A great open land."

Neurath finished his words, saying, "Where the bearer of light from Heaven fell when he was rejected by the Supreme One. The impact was gigantic and the waters flowed in, freezing it solid for a time."

Goliath replied, "I hear many stories, Neurath."

The giant smirked; his long head tilted mockingly

to the right. "And I tell you the truth, I came here as it is a consecrated venue, but it has not fulfilled my desires. My brides all have failed me in this hour of magnificence, at this holy site or not."

"Brides?" Goliath raised an eyebrow, guessing what had happened to the women who followed him. "I need some bones from you, but I need to see one of the girls."

"Yes, all of them, my wives." Neurath cleared his thick throat and gripped the stone barrier before him. His muscled arms rippled through a layer of fat as he spoke. "I can smell thousands of combatants beyond the lip of the valley, gathering up weapons and their valor enough to slay each other. What, are they here to kill my brides and me? Have they sent you to warn one of their kindred?" He laughed. "They shall not kill them. No, not one."

Neurath sounded coldly more confident than Goliath liked to hear. He also surmised Neurath would never deduce his true mission that day, so he asked, "May I see her, the girl Ahmee? She was once handmaiden to my mother at Gath and a servant to Eucimar on the sly. Orpah wants me to see about her welfare. Some great answer lies in her being."

The giant stared at Goliath for a long time with eyes that seemed to be suns, and then looked at the distant rim of the valley. "I don't see why not."

Goliath's heart skipped, for he never thought it would be so effortless. His mind filled with dreadful things, like the wives of Neurath, all pregnant and under the giant's control, taking up arms and clashing with the small force not far behind him.

A system of pulleys turned and the gates opened outward. Goliath drew his broadsword and waited. Neurath was nowhere to be seen, but the sunlight crept in to add illumination to the torchlight's in the chamber.

Slowly, Goliath moved in and then stopped. The

warrior's eyes scanned the walls over, searching out the many items around him. Frowning, he did find relief in that he was now freed of his mission...for Orpah implied that Goliath slay the server girl Ahmee if she be in peril, rather than let her be one with the cult of Neurath. However, what reality presented itself was a worse fate than Goliath's mission.

Upon the stone walls of the inner keep protruded several metal hooks, probably hundreds, he thought. On each one hung the body of a woman, most of them pregnant woman, all of them dead. From the height of the women on the walls, only an immense, powerful man could have speared them on such hooks. The hooks extended from many chests between floppy breasts. Others hung lopsided with a hook under a collarbone. A few of the bodies hung even more grotesquely, their infants having aborted and fallen free, yet still were attached to their mothers by a purple cord.

Goliath holstered his broadsword. When Neurath stepped down the stone steps, Goliath knew what his new mission entailed. Indeed, the giant had aged much in the years since they last met.

"Talk to her, then," Neurath instructed the Philistine as he strutted from the steps. "I believe it is this reddish headed swine over here? Yes! That would be her."

Goliath glanced over his shoulder and thought he could hear the cries of the small Philistine force, but he wasn't sure in the wind.

Neurath's eyes glowed a shade of amber. "Surely, you weren't here to rescue that cow for your sainted mother? You would have only a small chance..." the deep voice faded as he, too, heard the forces of Balzer gearing up across the valley. The giant showed no fear and gave out a loud sigh. "No, you truly weren't here to rescue her body, were you? Only a bastard like Goliath would come in here and kill her so that she couldn't escape with me, eh?"

"We have to do what we have to do to live, Neurath," Goliath replied, hands at his sides. "A simple life is not why I came unto you."

The amber eyes leered at him for a few seconds before Neurath asked, "No show of swords? No attack? No questions? You puzzle me. If I were in your place, I would want to know why all of these women were slain, great in the belly with child."

Goliath shrugged. "A crossbred from off this world, I didn't expect normal behavior."

Neurath's ire faded. "You should talk. You don't have children, do you Goliath?"

"No," Goliath coughed, nostrils touched by the odor of the dead. Though many bodies decayed, he felt surprised that no flies kissed the bodies.

"My father was one of the sons of God, like yours," Neurath said, looking at the six fingers on each hand of his long, sagging arms. "Amongst these tiny parasites, I am as close to a god as they can find. They followed me and begged to be the vessel of my children."

Goliath nodded, his eyes going to a series of stone containers along the far wall. "Most of these women aren't the most petite things I have ever seen, pregnancy not withstanding."

He grinned. "A small woman couldn't capture me, as you are familiar with. To my point, I never forced any woman to be my slave, and yet, the failing was thought to be theirs." Neurath turned to a small cul-de-sac behind the stone outcropping by the steps and opened a wooden door. From out of this place came a tiny, skeletal form with an enormous head. The freak, reptilian in skin, sported huge eyes and no nose. The dull slit of a mouth made Goliath's skin crawl. The frail body certainly wasn't threatening in any way, just eerie.

"The product of your unions?"

Philistine

Neurath snorted. "Apparently, my father and his brethren could make giants from mating with women on this filthy world, but if we do it in turn, this is the result." From out of the hidden spot flowed many more of these creatures. A swarm of them soon filtered out. Neurath gestured at the hanging women and said, "After more tests, I forsook my dream of fathering a superior race, of being a god. After that, there's not much left for me."

"It's a terrible thing when one produces something the world can do without." Goliath sighed, disengaging his sword and leaning on his javelin.

Neurath paid him little attention at this act. "To dream, to foster a passion and have it destroyed; it numbs one, doesn't it?"

The sound of the Philistines started to rise louder behind Goliath. The horrific offspring of Neurath looked past the warrior with their almond-shaped eyes and blinked. They looked to their father as if to ask for guidance.

"The filthy tribe with you will solve my problem," Neurath said quietly. "Now go away, Champion, before you injure yourself with that sword. Leave me to my melancholy and be gone. I will snicker at the coming combat between the mongrels under Samien and your righteous phallus Schlack."

Closer and closer, the berserk screams came to the mouth of the great Nebo Mountain. The skinny children of Neurath walked past Goliath and to where the gigantic gate should close. They made no effort to shut that gate.

Goliath said, "It isn't that easy now, Neurath," His eyes glanced at the hanging bodies and his ears took in the screams at the primal gods of the incoming force. "You have managed to get my undivided attention and give me fatalism for life. Mother was correct. You have provided truth to me in ways you cannot understand.

For that, we must dance. You have something else I need."

Neurath still showed only mirth in his expression as he waved at the hanging bodies and said, "They are cows, cattle, containers, not even worthy of my seed. You have talked to spirits and slain creatures all over this abysmal planet, Goliath. Tell me that I am so wrong?"

Goliath stepped forward and took up a defensive pose. "I never said you were. I want the bones of the Prophet."

Neurath squared his shoulders, equal in height to Goliath, and stepped a bit closer. He looked past Goliath and pointed at the oncoming soldiers. He turned to a series of containers on the wall, not far from the hanging women. Sacks of grain stacked a neat retaining wall around the boxes of bones. "So, take them. I don't care. They couldn't conjure enough magic to make me a god. They are in the second box. The other bones are ox heads and some extinct leviathan."

Goliath gazed at the boxes and then returned his look to Neurath.

Neurath said, "They cannot kill me with their numbers, so what can you do? I shall ascend my stairs and jump into the sandy plains beyond. Perhaps there, I can find comfort for my..."

His words stopped as Goliath let his cloak fall. "We may as well get this over with."

Neurath's eyes widened at Goliath, and the Philistines led by Balzer hit the first line of freakish children. Neurath stepped back, gritted his teeth, appearing like a shark sniffing blood. His concern stoked for his own situation, not the slaughter of his offspring. The splattering sounds behind Goliath did not seem to faze Neurath at all.

Balzer and the Philistines crushed the skulls of the freakish group as they stared quizzically at the hairy attackers. In only moments, they stood at the mouth of the cavern, staring at Goliath and Neurath. They didn't advance.

Neurath spoke loudly, "So you have seen what you wanted, affirmed your duty, and I have even offered the bones of the Prophet for your supper. What more is it you want of me?"

"I'm the last of my kind, do you hear me?" said Goliath.

Neurath stepped toward the boxes of bones, stopped and wore a puzzled look.

Goliath stepped forward and attacked, fully anticipating what Neurath would do. Goliath's sword swung up at the giant's right thigh, but Neurath's hand batted the flat of the blade back. Just as this blow arrived, Goliath stabbed forward with his javelin, striking the abdomen of the giant. The thick hide of Neurath scratched deeply, but never bled as this weapon was knocked away as well. With one enormous stride, Neurath reached out, grabbed Goliath by the shoulders, and spun him around. With reflexes like lightning, the giant swiped his hands down Goliath's arms, knocking the weapons from the hands of the champion.

Balzer raised his right arm. This action froze his folk in their movements to attack. Intent to see how Goliath performed at the hour of his death, they simply watched.

A hand in Goliath's helmet and another gripping one of his armored greaves, Neurath swung the champion off the floor of the cavern, causing the Philistines to gasp. No grace inhabited the move but the flabby giant tossed Goliath into the third container of bones. He landed across the case on his back, and the stone surface gave way. Floundering in the pieces, Goliaths boots crashed into the second bone box, ruining the container.

A single stride later, Neurath stood over him, and

reached down into the ruined box at his left. "Prophesy for me now." His left hand pulled up a skull and smashed it across the helm of the struggling giant. The bones shattered as Neurath chuckled, slapping Goliath across the face with the flat of his right hand as he pulled up a pelvic bone. "He's not as scary as he used to be." Neurath crushed the pelvis across Goliath's face.

A deep roar in his throat, Goliath shoved at Neurath, but the fat giant had surprising reflexes, and dodged the move. Goliath staggered out of the third bone box, but ended up on his knees.

Neurath reached down into the place where Goliath fell and pulled up a huge bone. This object made the Philistine soldiers gape, as they'd never beheld such a giant object. Neurath gripped the end of the bone with both hands and raised it high.

Goliath spun, turning over fast and avoided the blow as the bone crashed to the floor of the cavern. The Philistine swiped his leg under Neurath's, but only clipped one of his legs. Neurath hopped on one foot and stayed standing, yet dropped his weapon. When Goliath tried to rise, Neurath stabbed out with his left hand, poking Goliath in both his eyes. Hands to his face for a moment, Goliath swore and turned.

Neurath pulled Goliath off the ground and then grappled him to his breast. Goliath's feet dangled a moment, as Neurath bear hugged him tight, but not hard enough to break the spine. Lips close to Goliath's ear, Neurath whispered, "You slew beasts, but ne'er a child of the stars! Before I break your back, would you tell me how you did that feat?"

Goliath's huge hands had hold of the muscled forearms of Neurath as he gasped, "You ever hear that one needs a diamond to cut diamonds?"

A look of confusion spread across Neurath's long visage as Goliath brought his arms over the interlocked limbs of the giant and drew them backward. The giant released Goliath, screaming in agony. Goliath landed and stumbled, but never paused to be in awe of the sight of the bleeding giant...as did the Philistine band. The warrior attacked again with fresh weapons in his hands: Goliath gripped two dew nails of the creature in the third box, a set of curled bones wicked in their appearance. Again, he slashed at Neurath with the nails, this time lower on his body. This instance, Goliath went to one knee and swiped the backside of his small nail across the calf of Neurath. More violet essence flowed in a horrendous spout as ligaments severed and the giant fell to one knee.

Goliath slashed the nail across the chest of Neurath, tearing loose the right pectoral muscle and causing an even louder howl from his opponent.

Unfamiliar to such pain, Neurath retreated awkwardly, but Goliath did not pursue him. Sure of the ruse, Goliath waited and indeed, Neurath tried to leap on him. The move was sloppy and ill-timed, due to the injury to his calf. However, the giant did drape his body over Goliath, an act that looked to be a smothering one. Before the full weight of Neurath was on him, Goliath looked to throw a fist in the air. As he fell under the mass of the giant, Neurath burst into tears and screamed. Quickly, he pushed himself off Goliath to reveal the cause of his injury. Goliath had slit open the giant's abdomen; his intestines unraveled in thick, gory spirals onto the warrior.

The Philistines cheered as Neurath tumbled onto his backside and tried to shove himself away. Goliath arose, seized handfuls of the slippery intestines, and pulled. Even more of the giant's guts spilled onto the ground, and shouts even Philistines would hear in their sleep for ages echoed out. Goliath looked up at the nearest, lowest hook sporting a female body and threw the gut line up high. After several attempts, Goliath strung the guts of the giant over three hooks, making a further horror to the evil of the chamber.

Picking up his weapons, Goliath stepped forward. The eyes of the Neurath, full of tears and fear, glared at him.

Neurath screamed, "I don't want to die!"

Goliath stepped up onto the thighs of the giant. "Who does?" With that, he buried both the lance and the sword deep into Neurath through the gap in his midsection. Goliath stabbed, poked and ground his weapons. Neurath writhed under the points of the sword and lance, until suddenly, he ceased to move, a hand gripping the lance beam. Goliath nodded and stabbed deep again, certain he found the monster's heart. He then let his javelin fall and raised up his sword with both hands holding the pommel. One savage blow and Neurath's head fell free of his body.

Wiping off his weapons on the frock of the nearest hanging woman, Goliath took a few steps and his eyes met those of Abimelech, who stared at the twisted body of Ahmee. There were no tears. Goliath wished that there were.

Unsure if the stone box beyond the hanging bodies really held the bones of the Prophet, Goliath sighed. He emptied the sack of grain near the chest and started to load it up with the bones.

He walked out of the keep of Nebo with the bag of Moses' bones under his arm. He paused and handed the head of Neurath to Sadik, saying, "Strip this, won't you?"

As he left, from across the plain and mountainside a hissing sound rose, not unlike meat on a grill. Soon, this sound became a drone, a buzz.

The Philistine mass parted, flanking Goliath as he departed from the belly of Nebo and let in countless flies. The soldiers cheered his name over and over, for it was the only words that could come out of their mouths at such a spectacle. The giant never looked back, but Cairn and a few of the younger men did. They saw the swarms of insects blot out the bodies of the hanging women. In moments, the wives of Neurath lay in the cradle of the children of Ba'al Zebul.

CHAPTER TWENTY
MOLOCH AND REVELATIONS

"Please, my dear, be of good cheer," the steady voice of the old priest said to Akisha as she shivered on the reclining couch. "You're safe here at Ekron under the veils of Ba'al-Zebub."

Her face registered horror and she looked from the younger man who helped her flee Ashdod unto the olden men they met inside the shrine at Ekron.

"The champion, the giant..." she stammered, as if saying his name would make him appear. "He prays to and often sees Ba'al Zebul. Eucimar is his friend! How can I be safe here?"

The priest smiled and waved a hand in the air, carefree. "You have mistaken me. His god is the Lord of the Flies. Ba'al-*Zebub* is Lord of Dung."

"Aren't they all on the same side?"

"No, my darling, different aspects of analogous brethren. It's a common enough mistake. Our god favors us and we are privy to the grand scheme of things, certainly, to the majestic design you are involved in with various kings and priests."

Akisha whispered, "Malak said she would protect me, but that never stopped Yaggah, her devoted servant, from dying. Abimelech killed him and chopped him to pieces."

The priest again made a dismissive wave. He then bade her and the young novice from the temple of Dagon to follow him. The old man stepped into the stygian darkness of the inner temple and Akisha stopped, grabbing the robe of the novice in fistfuls.

"There is nothing to fear," the younger man assured her. "We are amongst friends here."

Still, she paused. "How can I not be afraid?"

With patience and buoyancy, the old man said, "I will show you in my caldron the means to calm you. You will see what awaits the mighty champion when he gets closer to Jericho. Come and see what lies within."

With halting steps, Akisha approached the stone well in the middle of the dim chamber. One hand gripping the young priest, the other one cradling her belly, Akisha peered over the lip of the limestone structure.

Though the seething interior looked like a swirling mass of excrement, soon solid images appeared. She jumped back, but the young priest forced her forward to see what revealed itself.

The old man said, "See, here the terrible domain of Moloch? Lady Bednukah knows they are coming near to her and is awaking now."

Akisha saw the three-breasted woman stretch and yawn. Eyes wide, Akisha then cried out as she saw the demon in the star. Again, the young priest held her fast as the scene blurred. The realm of Moloch faded away, replaced by a realm of light, purity and long, wooden paths one might even mistake for spokes in a wheel. They all had a beautiful woman at the end of each path. Every path led unto a point where a tall woman with long hair resided.

When Akisha heard her sing, she passed water and lost consciousness.

Philistine

Qorus patted the bundle Goliath strapped to Abimelech's horse. "All of that for a bag of bones?"

Goliath's head raised and looked back toward Mount Nebo. "Well, kind of. Why not?"

Mouth open, the young warrior hesitated and decided to not go on with his line of questioning. The look from Abimelech helped his decision.

Abimelech faced to the east and said, "Our scouts say the army of General Samien's mongrels is gathering out there in the wastes in earnest."

Goliath secured the last ropes and never looked up at his shield bearer. "Do they now?"

Captain Balzer wheeled his horse around by them and said, "If we are to make Jericho's ruins fast, we need to double-time it. We saw a force of the Israelites moving around in the distance. I think they are just concerned the mongrels aren't there for them."

Goliath muttered, "Stands to reason." He held his head up again and took a deep breath. "Great day to be alive, isn't it you bunch of bastards?"

The two dozen soldiers laughed and grouped around Goliath.

"If any of you want to go to the main force of the army, go on now," Goliath said, and his voice rose. "If you want to run off to a whorehouse and forget about the world, I won't hunt you down and nail you to a tree. Life is what we make it. You have stood by me in these past weeks and for that, I salute you. I'm going to face a bit of personal destiny that may destroy everyone near me. You can stand with me or not. There's a time coming soon where I will need some of you. Yes, that means you may die. I never promised you anything more than the army has. But come along with me this day and I can say that in the end, men will fear you more than others. Women may hide from you, but the mystery of what will come this day will heighten their looks, soften their hearts and loosen their girdles. After this day, you will either be dead or more alive than ever before."

The men cheered and a few laughs rippled out.

"Then let us go unto the Domain of Moloch. All of the nightmares you have had as children? Get ready to face them and slay those who gave them unto you."

*****

General Schlack relieved himself by a grove of trees and then adjusted his tunic. His army swelled as they traveled out of Ashkelon, both picking up small numbers of troops from villages and greater divisions down from Ashdod and up from Gaza. They started their trek across Israelite territory aiming for a confrontation with troops amassing beyond Jericho. Emissaries from King Saul met the officers and were informed they should stand aside.

As Schlack stalked back to his horse, a captain approached, bowed, saluted and said, "General, sir, our spies say the opposing forces are gathering at Rabboth-Ammon."

He nodded and threw himself onto the horse again. "Scum of the earth come to test us. Ammonites, Edmonites, the outcasts of Assyria and Moabites...bah. What could hold a confederation like that together? Certainly not the balls of Samien."

The solider replied, "They must have a powerful

leader or a fine god to inspire such actions."

The General eyed him and pondered his words. "I hope not. In any case, they will meet their damned god soon enough. I shall not be intimidated by bastards." He paused for a moment and asked, "What of the forces that went out before them all, Goliath and the rest?"

"Strange, sir, but reports are that they are now on a course for Jericho, but went to Gath, then Nebo first."

"I see."

"From the men from Ashdod there are terrible reports of murder in the temple of Dagon. It is true that a solider dressed in priests vestments slew everyone in the temple."

"I've heard."

"No, but he was a big man."

Thoughts of what it all meant swam in his mind, but Schlack asked, "Everyone in the temple? Huh."

"Akisha escaped unto Ekron, sir. The champion's beloved has escaped."

Schlack nodded at the soldier and turned his horse from him.

The soldier called out, "Sir, does Goliath go to offer himself as the champion in a challenge to the rabble? Will he throw down against their greatest warrior so we won't have to fight?"

"Perhaps, but I think Samien will strike him down if he does such a thing."

*****

It was near to dawn when Goliath arrived at the edge of Jericho. They took care not to approach quickly and arouse great concern to any watching.

A small army of priests and novices stood around

the hidden entrance to the temple of Moloch.

Goliath jogged amongst the Philistine detachment's horses. When the soldiers stopped to size up the priestly opposition, Goliath weaved to the front of the band, eyes on the sacks on Abimelech's horse and the bundle Hasana carried against her breasts..

"Two dozen of you versus three dozen novices, slaves and assheads." Goliath coughed a disgusted laugh. "Cut them all down." He then walked to a ruined pillar, near to as tall as himself. Although blood stained the base of it and flowers wreathed the pillar, Goliath kicked it over. Those of Moloch lowered their spears, but Goliath picked up the pillar under his arm. "The time for playing politics is over."

Ten of the Philistines raised their bows, notched arrows and fired. Their projectiles struck the main members of the priesthood in their chests. They selected their targets well and struck down the men of power. They fell, lungs pierced, on the hillside above the ruined entrance.

In the moment their leaders fell slain, the novices panicked. The other Philistines dismounted and charged, a few throwing lances at the alarmed novices. A couple of these spears missed but many buried themselves in the bellies targeted. Captain Balzer called his men into action and they held no mercy for the priests or their students. Swords out, the Philistines made fast work of the rest. Even Hasana drew her blade and clipped the legs of a fleeing novice. He reeled in the ruins, begging for his life. Hasana delivered the kill shot to the youth's breastbone and never dropped her bundle.

Armed up with the pillar, Goliath shouted for them to clear a path. He aimed the pillar at the narrow stone entrance while a few of the better-armed guards of Moloch moved forward from the surrounding rocks into the Philistine force. Goliath blinked as these hired men stabbed and cut down two of the Philistine soldiers.

In unison, Abimelech and Qorus said, "Sonofabitch," and swung their swords. Arms flew and the rented killers killed no more.

Goliath leveled the pillar at the entrance to the Domain and roared. He ran, all force in one blow, and drove the pillar through the walls that positioned themselves to make easy access to the underground realm difficult. His stone ram crashed through the first wall and toppled the next one, which fell over into the next wall, and so on.

The giant dug like a child in the sand, throwing rocks and debris to one side, ripping out sections of the hallway where no sun had shone for years. Knee deep in the rubble, Goliath picked up the further damaged pillar and reared back again. He slung it sideways and it penetrated another wall. This time, only darkness flowed out. Goliath turned and yelled at the men. A wicked grin spread over his rugged face and his eyes gleamed with excitement.

"I'm through," he exclaimed.

Abimelech staggered through the ruins to get closer to his master. On one of the shattered walls a priest emerged, holding a dagger. Sadik moved in fast and struck with a small Amalekite hatchet. Over and over, Sadik hit the flailing priest in the guts. Goliath threw portions of wall out as the screaming cleric refused to die. Sadik started to laugh, but never stopped swinging. Abimelech turned, wore a sour look, gave the resilient priest a harsh kick that half twisted his head about and stopped his movements.

"I'm with you, sire," Abimelech said, sword at the ready.

Goliath touched the cinch strap on his chest, the one that ran next to the javelin holder, and pulled the bag of bones nearer to his back. The giant reached out and Abimelech handed him another bag, a smaller one covered in canvas. He eyed Abimelech and then Qorus who moved up behind him.

Captain Balzer joined then and affirmed, "They are all done, sir."

"Good, now the tough part begins."

Just before Goliath ripped the wall open further, they all heard a woman's laughter. Bubbly, hot and hysterical, yet, so devoid of humor it inspired the desire to run. Cairn, Hasana, and Sadik all sported quivering lips, but never fled.

A laugh broke from Goliath as he headed through the breach. Abimelech followed his master, sword and shield high, but never smiled.

Goliath collided with a couple stout eunuchs as he moved through the breech. Each of these men held bludgeons made of bronze. Goliath stumbled, arms confused, and crashed to the floor of the huge chamber. One of the eunuchs staggered from the giant's bulk, hands on his face, nose obliterated by a random shot from the flailing champion. He turned and his eyes bulged more, mainly due to the sword Abimelech drove through his abdomen, suddenly turning in a clockwise direction.

More husky eunuchs surrounded the Philistines as they descended from the breech. Qorus buried his sword in the head of one of them, making it twist and splitting the skull away. Another eunuch boxed Qorus's ears, sending the young warrior to the floor not far from Goliath. A swinging bronze bludgeon impacted on Balzer's shield, sending him back into the grip of his men. Only Cairn's shield saved him from such a blow as well. He sprawled to the floor at the feet of these huge men in loincloths.

Abimelech armed up the massive shield of Goliath and swiped out at their enemies. He took out three of eunuchs at the knees, gouging wicked gaps in their joints with a savage move.

Balzer charged forward, but stumbled over the prone form of Cairn. More eunuchs brought their bludgeons to bear and Cairn sat up, striking with his sword. The blade found a home in the chest of the nearest eunuch, but when Cairn rose up to attack anew, he fell over the legs of Captain Balzer. One of the injured eunuchs raised his bludgeon and smashed Cairn's skull. He fell to the floor like a rag doll, his bent helmet and ruined head bouncing once. His legs twitched twice and the sword in his hand echoed lightly as it fell from his hand on the stone floor.

Bednukah's cackling voice rebounded in the chamber as Sadik knelt next to Cairn, his hand on the pit of his back. Sadik pulled the hatchet and threw it, end over end, into the forehead of the injured guard that slew his friend. The blade missed and only the handle of the hatchet smacked the eunuch. The momentary confusion allowed Sadik to slice and remove the windpipe of his target.

The demon next to the Lady glowed green as white flames surrounded his reptilian form to the waist. She waved her arms in the air and the six sides of the star encasing the demon glowed purple. The creature wore a grim look as red flashes like lighting flew from his body and bounced around the vast room.

Once this lightning cleared it was Goliath alone that staggered to his feet. The others lay, breathing, but felled from the power surge.

Bednukah dried tears from her eyes, her hilarity great. "My, but this is an amusing treat for me and Amazarak. What else have you brought me to amuse myself, bastard of the stars?"

Though Goliath never answered her, he did hold up the smaller of his two sacks. Once he opened the small bag, he held up the skull of Neurath for her to see.

Bednukah and Amazarak both gave the object a quizzical look.

Goliath then looked back at Hasana. On her knees, still shaking from the bolt of power, she threw him her bundle, underhanded. Goliath caught the sack and opened it. When he drew out the head of Eucimar, the giant grinned.

When Eucimar's eyes opened, sly smiles broke out across the faces of the Lady and her demon.

When Eucimar's mouth opened and he vomited a long stream of maggots, hilarity ensued again from those serving Moloch.

*****

King Vyndekay refused any more bulletins from the seers and tried to rest. In the night, all he could hear were screams and laughter in his dreams. Never a man for strong drink in excess, Vyndekay drank several mugs of wine before sleep would come to him.

When sleep did come, he found himself on a battlefield many years before. When the King looked down he saw the dead body of his son Kedvybaal, slain in a savage war with the Israelites and one of their judges. Vyndekay could only stagger toward one of the stone slabs in the nearby country. Through twisted bodies and a sea of ruined, lamenting humanity that did not realize it was as good as dead, Vyndekay had staggered, bearing his son. Though not its original purpose to be a reclining couch, Vyndekay used it as such and lay down his son on the massive slab. He looked across the meadow, trying to shut out the cries of the dying. Kneeling before the block, the stench of guts in his nostrils, he beat his fists on the rock surface.

Never live too long, his father had warned him. *Never see your children die.*

When he jerked himself awake, he stood in the room of his small children, the little girls born of his last wife. He stood near the form of Emana, the one the goddess raised from the dead. Emana's chest barely raised and lowered.

Eyes closed to hide her pallid features, Vyndekay whispered, "Anything but to see another die." With those words, he knew that is what doomed him. A fighting man in his youth, Vyndekay let himself fall into the weakness of women and children.

He tried to bury the regret and drown it in more wine. The light of morning brought him some hope, but still terror lurked at the edges of his mind.

There needed a new sense of order and a new way of the gods. The olden way had only brought them this average existence and a usurper's spot on the coastline. Would the goddess keep her words?

He was so tired.

*****

Samien rode up and down his lines as they started to fall into regular formations. True, his overall force didn't get the full time to train or drill he desired, yet his confidence ran high. It wasn't just the promise of the goddess. Few in the Confederation army were aliens to military works. Though many citizens arose to join his cause, not as many as he hoped, and too many foreign men to his taste, the great majority were soldiers at one time or another, so they'd serve him well. Samien's second-in-command, Baldassare, required anyone of greater experience to have the greener fighters or untrained men near to them. Samien rode down the lines, looking at the varied divisions of men and nodded. He wondered how long the Philistines' patience would last with a foreign rookie nearby, but he hoped they'd stay unified long enough.

Baldassare rode up and looked him in the face for a moment before scanning across the valley. Dust rose in the distance. "The Philistines are here, curling around the ruins of Jericho."

"How many?"

"All of them, I think," The Colonel grinned.

Rigid on his mount, Samien spat to his left and said, "There aren't enough palm trees here to hide them all."

After a nod, Baldassare declared, "We shall try to get them out in the open more as fighting in the ruins is madness."

"The Jordan River nearby, the Dead Sea ten miles at our backs, it's a day smelling of great revolution," said Samien. "The goddess is foremost in my mind, but there seems confusion in my dreams. No matter. I'm a fighter and today, we fight. I'll cast down these fools who destroy our folk."

Baldassare grinned. He was a fighting man as well and enjoyed what was about to come. "The men are ready even if they look varied."

"The Hittite bowmen look ready to kill everyone," Samien deadpanned to his second.

Baldassare raised an eyebrow to the section of these archers, all cursing and ready to do war. Their leaders soon divided them into different groups to go down the lines and strike at different spots. "The Moabite axes may get a few Edomite spearmen, but they are ready to go."

Samien replied, "We had enough trouble keeping

them separated from the regular Assyrian swordsmen."

"Why do they hate each other so?"

Samien threw up a hand. "Why do any of us hate each other? Their fear is more primal and based on personal space. The destruction of the Philistines must happen as they are interlopers unto this land of mine, a real Canaanite. The Sea Peoples have no claim to this place other than that they chose to land here and fight."

"They've fought well."

"They will die beautifully, then. By the power of the old goddess and the forces that slumber under the land, I shall see their places laid so to waste Ereshkigal, goddess of the underworld, will not abide there."

Baldassare stated in a quiet voice, "Our numbers are greater than the force they send out."

"But you know the ferocity of the Philistines."

Baldassare nodded and said, "And if not for the confused mettle of their Generals and leaders, I'd worry more."

Samien smirked. "Their traitors think they are removing a power structure and killing their champion, thus changing the way of things. The fools. They don't know I plan to cut the throat of every Philistine in the land."

Baldassare took on a look of mocking surprise. "Whatever will the priests say?"

Samien grinned and then through snarled lips said, "I shall slay them all as well. The priests and their stone idols will be crushed to the ground so well no one will ever miss them." He then looked north and said, "After the Philistines, our Confederation will turn our swords north."

His second nodded. "The Sea Peoples aren't the only interlopers on this land."

Samien nodded, touched the necklace around his neck and said, "Indeed."

Steven Shrewsbury

*****

Goliath shifted his feet, in a slight stupor from the bolts emitted by Amazarak, and still held the head of Eucimar by the locks. The skull under his left arm, his right hand flexed, and he hadn't realized he'd dropped his javelin in the shock wave. He heard Eucimar chanting and cursing, truly, beginning his war with Lady Bednukah. Maggots coated the floor at his boots.

She yelled out in a voice that rolled like thunder, "You are fools, all of you, to fence with me."

The last of the maggots out of his mouth, Eucimar retorted, "Then you have little to fear from me, no?"

Goliath set Eucimar on the floor and grabbed at his javelin as two stout figures emerged from the pool by the owl. He missed his lance, fingers still numb. He eyed the demon in the star who made no attempt to attack. Goliath grabbed the shaft of the javelin just in time to use it to block two men in loincloths from the pool. Ten more of these attackers came out of boats across from the great image of Moloch. He shoved this first man back, javelin across his chest, and swung the head out, clipping the jugular vein of the next man. This attacker clasped his neck, stunned over the fact he was about to die.

Eucimar's voice rose and when the next blast of lightning came from Amazarak, it bounced from the area of the Philistines.

Abimelech's head arose from the floor and his body jerked. The others still lay motionless. His eyes gaped at Bednukah. Tall, lithe, fair-haired, and bouncy, her outline made him gape, even if her sorceress ways gave off a Stygian bent. She walked in a small semicircle with an arrogant gait, though, fluttering lustrous hands in the air, causing fire and plumes of glowing objects to appear from Amazarak. Her sensual, gleaming body strutted nearer to the stationary figure Amazarak. His luminosity changed colors every moment or two.

One of the Philistine warriors awoke and screamed out in panic. When Abimelech and Goliath tried to tell him to stay with them, he bolted, running for the pool before the great image of Moloch. Flame shot from the demon and struck the soldier in a single beam of light. The soldier smoked, and soon his flesh boiled and seeped through the chainmail links in his armor.

This creature gave Abimelech a disdainful look and vomited a spurt of bile out of the star. This phlegm rolled and took on mass, growing larger all the time. They saw the ball of spit transform fast, suddenly sprouting a spine, scales and wings...and then take on the appearance of a dragon the size of a man.

The lady shouted, "What a pathetic challenge! I will blight your land for a thousand years!"

The tiny dragon pointed its spade-shaped skull at the Philistines. Leathery lips peeled back into a mocking grin. Rows of teeth parted and the diminutive dragon aimed his fiery breath at Goliath and the dangling head. Eucimar's voice raised in pitch, and the stream of flame split apart before it ever reached them.

The creature then turned its face toward Abimelech and spewed flame again. Although barely awake, the warrior pulled up Goliath's shield and slumped down. The great cover repelled the blast emitted by the dragon, and even sent the spray onto one of the attacking eunuchs. The bald man screamed, his flesh aflame, and he stumbled into the river that ran before the Owl.

The champion advanced and thrust his javelin through the creature, causing it to shriek. Eyes wide, it appeared surprised at this predicament. Goliath felt glad that it had real flesh to harm. After he released his javelin, Goliath pulled his sword from over his back and kept that path of travel going...dropping it across the long neck of the creature. The blade never severed the neck, but the beast flopped to the floor. The dragon's mouth puckered in like a fist, but no flames came out. The neck, crooked, refused to move.

Suddenly the dragon stretched flush and an inferno ejaculated out of its backside. From under its tail, the stream of combustion continued as the beast fell to the ground. It lay still, flames slowly ebbing away from the hindquarters, and Bednukah couldn't hide her look of astonishment. In moments, the creature returned to spit and oozed away into the darkness.

Bednukah looked puzzled while the demon beside her took on an appearance of amusement. Smiling, his chest heaving, the demon said to her, "I can generate creatures for you, my rotten jailer, but I cannot teach them to fight."

Eyes afire and lips shooting spittle, she retorted at the demon, "Mind your mouth or you shall return to the abyss! Does this young one realize what power I command?" she asked, but no one was certain whom she addressed. "Why, I could call forth any number of minions via the power of my dark servant! With but a word or desire I could send forth solar scarabs, berserker wasps or feral harpies unimagined, soaked in poisonous ooze! However, in this case, this challenge doesn't rate that much blood."

Bednukah raised her hands and balls of flame started to cultivate there...sapped off the sulfurous nimbus of the demon beside her.

Spheres of fire flew and almost singed Goliath as he strode, bent over, shifting his body from side to side. Closer she came to them, walking away from her demon, toward the edge of her dais. As she did so, the fireballs grew smaller. She paused, looking down into the rigid faces of two of the men at arms who died and remained on their knees. With a cackle, her smoking hands extended and their bodies floated up to her touch. She clutched the heads and their skulls split like rotten timber. When the pieces of the skulls and bodies fell away, the gray organ left over remained erect, and pulsed purple under her touch. Inhaling and letting a guttural roar escape, she drooled as the brains grew three times their size, puffing up like clouds. She dropped them and they halted before striking the floor, only to sprout four legs each. These new creations dropped on their former hosts and absorbed the bodies. The brain-creatures again tripled in size.

Heads shaking and bodies starting to loosen from the beam attack, the Philistines awoke to see these beasts striding forth. Several of the men couldn't help but cry out in terror.

Watching these monstrosities learn to walk on their fresh legs, Goliath thought she was getting close to the edge up there, arrogant in her power, leaving the place of safety. All of his dodges and shoulder rolls could only help him for so long from the fireballs. She stopped in her tracks and even Amazarak's brow lifted as they peered at the gap on the floor between them.

The maggots Eucimar puked onto the floor had grown fat and even the walking brains Bednukah brought out avoided these things. Each bloated maggot burst and a swarm of flies spewed from within. They scattered and flew around the chamber.

The rhythm of Bednukah's triple breasts stopped. Several of the flies flew across her face and she swatted, stumbling. She shrieked, turned and ran back toward her creature, who laughed at her again.

"They burn," she screamed.

Abimelech moved out, seconded by Qorus and

Sadik, and struck more of the eunuchs. Balzer ordered the archers to fix arrows and attack. Their arrows never hit the Lady or the demon, always flying away, but Balzer ordered them to hit the brains or the eunuchs. In a moment, the shafts struck one of the brain beasts, but couldn't make it fall.

Inadvertently, in his attempt to avoid the lady's fireballs, Goliath stomped on one of the brain creatures. It exploded into a puff of gray dust and lavender juice, and all of their ears popped as it died.

With great curses to all, Bednukah wiped her eyes and started to hurl flame globes again. From deep in her bosom came chants and curses, causing the host of insects to arise in the air between the demon and Goliath.

The giant set his feet, sucking air fast.

Eucimar hissed as Goliath raised the head, "Face him."

In the air, the swarm of flies drew dense and started to take on a shape. This figure forming in the air became humanoid and sported six wings, but the face featured enormous insectoid eyes.

Bednukah smiled, spat, then shouted, "You'll have to do more than a manifestation of Ba'al Zebul."

Amazarak roared and his green flames billowed from his star. The image of Ba'al Zebul thinned, became more skeletal, but didn't vanish.

"Tsk, tsk, I am through with this worm and his games," Bednukah snorted and spread her arms wide. "I call upon the Scarlones of the Waters to aide me!"

While monstrous forms started to outline themselves from the waters in the pool before Moloch, Goliath sensed time grew short. In his mind's eye, he could see the water creatures envelope the men and drown them. Still with the skull of Neurath under his arm, he muttered, "One shot," and then started to dash toward Bednukah and her devil.

The demon smiled as the champion dropped his sword. Amazarak watched casually when Goliath crashed straight through the first watery Scarlones creatures that climbed free of their birthing spot in the pool. One Scarlone took the shape of a giant kitten, yet it never slowed the giant nor did it have time to wrap about him for a drowning. Goliath then stopped, planted his feet as a crawling brain launched itself at him, legs out. Goliath pulled the bag of bones from his back and swung it fast. The brain stuck to it, legs dug in. He then kept on running forward.

Shaking his eerie visage from side to side, the demon said, "Stones he has, my dire jailer, and not just in his bag."

Bednukah flared her nostrils, expelling mucus. "He is drunk or mad, look at him. What can he hope to do?"

Despite her mocking, he refused to stop. In her overconfidence, she allowed him to get reasonably close. She then commanded the demon to shield them, which he did. Both muscled arms of Amazarak went up and a faint yellow glow stretched across their bodies, but not to encompass them.

Goliath drew back and lobbed the bag of bones, brain creature and all, through the air. When he flung this overhand, he twisted the opposite way and sidearmed the skull of Neurath through the air.

Bednukah giggled, covering her mouth to suppress majestic laughter.

The weighted bag, traveling toward her, fell dismally short of the target, but struck the shield. It plummeted just shy of the demon, hitting near the drawn out edge of the six-pointed star. The brain creation splattered on impact and the heavy bag rolled off the bottom lip of the magick shield.

The skull of Neurath, however, arrived not at the

Lady, nor the demon...but traveled end over end and struck the bottom of the shield...a barrier that didn't quite reach to the floor. The skull glanced off the lower portion of the shield and bounced, skidded and then floated in the air. A buzz sliced the air from the host of flies now clustered within and about the skull of the Nephilum...rolling it into the diaphanously kept mixture of the salty star around Amazarak.

The mystic line, now imperfect, was broken by the skull of Neurath. A silence, not unlike the echo following thunder, rippled through the Domain of Moloch. All attention focused on Amazarak and the gaping Lady.

The demon's cage open, his eyes flared emerald green at the imperfect portion. A great inrush of air, like a heavy wind, blew past the Philistines and even knocked Balzer to the floor. Even the Scarlone creatures stopped, water running through their myriad shapes, curious at what would happen next.

Six leathery wings unfolded from Amazarak's spine. A yellow sap ran all across his body and the scales fell away from the demonic form. Underneath the reptilian shell lay an identical likeness, yet colored gold and white. He immediately faced Bednukah, arms out and mouth open. Amazarak arose from the floor, the nails on his saurian claws falling away, the dust of the star blown away completely.

"Stop," she commanded, eyes wide.

"No," Amazarak replied in a soft voice, but the word hung like an echo itself and bounced around the chamber, nearly hurting their ears. Still, more sections of Amazarak fell away, but his glowing form remained a hideous combination of beast and mankind.

Goliath stumbled backwards and armed up his sword. He saw Hasana grab Eucimar by the hair and hug him to her bosom. "Get back," Goliath shouted at her and the rest.

Levitating away from his prison, Amazarak wiggled the fingers on his outstretched hands. This action let his curved nails lengthen, then fall off. Amazarak grinned a mouth of canines, which also started to fall away in a shower, revealing a normal set of humanoid teeth behind them. "A pity, but I don't need the nails for you, Lady."

Though she tried to backpedal away, the lady ascended off the floor and into the arms of the demon. He embraced her, melting the sorceress' red hair from her willowy body. Beams of light shot out from Amazarak's back, looking like a cross between a porcupine and starlight, as his body continued to transform. Her shrill screams blended with his guttural groan of pleasure. Everywhere one of these beams of light struck poked holes and burned an out, letting the light through to the outside world. The beams that aimed lower buried deep into the earth.

Goliath fell down to his buttocks near to Abimelech, Balzer and Qorus. They remained fixated on the spectacle before them.

The ceiling blew away and the sunlight rushed in, but the cloud of dust soon blocked out much of the welcomed glow. Though a rain of fragments and dust fell all around the small force of Philistines, beams of power leaving the body of the freed demon pulverized larger hunks.

The creature arose higher in the dais, laughing, still holding his jailer and former mistress. Amazarak's smile faded. His thumbnails, though human now, grew longer and glinted, razor sharp. Amazarak used these appendages as he peeled Bednukah like a banana, slowly and deliberately in front of them. From the scalp down, he hummed a song as he ripped her skin off. She gagged, out of air for screams, and vomited a green bile over her skinless breasts. Dropping the strips of the sorceress's skin to the floor below, his eyes glowed purple and shot two beams at the huge image of Moloch by the now muddy pool of water. When the power of Amazarak lifted the giant idol in the air, the Scarlone creatures dissipated.

"A gift unto you," Amazarak said and stared down at Goliath. "My son."

Moloch dropped and smashed into the flooring not far from where the demon's star cage once sat. The idol never fragmented, but kept going, crashing through the floor and falling further below the surface.

The fiend roared with laughter and spiraled up into the daylight. He soon vanished, but more of the Lady's skinless flesh dropped to the floor near the new opening. It took but a moment for the image of Ba'al Zebul to reform in full, float near her pieces, stop and swarm across the ruined body.

As the echo of the departing one bounded across the sky, the shade of insects dispersed from the Lady, left as bones. The next instant, Ba'al Zebul floated over the opening in the chamber made by the falling idol. The head in the formation of flies faced Goliath and then turned down as if to peer into the earth itself.

Qorus sucked air and tried to laugh as he said, "I cannot believe it! I'd not have believed it if I didn't see it."

When Goliath crawled toward the fresh fissure on his all fours, Balzer agreed with Qorus. "Unreal, by the gods, we have seen the Lady destroyed."

Abimelech got to his feet, wavered, but walked after his master, who still approached the break in the floor of the now sunlit chamber. He said to no one, "I never thought the sky could be so beautiful."

Goliath stopped at the edge of the new chasm and agreed. "It seemed so far away for a time, didn't it?"

Abimelech joined him and knelt by the perimeter of

the gap. They exchanged glances and then looked again down into the breech.

The utter gloom and nebulous shapes of the Domain of Moloch couldn't have been a bigger contrast to what lay beneath it. The perfect gray stones and white linens of the figures below held the Philistines breathless.

Goliath turned over, lay on his back and closed his eyes.

Abimelech could barely form words as he said, "Sire, the formation they take, the lines and the figure in the middle..."

"Yes," Goliath sighed and wouldn't open his eyes. "It's a wheel."

Balzer groaned, eyes wide. "Damn!"

"Indeed. The big gal in the middle of that wheel? That's my sister, Malak, apparently."

"Sister?" Sadik asked, voice shaking.

"Our work isn't over, yet."

CHAPTER TWENTY-ONE
WHEEL OF BLOOD

Vyndekay tired of listening to oracles and departed from the house of Dagon. He longed to talk to Kmentosi, to hear reassuring words, but soon, had to laugh at his own maudlin ways

He strode back to his household and found most of the servants out. His latest wife tended to the new baby, but he found his daughter Emana in the sewing room. She kept turning the spinning wheel. Her vacant eyes stared at it.

"Emana?" he said. "Come play with your baby brother, don't get in the way of the servants."

She arose and still gaped at the wheel. Eyes empty she looked up at her father.

*****

The men gathered about the new rift in the Domain of Moloch and stared inside. Hasana held Eucimar so he could look and the head babbled to Goliath. The giant looked over to the edge of the floor, where Sadik knelt beside the corpse of Cairn. *They were such friends,*

Goliath lamented for a moment.

"Sadik," Goliath called out and looked back down. "Come near to us. We will need you."

The young solder took his hand from his fallen friend's arm and stood, jaw jutting out, before approaching the chasm.

The giant kept nodding but Captain Balzer said, "Look, there at the sculptures all around the distance edges of the vast realm. How many must there be?"

Eucimar's voice rose, saying, "They are not sculptures. This is the realm of a gorgon."

"My sister," said Goliath steadily. "Malak."

Qorus stepped back a little, but his pride wouldn't let him run, like his young legs wanted to. "Those are men? The sculptures down there are really guys? Why are we staring in there if the sister can turn us to stone?"

All of the men turned their heads from the low temple and long beams that formed the wheel.

Goliath said, "It isn't like the legends, you hearty pricks. That isn't how it goes to look on her and be changed. I've heard of other gorgons and that's all campfire tales."

Qorus refused to look again but asked, "Are all of those women down there like her, gorgons?"

Goliath shook his head and gestured at the figure at the center of the wheel. "She is the last one."

Eucimar added, "Those look to be vestal virgins, pure focus points of directing her natural mental power. That is all their pure lives are is untouched vessels for direction, like driving on a clean path."

Balzer peeped in again and said, "She doesn't look like the legends. She looks rather fetching really."

Goliath frowned at him. "I'll put in a good word for you."

Abimelech wondered, "Why are they in such a state? They don't seem to notice the ceiling blew away.

Are they stone as well?"

Eucimar said as Hasana petted his hair, "They're in repose or in heavy meditation. Their minds are focused and as one. I can feel their power like the beat of a dozen hearts."

Balzer looked at Eucimar. "Their minds are somewhere else?"

Qorus asked, "Elsewhere? Where are they?"

Goliath rolled over and thumbed his beard. "Better still, what are they doing?"

Balzer stiffened his spine and cocked his head as the distant echoes of a commotion filtered down from the surface. "The bastard army of Samien is a confederation and worships something. We thought it was Moloch and the three-titted bitch. Something is bringing those dogs together as one."

After a fast nod Qorus said, "The power of the demon is gone and something tells me Samien's army and the will of these below remains unbroken."

Goliath mused aloud, "And yet look down there, the ladies in white all concentrate and never move."

"As good as dead?" Qorus offered.

Sadik asked, "Are they some sort of goddesses or just priestesses?"

Goliath drew his knees to his chest, then nudged the head with his toe and said, "Eucimar?"

Eucimar glared down at the women at each station of the wheel and said, "They are in dedicated, fervent prayer, focusing all of their power and that of their mistress down the beams."

Abimelech said, "Their magick is their purity and their ability to focus the power of their mistress?"

Eucimar blinked hard. "Yes, I cannot nod, but yes. It seems this Malak chose to focus on being a wizard and not a warrior. Her ability is naturally more emphatic with the spirit realm, like Goliath, as her linage is from there."

Qorus faced the sky. "That thing, the demon Amazarak, it called you...its son?"

Goliath never looked at him. "Apparently, that Seraphim had a big heart when they thought Malak dead at my birth. I don't comprehend how she has power nor do I think it will matter in the end. It's me who has to confront her. The power of the demon, our fallen father, shielded her presence from all wizards."

Eucimar's eyes turned around in a circle. "Something warned you, sent those dreams, not just your sister trying to slay you. Was Amazarak warning you? He defied his jailer and warned you. He does have a soft heart still."

Goliath never answered, only focused his brooding eyes below.

Qorus persisted, "She is your sister? Why does she want us all dead?"

A dull silence reigned long enough for them to hear the sounds of trumpets of distant armies as they approached.

Balzer offered, "Jealousy? Goliath is revered and she has sought a new faith with this Akisha to obscure his self?"

Goliath arose and sighed. "Why does she want me dead? Why? Why not? Kingdoms and families are crushed on less than family hatred."

Qorus looked at the stone figures beyond the virgins. "How does she change men to stone? If the legends aren't true and we won't turn to stone for looking on her, how does she do it?"

Abimelech squinted down into the realm. "They're not standing nor fleeing, but at odd angles and poses."

The giant strode along the edge and then looked up at soldiers that sat above them outside. He then wondered after the sunlit areas about Jericho. "Do the armies gather in closer?"

"Yes," one of the soldiers above confirmed. "The Philistines gather in from the west and the mongrels to the east."

"I can smell them all," Goliath mumbled. He then said in a louder voice, "We will soon join the battle above, but there's one more thing I must ask of you all. Come down here all of you."

The sound of the warring factions closing in started to make the younger soldiers shake.

Sadik looked down the line of the men and at Goliath, ready to address them. "Lord Goliath, Champion of all Philistines, are we going to die?"

Loud, raw and harsh, Goliath answered him.

"Yes, you shall die. We all must die, from the moment you fell from your mother you started to die. We are surrounded on all sides by the factions of our own land, many of whom wish to see me, and you all by association, dead. The mongrel army led by Samien also closes in, seeking death of all Philistines and for me as a sacrifice to a new way, a new order from those who glean power from my sister.

"Look, unto the sky. You see the clouds where archfiend Amazarak ascended and flew away from his appointment with the abyss? You see what I see: the form of the dragon, the old fiend who inspired evil and wants the death of this world. His imperfection is why I cannot have a son or daughter that's normal in the next generation. His darkness and anger in the universe is why I am as I am, a misanthrope, a mistake of power from the fallen host unto the homunculi of the true Creator God. The dragon has saw fit to see I can be no more and through that bitch sister of mine, that we all shall fall.

"But hear me, if you call yourselves men. Shall you die like Philistines, like men with balls tight and hard, or shall you go out to the abyss on your knees, mewling for mama's teat like a runt? I have news for you, your mothers are all dead and sucking cocks in flames. This is all there will be for us. There is no tomorrow. This is the last day of the rest of your lives. Feel the call of your blood and the call of your folk."

Goliath started to thud the ball of his javelin into the flooring between his legs. The steady beat never ceased.

"We shall go down and destroy the power of the one controlled by the dragon. We will march with one heart, one beat, one purpose and destroy the plans of the dragon. For you see, I cannot slay the dragon, he is eternal, but his children like ones I'd foster, are not. Dragons live forever, Sadik, but not so for little boys."

The driving beat of his javelin carried on, louder as he spoke.

"We shall march down and break the power link with the vestal virgins. Philistines, you will not use the swords on your backs for this, but the one that swings between your hips. All of that purity and might will be halved. You are a dozen in number and there are a dozen ladies on the beams attending my sister. The God of all gods has seen to this as a sign unto me. If I am wrong, if I am leading you all into Hell itself..." The javelin rested, the beat stopped and the dozen Philistines all jumped a little as Goliath hissed, "They are going to wish they sent me to heaven."

They all raised their hands and roared.

Goliath turned from them, pointed to the sky and said, "The dragon seeks our destruction. He shall have it. Abimelech! To my side! All of you behind me, for I shall never send you where I will not go first." Goliath dropped his kilt and let his manhood swing free. The others did likewise. "For your people, for your god and for your selves, follow me. Here comes the night!"

Philistine

All of them shouted the name of *Goliath* as they leapt into the realm of Malak, naked, roaring as they selected a praying vestal virgin on the wheel.

In the realm of Moloch, Eucimar's eyes rolled back in his head.

Only then did Malak look up from her prayer pose. Beautiful and sinister at the same time, Goliath's sister wore a look of confusion, and then winked at him. She lay back, spread her legs and offered up her sex.

All around them at the points of the wheel, screams rang out as the Philistines pulled the vestal virgins from their prayers and did what warriors did second best.

Goliath stood over Malak. He went to one knee and took her left hand.

"Come inside me, Big Brother," she cooed in a husky tone. "Let us become one."

Goliath felt her long nails on his skin and his member bounced off her leg. All around her were the stone sculptures, of men. Most with horrific looks on their faces, but all in a laying position, most naked, the stone figures told him many tales.

He squeezed her hand gently and she smiled wider.

"No questions? No threats? No curiosities?"

Goliath had too many questions, but felt the answers wouldn't make him happy.

He let out a huge roar and in moments, Malak joined him, screaming.

In seconds, the two were quiet.

*****

Vyndekay slumbered in the day, this time out of necessity as sleep so eluded him that previous night. This time though terrible pain awoke him. He flew off his bed mat and staggered. Between his legs blood squirted and it felt as it his knees were tied to his chest.

The King stumbled into the hallway, eyes facing the children's room. Blood smeared the walls by the door. King Vyndekay grabbed his crotch and realized his manhood was injured, if not mutilated bad. He crawled to the door of the nursery and peered in.

He saw the baby's cradle, scarlet staining it, and a slender body on the floor near the corner. By the hair, he guessed it to be his latest wife.

Vyndekay sank to his knees and then flopped to his back. When he tried to rise, he failed. It was then he saw the figure of Emana walk from his room. Both of her hands were bloody and wet, just like her mouth. In her left hand was the arm of an infant. In her other hand was the shaft of his penis.

Emana said, "The goddess is gone and her promises no more. She reanimated this flesh, but I wanted you to know who slew you this day. It was you that sent me on that mission and caused Zorn to take my body away. Suffer, now, as I have suffered."

"Eucimar..." Vyndekay stammered as his head fell back to the floor.

*****

The host of Philistine artillery catapults released their large rocks and smashed into Samien's front causing many of the warriors in the wedge to scatter and withdraw. However, most lines held as the battle-hardened veterans of the Philistine infantry progressed, uniform in purpose, holding up shields to fend off the projectiles of the Ammonite slingers.

The forces of Samien assembled in front never

flinched in the face of this battle and waded in with doom-expectant resolve. Spears lowered, shields ready, they met the challenge as the arrows launched both behind them and before them.

Philistine cavalry materialized on each end of the infantry's body. The mass of enemy fighters progressed almost like a long-living creature. The sound of hooves mingled with the sandaled slapping march of the Philistine infantry, but the Confederation never ran.

Along with Samien, men equally as large and sinewy of muscle charged forward. Throughout their very being, power surged with each bloodthirsty war cry. They ran into the range of the artillery from afar, and dozens of them perished, crushed by the rocks smashing into the ground. As the battle lines neared, the barrage of pulverizing boulders ceased.

The berserker force of Amorites that had curled around advanced and threw themselves into the rear of the Philistine army. Nearly two thousand screaming men brandished stone axes and clubs, and attacked assembled units of Philistine pikemen that guarded the rear. The savage killers overlapped into other formations, hitting infantry and archers. Usually, a charging foe was softened up by the military with artillery and projectiles from archers or the longbow classes. These Amorites, though, had scrambled cross country to head up a rear charge. Several new recruits and former Philistine regulars followed in their wake, picking at ones the crazed warriors maimed or missed.

The javelins of the Philistine infantry rained from the sky on the main Confederation body. These dire shafts of death slayed several of Samien's men in the fray, and many lodged in their heavy shields. The long, soft-metal covers bent from the javelins' own burdensome weight, causing the warriors to discard their now useless and cumbersome shields.

The Philistine archers leashed volley after volley of arrows, and Samien saw the infantry draw their short swords, almost as one man. The Ammonites answered with their own slings, filling the sky.

The manner of Samien's Confederate army was vile and unpredictable. Solid units of trained Philistine pikemen, well skilled in fighting with longer spears, met this initial force. Of the ten thousand, there were hundreds of pikemen, but now they divided their ranks to separate parts of the army. One force of pikemen stood, supported by a thousand regular infantry fighters with crude bronze short swords and long shields. Hundreds of archers tried to get ready again, but only a few dozen managed to loose arrows as the Confederate thrust hit.

The Confederate army rushed headlong into the Philistine lines with brute strength their ally. Their own archers and spearmen launching an air war as they ran, the last of the spears and projectiles crashed into their shields, but this did not slow the charge of savage warriors whatsoever. They rushed pell-mell into the Philistine lines at full death-charge, and the formations of Schlack's men indeed bent inward like a weakened iron bar, as their own javelins had bent when they struck shields.

The heavy slaughter ensued, destroying a hundred pikemen and two hundred infantry in an instant. Many of the Edomites died, but their push was irresistible.

The on-sweeping hordes attacked with communal entreaties to their gods, their push causing a few hundred in the cavalry to retreat and take up a different position. With great valor, the pikemen and infantry fought.

Each side met the attack, struggled, and died hard. The berserker force was only stopped by the armored legion, a thousand elite men of Schlack's in stern body armor, fighting with shields. Many of these men of

Philistine

Philistia perished, but there were more to fill their gap as they went down.

An auxiliary cavalry charge, led by Schlack himself, supported by more units of the armored men, stopped the rear attack of the savages cold. The terrible fighting went on, but the Confederates' aft attack stopped.

The dozen Philistine soldiers then arose from the ruins of Jericho. Their kilts and trousers on, weapons drawn, each quickly understood where the fight was at. Much of the seething war spilled around the ruins of Jericho, trying to avoid it.

Weapons at the ready, Balzer and Qorus jumped into the fray to aid their Philistine brothers. Qorus slashed many times, drawing blood with every stroke, but watched helplessly as superior numbers surrounded his brothers.

Abimelech armed up the champion's shield and created his own opening. Slipping into the gap, Abimelech waved off a slashing short sword from a man with olive-colored skin as he impaled an Ammonite soldier in the right side. The invader's black eyes flared with a dying expression of shock. Dodging a hail of arrows, Abimelech stepped on the stunned face of the Ammonite before moving on into the red maelstrom of battle.

The echoes of violent death filled their ears. The clang of sword on shields, the crushing sound of axes breaking helmets, the cries of agony, and the squelching wetness of dismemberments passed from the outside world into the hollow part of his soul. The shield bearer felt warm. He'd been here before.

A large group of Philistines, led in the fray by Balzer as their leader, fell under a Moabite ax group, feigned retreat, then charged anew into the lines of Confederates. Balzer focused so on his task, that he divorced himself from the emotion of what transpired.

He shouted at the gods as his compatriot Qorus slipped to one knee due to a slick of entrails. Qorus laughed as he killed an opponent, a Philistine who'd defected to Samien's side.

General Schlack led a few hundred of the cavalrymen directly at the left flank of the forces. His hope to break them fast with a show of power remained. Indeed, fear couldn't be wiped from the face of the regulars of the Confederacy.

Nevertheless, the Confederates, drunk on Samien's initial successful thrusts, went on into the killing maw against their former leader. Even those far behind in the ruins cheered and shouted their encouragement as the fight went on.

With a flashing sword and a heavy spear, Abimelech cut two riders down. He stabbed, slashed and fought like a man possessed, never caring as spouting blood painted his light armor. In time, he chopped the kidneys from an Assyrian rider and leapt onto the back of his horse. Almost elegant in his acts of murder, Abimelech wasn't denied. Both his blade and his spear dropped on either side of himself, both finding homes in the shoulders of pikemen that'd rushed to him and hesitated. Abimelech ended their fears forever. A loud chunk sound echoed as the blades found flesh. Armor rent, collarbones collapsed as the blades crunched down into the ribs and tender flesh of the attackers.

Facing his enemies anew, the press of bodies and horses became greater and Abimelech lost his sword in the tussle. He grabbed up the pieces of two broken lances. Spear planted in the hoof of a nearby offending horse, Abimelech swished the new broken pieces like swords across the front of his body, twirled them on his fingers before holding them tight and driving the split ends into the exposed necks of two towering Amorites. Twin founts of blood spurted from the impact points, criss-crossing in front of Abimelech, splattering the dead and the still living, soaking his mount's mane.

Blind in his odium of Schlack, Qorus skewered a horseman, mounted up and charged forward. Ravenous for the ultimate kill, all of his senses flared at the sight of the warring man, killing everyone around him, dropping the blades so often one would think he was chopping logs. Several of those in the Confederate cavalry fled rather than attack Schlack. The General was quickly aided by his warriors buoyed by his undaunted bravery. It was the wedge they needed and they drove it deep into the side of the main body of Samien's army. The edges of the main force started to disperse, perplexed and pushed away by a crush of bodies, also confused.

Qorus fought their common enemy and his skin crawled as he reached Schlack. The armored veteran never flinched, as Qorus fought for him, against the Confederates, but recognition lit in the General's eyes. He didn't seem surprised when Qorus attacked him. Schlack gritted his teeth, reached out with his blade and blocked Qorus's first sword thrust. Schlack even kicked the young warrior in the hip as he passed his horse. Qorus's fury went white as he saw that even in the midst of a war, Schlack played with him. Qorus heard him laughing as he kicked a foreign pikeman, caving in his ribs.

Again, he charged the General. Again, Schlack repelled him with sword and shield. Qorus reined back, flummoxed. Schlack snatched a lance out of the turf just as Abimelech rode up, seeming to put himself between the two men. Qorus read the face of Schlack and believed that the General meant to impale the champion's shield bearer. No shock overcame him when Abimelech pivoted on horseback, causing the lance to miss his side. Abimelech then swung his sword down, snapping the lance. Abimelech's momentum carried him close to Schlack and an overhand smash from the General's gloved fist landed. The brain buster caused Abimelech to falter in the saddle and tumble backwards from his mount. Twirling, he landed on his back and then rolled on all fours. Shaking the cobwebs free, Abimelech tried to rise, but his head hung. He never knew Schlack sliced at him with a sword and missed his head.

Qorus then shouted a single word at him. Schlack raised his head up to look. The blade of Qorus fell. The General howled as he heard a brittle crunch and the sword bit to bone depth and beyond in his own neck. His hand grabbed at the blade, still lodged in his armor and neck. General Schlack went off his horse and slammed to the battlefield.

"You..." Schlack gurgled as Qorus stood over him and Abimelech got to his knees. "...you're a dog..."

Qorus gripped his sword and raised it high. "I'm a Philistine."

Sadik lost count of how many times he broke a sword or lance and acquired another. He fought for a spell with a curved Ammonite blade, but gladly discarded it for a Philistine sword and a small tomahawk gleaned from a dying Amalekite. He limped as his ankle bled badly from a horse's hoof strike and his left ear was missing. Still, the youth fought on.

The young soldier never realized the horse he maimed was that of Colonel Baldassare. The Confederate Colonel screamed, as he lay pinned under the dying animal, his left leg broken. Sadik did recognize Baldassare, but didn't let that stop him from dropping the tomahawk in the Colonel's chest. Sadik expected the man to die fast, but his opponent smiled. Sadik thought for an instant he struck a plate, as the tomahawk hit a hard surface. Pain shot up through Sadik's good leg as Baldassare slit him open, striking a dagger into his bare calf and slitting him past his knee. Sadik fell, gasping in pain, looking over at Baldassare.

The chest of the Colonel never bled around his heart.

Sadik wore the look of amazement when the Moabite ax man chopped his head free from his shoulders.

Several Confederates pulled Baldassare from under his mount and Samien rode up to the scene. The Colonel croaked, "How fair we, sir?"

Bloody, but full of the killing rage, Samien replied, "It goes on. I must rejoin."

A soldier pointed to the ruins of Jericho. "Look, General! The champion rises!"

Though the craze of the war ran intense, many stopped on either side of the rubble as Goliath emerged from the ruins of the Domain of Moloch. He bore a huge statue in his arms. Well, most thought it was, anyway, and it got the attention of thousands of warriors on either side. He waited for no audience reaction as he raised the image above his head and cast it far from himself.

Back to his feet, Abimelech saw the stone image of Malak fly and crash through ruined pillars. The gorgon shattered into dozens of pieces, but not before Abimelech noted something fascinating. The image of Malak had her left hand inserted into her crotch.

Baldassare cried out and his throat became dry. Samien looked down from his mount at his Colonel, hand to where his heart should be.

*****

Hands empty, Goliath roared at the heavens, and slammed several riders nearby from their horses. This gave Abimelech a chance to scramble back to the ruins, take up Goliath's weapons and present them to his master.

"Thank you, my good and faithful servant," Goliath told him as Abimelech took up the shield again.

Abimelech stood beside his master and they faced General Samien, surrounded by a dozen warriors all holding bloody weapons.

Goliath donned his helmet and said, "Let us enjoy the rest of the day."

"As you wish, sire," Abimelech agreed.

Goliath and Abimelech faced the vulgar display of violence on the plain, laughing. They charged into the fray toward General Samien and overwhelming odds.

Philistine

EPILOGUE
CONSUMMATED

The following is a rather fanciful translation of tablets GATH3A-E discovered by Dr. Elijah Blackthorn from Miskatonic University. It's the only one of the tablets completely intact, thus, the first-person account is retained, unlike the above epic that was pieced together in fragments by Blackthorn's students and told in third person. The following appears claimed as real testimony from Abimelech, shield bearer of the Champion of the Philistines, the first in a huge cache found in ruins at Mount Nebo. Again, the fanciful verbiage is that of the students.

On the morn after the great defeat of General Samien's uprising, we arose and left the others encamped. What remained of our troop traveled to the outskirts of Ekron. This locale thrived under Philistine rule despite all attempts by the Israeli tribe of Judah to dispel them. Many small dwellings and a fine marketplace lay in view as we approached. At the edge of the community sat the small rounded stone temple dedicated to Baal.

When the priests of Baal saw us approach (or

rather the specter of Goliath) their faces turned fraught with terror. Their russet robes flitted in the morning light, but they soon stood fast in an orderly column. Servants scurried, a few grabbing goats in nearby pens, perhaps for food, perhaps for a sacrifice to my master.

Before Balzer could make his request to the high priest, Goliath called, "Send her out, and I'll spare your lives. You're but fools to the wills of others. My sister Malak is dead and so is the entire opposing army. Samien's head will soon be on display in the city of Gath. What're a few more deaths on this week?" Truly, Goliath sported no fright for the priests that most men would flee from in terror.

The high priest of Baal came out of the temple along with a few nervous-looking novices. With him was the priest of Dagon, Nekimai. He was an older man and said in a firm voice, "Akisha is gone, great Goliath. She has gone into the wilderness with the Prophet."

Hands on his waist belt, Goliath laughed in the face of the priest. "She who would be venerated a goddess will find no respite this day. I'm sad to see more than one stripe of you together on this matter. When did Akisha leave? Where is your King, Ladral? Why didn't he stop this?"

"In the night," Nekimai confessed, pulling his dark green vestments around him to shield the rising wind. His faced soured as he noted the head of Eucimar carried in an infant's strap about the neck of Hasana. "The King... well, we couldn't detain her with the Prophet. She cannot be far, in her condition." He gestured at the hills to the east. "Yesterday, she screamed in horror and we thought that the child was lost. Then, the Prophet came."

Three great strides separated Goliath from us, and then he paused. He faced me and said, "Come with me, Abi. I need only your eyes at my back. You others, butcher up some food, for I'm sure these men of the gods will give us wine to drink."

The priest of Baal called out, stopping us with a desperate voice. "Return her to us and we will care for her as she deserves!"

Goliath's features darkened and he leered at the cleric, "She will be well taken care of, priest. Go in and pray for her deliverance and I'll show you the effectiveness of Ba'al *Zebul's* power." Again, Goliath teetered at the point of silliness when talking of the gods. He then took off his bronze helm. "Do you have a good blacksmith in this city? The nose guard application Kikron made for me was struck off in the great battle." The priests exchanged glances and Goliath donned his helmet anew. "Bah, to Hell with you all." He then started to jog and I had to run fast to keep up with him.

"Master," I asked, breathing hard, but keeping in his stride. "Why do you scorn the priests so, still?"

"The celebrant should spread his seed on his altar," Goliath said in a mocking voice. "At least then he'll have something to show for his efforts." His eyes searched the hills. "You have been with me most of my life, Abimelech."

I nodded, used to his powerful strides, for keeping up with him kept me in condition. "I have been proud to carry your shield and write of you all of my days, Lord."

Goliath continued with his domineering tenor, "You know what I feel of men and their gods."

"I was unsure of your intent this day, sire."

Once over the hills, Goliath slowed to a walk and looked down on me. "All the images of stone or earth cannot save Philistia this day. Truly, Akisha will be the Queen of Heaven before the sun sets. You have heard tell of the demise of Vyndekay."

"You think that the Prophet of the Israelite God will..." My voice faded, guessing at his objective at last.

He smiled, his savage teeth like that of a tiger's under his wild mustache. "You are wise, Abi, not a lamb like the others. You will not be a whelp at my actions."

"I am as I must be, sire."

We traveled for most of the afternoon, but at last, found a small encampment. A tall, elderly man dressed in a dusty robe sat by a fire. With him was a female, robed in a russet cloak not unlike that of the Ekron priesthood. When we approached, both stood. The woman, great with child, indeed was Akisha, the reason for our trip to Ekron from the battlefield. At long last, we found her, after hearing tales of her self from the farthest reaches of the region.

The old man showed no panic in his face for the enormous one walking to him, unlike the woman. She practically screamed and ran, but froze in her steps. It was as if she were uncertain if to hide behind the Prophet or run. Did she comprehend both eventualities were fruitless? She looked at me and knew she'd not go far.

"Behold, woman, thy benefactor," Goliath snapped in an annoyed voice. He stared at the aged man and said, "Today, great Prophet of renown, I'll fulfill the edicts of your God."

Not flinching, the Prophet replied, "That may be, for the will of God isn't for men to make. We are but his instruments. He is the potter and we are the clay."

Goliath unsheathed his sword and stared down at the woman. "Agreed and well said, mystic. For you know how it is with gods. What they create, they can destroy." The giant reached out and snatched the woman by the shoulder with his left hand. "Akisha, did you think you could keep my offspring from me?"

The woman's tear-soaked eyes grew large as she begged, "Mercy..."

"Now it's mercy you desire?" His nostrils flared as he laughed with cruel accents. "That isn't the ballad you sang before I came back to these shores, eh? You desired to be venerated as one of the goddesses and your offspring enshrined as a living deity, worthy of laud and sacrifice. Was this to be bestowed because you actually could accommodate one such as me? I foolishly fell for your wiles that night at the grand party. I must say, the babe grew in you fast enough."

"Do not take my baby from me. Please, let me have our baby."

"I would not dream of it." With a single quick thrust, his great sword rose up and he impaled her through the abdomen. The angle proved awkward and the blade clipped her at first, then delved in further, shooting far out of her back beside her spine. When his wrist twisted, Akisha's eyes turned back in her head and with a single gasp, Akisha died. Goliath pulled her close and she exhaled loud, long tresses flying over his chest. He patted her on the back, kissed the crown of her head and closed his eyes. In a few moments, Goliath released her, letting his sword wilt. Akisha slid off his blade, leaving a trail of crimson and grisly bits behind on it.

We stared at the sight and I felt drained, knowing this was the culmination of his passionate mission. Goliath then said, "I told you all the prayers to Baal or Dagon couldn't stop her destiny."

"You decide who gets to live or die?" the Prophet asked, no emotion in his face.

"When they come out of my thighs, yes," the giant muttered. "I'll choose who gets to be worshiped as a god, too, if I can help it. In this matter, I could. Priests are whores and donkeys. They worship of progeny and the provider of one descended from the sons of God. I'll leave no trace of my self to infect this planet, for my father and his brothers abandoned me here. You see, Prophet, we both desired the same thing, the demise of my family line. I just made your day easier."

As Goliath wiped her blood and the child's guts off on Akisha's cloak, the Prophet said, "Destiny comes for us all, Goliath, even those descended from the fallen ones from the sky."

"True," Goliath smiled and then winked at him. "But not today, Samuel."

We turned and left Samuel in the wilderness.

I asked Goliath, "Would the old one really have slain her?"

Goliath shrugged. "That one is a truly strong man. You breathe because of him, remember? I heard he beheaded Agag the Amalekite in spite of Israelite King Saul. Who knows the foundation in the Prophet Samuel's innards? I think Akisha would've suffered a similar fate, but I needed to be certain."

We walked back to Ekron and Goliath wasn't exactly true to his word. He didn't spare the priests of Baal or the man from Dagon's temple who were going to venerate Akisha as a goddess and probably enshrine his son. Thus, word went to many in the Philistine culture that such a practice wouldn't be prudent.

After feasting in Ekron, we returned to Gath where the remains of our great army amassed. There was talk in the air we would soon turn out blades to attack the Israelites at the Esdraelon valley to rid the country of them once and for all.

"No dreams for me, just roaming free
Red wine and battle's roar
I'll breast the gales and ride the trails...
'til I can ride no more..."

Robert E. Howard

PHILISTINE Bibliography

Dothan, Trude and Moshe. *People of the Sea: The Search for the Philistines* (1992)

Kingsley, Rebecca. *Gods and Pharaohs of Ancient Egypt* (1998)

Landau, Elaine. *The Assyrians* (1997)

O'Connell, Robert L. *Soul of the Sword* (2002)

Redford, Donald B. *Egypt, Canaan, and Israel in Ancient Times* (1992)

Sanders, N.K. *The Sea Peoples: Warriors of the Ancient Mediterranean* (1978)

Velikovsky, Immanuel. *Peoples of the Sea* (1977)

A special thanks to the ladies and men of the Pontiac Public Library that acquired rare volumes for me.

About the Author

    Steven L. Shrewsbury, from Central Illinois, enjoys football, history, politics and good fiction. Over 300 of his short stories have been published in print or digital media. His small press novels include OVERKILL, HELL BILLY, THRALL, BAD MAGICK, BEDLAM UNLEASHED, STRONGER THAN DEATH, HAWG, TORMENTOR, GODFORSAKEN, the forthcoming PHILISTINE and BLACK SON RISING. These titles run from horror to historical high fantasy. He tries to drown out the rumors that he is Robert E. Howard reincarnated with beer. When not wrangling his sons, he can be found outside in his happy place.

Transcend reality with Seventh Star Press!

On the following pages we would like to introduce you to some of our titles featuring Sword and Sorcery, Post-Apocalyptic Fantasy, Epic Fantasy, YA Fantasy, and more!

To get more information on Seventh Star Press and our titles, please visit:

www.seventhstarpress.com

or connect with us at:
www.twitter.com/7thstarpress
www.facebook.com/seventhstarpress

Want Sword and Sorcery?
Pick up the anthologies *Thunder on the Battlefield:*
Sword, and *Thunder on the Battlefield: Sorcery,*
from editor James R. Tuck!
(author of the Deacon Chalk novels)
Available in print and eBook!

Thunder on the Battlefield: Sword
Softcover: 978-1-937929-24-4
eBook: 978-1-937929-25-1

Thunder on the Battlefield: Sorcery
Softcover: 978-1-937929-26-8
eBook: 978-1-937929-27-5

Gorias La Gaul adventures from Steven Shrewsbury!
Enter an ancient world of heroes, blood, and steel in the
tales of Gorias La Gaul! Hard-hitting Sword & Sorcery in
the vein of Robert E. Howard!.

Softcover ISBN: 9781937929800   Softcover ISBN: 9780983108634

eBook ISBN: 9781937929831   eBook ISBN: 9780983108641

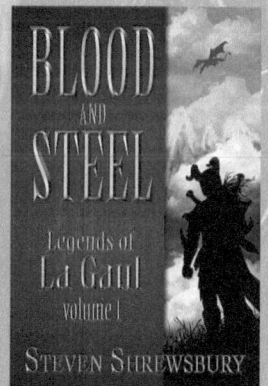

Softcover: 978-1-937929-28-2

eBook: 978-1-937929-29-9

Action-driven Fantasy from D.A. Adams!
Begin your journey into The Brotherhood of Dwarves, the
popular YA Fantasy series from D.A. Adams. An action-
filled saga where the dwarves are not just sidekicks!

Softcover ISBN: 9781937929916   Softcover ISBN: 9781937929923

eBook ISBN: 9781937929930   eBook ISBN: 9781937929-947

Explore post-apocalyptic fantasy worlds!
Read the Seventh Star Press anthology *The End
Was Not the End*, from editor Joshua H. Leet!

softcover ISBN: 978-1-937929-07-7
eBook ISBN: 978-1-937929-15-2

Chronicles of Ave Now Available!
Be sure to check out the novella-sized single-
author collections of short stories from Seventh
Star Press!

Now Available!

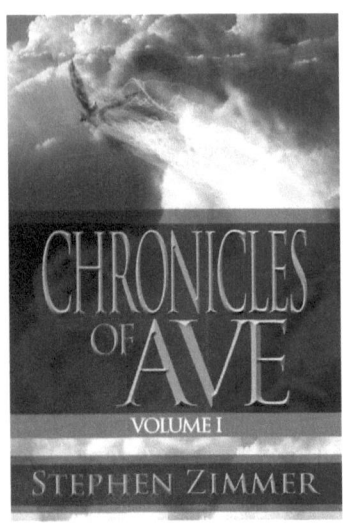

Have many action-driven fantasy adventures in
the world of Ave in Stephen Zimmer's
Chronicles of Ave, Volume 1.

Softcover: 978-1-937929-30-5
eBook: 978-1-937929-31-2

Grand Epic Fantasy from Stephen Zimmer!
Explore the world of Ave in the Fires in Eden Series from
Stephen Zimmer! Epic Fantasy for those who enjoy authors
like George R.R. Martin and Steven Erikson!

Softcover ISBN: 9780982565612

eBook ISBN: 9780982565698

Softcover ISBN: 9780983108627   Softcover ISBN 9781937929855

eBook ISBN: 9780983108610   eBook ISBN 9781937929862

YA Fantasy From Jackie Gamber!
The highly-acclaimed Leland Dragon Series from Jackie
Gamber! Strong character-driven YA Fantasy for those
who enjoy authors such as Christopher Paolini.

Softcover ISBN: 9780983108672

eBook ISBN: 9780983108696

Softcover ISBN: 9781937929893

eBook ISBN: 9781937929817

www.ingramcontent.com/pod-product-compliance
Lightning Source LLC
Chambersburg PA
CBHW032300020726
47495CB00001B/190